REBECCA CAMPBELL

Alice's Secret Garden

HarperCollins*Publishers*

HarperCollins*Publishers*
77–85 Fulham Palace Road,
Hammersmith, London W6 8JB

www.**fire**and**water**.com
A Paperback Original 2003
1 3 5 7 9 8 6 4 2

A catalogue record for this book
is available from the British Library

ISBN 0 00 711814 7

Typeset in Meridien by Palimpsest Book Production Ltd,
Polmont, Stirlingshire

Printed and bound in Great Britain by
Clays Ltd, St Ives plc

ACKNOWLEDGEMENTS

I would like to thank Susan Opie at HarperCollins and Stephanie Cabot at William Morris for their labour pains.

Thanks also to two sets of grandparents: Patrick and Margaret McGowan and John and Paddy Campbell.

Finally, thanks to Anthony, who held the hand that held the pen.

I dreamt it last night that my true love came in,
So softly he entered, his feet made no din;
He came close beside me, and this he did say
'It will not be long love, love, till our wedding day.'

Based on 'She Moved Through the Fair'
– Padraic Colum

The last and best Cure of Love Melancholy is, to let them
have their Desire.

Robert Burton, *The Anatomy of Melancholy*

ONE

She Moved Through the Fair

Alice had been thinking about the Dead Boy for nearly six months before anyone else at Enderby's found out about him. And that was funny, because for those six months the Dead Boy was the most important thing in Alice's life: more important than her job in the Book Department, looking after Natural History; more important than her mother in the tiny flat in St John's Wood; more important than her friends, her living friends, scattered around London.

Alice had never spoken to the Dead Boy. She had never felt, as she longed to feel, the fine dense blackness of his hair as it swept with such sensuous, careless, charm across his face, across her face. She had never touched the full Slavic lips that fell so easily into a pout – not the pout of a spoilt child or of a sulking teenager, but a little 'o', a pout of pure surprise, surprise at the onrush of death. She had never brushed her own lips against those high cheekbones, cheekbones which would have looked cruel, tyrannical, implacable, had they not slid into the fine smiling lines around the eyes. The eyes, to Alice, were something of a mystery. No matter how many times she replayed the incident, winding backwards and forwards, slowing it down or speeding it up, panning back to take in the whole street, or the whole of London, or zooming into ultra close-up, she could not settle on the colour of the eyes. It was not even the precise shade that was in question – it was not some unimportant semantic quibble about hazel or chestnut or rowan – it was that Alice could not even decide if they were blue or brown, dark or light. Sometimes they would burn through her with an intense cobalt light, or dazzle with shimmering bright crystal; at others they would fold in on themselves in wave after wave of growing darkness, like evening falling on a forest.

Had Alice known the Dead Boy for more than four seconds, or had she never gone for that seemingly harmless stroll, but rather sat on the imposing steps at Enderby's with Andrew that lunchtime, as she often did, to eat a sandwich and breathe in the petrol fumes, while they talked about the oddness of people, and he tried to think of something clever and nice to say that wouldn't trumpet his devotion in her ear like an elephant in musth, then everything would have been different.

Back in the office that afternoon, the afternoon when everything changed, Alice was surprised to find that nobody noticed anything different about her. It seemed that none could see the penumbra of light around her, or sense the dramatic transformations that had taken place within her.

But no, nothing. The only comment as she made her way slowly, like a bride, to her desk, was one of Pamela's deafening whispers:

'Alice, where have you been?'

Pamela, or Pammy, or Spam, as she was known with varying degrees of affection, had been there longer than anyone, and was seen as a sort of retaining wall which couldn't be demolished without dire, if unspecified, consequences. Of course it was possible that she retained nothing at all, supporting only her own weight, which was considerable. Originally she had typed letters, but now that everyone did that for themselves her main responsibility was ordering the rubber bands which spilled and coiled in pointless abundance from every drawer, like intestines after a battle.

'Mr Crumlish has been around. He's got one of his faces on. You know, the one like Easter Island. He'll be using one of those thingummy bobs . . . metaphors on you if you're not careful.'

Mr Crumlish was then still part of the ill-defined strata of middle managers within Books, or, to give it its full title, Books, Manuscripts and other Printed Matter. Books was the smallest department in Enderby's, the fifth biggest auction house in London, which is quite as unimpressive as it sounds. The office, an ornate Florentine palazzo, complete with dirty windows, and spluttering drains, and the grand statue of its founder, the buccaneering Mungo Enderby (1772–1861) in half armour, was the one relic of the glory days, back in the nineteen-twenties when Enderby's was briefly acknowledged as one of the Big Three. But then came the scandals: the famous fraud case; the fake Canaletto; the 1949 public indecency charge against Ashley Enderby. And so eventually the Americans had come, or rather the Americans who ran the business for the Japanese bank which bought, at bargain basement rates, fifty-one per cent of Enderby's. Ashley Enderby had died without issue, alone in Marrakech, befuddled with intoxicants, and the family share had gone to the Brooksbanks, obscurely related by marriage. The Brooksbanks, whose interests were principally rural, were content for the Americans and Japanese to take the decisions while they drew off what they could in the form of profit and prestige. Only one Brooksbank was still involved in any practical sense in the running of the company, and he only in the way that the froth is technically still part of the beer. But he was, at least, a link of sorts with the past.

'Alice, where have you been?' repeated Pamela, looking perplexed, the second of her two facial expressions after her more familiar vacuous jollity.

But Alice couldn't think of anything to say back to Pamela, and nor could she meet her vacantly inquisitive stare. Where *had* she been? To heaven. To hell. Nowhere special.

To begin with not even Andrew, the closest thing she had to a friend at Enderby's, noticed anything unusual. But he was preoccupied with his work that afternoon and was soon called in to a meeting, which lasted for the rest of the day. And of course Alice was still quite new then, and generally perceived to be a little strange. The problem had been summed up for her two months earlier, on a bright, cold February morning, by Mr Crumlish, whom Alice was destined never to call by his first name, Garnet. Mr Crumlish was showing Alice 'the ropes', a phrase he used with such relish she assumed she felt it to be an expression of thrilling vulgarity.

'You see, if we leave aside dear, dear Spammy over there,' – at this point Crumlish toodled with his fingertips over to where Pam was arranging paperclips; she burst into gales of girlish laughter, which set off curious seismic events in the various pendulous and drooping zones of her body: a small tremor about her middle; a major quake in the jowls; a volcanic eruption of spittle at the lips, and a devastating bust-tsunami – 'everybody here is either a Toff or a Tart or a Swot. Oh. Are you allowed three "eithers"? I can't remember. Anyway, *I*, of course, am a Toff. We don't know very much, but the gentry *do* like one of their own to deal with. Not perhaps when it comes to going on a *rummage*:

4

then they seem to prefer it if you act like staff, and you think yourself lucky if cook gives you a chipped mug in the kitchen. But when they bring in one of their gewgaws for a valuation they appreciate the rich and heady aroma of old money.'

Alice was clearly supposed to be shocked by Mr Crumlish's performance. But she noticed that the people in the office, the twenty or so men and women arranged in clumps about the room, paid him no attention, despite the arch and actorly projection of his voice. She assumed that they had heard it all before; perhaps received the same initiation themselves.

'Ophelia,' continued Mr Crumlish, 'is, as you can see, a Tart. Pretty, pretty, pretty.'

With each 'pretty', Mr Crumlish twitched the hem of his pin-striped suit, flashing the vivid lilac lining.

Alice quickly glanced in the direction that Mr Crumlish had flicked his thin wrist. She saw a young woman of astonishing, languorous beauty, playing idly with her long dark hair. She seemed to have nothing else to do. Alice instantly felt shabby: her own long hair was cheaply cut, underconditioned, and prone to acts of reckless rebellion; her clothes were ill-matched, picked up as the sales were entering the please please please don't buy me phase.

'The Tarts,' continued Mr Crumlish, breaking the spell that Ophelia's beauty had cast over Alice, 'tend not to know very much either, but they *are* easy on the eye, and it's so much cheaper than getting the decorators in. Anyway, what else would they do with their History of Art degrees? The Swots, on the contrary, know everything; not everything about everything, but everything about something. Couldn't do without the Swots. *Could* do without the smell.'

'The smell?' Alice was mystified.

'You know, the stale, composty, damp-tweed aroma, combined with the smell of a shirt worn for a *second*, or even *third*, day, mixed finally with the faint, sweet tang of distressingly recent onanism. I present to you Mister Cedric Clerihew.' He pronounced Cedric 'seed-rick', which Alice hadn't heard before. She had no way of knowing if Crumlish was being amusing. Clerihew certainly wasn't going to put her right. He was a small round person, like a globule of some unappetising but not actively repulsive liquid. Like many round people, his age was difficult to estimate, but certainly above twenty and below forty. He was very neatly dressed, almost like a boy receiving his first Holy Communion. He smiled and sweated towards Alice, but Crumlish swept her on and away before he had the chance to speak to her, or reach out with his little hands, the fingers of which looked a knuckle shorter than the usual complement.

'Poor boy,' said Crumlish, this time in a voice that only Alice could hear, 'one day he might, by pure good fortune, stumble upon the right posterior, but, until that happy time, he licks in vain.'

Alice giggled too loudly, hiding her wide mouth behind her hand. A couple of faces turned, Ophelia's among them. She performed what must have been a very deliberate up-and-down look of dismissal. Anyone who'd cared to glance towards Clerihew would have seen him staring intently at his desk, his face red, his mouth set hard. Mr Crumlish, pleased with the response, moved Alice on through the large, book-splattered room.

'But you, Alice, what are *you*? Not, obviously, one of the Tarts. I'm afraid your degree, what was it? Of course, *Zoology* of all things, suggests that. Not to mention your commendable lack of vanity.'

As was perhaps intended, Alice took the statement that she lacked vanity as a hint that she ought to rectify the deficit.

'Nor, despite your name, which, between the two of us I don't *entirely* believe, do you appear to be one of us . . . I mean a Toff. That only leaves the Swots. And, my dear *Alice*, you really are far too fragrant to be a Swot. I fear you may be *sui generis*, which is frightfully inconvenient for the . . . oh, what is the word? A putting-things-into-classes person?'

'A taxonomist. Was that a test, Mr Crumlish?'

All the while they had been winding their way between the desks, each carrying its burden of computer and heavy reference books. In the far corner they finally came to two facing desks with a low partition between them. One was free, and the other occupied by a young man who might have been handsome had the frown lines been etched a little less deeply.

'Oh,' said Mr Crumlish. 'I've got it all wrong. There's a fourth category. As well as the Tarts and the Toffs and the Swots, we've recently acquired our first Oik. And look, he's to be your intimate desk chum. How affecting. Alice, meet Andrew Heathley. I suspect his *mates* call him "Andy". Andrew, this is Alice Sui Generis. Be gentle with her.'

Andrew scowled yet more heavily, and Alice was convinced that a brute impulse to hurl a profoundly unacceptable insult in the face of Mr Crumlish had been forced down into some subterranean chamber of the mind. She doubted it would be lonely.

'Hello,' he said, smiling the frowny smile which was soon to become so familiar to Alice.

'Hello,' replied Alice, a little intimidated by Andrew's apparent seriousness.

'You've had the tour from Crumlish. I presume you got the Tarts and Toffs stuff. I had that when I joined. I suppose I ought to be flattered that I've entered the pantheon.'

'Are you really an Oik? Whatever an Oik is.'

'I think he means I'm a socialist. From the "North".'

7

'Seems like a funny sort of place for a socialist to be working. If you are. I mean a socialist, not working.'

'It is. A bloody funny sort of place.'

'How did you come to be here?'

'Oh Christ, life story time already. Well, I was doing a PhD on . . . oh, stuff, but I ran out of funding. There was a girlfriend who worked here. A vacancy came up. They never advertise them: there's usually one of Crumlish's Toffs grown in a pod in the basement ready to step in. Somehow they screwed up and I got the job.'

Alice wondered at the strange way Andrew referred to 'a' girlfriend, but she could hardly ask any more personal questions on her first day. Months later when she asked about the girlfriend, Andrew replied only that she was tall, and had gone to the other place, by which he meant, she supposed, Christie's, rather than heaven or the House of Lords.

As for Andrew, as soon as he saw Alice walking towards him, looking charmingly flustered by the Crumlish routine, he knew that he was going to fall for her. Just how far he couldn't even guess, although he had a brief and blurry vision of precipices. Not that having Andrew fall for you was particularly difficult. At that time he was principally (and hopelessly) in lust with Ophelia and subordinately (and, had he but known it, more promisingly) keen on a girl called Tessa, who would occasionally wander through Books on unspecified errands.

'You know, I haven't much of a clue what I'm supposed to be doing,' said Alice, once she had sat down and unpacked her pencil case and reached around on both sides in vain pursuit of the computer's on button.

'Oh don't worry, nobody does to begin with. Or sometimes ever. I can show you where the canteen is, and where to make tea, and where the bogs are. You'll pick up everything else as you go. You're our new Science and Natural History bod, aren't you?'

'Mm. I think they want me to do some Travel as well, but I don't know much about that.'

'Well, you're not quite what I was expecting. Usually the . . . people on the Science side are . . . well, you know. I can help you a bit with the Travel.'

'Is Travel your main responsibility?'

'Yes, no. Well, I do everything, really. An expert generalist. Or a general expert. And, by the way, when Crumlish says "recently acquired", he means I've been here for less than ten years, not that I joined last week.'

Andrew was losing his focus a little. Alice, although not quite beautiful, had the kind of face that made you want to look at it, that made you think that things would be all right, or at least a little better, if you spent another minute or so just looking. Andrew had to struggle hard against the urge to stare baldly at her. He broke loose by looking at her clothes. Most of the younger Enderby girls were *Vogue* perfect. Not Alice. He couldn't quite put his finger on what was wrong, but he knew that either the right sort of directed intelligence, or the time, or the money was missing. It made him like her more by, in his own reckoning, about seven per cent. It also made him feel more comfortable: at least she wasn't *perfect* like Ophelia, and soon they were chatting about nothing in particular, which was how most days were spent in the Books department.

And so Alice's first day at Enderby's had been only mildly traumatic and if she never did *quite* fit in, she at least, in those two months before she fell in love with the Dead Boy, found a place as one of those who were officially permitted not to fit in.

The same, alas, could not be said for Mr Crumlish who,

for all his protestations, was not a Toff, but an Edinburgh council-estate boy, whose brilliance and taste had doomed him to alienation from his own people, and yet never quite achieved for him acceptance in the world to which he aspired, the world of the beautiful and the clever and the rich. Perhaps it was the name, Garnet, that had sealed his fate. His father, a merchant seaman, had brought one of the semi-precious stones back from a distant port for his wife, and she had so loved its profound crimson opacity that she had insisted that the unborn child should carry the name. Had he been a simple John, or Davey, or Robert, then a different life might have been his.

It was the Americans who insisted on his dismissal. They acted, of course, through Oakley, the Head of Books.

Oakley had been promoted from the documents basement, where he acted as a Cerberus to its Hades. No one in Books (or anywhere else in Enderby's), with the exception of those unfortunate clericals who'd been forced to request a document from storage, had ever heard of Oakley. He had, however, one asset which, from the American perspective, set him aside from, or rather above, his more knowledgeable, refined, cultured, eloquent, sophisticated, amusing and able colleagues: a qualification in Business Studies. That qualification, vaguely defined as a 'diploma', had been awarded by the Llandudno Business School, an institution which usefully allowed itself to be abbreviated to the LBS, and thereby readily confused with other, possibly more august institutions. On his elevation to Head of Books, Oakley had become simultaneously more English and more American; the former accomplished by the rapid purchase of a pin-striped suit, and the latter by a studied replacement of the word 'arse' by 'ass' in his vocabulary. Alice would eventually come to agree with the general view of those who worked in Books that he was a fawning toady to those above him at Enderby's and a ruthless tyrant to those below; a snob and a fool.

When asked, at his first monthly round-up, by the American management to give an appraisal of his 'team', Oakley had initially replied that they were all 'top drawer', which he hoped would reflect well on himself.

'But what about that guy Crumlish?' asked Madeleine Illkempt, aka The Slayer. 'All he seems to do is file expenses claims and make inappropriate personal remarks. And to be frank, we don't care at all what you people do in private but his kind of open . . . display in the work environment just isn't efficient.'

'Ah, Mr Crumlish,' said Oakley, rapidly assessing what it was that The Slayer wanted to hear. 'Well, I did feel it was my duty to . . . protect . . . to . . . but of course, yes, there have been one or two . . . problems.' And if there weren't, he knew how to go about manufacturing some.

And so Alice never got to call Mr Crumlish, Garnet. But she had liked him, and she never forgot that the Books department at Enderby's auction house was made up of Toffs, Tarts and Swots, or that she was *sui generis*.

TWO

The Secret Garden of Alice Duclos

Alice was in the garden again. She looked back and saw the low arch and the little green door through which she must have entered. The garden was her special place. Its high brick wall kept out the wind and the world. Its paths wove complicated patterns, which, once deciphered, would tell her the answers to all of her questions. The roses, always in bud and never blooming, dwelt partly in the garden, and partly in fairytales, guarding princesses, holding the impure or the unwary forever in their gauzy tangles. At the heart of everything stood the dead stone fountain and the dark green pool.

She reached up and felt her father's soft hands; felt with her fingertips for his smooth, clean nails. The sensation filled her with excitement and yet soothed her.

'Daddy, can we go to the fish?' she said, but she knew he would not answer. And then she was looking down through the shadows to where the long lazy goldfish slid and turned amid the darker green of the weeds. She could see the shape of her father reflected in the water, but the details were lost in the murk and silt.

'Don't the fish get cold, Daddy?' she asked, but again she

knew that there would be no answer. She looked up to where his face should have been, but the sky was pure white and dazzled her eyes after the darkness of the water. She would close her eyes in the dream to shut out the light and, as her dream eyes closed, so her waking eyes would open onto the world.

It was a dream, but not a dream. She could summon the vision when she was awake, sometimes as she lay in bed at night, sometimes as she sat and stared at the computer screen on her desk at work, and once in the garden she would try to drive the dream on to the point at which she would see her father's face, and know him again. The dream was a dream of love and a dream of loss. But then so was the other dream. The dream of the Dead Boy.

The garden of Alice's dream was a distillation of the many gardens of her early childhood. Her father, Francis Duclos, was a doctor, specialising in infectious diseases. The fever hospitals he moved between all had huge grounds, acres of parkland with great horse chestnut and yew trees and lines of dense privet. But the killers of the past: diphtheria, measles, scarlet fever, even TB, had vanished or been attenuated, and so the long wards and the open grounds and secret gardens were empty. Duclos found himself in a branch of medicine without a future, and yet for him it was the only medicine, the only life there could be. He wanted to grapple with the invisible enemy, to fire his magic bullets at the tenacious and merciless microbes.

Around the core of the dream-memory, other memories would form: less vividly hyper-real, perhaps, but more soundly based in hard, nuggety reality. She remembered collecting conkers for their beauty. There were no other children allowed in the grounds and so, but for the occasional foray over the wall by the local urchins, she had the trees

13

and their fruit to herself. She could still remember the intense biscuity smell of the newly opened chestnut and its dark iridescence. Her father showed her how to twist off the shell, and would have taught her how to string them, and ready them for warfare, but she could not allow their irregular organic perfection to be destroyed by the awl. She remembered cutting her wrist when she and an older cousin, come from France for the holidays, broke a pane in the hospital greenhouse to plunder tomatoes. The cousin burst into tears at the sight of her blood, and Alice had to guide him home. She remembered her father making her wrist better, calmly sewing the edges of the cut together. She saw again the white fingers working the needle, and she remembered that she had not been afraid, but she forgot that she had cried from the pain. She remembered living in a big old house that was always cold. There were better memories of a room in the nurses' home; memories of running through the long corridors pretending to be Tarzan (who, after all, would ever want to be Jane?) with a toy knife stuck in her green knickers.

Alice's mother never had a role in her memories. Alice's mother was too much part of her present to belong to her past. The past was for the good and beautiful things, worn smooth with the years. The past was for the dead, the sacred dead. Alice could, however, remember her mother's special friend, one of the patients, a boy called Gulliver. He was dying from some intractable strain of consumption. Alice remembered his glistening eyes, and the dark circles around them, and his long, straining neck and she feared him because on the only occasion Alice had seen him smile, his lips peeled back to reveal his bright red gums.

After the death of her father, Alice and her mother had moved to a small flat in St John's Wood. Kitty was from a prosperous family, with what she always described as 'good connections', although to whom or what was never specified. She was sharp-faced, and had once been very pretty. Her marriage to the tall, handsome doctor seemed like a good one, until he decided to abandon London for draughty, remote prisons, millions of miles from theatres and restaurants and dinner parties.

She snatched at the opportunity to return to London, the opportunity wrought by his death. Using every penny that they had saved, she bought the little flat, back here, where the people were, where the life was. It was a shame that London had moved on so much in the ten years that she had been away. Her friends had new friends. The *places* were all different. The invitations wouldn't come. The romance that she expected never happened, apart from one or two crooks out, she eventually convinced herself, to purloin what little money she had left. The years passed and she found herself becoming old.

At times she blamed dull, strange little Alice. She took her away from the expensive private school, little knowing that Alice had hated it, despising the catering and grooming skills it seemed intent on imparting, loathing the silly girls who talked of nothing but ponies and lacrosse. The fact that Alice actually seemed to *enjoy* the local comprehensive confirmed Kitty's doubts about her, doubts amplified by the child's interest in science, in the horrid creepy-crawly world of beetles and locusts and dissected rats. So like her father. Such a disappointment. And as Alice grew so Kitty shrank. She went out less and less, although she dressed immaculately for each evening in with the television and the dry martinis.

Alice could never blame her mother for being what she was; but nor could she love her. The sense of duty she had absorbed from her father prevented her from taking up the place at Cambridge, and she went instead to Imperial

College, living all the while in the little flat. However much her mother pursed her lips, and rolled her eyes and criticised ('How did I make such a dreary, dowdy thing as you?'), Alice could not leave her on her own. She cooked her meals, and paid, out of her meagre student loan, for a girl to come in twice a week during the day, ostensibly to tidy, but really to act as company. These acts of charity were undertaken not with the kind of glad and cheerful heart that would have made them glow in Alice's own eyes, but with the sense of a heavy duty performed joylessly, and this deprived her even of that sense of wellbeing which comes from the knowledge of being virtuous.

Bizarrely it was Kitty who helped to get Alice the job at Enderby's. Secretly fearing that Alice would leave her forever to go and pursue her vile zoophylliac interests in some shamingly out-of-the-way place, Kitty had roused herself, called all of her few surviving acquaintances, pulled whatever strings remained in reach, and arranged a lunch with a reasonably senior Enderby's panjandrum. Alice well remembered the two hours of preparation (not including hair). Her attempts to help were met with screeches, and agonising nips from the long red talons. Kitty eventually emerged looking stretched and gaunt and frightening. Alice suspected that the combination of pearls and diamonds (Kitty still had some very old and, taken individually, rather beautiful jewellery) might have been *wrong*, but she knew better than to say anything.

The Enderby's man was none other than Parry Brooksbank, a younger son of impeccable manners but limited intelligence, who existed principally for this sort of task. He had no idea of quite what he was in for when he found himself steered towards a lunch with 'Old Crawley's daughter, Kitty' by one of his colleagues. He'd never heard of Old Crawley, and assumed the daughter was another more or less marriageable girl dangled before him as part of some Machiavellian plot by the Family, who seemed incapable of understanding that he was utterly, immovably and happily *confirmed*.

He was initially pleased to see the very definitely unmarriageable Kitty. 'P-post p-post-menopausal, I'd have s-said,' as he put it, a *little* unfairly, to his partner, Seamus. 'Looked like Mrs Simpson after a night on the ch-cherry brandy.'

Brooksbank had begun affecting a stammer as a teenager in an attempt to appear more interesting. It was now more or less second nature, although he occasionally forgot which consonants he was supposed to have trouble with.

'Marge?'

'No, dear b-boy, the *other* Mrs Simpson.'

To Kitty herself he was, of course, the soul of charm. Entertaining wealthy eccentrics was just part of the job, and one (perhaps the only one) at which he excelled. He paid close, almost minute-taking, attention to the rambling anecdotes about people of whom he had never or only dimly heard. Most of the stories culminated in Kitty's triumph over some enemy: a rival hostess or impertinent tradesman. He noted with little interest that all of her stories took place in the ancient or very recent past, with nothing filling the middle distance, and put it down to some sub-variant of senile dementia. However, once Brooksbank had established that Kitty was neither a potential threat to his mental or domestic equilibrium, nor, despite appearances, *amusingly* mad, his mind began to drift, helped along by the second bottle of surprisingly good Argentinian red (even Claridges were looking Westward now). Seamus, so *broad*, and yet so sweet; what a find he'd been. Really must go back to . . .

And then, with a start, accompanied by a quite-possibly audible click made by some intricately wrought cartilaginous

17

structure at the back of his nose, Brooksbank realised, an hour into the lunch, that Kitty had reached The Point.

'. . . and her degree was of the first class, you know, the only one they gave out that year. But after all I've told you about our history, you'll admit that she shouldn't be looking at molluscs and woodlice?'

Brooksbank, driving away other visions entirely, wondered what it might have been about the girl's background that made such investigations inappropriate. Something to do with gardening, perhaps?

'No, I quite see. Fearful creatures. Do terrible things to one's radishes and lettuces.'

'I'm so pleased you understand,' said Kitty, looking at him as if he'd just started to caress his own nipples. 'So you'll be able to arrange it then?'

Arrange it? What could the ridiculous old hag be talking about?

'Oh, I expect I'll ah um,' he said, playing for time as he scrolled through his longish list of meaningless and/or ambiguous platitudes. He was looking for one that would work something like: well, you could take it to mean yes, but equally, I could explain it back to you and if necessary the courts, at some stage in the future as, in no way, not at all, you must be joking, forget about it, couldn't possibly do that kind of thing, against all the rules, more than my job's worth. What came out was, 'y-yes, yes, of course.'

'Oh good! When will the interview be – I know it's a formality you have to go through . . .'

'You didn't cave in did you, Parry?' said Seamus that night as they lay together on the sofa watching *Coronation Street*.

'Well,' he replied, 'as it happens there is a small recruitment exercise under way . . .'

'You old softie.'

'Anything for an easy life. P-pass the Maltesers.'

From Kitty's perspective the lunch had been a triumph. The rather handsome, silver-haired fellow had obviously adored her.

'You should have seen the far-away look in his eyes,' she said to a not-really-listening Alice, whose eyes had something of the same character. 'Nice to know I can still bedazzle. You know, before I was married . . .'

She was not in the least surprised when the letter came inviting Alice in for an 'informal chat'. Alice, on the other hand, was astounded. She had only agreed to the idea on the assumption that Kitty's project was doomed to failure. She wanted to do research in some aspect of island bio-geography and had applied to Sheffield and Southampton, proposing to launch herself into field trips to the islands of Mauritius and Reunion, exquisitely isolated in the Indian Ocean. Why would she want to work in a silly office in London, selling old things to very rich people? There was a world of seething, replicating life out there to be studied, catalogued and understood. If it wasn't her father's work, it was at least work that he would comprehend and respect. What would he make of her dusting down ornate picture frames, or whatever else happened in a place like Enderby's?

It was only when the issue of the great auk arose that Alice began to think that she might actually want the job and, more importantly, when the job began to think that it might want Alice.

'What do you make of this?'

The man, tall and craning and unhappily bald (a baldness for which he tried vainly to compensate with one of the last heterosexual moustaches in London outside of the police and fire services), held out a large book open at a

19

picture of an ungainly black and white bird, like a penguin painted by someone relying on second-hand witness accounts.

Alice, who had been bored by the questions about her experience and qualifications, almost leapt in the air.

'It's an auk, the great auk! It's so sad.'

The panel members exchanged a variety of smiles, raised eyebrows and ear-wiggles.

'Well it is, actually,' said the moustache. 'Very good. But we're more interested in what you make of the plate, and the *book*, if you take my meaning, in which it appears. Could you give us your impressions as to *value*, for example?'

This was an extraordinary piece of luck, although whether ultimately good or bad Alice would never be able to say. A request for practical information about almost any other book would have left Alice perplexed. She loved books – not just the scientific works in which she lived, but also the wider humanist canon that she had absorbed (a *little* erratically) through her father. But books as objects didn't much interest her, beyond a vague desire, which she recognised as feminine weakness, to arrange them according to colour rather than subject matter or author.

The great auk, however, did interest her. It was the world's unluckiest animal. It had the misfortune, first of all, to taste (to half-starved codfishermen battered by arctic storms) good. Its eggs were large and delicious. You could squeeze a useful, if smelly, oil from its flesh. It lived in places taxing, but not impossible, to reach. It had a trusting and gentle demeanour, making it simple to harvest. It had once nested in millions, but the cliffs and islands where it waddled were gradually stripped by hardy sea folk (and later scientific egg collectors, eager to bag an auk shell before the creature went the way of the dodo) until the very last survivors clustered together on one rocky islet off the coast of Iceland. Which happened to be a volcano. Which happened to blow up. Alice came across the story in her research on island biodiversity, and had to leave the library to go for a good cry in the park.

The question had been a trick one, contravening one of the unwritten rules of interviewing. But then that was Colin Oakley, who liked to show his masters how ruthless he could be in their cause. The plate was a reproduction of an old watercolour of the auk, but the book was relatively new. New, but printed privately as a limited edition. Would Alice fall into the trap of overestimating the value based on a false assumption of age? Or would she take it to be a worthless modern work, of some interest, perhaps, to auk-enthusiasts, but none at all to book collectors? Well neither, as it turned out. She had read an article in a Sunday newspaper about the author, and his lonely, monomaniacal interest in the auk. She knew that the book was a modern limited edition. She knew its approximate value. She made the right sort of cautious noises about checking just how limited the edition was, and having to scan the internet for any information on recent sales, but when pressed for a number, hit happily on exactly the figure the panel had before them.

She then realised that a pun had been staring her in the face for a while without her fully noticing.

'Of course,' she said, a little shy smile making her look as pretty as she ever would, which was really quite pretty, 'we'd have to wait to see what it actually reached at . . . auk-shun.'

There was a worrying moment or two, in which Alice seriously contemplated simply walking out, before the panel decided to laugh, but once underway the general chortle acquired enough momentum to last for a good ten seconds.

'It'd be handy having a scientist around. You know, for facts and suchlike.'

The panel were having a final round-up.

'Mmm, she certainly knew her stuff when it came to auks.'

'And seemed to have a reasonable sense of humour.'

'For a scientist.'

'Not bad-looking either.'

'For a scientist.'

'And of course there's Old Crawley to think about.'

'Crawley, of course.'

'Ah yes, good Old Crawley.'

So Alice got the job, despite the fact that none of the panel members ever had a clear idea of who or what Old Crawley might have been.

Alice approached the body that had agreed to fund her research. She half wanted them to say that no, they really couldn't defer her award, and who did she think she was anyway, even to ask. But in the event they were horribly decent and agreed that her funding was available for any time over the next year, after which she would have to reapply. It made her think of the tutor who'd first suggested that she stay in research. 'They always like to have a girlie or two on their books,' she'd said with minimal bitterness. 'Makes it look like they have a decent equal opps policy.'

So Alice told herself that she could do the job for a year, save some money, have some fun, and then carry on with her research. After all, she was only twenty-four. Mauritius wasn't going anywhere. And just how many species of snail could go extinct in a mere twelve months?

The plan, had it not been for the intercession of the Dead Boy, might well have worked out. As it was, everything changed when Alice entered her dreamtime.

Why her? Why then? Why the Dead Boy? The questions drifted through her mind but never pressed her to answer, never forced the issue. If someone had taken her face in their hands with gentle pressure and implored her to say what it was about her, Alice Duclos, that had made her vulnerable to this obsession, then she might have tried to say something about her father, something about the rotten, death-filled, loveless cavity where he had been, that marked his loss. She might have said something about the bitter wilderness, the tedium, the endless ache of her life with Kitty. She might have said those things, or she might only have pulled away, her eyes empty.

Whatever it was, Alice's plans dried and shrivelled and blew away, and she stayed at Enderby's. It certainly wasn't that she'd fallen in love with her job; it was more that her life came to a kind of a stop when she saw the Dead Boy; everything became frozen, petrified. She didn't want change; she most emphatically didn't want Sheffield. What she wanted was to think about her boy, to imagine his life, to invent a life together with him. Working at Enderby's was a link to the Dead Boy, because that's where she was when she found him, but it also left her with the time to live in her imaginary world. She wasn't stretched or tested. Her colleagues presented no real difficulties or challenges, and she found that she could function perfectly well with only a fraction of her consciousness above the surface, in the waking, office world.

The main problem had been Andrew. At some point during the two months of innocence before things changed, she had gradually become aware that he might like her, although she never fully admitted it to herself. And he was nice. Well, no, not *nice*, but funny and interesting. They'd even had a sort of a date.

'I hate parks,' Andrew said one afternoon. Alice had brought him a mug of tea, as it was her turn. They had a little running joke about how terrible her tea was – too milky, and not brewed for long enough. 'You've got to shqueeze the bag,' he'd say in a comical version of his northern accent, and she'd pretend to get huffy about his ingratitude.

'What's wrong with parks? I don't think I could survive in London without them. It's the only way to escape the clamour and rush.'

'Yeah, well, that's the cliché, but it's just a thing that people say without meaning it, or thinking about it at all. Parks are full of weirdos, and people doing t'ai chi, and old codgers with nowhere to go, and dogs, and pigeons with gammy legs, and people snogging as if nobody can see them. The ground's always wet, and there're trees and shrubbery and stuff all over the place. When did anyone ever have a decent conversation in the park? No, parks are for losers. There's that Larkin poem, you know, about turning over your failures by some bed of lobelias.'

Alice was laughing.

'Have you ever actually *been* to a park?'

'Yeah, loads.'

'Which ones?'

'You know, just parks. The regent thing. And that other one, the green one. No, not really. I told you, I don't like them, I prefer to get drunk sitting down in the corner of a pub, not standing up with a can of Special Brew, and a gang of old men with bandaged heads, and piss stains down the front of their trousers.'

'There's a beautiful one that I used to go to when I was young. We used to bunk off from PE lessons and sit in the grass and eat ice cream. It saved me, in a way, because I used to live in the country when I was very little, and London was . . . difficult. I still go there sometimes. I think even you'd like it. It has an aviary, and an enclosure with wallabies, and an old-fashioned bandstand. It's not really a Special Brew kind of park. More cream tea.'

Now Andrew was laughing, but his eyes had narrowed. He'd suddenly realised that this was the fabled shot-to-nothing, the freebie, the chance to ask Alice out without actually *seeming* to ask her out. No declaration of intent was needed, no fear of rejection, no embarrassment at all. This could all be passed off as an innocent trip to the park. A mere matter of friendship. But still, how to ask her. Words. What happened to them when you needed them? And anyway, it wasn't true that there was nothing to lose. What if she didn't even want to be friends? Wasn't that worse than not wanting to go out with him? (On balance, he decided that it *wasn't* worse, but only by between six and eleven per cent, depending on other variables.)

'*Wallabies*,' he said, after a few moments of computation. 'You're winding me up. No? Well, if you say so. I've always liked the idea of wallabies. Little kangaroos. Charming fellows. Mmmm. It is, you know, on this plane of existence, isn't it?'

Alice already had a reputation for being a little dreamy, which Andrew used occasionally to tease her with, staying, he hoped, on the right side of being an arse.

'Yes, Golders Hill Park. It's a sort of offshoot of Hampstead Heath. But without the men having sex with each other in the bushes.'

'Why don't you show me round it? You know, the wallabies and the cream teas?'

With sublime ease the date was arranged for the next day, Saturday. Andrew's pleasure at this was dulled after he became aware that the divine and/or profane Ophelia had been listening to the conversation. Although he didn't have the nerve to look directly at her, he could easily picture the aspect of disdain into which her exquisite features so easily fell. For a moment his mind projected Ophelia's contemptuous sneer onto Alice's open and innocent face, where it

curled like an obscene wound. The vision made him hate
Ophelia, but he would still have given a month's salary for
the chance to pin her down on an unmade bed and . . .

'I'll meet you by the flamingos,' said Alice.

And it was that lunchtime, Friday 14th April, that she
found the Dead Boy.

Andrew couldn't put his finger on what had changed, but
it was clear that things were different as soon as he saw
her. He would have noticed the difference if he hadn't had
meetings on the Friday afternoon, and he deliberately spent
the time in between appointments away from his desk, just
in case Alice should change her mind. After all, that's what
girls did, sometimes, didn't they?

He'd been watching the flamingos for about ten minutes,
thinking what ugly organisms they were, close up, with
their birth-defect, upside-downy faces, and trying to work
out why they would want to stand on one leg. Something
to do with heat conservation? Showing off to lady
flamingos? Just because they could? And then Alice
appeared, wordlessly. Her eyes wouldn't meet his, which
wasn't like her at all, and she was dressed in something
beyond her usual endearing simplicity in a combination of
heavy top and light skirt and idiot-grade, lumpen brown
shoes.

'Alice, hello,' he said. 'Lucky you got here. The flamingos
were starting to get bored with my conversation. And to be
honest even I can only take so much small talk about
whatchacallit, plankton.'

There was a profoundly disconcerting pause before Alice
said, 'I'm sorry.' Andrew couldn't think what she was apolo-
gising for, but it seemed a strange sort of greeting. The park
was, as Alice had said, very pretty. There really were wallabies, or one at least, accompanied by what Alice said

without looking was a capybara, a big brown thing like a guinea pig on steroids. There was a bandstand with a large sign warning people to stay away. Although it was a chilly April morning, the sun shone in its weak-willed way, and it ought to have been fun.

But for Alice.

Andrew became increasingly frantic in his attempts to break through her . . . her what exactly? Reserve? No, she'd never been reserved, and that wasn't it now. Veneer? God no. A cloud. For some reason Andrew remembered the derivation of 'glamour' which was originally a Scots word for an enveloping, obscuring cloud or mist, conjured up by a spell. So that was it: here in her mad-auntie clothes, Alice had acquired a glamour. Having a word for it didn't help. His capering produced one brief smile, one moment of flickering recognition in her eyes. They were walking slowly around the aviary when Andrew was confronted by a tastelessly plumed, gangly bird, about a yard high, with a frill of what looked like 1960s eye make-up around its head.

'What's that one called?' he asked.

'It's a crane.'

'A crane! Amazing. It doesn't look strong enough.'

There was a pause before Alice registered what he'd said. 'Strong enough?'

'You know, to do all that lifting, for buildings and things.'

She crystallised for a second, before deliquescing back into some unreachable place, behind the cloud, behind the glamorous cloud.

The last thing Alice said to him as they parted was, 'I'm sorry.'

THREE

The Death of a Boy

Ships, towers, domes, theatres, and temples lay open to the sky. From up here she could see the whole of the great city stretching away from her on every side: glass pyramids, sky-scrapers in gleaming, beaten bronze and bright chromium, towers of intricate wrought iron, ecstatic arcs of light, bridging gulfs and chasms. And lower down, miles below her, acre after acre of teeming tenements rich, like a coral reef, with life, blooming and billowing in the clear currents of air. Lower still, she could just make out the network of placid brown canals, with their longboats, and oared Venetian barges, crusted with gold and sugar icing, laden with aromatic cargoes of spice and opium. Blue airships, borne on plumes of white canvas, sailed serenely above and between the towers, and she could see the children waving from the small windows, giddy and hectic with the thrill of flight. From here there was no noise, none of the roar and throb of the city, just the sighing of the cirrus clouds and the blood murmuring in her ears.

But this was too high: she couldn't see what she wanted to see. Up here she was blinded by all the beauty and the splendour. She closed her eyes and thought herself closer to the ground, closer to the heart of things. She felt for the place, gently, timidly, like a tongue feeling for a point of tenderness. She opened her eyes into a layer of cloud. But no, not cloud: thick, choking smog, dirty with flakes of ash and busy particles of soot. She thought herself lower. Noises reached her: a harlot's curse, the screams of a newborn baby, a hammering of iron upon iron.

And further down she plunged, hoping to drown the cries of the wretched with the rush of wind in her face. She opened her eyes again. Here was the street she had walked down so many times. She saw the cafés spilling tables out onto pavements, desperate to make the most of the spring sunshine; she saw the mannequins in the windows of French Connection, Hobbs, Gap, all eager for summer, in light dresses and swimwear. Queues formed at the cashpoints, each one headed by a bewildered old lady, randomly pressing buttons.

She hovered just below the roofs, close enough to feel the noise of the traffic: the buses and taxis and cars; close enough to hear the clip of heels, the jingle of change; close enough to see the faces, blank or anxious, smiling, wincing, cursing, laughing, of people pushing their way to the cafés and shops, all desperate to do what must be done this lunchtime. From here she could see directly into the windows of the rooms above the shops, but they stared blankly back, refusing to give up their secrets.

She didn't have to wait long before she saw him, moving like a dream of beauty through the world of things. Instantly, the street and the other people lost their vibrancy, became muted and grey. He was dressed in a long black coat, which swept behind him as if he were walking into a strong breeze. Beneath the coat she could see a white shirt, which flickered, becoming now soft swan's down and now shimmering chain-mail. The breeze which blew back his coat also caught thick strands of his long hair. But Alice made the wind stop: the image was false, too clearly derived from advertising or shallow girlish fantasies.

The boy's slow, long strides took him steadily towards the crossing. The people before him dissolved as he passed, or melted into the pavement: he was the only real, solid thing in this world. And look, there, on this side of the road, Alice coming. So innocent in her dreaming: nothing there to cloud her thoughts or crush her will. She's thinking about some silliness of Andrew's (was it the time he'd tampered with the auto-correct function on Clerihew's word-processor, so that whenever he typed 'Cedric Clerihew' at the end of a memo or letter, what came out was 'Cedric King of the Visigoths, Emperor of all the Byzantines, and Lord of the High Seas Clerihew'? – the watching Alice smiled even now). Or perhaps she's planning a mollusc hunt on faraway Mauritius. How easy the world had been then, how infinite in wonder and hope and opportunity.

The innocent Alice paused at the crossing, and the watching Alice looked for her boy.

When she replayed the incident, as she so often did, she could never quite see clearly enough to understand what had happened, why the car hadn't stopped, why he hadn't seen it approach. But there he was now, pellucid in the shade. This time she would learn the truth. And before she, the waiting Alice, had seen him, he had looked at her, paused for a moment, and then stepped out into the road.

The car must have come from his right. Alice looked, and there she saw it. Metallic blue; something nondescript; a badge she did not recognise. There was a thick crusting of grime around the butterfly pattern of the wipers. And coming too fast. The boy again. He was still looking at her, confident on the crossing. But now he sensed that something was wrong. He was alone. Where were the others?

Just as Alice, the waiting Alice, saw him for the first time, registered his presence, his beauty, he turned away from her to the car. The watching Alice peered down through the screen to the driver: a young woman, blonde, smart, untroubled, looking ahead. Looking but not seeing. But seeing now. Seeing him. Her body tensed and she stamped down on the brake. Tyres screeching. The boy absorbed the car, the truth of the car, and turned slowly – so slowly she realised there must be some distortion in her perception – back towards Alice. And he smiled.

What could that smile have meant? The waiting Alice wondered; the watching Alice wondered; and later the Alice who replayed the visions of the waiting Alice and the watching Alice wondered. Was it some reckless, adolescent bravado – a determination to show no fear in the eyes of the world? Was it a smile of sadness for the world that he was leaving? Was it a smile of love for Alice, a love engendered in that moment of desire and death? All seemed to carry something of the truth, but none to fully contain it. There was something else. Something darker. Something in the boy that said – but how could it be? – that said yes, yes.

FOUR

Odette and Alice

Odette was worried. This was unusual, because Odette was
not a worrier. Not that she was unnaturally cold or heartless (she was, in fact, a reliable source of solid, practical help
to those in need), but rather because she looked on worry
as hopelessly inefficient, and nobody had ever doubted
Odette Bach's efficiency. The tale is still told in her family
of how, at one of the irregular Bach gatherings to celebrate
a birth or a death or a marriage or an unexpected recovery
from cancer of the colon, the young Odette (accounts vary
as to whether she was seven, five, or a wholly unlikely
three) had replied to the 'and what do want to do when
you grow up' question, fired at her by an unwary aunt or
uncle, with 'I'd like to work in the City', thereby greatly
amusing the throng, but dismaying her parents: a social
worker and a music teacher, famed in the family for their
shabby furnishings and interest in Culture.

Unlike many of the women who did well in the City,
Odette neither ingratiated herself with her male colleagues
by excessive drinking and swearing, nor slept and flirted her
way to promotion. She simply did everything that was asked
of her supremely well. Nor did she work the insane hours

that had become accepted as normal in the City. And those who would see her walk from her desk at six-thirty every night would feel not the customary superiority over a 'light-weight' who couldn't hack it, but a cringing knowledge that they were only left still toiling because of *their* inefficiency.

Odette had only three close friends: Frankie, a psychiatric nurse, Jodie, an all-kinds-of-things, but currently an interior decorator, and Alice, the focus of her current, highly atypical concern.

Alice was the last to join the group. It had begun years before when Jodie, Odette and Frankie, who'd met at college, had taken an early season bargain holiday to Mykonos, unaware that its reputation as a party island was qualified by the fact that most of those partying, back in those days, were gay men. Frankie had spent two fruitless nights attempting to convert the impeccably turned out and exquisitely toned clubbers to the joys of heterosexual love, as Jodie and Odette rolled their eyes and consoled themselves with the lovely view of the harbour, when they spied the darkly attractive young woman evidently on holiday with her mother. They took pity on the girl, and dragged her out with them, despite her protestations that she must look after Mummy. What followed was two weeks of first shy, then warm, and finally hilarious bonding. As so often, the injection of new blood reinvigorated the gang, as the relations between them all shifted subtly. The nights were spent dancing, and perfect days followed, dozing on the beach, lulled by the shushing of the sea. Frankie moved on, with more success, to the locals, but the focus remained themselves. At the end they all agreed it was the best, just utterly and completely the best ever. Even Kitty had enjoyed herself, and was quite content to see Alice disappear with her new friends, leaving her among the polite and handsome young men of Mykonos.

From the beginning Alice had always, of course, been a little odd. It was part of her charm, one of the reasons why they loved her. She was the one who, when their little group of friends would meet for a drink or a meal, would jolt them from their discussion of house prices and handbags with a dreamy soliloquy about beauty or truth or the extinction of a rare species of gaily-coloured mollusc, once indigenous to one of the scattered islands of the Indian Ocean, but now gone forever.

Odd, but not *this* odd.

It had begun back in the spring, not too long after Alice had joined, to everyone's amazement, that toffee-nosed auction house. She hardly now ever said anything, just sat and smiled. Or sat and didn't smile. She'd recently missed two of their regular get-togethers, and when she came to the last meeting, coffee and cakes for lunch at Vals in Soho, she sat throughout the hour-and-a-half of gossip silent but for a blank 'no, fine' when Jodie had asked her, without really thinking about it, sometime around the halfway point, if anything was the matter. More significantly, Alice, normally an enthusiastic scoffer of pastries, had left untouched the *tarte au citron* she had murmuringly ordered.

Among the four of them, Odette was the one who was known for her ability to miss the subtle (or not so subtle) moods of the others, to fail to spot a new hair colour, or romance. But it was she who said to the other two, once Alice slipped away ('my . . . I have work . . . I must go'):

'There's something wrong with Alice.'

'Alice?' said Frankie. 'Yes of course there is. She's fucking mental.' One of Frankie's 'things' was too throw around unpleasantly derogatory terms for the mentally ill. 'It's why we love her.' She smiled her smile, defiantly showing the gap between her two front teeth. She was dressed in her usual costume of long, flapping skirt and bat-like membranous top;

a combination which emphasised her enormous presence. Her nails were painted deep purple, a shade lighter than was normal for her ('just felt like something sunshiny today'). Frankie had chosen her career largely because it would annoy her parents, Oxford academics who could never see the point of sullying themselves with anything that happened outside college life. Frankie was huge, not at all overweight, but just impressively tall and wide and looming, and her personality succeeded in entirely filling her frame. Her long dark-blonde hair writhed and squirmed over her shoulders, with occasional forays skywards. She'd been amusing them all (but for Alice) with another story about her complex and adventurous love life, and, like all of her stories, it had ended with her face down in a gutter, moaning and railing, legs splayed, knickers nowhere to be found. She'd used the opportunity to say again that if Odette was the brains of their little group, Alice the heart, and Jodie the pretty little sling-back mules, then she, Frankie, was its pelvis.

'No, not wrong in general,' said Odette, 'wrong *now*. And not just now. For months.'

'You mean because she's been quiet?' said Jodie, delicately wiping the corner of her mouth with a little finger. 'But you know she just *is* quiet sometimes.'

Jodie was a chameleon, able to look at home wherever she found herself. She was wearing a simple blue dress that might well look cheap and cheerful to anyone not used to spending a thousand pounds on an outfit. But those who knew, knew.

'Not quiet like *this*.'

'Well, I suppose she was a *bit* funny, even for her. I know, she's in love!' That was Frankie's explanation for everything, except where people were in love, in which case she would cynically invoke lust or economics.

'If it's love it doesn't seem to be making her very happy.'

35

'Does it ever, for anyone?' said Jodie, wistfully, although it had, in fact, made her perfectly happy, coming as it did in her case with a pretty house in Sevenoaks and an angst-free Platinum Amex.

'I think she'd have told us about it if there was someone new. I mean someone at all. It's not as if there've been many,' said Frankie. She immediately regretted saying that as it could apply equally to Odette, and she certainly hadn't meant to be bitchy.

Odette picked up her bag. 'I don't think it's love. Not the ordinary sort, anyway. I'm going after her.'

'She'll be long gone, you'll never catch her,' said Jodie or Frankie, or both together; Odette wasn't listening.

Running from the café, she turned left towards Piccadilly. Luckily, she just caught sight of Alice's dark hair bobbing down the street.

'Hi, Alice,' she said when she reached her, a little out of breath. 'I thought I'd walk this way with you.'

Alice looked at her with what might have been suspicion in her eyes. It was something that Odette had never seen there before.

'Well . . . I was just . . . yes, walk with me, of course.'

'Alice, there's something wrong. You're behaving so strangely. I'm worried.'

That wasn't supposed to have happened: she'd so meant to be subtle. But something about Alice made strategies useless.

'You shouldn't worry.'

'Look, Alice, I have to get back to work, but can't we meet one evening? Just the two of us – not the others. You know, the thing is, I'd like to talk . . . to get your advice about something. If it's easier for you I can come to your flat . . .'

'No! Not there. Sorry, I didn't mean to . . . I don't mind where we meet.'

Odette named a wine bar in neutral territory, and they arranged to meet in two days. They kissed stiffly as they parted.

Perhaps Odette's greater than usual sensitivity was a consequence of the recent developments in her own love life – these developments had been the main talking points of the girls over the coffee and cakes. The key to Odette's career success had been the ruthless excision of the superfluous. She had trimmed from her life all that was not central: anything frivolous, wasteful, unproductive, weak, and among those things abandoned as inessential was romance. There had been a single, unsatisfactory relationship at university with a lecturer, drawn by her intensity and unexpected willingness to be educated. Since then nothing, unless you were to count the single date with a man who claimed to make scale models of Stonehenge to sell as garden furniture.

But now, at twenty-eight, Odette decided that it was time to act. Her group outside work, sensibly-shoed Alice and the other girls, and the few helpless boys she knew, busy trying to be Something in the Arts, offered nothing promising: she abhorred the idea of a milksop. She wanted a man whose ideas would challenge her own, someone who would stand up to her, someone who could make her proud and, yes, perhaps even a little fearful. Someone with a cock ramrod hard and piston fast. Well, not perhaps the last, which Frankie had helpfully added to her list.

It had to be work. That was where the agreeably packaged testosterone lived. But she had to choose carefully. Anyone superior was out of the question: she could not bear the thought that the office gossips would say she was finally using her sex as a crowbar. She knew most of her close colleagues far too well to make them interesting in that way. And anyone too junior would create all kinds of moral and aesthetic problems.

But then there had arrived the new boy, Matthew Mindbrace, the one who everyone had difficulty in placing precisely. He was spoken of as a loose cannon, or rogue elephant, or sometimes as a loose elephant. It was rumoured that he may have been brought in to 'sort the wheat from the chaff'. He still carried with him the fresh bloom of Harvard Business School. Bright, everyone agreed on that. Carefully cut unruly hair, forever loosening itself from the imprisoning gel, which suggested a passionate nature only with difficulty suppressed. He'd smiled a shy, dimply smile at Odette on his first day, and she responded with her own modest work smile, a smile in which the corners of her mouth turned very slightly down, rather than up.

'Hi, I'm Matt,' he'd said, in an accent that was impossible to pin down, but *may* have been English. 'I'm told you're the Oracle. Or is it the Sybil? I get confused with my Greeks and Romans.'

Odette wasn't sure if she was being laughed at. What was the Sybil? She had a feeling it may have been some kind of hag. She thought about making a witty reply, and then said, 'If it's a matter of orientation, I should go to Mr Henshaw,' before returning her attention to the yen.

But that had been two months ago, and now she found that she wanted a boyfriend.

'Matt,' she wrote in her email, 'I'd like to discuss some issues with you in the Blackfriar tonight at seven.'

The evening was awkward, despite the wine. Matt turned out to have a surprisingly inadequate bladder, and kept disappearing to the gents, leaving Odette alone in the busy pub. But at eleven o'clock they went back to her flat in Putney and made love twice, painfully.

All things considered, a comparatively successful first date.

She'd mentioned Matt in passing during the lunch, half hoping that one of the girls would pick up on it, as she didn't want to make any 'I've got a new boyfriend' type public declarations, just in case things didn't work out. And of course Jodie did, to good-natured whoops of encouragement, and crude (ironic-crude, naturally, rather than crude-crude) suggestions. She'd downplayed the weak bladder.

But joking with the whole gang wasn't quite what she wanted, and the quiet meeting with Alice seemed like a much better opportunity to talk through strategies and feelings and fears. It would also, she surmised, help to draw out Alice, giving her the opportunity to share her thoughts reciprocally, rather than have them extracted by emotional dentistry.

The wine bar was studiedly neutral, any suggestion of character or individuality rigorously bleached away. They were both on time. This was quite usual for Odette, who despaired at the modern idea that half an hour late didn't count as late at all. Alice had always (even in her pre-Dead Boy period) been more erratic, as likely to arrive pointlessly early as extravagantly late. Odette immediately sensed that something – she shied away from the term, which was very unOdettish, but it kept coming back to her – something *momentous* was going to take place. She ran through the possibilities: Alice was gay; Alice was taking the veil; Alice was dying from a rare blood disease. They ordered a bottle of something white and sat down. Odette squeezed Alice's hand, and decided to begin by sharing her feelings.

'Do you mind if I tell you about my boy?'

Alice's eyes opened a little more widely, as if she'd just seen some unexpected nudity in the middle of a Jane Austen adaptation.

'Yes, of course. I'd like that.' Alice hadn't taken part in the discussion during lunch, but she'd picked up that Odette had a new lover.

'I work with him. I like him. I don't know, but I think he might be . . . well, I hate to use the cliché, but you know sometimes you have to . . . the one.'

Alice smiled. 'What's he like?'

'Well, he's American, but he was brought up in England. Or English and brought up in America. I've been trying to piece it together, but he doesn't talk much about himself. It's one of his better qualities. He's very good-looking, in that preppy kind of way I don't like, except with him. He's quite funny. You know, observationally funny, not jokes or anything.' All that came out at breakneck speed.

'Oh, Odette, I'm really pleased. You've been waiting so long for this.'

'I haven't really. I mean, been waiting. That implies I was just hanging round, twiddling my thumbs like a desperate spinster until Mr Right showed up. That's not me; that's the opposite of me. It's only been the past couple of months that . . . well, you know, biological clocks and all that. Or maybe just boredom. There's got to be more to life than spreadsheets and *ER*. I'd forgotten about how exciting it, you know, sex, can be, how it takes your mind off all the everyday crap. I *so* don't care if the yoghurt's past its sell-by date, or if Starbucks have messed up my morning latte, or if my mum's said something stupid. It's wonderful. But I'd also forgotten about the fear.'

'The fear?' Alice spoke as though she knew something about fear.

'Yes, you know the losing-them fear. I was fine before without him, but now . . . well, it'd be awful to have to go back to . . . to what I did . . . I had before.'

Alice felt little electric jolts whenever something Odette said connected with her own feelings. Electric jolts separated by an ugly void. Alice knew that she was in danger of failing in friendship, failing to see the other as anything but an

40

echoing chamber for her own obsessions. It was partly her horror and revulsion at this failure that had driven Alice further towards reclusion: better, surely, to inch herself out of the world of human love and friendship than to stand damned for her emotional autism? And she had a place to which she could retreat: into the dark arms of her boy, her demon lover, ageless in his underworld.

But it was different with Odette. At some level she realised that Odette's declaration was part of an attempt to reach out to her, an invitation to join in with a revelation of her own. And how she wanted to share. She looked at Odette's sensible, boyish, pretty face and succumbed to a sudden surge of love, which subsided to leave the tips of her fingers thrumming gently.

'Odette, you're such a wonderful person. Why should this boy . . .'

'Matt.'

'. . . this boy, Matt, ever want to leave you? You're the cleverest, sensiblest . . . prettiest person I know.'

The prettiest may not have been strictly correct, but it had, for Alice, an emotional truth.

'That's incredibly sweet of you, Alice. But the trouble is that no man ever stayed with a woman because she was sensible or clever . . .'

'You're leaving out pretty.'

Odette brushed it away. 'Whatever. And somehow I feel that he's not really committed to me. That makes it sound as though I want . . . well. All I mean is that I can't help feeling he just sees me as a bit of a fling, as a way of keeping his hand in until something or someone else comes along. There. Oh God, I sound like a typical female whiner. I'll be writing to *Marie Claire* next.'

Alice laughed. 'Don't worry, being in love . . . oh, I didn't mean to assume that you love him, I just meant . . .'

'It's all right, go on; we'll use "love" as a general term covering all emotional, romantic or sexual feelings directed towards another person. Scientific enough for you?'

'Quite scientific enough. Everyone's allowed to go a bit mad when they're in love. I know . . . I know that I have.'

There it was. She'd said it. They both knew that once the first words had been spoken, the whole story would inevitably emerge. But Odette was anxious not to ruin things by forcing the issue. She waited for a few seconds to see if anything would emerge, and when it didn't, she said:

'So then, what do you think I should do?'

'You mean to . . . what? Help things along a little?'

'Yes, I think that's what I mean.'

Alice's eyes came alive. She was delighted to have been asked for her advice, especially by Odette, to whom she had always ever so slightly looked up.

'Perhaps you don't have to do anything. Perhaps you're already doing exactly what you should be doing. Just being you.'

'I know that's sensible. It's exactly what I'd say to you . . . to someone else in the same situation. But you must trust me: that won't work here. Something needs to be injected, some, I don't know, glamour, or something. Something urgent . . . special . . . magical.'

'Heavens, Odette,' said Alice, laughing again. 'You've so come to the wrong person for advice about that sort of thing. I know even less, I mean less than you, about love and boys and things.'

'But I think you know about magic.'

They both paused and looked at each other, glasses symmetrically raised at chin height. Then Alice had an inspiration.

'Oh, if it's magic you want, why not take him to Venice?'

'Venice! I've never been. Isn't it a huge cliché?'

'Well, *I've* only been once, but it's just so miraculously beautiful, treated as an object. And I don't even mean the galleries, although you shouldn't miss the Academia. I went with the school. The canals were smelly, and horrid men pinched your bottom, and leered, but nothing could take away from the wonder of it. If it's romance and magic you want, Venice has to be the place.'

'Well, it's certainly an idea. And what else am I supposed to spend my bonus on? It may just be that you're a genius, Alice Duclos. You must know more about love than you claim.'

Alice drained her glass and looked down at the polished wooden table.

'Odette, when you asked the other day if I was okay, if anything was wrong, I should have told you about the . . . thing that happened.'

'Alice darling, you know you don't have to tell me anything you don't want to. You don't owe me a confidence because I told you about Matt.'

'I know. It isn't that. I think I do want to tell you. I can't talk to Mummy about it. Not yet. Probably not ever. And there's nobody else. The thing is that I'm in love with a dead boy. I saw him killed. He was knocked down close to the office. We looked at each other just before the car hit him. He smiled and closed his eyes. It sounds insane, but I know that he loved me in those moments before he died. His face was so peaceful, so beautiful. Odette, I can't ever forget him. Every night I dream about him. Whenever I close my eyes, he's there. I know him better than I know any living person. He's in me like blood.'

The noise, even the light, from the bar were instantly shut out. The table became the centre of a tiny universe, with nothing but the two of them centred there. Odette tried hard to keep the shock from showing in her face. This explained everything. And so was Alice genuinely mad after

43

all? This kind of obsession was so far beyond her experience, her understanding. But Alice seemed to be able to function perfectly well, apart from the distance, the growing isolation. And wasn't her love for this dead boy just an extreme form of the kind of intoxication they all felt when in love? Oh God, what to do, what to do? For Alice's sake, she must be sensible, she must be practical.

'Did you ever try to find out who he was?'

'Try? . . . No. How could I? Why should I?'

'Perhaps it might help?' What Odette meant was perhaps it might help to get him out of your system. It wasn't much, but it was something.

Alice's thoughts went on a different track. Help, perhaps, to know him more. Help to deepen and strengthen her love.

'But I don't know how to find things out about people, about people who . . .'

'I don't think it's very hard. I have a friend, an acquaintance really, a journalist. I'm sure she could find out. It's the sort of thing they do. When and where did he . . . was the accident?'

Alice told her, unhesitatingly. The date, the time, the place: all were cauterised in her memory.

And so it was agreed that Odette would ask her journalist to find out what she could about the Dead Boy. Alice felt a curious and not unpleasant numbness, the sort of vagueness she felt after her exams, but before the results had come out. It carried her through the next two weeks, until Odette called her.

Kitty answered the phone, and called out a simple, brutal 'You,' before leaving the phone dangling in the hall.

'He was a refugee from Bosnia. He came in 1991 as a fifteen-year-old, and so he was twenty-four. There's an address and a phone number. I don't know how Sarah managed to get that; boy, she's good.'

Alice wrote everything down in her red velvet address book.

'Thank you, Odette. This . . . matters a lot to me.'

'What will you do?'

'I don't know. What did you do about Venice?'

'Venice? Well, I've booked it! It was such a great idea. I'd love to talk tactics with you.'

But before they had the chance to speak, Kitty called out: 'Alice, you've been gossiping for long enough. I am expecting a very important call.' Alice knew that she wasn't; or at least that the *expectation* was false. But it was futile to argue.

'Yes, tactics. We'll talk tactics.'

FIVE

The Prior History of
Andrew Heathley

Andrew was sitting with his last surviving college friend, Leo Kurtz, in the Red Dragon of Glendower, a public house in Finsbury Park equally inconvenient for both of them but possessed of certain pleasant associations and, crucially, lacking a jukebox. The principal pleasant association was Zoë, a barmaid who'd worked there for one golden summer two years previously and who was, they both instantly decided, the most beautiful girl in London. Zoë had gone, returning to a course in Media Studies at Manchester University, but had left behind her a sweet white radiance which lifted the grimy old pub into a sort of Parthenon in their eyes.

Leo had a face made for swashbuckling villainy, long and slightly twisted, as if flinching from the light slap of a woman's gloved hand. His hair, black and thick, stood proudly on his head like the bristles on a goaded boar. He wore a black polo-neck jumper, recklessly challenging all comers to fuck off and read *Being and Nothingness* before they thought to interrupt *his* flow. Both Leo and Andrew were nursing pints of soapy brown fluid, mumbled complaints against which took up approximately one-third of all their

46

conversation. At the moment, however, the object of their discourse was the new quiz machine, installed by the brewery in an unwelcome attempt to move with the times. A large figure was hunched over the glowing screen, which was clearly visible to Andrew and Leo. Leo was in full flow, his long face oscillating between extreme animation and a sort of laminated inertia. His voice, when not deliberately made sinister or mocking, or contorted with bile, had a surprising depth and beauty.

'It's all to do with the compartmentalisation of knowledge. You see that *fop*' – one of Leo's commoner terms of abuse, not intended to suggest dandyism or effeminacy, merely irrelevance – 'just got the right date for the Battle of Waterloo. He had the choice of 1066, 1745, 1815 and 1939. He's probably played that thing a thousand times, and he's tried all the other options, and he knows that the right answer, the answer that lets him carry on, is 1815.'

'So what?' Andrew was usually up for this sort of thing, but tonight his mind was occupied with other matters.

'So what? *So what?* Don't you see that 1815, one of the most crucial years in European, no, fuck it, in *world* history, has become nothing more than the answer to the question, *What year was the Battle of Waterloo?* All of the complex historical reality, the treaties, the lives, the pain, the power, it's all gone. All that's left is the simple question and the simple answer.'

'So what?'

'Don't you get it? It's the end of any kind of organic understanding of our society. All these facts are shaken loose of their true social setting and given a new context, the context of the quiz. What was the *real* context of the Battle of Waterloo? Revolution, the Terror, the rise of Napoleon, blahdy blah and then the restoration of the Bourbons, and the general crushing of dissent and reform up to 1848. But now how does that guy, and almost anyone else that ever comes up against the date 1815, see it?'

'I strongly fear and suspect that I'm about to find out.'

Leo paused for a megalithic second, considered asking Andrew *exactly what the fuck was the matter with him*, and then compelled by the momentum of his analysis went on:

'The setting now, the context is: *which Spice Girl had the first solo number one?* And, *which Coronation Street character fathered an illegitimate baby in 1968?* And *which was the first English team to complete the FA Cup and League Double?* You see, it's all isolated fragments, cut out of their setting. That's what trivia means. In the old days we had general knowledge, and it might have been the reserve of dullards, but at least it was all about connecting up. Now we have *trivia* and it's all about . . .'

'The trivial?'

'Exactly. Look, just what the fuck is the matter with you?'

'Me? Nothing, I'm just not in the mood to play tutorials. Save it for your students.'

'Ah, I see. It's chick-related. Is it still the weird girl in the office?'

'What weird girl? There isn't a weird girl.'

'You know who I mean, the one you had the date with, the one with the eyes?'

Leo accompanied this question with a wiggling two-fingered gesture in front of his face, as if to suggest strange mystical powers in the organs under consideration.

Andrew, of course, knew exactly who Leo was talking about. He knew because he'd been talking about her himself for the best part of eight months.

'It wasn't a date, it was a disaster. And I wouldn't call her weird. She's just a bit . . .'

'Mad?'

'Mad? Maybe, a bit.'

'Mad madness-of-King-George mad?'

'God no, not madness-of-King-George mad.'

'How boring. So you mean mad in the usual mad-woman mad way, the not getting your jokes kind of way, and suddenly saying out of the blue "why don't *we* ever go to Venice" kind of way, and thinking that whenever you make a general point in an argument it's somehow directed at them kind of way.'

'No, no and no. She's not mad like that. In fact the opposite. We used to have quite a laugh together, in the early days. Maybe I don't mean mad at all. At least not in any of those ways. Maybe I just mean . . . strange.'

'Ah, strange-but-interesting-mad. The most dangerous sort. They suck you in, and they can appear enchanting to begin with, and sexy as anything, but in the end the mad bit always breaks through and then they come at you with a mattock or leave dog excrementia in your pyjama pockets.'

'No, no, Alice isn't like that. I can't really see her with a mattock, whatever a mattock is. I shouldn't have said mad at all, *or* strange. Scratch mad and strange. It's more that when she's there, she somehow isn't really there. No, I mean the other way round – it's *we* that aren't really there, or we're sort of semi-transparent and she sees through us to the things that *are* really there.'

'So far so Neoplatonic. You'll be giving us the parable of the cave next.'

'And she sort of says stuff, stuff that *should* make you laugh in her face, but you can't because . . . she's got some kind of . . .'

Leo did his two-fingered eye-wiggling thing again, accompanied this time by a head wobble.

'I'm not really getting it across, am I? I'll give you a for-instance. You know how she deals with all the science and nature stuff?'

'I think you might have mentioned it, like about a million times.'

'Well, we've got a fucking massive, and I mean massive, job on. You've heard of John James Audubon?'

'Yeah, I think so. Some kind of bird-watcher fellow.'

'Yes, but also a pretty good artist. Anyway, there's a reclusive aristo down in the Quantocks with a copy of Audubon's *Birds of America*, which is, you know, *the* most expensive book in the world. We're talking five million quid here. Apparently he wants to sell, and if we can get it, then it might just be enough to stop the Americans from sacking us *all*. So we're heavily into the research. As I said, it's Alice's area, but I'm in as well, because she's still pretty junior, and she sort of comes under me.' (Here Leo contemplated one of his famous leers, complete with the sound of moist membranous flesh plapping and slithering, but decided that this was not the time.) 'We're looking at some repros of the plates, which are about the size of a duvet. A few of the others have gathered round, because they know how hot the whole thing is. We're looking at something called the Carolina parrot, but Alice says it's actually a lorikeet. And, you know, although it's not my period, or subject matter I could see it wasn't bad – plenty of energy and panache in the execution, and certainly a notch up from the Lewis *Birds of Great Britain and Ireland* . . .'

'Mmmnyaah,' said Leo, drawing deeply on a phantom briar pipe.

'Okay, I'll get on with it. But then Alice says, and believe me it was one of those times when you didn't know if it was going to end in us all laughing till our tonsils fell out or in a group hug and years of counselling, she says, "You know why they are so alive, don't you, the Audubon plates?" And I thought she was going to talk about the vibrancy of the watercolours, or the grace of the line, or whatever, but she says, "It's because Audubon painted them in death. He shot the birds and had them stuffed and mounted . . ."' (At this point Leo couldn't stop himself and about two-sevenths of a leer emerged, along with a solitary plap, but Andrew was too fervid to notice.) '". . . and that is why they are so intense, so perfect, so *alive*. You see it is only because they were dead that they could be authentically, mesmerically alive." And nobody knew what to do, and then everyone drifted off, leaving just the two of us. Thank Christ Ophelia turned up to wave her hair around, or God knows what I'd have done.'

'You know I really think we are talking madness-of-King-George mad after all,' said Leo, because he knew it was expected of him. And then, because it was time, 'Another pint of Old Shagpiss? Or shall we try the guest ale, which this week, according to the board, is the famous old Bodkin and Feltcher's Whale Gism, at 9.7 per cent proof?'

The eight months that had passed since Alice had joined Enderby's had been uncomfortably intense ones for Andrew. His brief account of how he came to be in quite so unsuitable (from his own perspective and background) a place as Enderby's was accurate, as far as it went, but missed out the various psychodramas, failures, reversals that led up to it. Like Alice he was an only child, but there the resemblance ended. He was brought up in a small mining town in Nottinghamshire, where his father was a collier, until the pit closed, whereupon he opened a shop selling fishing tackle and buckets of maggots, which used up all of his redundancy without supplying any kind of adequate income.

Like most miners, Andrew's dad had a reverence for learning, and watched proudly as his son sailed through every exam he ever sat, and became the first boy from the town to go to Oxford. School had been easy for Andrew, not just because he was the cleverest boy in his or any other year – that, on its own could have been a fast track to getting his face punched on a more or less daily basis. No, what made Andrew's life a joy was being a cricketing prodigy, as sporting prowess was the only sure way for a brainy kid to escape the regulation clattering. Every Saturday and Sunday of the summer season would see Andrew gliding across the little cricket pitches of the local villages and towns, hurling himself fearlessly on long slides around the boundary, or dancing down the wicket to flick and drive the quickest of the bowlers. Standing in the slips, he'd dream of catching the swallows that hawked for midges in the outfield as the sun burned red through the white plumes of mist billowing from distant cooling towers, and yet he'd still have time to take the real snicks and edges, to gasps of delight from his burly team-mates.

It was in the concrete pavilion of the local ground that he lost his virginity to an older (and considerably larger) girl called Jan, who worked behind the counter in the bakery. He wasn't entirely sure that he *had* lost his virginity, but she seemed confident enough, and forever after let him have an extra barm cake or free sausage roll whenever his mum sent him in for a loaf. In any case it at least gave him a start, and put him a notch above most of the other boys when he went, late that September, to college.

There was no good reason for his relative failure at Oxford. The failure was not academic: he was still able, despite doing the bare minimum to escape censure, to pick up a First in PPE. It was more that he passed through the University without making an impact, without finding himself in any exciting group, or movement, or even mood. He gave up sport. Nobody was interested in his kind of politics; nobody found him particularly clever or funny any more – there were too many semi-professionally funny and

52

clever people around. Ditto beauty. His friends were all pleasant, and helped to pass the time, but he never fell in love with any of them, nor with the frizzy-haired swotty girls he tended to consort of his circle, few of whom were prepared to go much beyond what he termed 'moist digitation'.

Life as a postgraduate in Brighton was a little better, largely because of his success, by virtue of taking some tutorials, in bedding a slightly foxier class of student. Nevertheless, when his money ran out and it became clear that there were few, if any, jobs available to which his thesis, even if he ever managed to submit it, was likely to prove a passport, life again seemed to lose its savour. For no very good reason he moved away from cosy Brighton and into one of the two attic rooms in a large falling-down house in Crouch End, where he worked fitfully at his bibliography, living principally off whichever type of cereal happened to be open in the kitchen.

Karen, the Tall Girl, who lived in the other attic room, rescued him in more ways than one, and it was only partially to Andrew's credit that he was sorry to have treated her so badly (part of the badness related to a failed attempt to palm her off on to the ever-eager Leo). Andrew's appraisal of his own appeal was fair, if perhaps a little stern. He estimated that he was at the top of the second division of attractiveness, which meant that he could count on the second, third and fourth division girls and had a fighting chance of picking off the odd slumming first-divisioner, particularly if he happened to be in one of his world-conquering moods, when a spurt of self-confidence would lend his tongue wings and provide a handy thermal on which to soar. It was certainly the case that by any objective measure he was a poor lover, prone to an analyst's dream of dysfunctions and fiascos, from outright no-shows, through prematurity, to hopelessly elongated dry runs. Yet somehow sexual intimacy lent him a sweetness and vulnerability and charm which left his partners helpless and, more often than not, love struck. Karen assisted with the bibliography, tidied his room, advised on how to move on from his now dated student-trendy look without ironing out too many of his 'endearing' idiosyncrasies (for example the faint, though discernible, tendency towards Edwardianism in his pants, boots, and sideburns) and finally, through a careful monitoring of the office airwaves, got him the chance of the interview in the Enderby's Books department, where she worked. Despite a good degree in history, Karen was stuck in the secretarial grade at Enderby's, from which it was almost impossible to escape into the hallowed realm of the Expert.

Two further pieces of good luck were necessary to Andrew's unexpected success before the panel. The first was that he happened to have one of his better, thermal-borne days. He managed to persuade the three wise men and one foolish virgin that his protestations of ignorance about deciphering eighteenth-century handwriting and his confusion about roman numerals beyond XV were the product of excessive modesty and he made two good book-related jokes, only one of which he'd prepared in advance. The second (or rather third, if we include Karen) piece of good fortune was that the pre-interview favourite, for whom Andrew and the other two anaemic boys on the shortlist were supposed only to be makeweights, turned up wearing a cloak and a floppy hat, which he refused to take off.

Four years of steady progress followed, with numberless trips to country houses, forced to sell the library to finance a new roof or fund a venture into bakewell tart mass-production, or poodle-rearing. Four years of inhaling dust and squinting at woodcuts. Four years of politely telling callers to Bond Street that their stack of *Bunties* from the 1970s were no, sadly not worth any more than sentimental value, or that the ninth impression of Rider Haggard's *She* was not a valuable collector's piece despite being over a hundred years old. Four years of looking for that rare first edition among the dross: a *Casino Royale* or a *Brighton Rock* in its dust jacket. But only one more year of Karen, who left, frustrated by both Andrew and Enderby's.

When Alice arrived, Andrew was still heavily into his infatuation with Ophelia. None of his standard methods had worked with her: the looking-helpless-by-the-photocopier-bumblingly-eccentric-but-also-quite-cool persona he'd perfected simply rendered him invisible to her. His little puns and humorous spoonerisms sounded in her ears like the jabbering of an idiot, and his learning counted for nothing in her world, where a trip to the hairdresser's lasted half the day and cost two hundred and fifty pounds, not including the coffee. Books meant nothing to her but the same could not be said for a title, and it was only when Andrew's friends started using *Doctor* Heathley (the thesis, bibliography and all, having been submitted, defended and, with minor corrections, accepted) as a way of amusing themselves at his expense, that he finally appeared, a dim green glimmer, on her radar.

Their only date was predictably disastrous. Andrew had never been out with anyone completely stupid before. He'd had girlfriends who'd left school at sixteen and never read a book, but they could all crack two jokes to his one and fizzed and bubbled with words and thoughts and laughter. Ophelia had only two topics of conversation: the fashion follies of the other women in the office (*'I* wouldn't wear that face with that bum' was one famous quip), and the cars driven by her boyfriends, or rather whichever clutch of management consultants, property developers and bankers were currently courting her. A typical exchange, screeched above the clamour in Quaglino's ('I couldn't believe it,' Ophelia would say on her next visit to the hairdresser's, 'I mean *Quaglino's*! You'd have thought it was 1997 or something'), ran:

'What kind of car do you drive, Andrew?'

'Well, actually I . . .'

'Richard drove a Mazda MX1, but I told him that was really a *girl's* sports car, so he bought a Mercedes *Kompressor* the very next day, which I thought was over-compensating. What did you say you drove?'

'I was saying that . . .'

'Phillip had a convertible Beetle that I couldn't make up my mind about, you know, whether the convertible bit made up for the Beetle bit . . .'

There was no question of a kiss, let alone a night of inept, but heartfelt fumbling. In fact, the only physical contact Andrew obtained from the exercise was a very public crushing hug from Pam, who whispered loudly and wetly in his ear that Ophelia wasn't good enough for him. Had anyone, he wondered, not heard about his humiliation? He did a quick calculation to work out how uncool the episode left him seeming to the eyes of Books and/or the world; the result came out at something close to the boiling point of lead, or, according to the traditional scale of one-to-ten, really very uncool indeed.

Yet more dishearteningly, the sure knowledge that Ophelia was one of the first division girls who would *not* be stooping to entertain a plucky second division contender only served to splash Tabasco on the hot chilli of his passion.

Nor did Alice's arrival lead to an immediate or complete transference of affection. The wandering Tessa, it is true, no longer played a role in his fantasy life, although a candle long burned brightly for *him* down in the Internet division, where she did clever technical things to facilitate on-line auctions. The trouble was that Ophelia was simply too damn beautiful – actress beautiful rather than supermodel beautiful, which allowed for the discernible and delectable presence of hips and buttocks and breasts – not to be, however critically and/or hopelessly, adored. The way he put it to Leo was that he *loved* ('don't cringe you fucking long-faced, cynical wanker') Alice, but *fancied* Ophelia, although he *did* allow for the possibility of a little bilateral seepage between the two (leer, plap, schleershp, mmpap, mmmpap, mmpap, from Leo).

And no, after The Disaster in the Park, he never got up the courage to ask Alice out on another date: the deepening, mystifying, otherness which enveloped her made it impossible. How do you ask the Sphinx out for a curry? What chat up lines can you use on Astarte, everyone's favourite Phoenician goddess of life and death? So, for eight months from February to September, Andrew yearned: and it was a yearning without respite, because to look away from Alice meant to look towards Ophelia.

And then came the Audubon. As soon as word reached him that an elusive copy of *The Birds of America* was up for grabs, he knew that it was his big chance, not only to increase the incline of his modest career graph, but also to spend time, no, more than time, to spend a *night* with Alice. In theory the Quantocks trip could be done in a day, but what if something unexpected cropped up? What if the deal was about to be closed and they had to rush off to catch the last train? Lord whoever-it-was might feel offended if he received a mere single day of flattery and cajoling. And for all they knew, the Other Place might already be on the trail, offering the usual inducements: the pretty girls (or boys), the promise of secret buyers, and fabulous wealth. No, this was a two-day job, with a night in (consulting the relevant page from the atlas), Nether Stowey or Crowcombe or Spaxton, assuming any of those hamlets could supply a comfy B&B. It wasn't that Andrew had any explicitly formulated plan of seduction. He just hoped that the simple fact of spending the time together would somehow meld them, or work some other magic. He got as far in his head as a boozy night with her in a thatched hostelry, hung with antique farming machinery (turnip spanglers, hay thrummers, perhaps even a many-bladed pig splayer), and there drew back, hoping vaguely that she might blurt out something about having always fancied him, no, dammit, *loved* him. That would see off the Ophelia problem.

Just love me back, my strange, my precious Alice, he thought, and I'm yours forever.

SIX

Quantock Bound

'Climb in,' said Andrew, smiling brightly. It wasn't one of his usual faces. Nor did it particularly suit the greasy grey skies, oozing drizzle like a fat man sweating over a meal.

Alice had been daydreaming. She'd been waiting on the pavement for ten minutes. Because she was by the busy road she saw, of course, the Dead Boy; saw him there for that second before he died, the second before she turned away. She had coping strategies now, and rather than cry out or turn away again, her face in her hands, she was able to drive out the bad thoughts by immersing herself in the Boy, breathing him like incense, drawing him in to her cells, until he was inside her and outside her and everywhere.

And now here was Andrew. In a car. And what a car.

It was perhaps fortunate that Andrew never had the chance to tell Ophelia about his car. Even Alice, who cared nothing for such things was vaguely aware that it was the sort of car that the kind of person who might be ashamed of having a crap car would be ashamed of. Andrew's attitude to his car was deeply ambivalent. He had enough intelligence and awareness to see that it was a completely crap car. And not just because it was a bottom-of-the-range 1979

Vauxhall Chevette two-door saloon. There were other reasons.

First of all there was the colour. Andrew would occasionally try to pass it off as mahogany, or chestnut, or dark tan, or burnt almond, or sienna, but the truth is that it was brown, and more than that, shit brown. Then there was the filth. The outside had never been cleaned in the year and a half that Andrew had owned it. His reasons for this were logical, if short-sighted. 'If I was going to be frying eggs on the bonnet, then I'd give it a wash,' he'd say. 'Or if I wanted to roll around on the roof wearing a cream linen suit. But I don't like fried eggs and I haven't got a cream linen suit.' And so layer on layer of crust had formed over the brown core, giving it yet more of an excremental aspect. In places, some of the outer layers had liquefied in the rain, and formed swirling patterns, before drying again, giving the effect of a lava flow, glooping its way towards Pompeii. The inside was slightly less filthy, although the exoskeletal remains of sweet and savoury snack products were lodged in most of the car's niches and inglenooks, and there was a faint vegetal aroma, unexorcisable by any number of pine-fresh car deodorisers, caused by a stray sprout, lost six months previously somewhere in the superstructure of the vehicle. The problem internally was more the décor, in particular the matching brown fun-fur seat covers, tufted and mangy now, but still able to drench a back in sweat in all climatic conditions short of a prolonged nuclear winter. Everything inside the car was ill-designed, adept only at spearing knees, jabbing kidneys, and catching and tearing clothing.

So yes, Andrew was aware of the fact that the car was a (barely) moving insult to all road users, a thing neither useful nor beautiful, a slovenly, casual V sign, thrown by the lazy seventies at the very William-Morris, utopian socialist, arts and crafts creed to which he felt most allegiance, indeed a thing both useless and ugly. But he loved it. He loved it not only because it was the physical manifestation of the fact that he had, after ten years of nervous trying, finally passed his test. But also because it needed him, *because* it was so bad. So *he* could insult it, hit it with sticks, spit at it in rage when it died at traffic lights or belched the black smoke that meant that yet again it was burning oil, but nobody else was allowed that privilege, and Andrew could be very unkind indeed to anyone who questioned the merits of the Merdemobile.

'Just sling your bag in the back,' he said, pointing to a rear seat overflowing with books and newspapers, but dominated by a headless porcelain dog, which Alice never got round to asking about. As she sank into the front passenger seat, her knees disconcertingly at about the same level as her shoulders, and her bottom gingerly aware, despite the intervening fun-fur, of individual springs, sprung all gone, he added, 'Welcome to the Merdemobile.'

Alice won instant points by neither gagging, nor laughing, nor leaping straight back out and running screaming down the road, all common responses. She did smile, however.

'Hello, Andrew. I really appreciate you collecting me. Why aren't you wearing your glasses?'

'I find it distracting if I can see too much when I'm driving.'

'Ah.'

Alice was more than a little amused by the sight of Andrew hunched over the wheel, squinting through the porridge-coloured windscreen. Also touched. You could say lots of things about Andrew, many of them tending towards the neutral or even hostile, but you could never say that he measured his worth by the quality of his material possessions.

'Sorry about the smell,' he said once she was settled.

'It's okay. Can hardly notice it. Cabbage?'

'Sprout actually. Lost one last Christmas in the back some-where. Just dematerialised.'

Something about the car, and Andrew's comically bad driving, put Alice at ease. Oddly comforted by the erratic choking of the engine, and the miscellaneous rattles and whistles coming from unseen corners of the interior, she stopped thinking about the Dead Boy, in either a good way or a bad way, and not thinking about the Dead Boy was something she hadn't done for a long time.

Why hadn't she taken the lift up to the fourth floor of the block of flats in Hackney, rung the bell, spoken to the family of her boy? Her memory of the trip was of watching her-self as if in a film, from the outside. She saw herself standing in the busy street, looking up to where she thought the flat must be, the address clutched in her hand as it had been throughout the long and unfamiliar journey, by tube and bus. The block was one of the thirties, rather than sixties, kind: almost elegant in red brick and white plaster. But its poverty was palpable. Perhaps it had been the stench from the lift well that had put her off. No. She couldn't blame that. The truth was that she feared what she might find, and even more she feared what she might lose.

And just standing there gave her a deep sensual fulfil-ment. This was the closest she had come since that day, the first day of her new life. Here the Boy had lived for those nine years before they came together. She felt his presence resonate through the walls and the earth and the air, like the huge silence after the death of a symphony. And standing there bathing in the glory of his resonance, Alice realised that one phase of her . . . madness . . . infatuation, was coming to an end. She felt a calm descend, a peace, a new clarity. The drug had been metabolised, had become part of

62

her. It was certainly not that it had become less important: no, it had entered her more deeply; but that left her superficially more able to cope with the surface of things. Yes, she knew that he would always now be there, but the unimportant parts of herself had been set free, her waking, conscious, living side. The side that had to sit in traffic with Andrew Heathley on a dull October morning.

There was a certain amount of hassle, as there always is, in getting out of London. Andrew thrust a flaking *A-Z* onto Alice's lap, and between them they managed to find every traffic cone in South-west London, but by the time they blundered onto the M3 they were laughing together in a way they hadn't done since before The Disaster in the Park, since before the Dead Boy. Andrew had a packet of jelly babies in the glove compartment, and Alice found herself greedily devouring them.

'Did I ever tell you about my friend Leo?' asked Andrew.

'I can't remember. Maybe.' So much of the past few months had passed through her consciousness without leaving a trace.

'Well, he has this theory,' he paused as they both winced over a gear change that sounded like the very gates of hell opening up right there in the car between them, 'about jelly babies. To be honest, he has a theory about everything, but his jelly baby theory is quite good. You know how everyone likes the black ones best?'

Alice was about to say that she actually found that she preferred the red ones, but that would ruin the tale. 'Yes.'

'Well, have you ever wondered why they don't just make them all black?'

'No, I haven't ever wondered that. But if it's true that people prefer them, it's surprising,' Alice replied, trying to help out.

'The thing is that apparently that's just what they tried back in the seventies: all-black bags of jelly babies. And guess what?'

'Nobody wanted them.'

'Of course, nobody wanted them. And why's that?'

'Um . . . because people like variety?'

'No, not that. At least not only that. This is the Leo bit. It's because of structuralism.'

'Oh, that's nice,' said Alice, unable to repress a reasonably naughty look.

'Yeah, okay, just listen. You see according to structuralist linguistics, everything only has a meaning in relation to everything else in the system. The word bus only means bus because it doesn't mean car, motorbike, elephant, whatever. There's no natural link between the word bus and the thing bus. It's just the way that language functions. You with me?'

'I think so.'

'So, with jelly babies, black ones only become *nice* in relation to the others, the yellows, oranges, greens and blues . . .'

'I don't think they have blue ones. Not in jelly babies.'

'Yellows, oranges and greens, then, if you *must*.'

'Sorry.'

'. . . that are not *nice*, or not *as* nice. In isolation, there is nothing *nice* about the black ones. Put another way, on their own, without the signifying system of the whole jelly baby family, the black ones cannot mean *nice*. So, to enjoy, to understand the *niceness* of the black ones, you need the *not niceness* of the others. Okay, you can laugh now and call me whatever kind of arse you want. But remember, it's not me but Leo who came out with all that bollocks.'

Alice had taken pleasure in the jelly baby tale and she wished that she could have made some more witty or clever contributions. She hated just sitting there and saying 'oh' and 'ah' and 'really' like the awe-struck wedding guest listening to the Ancient Mariner. The trouble was that although she felt more relaxed, less alienated than she had for many months, Alice had fallen out of the habit of conversation. At work, even with Andrew, she confined herself to mainly factual matters, relaying points of information, technical details, clear instructions. Apart, that is, from the occasional lapse into the 'death is life' kind of epiphany that so unnerved the office. Outside work she now hardly ever saw her old friends. She hadn't even spoken to Odette for several weeks, not since the phone call when she had passed on the address of the Dead Boy. She'd meant to tell Odette about her failure, when so close, to contact the family, and of how the experience had helped a little in reconciling her to the world. She put it off because she felt that she had let Odette down in some way. They'd never met to talk tactics for Odette's trip to Venice, or discuss how things were going with the preppy boyfriend. Had she gone already? She thought she must have done. When she finally got the courage up to telephone her, Odette's work extension just went dead, and she hadn't followed it up with a call to her flat. Thinking about it now, Alice felt a heavy pang of guilt and she made a firm mental note to call as soon as she was back from Somerset.

But even if she had seen Odette, sitting in quiet harmony with an old girlfriend was a very different thing to spending a three- or four-hour journey with a bright, prickly, funny, sensitive man like Andrew. And she found that she wanted to make him like her, wanted him to enjoy the journey. She stopped short of asking herself if perhaps this meant that she was waking from her dream of the Dead Boy; stopped because she knew that she didn't really want to

65

wake from the dream. But, for the journey at least, she would be awake.

Of course, questions. You asked questions. That would make her *appear* interesting without actually having to *be* interesting.

'You never told me what your PhD was about.'

They had hit the countryside, or rather some larger areas of green between the sprawl. It was one of those days when there aren't any clouds, but nor is there any sun, just a blanketing paleness.

'Christ, I can hardly remember. Ah, yes, ahem, full title, *The Sublime Machine*, colon, all-important colon, have to have a colon, *Conceptions of Masculine Beauty 1750–1850*.'

'Oh.'

'Yeah, I know, it's a killer, isn't it. Fat lot of good it did me.'

'Well, it got you into Enderby's.'

'That's what I mean. You can't believe how it's destroyed my credibility. All those years of railing against things, and hating people for having cushy jobs, and then I go and get one. It's ruined my life.' He smiled pleasantly at her. 'I do kind of half mean it though. It seems like such a frivolous thing that we do. Whenever I go home, back to Nottingham I mean, and I try to tell my parents what I do, they just don't get it.'

'I have the same sort of thing with my father.'

'You know I remember when poor old Crumlish showed me round on my first day and it was say hello to . . . and then some noise, and I'd have to say, who? And then he'd say very clearly and loudly PYRRHOUS, or BYSSHE, or FULVIA, or whatever, and then do a little smirk. When I told my dad there was actually a person called Horace, he laughed so hard he spilled a bucket of maggots.'

'Euw.'

'Fish bait. Did I never tell you about the tackle shop? Hang on, *your* father? I thought your father was dead.'

'He is, but I still talk to him.'

'Oh.'

There was a pause. Andrew didn't really think it was mad to talk to a dead parent, but he didn't know what he was supposed to say next. Alice broke the silence.

'Do you spend a lot of time thinking about male beauty?' She was trying very hard, and succeeded in pulling off the naughty/innocent face she had once specialised in when talking to boys at college.

Andrew ignored the half tease. He'd been mocked about the feyness of his research too often for it to bother him, but no one ever thought he was gay. It rather annoyed him.

'God no, not any more. Not that I ever did, really. There was just a gap in the research. You know, tonnes of stuff on changes in female beauty, but nothing academic on the blokes, despite the fact that, off and on, men have been just as much the focus of the adoring gaze as women, and just as likely to be described as beautiful.'

The adoring gaze. Yes, Alice knew about the adoring gaze.

'So what do you think beauty is then, as you're the expert?'

'Well, I certainly don't think it's any particular type of face, or shape of body. There's been loads of scientific, or rather cod-scientific, research trying to pin beauty down in terms of facial geometry, and tie it all in to our genes, but it just hasn't come up with anything persuasive.'

'It's funny, but I actually know quite a lot about this. The biological side.'

'Really? Yeah, I suppose you might.'

'You see there are various theories that suggest that being . . . nicely turned out, if you're a bird, or a guppy, say, (Alice at this point remembered that she used, when much

67

younger, to do a rather fetching guppy face, which never failed to amuse, even if no boy could ever truly fancy her again after seeing it. She quickly decided against doing it now) means that you've got strong, healthy genes, so you can get enough to eat, and haven't got parasites. And as for things like peacock's tails, well the fact that you've been able to carry that lot around with you for a while and not *get* eaten means that you must be pretty tough. So in either case, the lady guppy or peacock will want a piece of the genetic action.'

'God, I love girls that know stuff! I can't believe we have an overlap.'

'Not much. Just one lecture's worth. But back to beauty. If you don't think it's the gene thing, then what is it?'

'Well, you're not going to like this, being a science dolly . . .'

Alice did a head-on-one-side pretend pout, looking, Andrew thought, suddenly very, very kissable, weirdness and talking to dead dad notwithstanding.

'. . . dolly . . . what was I saying? Oh yep. Well, it's all just a way of talking. Oh, and writing, and painting. My view, I say *my* view, but I actually only got a handle on the theoretical side by talking it through with Leo. Did I mention that he was a genius?'

'I think it was implied or suggested at some point.'

'Well, *our* view is that beauty dwells in language: it's a series of conventions, or clusters of ideas, that live and move in our culture, and determine how we think and talk about beauty.'

Alice made a polite but distinct scoffing noise.

'So you're saying that when you look at someone and think, mmmmm, then there's no biological basis for that, it's all just a cultural convention? You're insane, or you've never been in love, or even . . . just fancied someone.'

Alice was enjoying the discussion; she could feel some of her old zest for ideas creeping back. She was also fairly sure that Andrew was talking rot. Behind the lightness, however, there was another, darker, reason for her pleasure. They were talking about beauty, and beauty meant talking about her Boy, her Dead Boy.

'No, no, of course you're right that even in humans, sexual attraction is biological, and you could probably trace it back to the need to reproduce, but what I'm talking about is what happens when we start to reflect on our . . . urges, to try to find meaning or structure. What happens as soon as you look at someone you find attractive?'

'I . . .'

'Yes, you give them a word, such as beautiful, and then wham, you find yourself smack in the middle of three thousand years of Western culture, you're in Plato's dialogues, you're in the songs of the troubadours, you're in Shakespeare, in Shelley, in Keats. Your thoughts and certainly your words aren't yours any more, they're part of the great conversation.'

'Talking of the great conversation . . .'

'What? Oh, damn, sorry, I'm ranting, aren't I? I must have had a couple of years of thesis stuff pent-up inside.'

'It's okay. It's an interesting subject, beauty. I just wish I had some.'

'Oh come on!'

'That probably sounded like false modesty. I know I'm not hideous, everything in the right place and things, but I'm not beautiful, not in the way that transforms everything, not in the adoring gaze way you were talking about.'

'For heaven's sake, Alice, you're the . . .' and Andrew only just stopped himself from saying 'you're the second most beautiful girl in the office', which he knew was more than any girl could take, be she hunchbacked, begoitred, or

69

scrofulous. Unfortunately, he couldn't stop himself from quickly physically running through hunchbacked, begoitred, or scrofulous as he drove.

Alice laughed.

'What were you doing?'

'Eh?'

'You did a funny thing with your back, and you pulled a silly face. You stopped yourself saying something, didn't you?'

In the moment he had to gather his thoughts, Andrew realised that he couldn't correct 'second most' even to 'most'. It would sound either insincere (which he could live with) or desperate (which he'd rather do without).

'I was just going to say that you're not bad-looking for a geek. At least you haven't got mad hair.'

Andrew's hair was the thing he thought most about, after breasts and books.

'Here we go!' Alice had heard quite a lot about Andrew's hair: he'd start most mornings by complaining about it over his coffee.

'Well, it's okay for you. At least all of yours is pulling in the same direction. You're not being subtly undermined from within. You must have seen it – whenever I'm trying to be serious it deliberately looks silly, curling off in all directions, and making obscene gestures. And then when I'm trying to be funny, it goes all sensible, and makes me look like a fucking Mormon missionary. I hate my hair.'

Andrew's hair *was*, in fact, quite silly.

'I think your hair's lovely,' said Alice, which pleased Andrew for about ten miles.

'I've just realised,' said Andrew, after a long disquisition on why he'd stopped playing sport, in which his fear of mediocrity, the death of artistry, and the question mark hovering

70

over his groin ('I have the thighs of a Titan, but the groin of a weak-willed girl' was how he put it) all featured, 'that I've been talking about me and my stuff for hours. Unforgivable rudeness. And boring. It's your turn.'

'What, to be boring?'

He looked at her and smiled sweetly. 'If that's what you want, then go ahead and be boring. I'm all ears.'

'That's not fair. You can't simply order someone to be boring just like that. What if I accidentally start being interesting?'

'I'll blow this whistle,' said Andrew, holding up an invisible whistle by its invisible string. 'Why don't you tell me why you gave up science and became a slave in the temple of Mammary. I mean *Mammon*. I said *Mammon*.'

'It was only ever meant to be a temporary thing. I still hope to go back to research, when, when . . .' She thought for a moment about telling Andrew some of the truth. But this wasn't the time. Instead she simply went off on another tack, explaining the joys of island biology, pointing out the paradox that islands are both fast-burning engines of evolution, churning out new species, and yet strangely impoverished when compared to similar sized areas within larger landmasses.

'If you take an island of fifty square kilometres, it might have twenty species of bird found nowhere else, but that's it. In a fifty kilometre section of Amazonian rainforest, you could have a thousand species. So islands are fascinating from an evolutionary perspective, but much less useful than continuous landmasses for biodiversity. I note that you haven't blown your whistle yet for me being interesting. It's lucky I haven't told you about my M.Sc. thesis on the subvarieties of land snails to be found in the Scilly Isles.' They both laughed.

'I can't wait till I tell Leo about you and the snails. He's already half obsessed with you and that'll really get him going.'

Alice and Andrew exchanged glances. Andrew wasn't sure if he'd *deliberately* suggested that the obsession was really his own. Couldn't even say if she'd picked up any suggestion at all. But he did know that the sight of Alice's face, calm and lovely amid the filth and litter all around her, made him want to pull over on to the hard shoulder and declare his adoration, quite possibly accompanied by weeping and the recitation of appropriate verses from the Romantic canon. Instead he scraped around for that elusive fourth gear, like Alice in being so close and yet so unobtainable, until the moment had passed.

Sometime during the fourth hour (an exit from the motorway was missed when Andrew stretched for the last of the jelly babies) as flat fields hunched into shoulders, and the road began to wind and dip, Andrew finally got round to talking tactics for the rummage.

'Let's go over it again. What do we know?'

'About the seller or about the work?'

'Let's start with the work.' Andrew's apparently business-like manner was at that point slightly undermined by a wild swerve to avoid some almost certainly imaginary obstruction in the road.

'Christ! What was that? A hedgehog?' he said.

'I don't think it was an anything,' replied Alice, showing more savoir-faire than she felt. 'Are you sure about not wearing your . . . never mind. Okay. Audubon's *Birds of America*: first edition. Four hundred and thirty-um-five life-sized illustrations, double elephant folio – thirty inches by forty. Produced in four volumes, 1827 to 1838. Based on his watercolours, done partly in the field, partly in the studio.' (Andrew glanced over to see if there would be any maudlin dreaminess here, and was relieved to find not. Alice had on her competent face, which was one of his favourites.) 'No one was interested in America, where his lack of either scientific or artistic training was held against him, so came over here, and had his paintings and drawings engraved on copperplate and hand coloured. Still, most of them ended up in the States, with a few dotted around Britain and France. Cost a hundred and seventy-five pounds, or a thousand dollars, at the time, which meant that you had to be very wealthy to afford a set. Altogether maybe a couple of hundred sets in the world, last one sold in ninety-eight for seven million dollars.'

'Very good,' he said, clapping, which was unwise, and very nearly fatal. Luckily the other vehicle, a tractor pulling a trailer of steepling manure, was slow moving.

If it sounded a little bit like a test, that's because it was. Oakley had asked Andrew to report back to him on how well Alice performed on this trip. Andrew himself was under a lot of pressure. Garnet Crumlish's post had never been filled: the vacancy was left open, partly to save money, partly to encourage commitment and compliance from those who might feel themselves to be in the running. Internally, Andrew, Clerihew, Ophelia and Alice, had all been tipped as hopefuls. The inclusion of Ophelia (useless) and Alice (newish) was a goad to Andrew and however much he downplayed his commitment to the job, he knew that there was precious little for him if he found his name on the next, no doubt long, list of those whose services, experience, knowledge and love were no longer required by Enderby's. He imagined brushing bluebottles from the top of rows of cheap editions of the Waverley novels, or the collected works of Edgar Bulwer-Lytton, in a smelly second-hand bookshop in . . . where? After the failure to get the Audubon, the Bloomsbury dealers wouldn't touch him, nor even the Charing Cross Road. What did that leave – Hampstead? Golders Green? Stoke-on-Trent? Hull? Inverness? Stockholm? Reykjavik?

'Made Audubon a celebrity in Europe,' Alice continued. 'He met Scott and various other influential people. Granted membership of the Linnaean Society, that sort of thing. But the project wasn't a great commercial success. Too many subscribers dropped out, or, like the King, never paid up.'

'Which king?'

'Oh God, I don't know – one of the Georges?'

'Aha! A weak spot.'

'Does it matter? Anyway, you're history and I'm science, remember. I'm not supposed to know.'

'I think you'll find,' said Andrew rather sniffily, 'that a William sneaked in between George III and Victoria.'

Alice ignored him and went on.

'So, when Audubon went back to America, he set out on a cheaper octavo edition, this time lithographs, again hand coloured. Still a beautiful object.'

'And worth?'

'Forty thousand pounds. Perhaps fifty, with a following wind,' said Alice in a subtle pastiche of Andrew's way of talking.

'And we don't know which this is,' he replied, making a mental note to pay her back for that.

'And we don't know which this is. All we got was a handwritten note from the seller, stating that he had a complete *Birds of America*, and some other books, and would we care to do a valuation.'

'So that's what we've come to look at – check out the Audubon, pray, but not dare hope, that it's the double elephant, and have a sniff through the other rubbish he wants to dump. What do we know about the punter?'

'Well, his name's Lynden, and he's a baronet.'

74

'Which means?'

'He's the lowest rank of hereditary nobility, doesn't get to sit in the House of Lords, but we call him "Sir".'

'Actually I try to avoid calling them anything. Saves embarrassment all round. What else?'

'Seems to be a bit of a recluse. Nobody in the office had ever heard of him, except Ophelia who keeps tracks on those sorts of things. She didn't spell it out, but she suggested that there was some sort of distant family connection there, although she may just have been . . . well, doing whatever it is that she does.'

Andrew pictured her doing whatever it was that she did, or rather something that he liked to think about her doing. It involved a shower and a bar of soap. 'She,' continued Alice, unaware, 'said that Lynden's great grandfather bought the title from Lloyd George, and given that he only ran to a baronetcy, it suggests the family wasn't *that* wealthy, which in turn suggests the second, or subsequent edition, rather than the original. Oh, and there's the house, which is famous.'

'Oh, what is it? Tudor? Palladian? Victorian gothic? Ranch-style bungalow? Wigwam?'

'Do you really not know, or is this still part of my . . . assessment?'

'Oh, um ah,' burbled Andrew. Alice wasn't meant to know about the reporting-back side of things. Would she think him a snitch? 'No, I really don't know about the house. I know we're always supposed to see if it's in *Pevsner*, but I can never be bothered. I just wing it, and talk about new cures for deathwatch, and the best grade of rubber for a Wellington boot, and how to shift dried-on pigshit from the rear axle of the Range Rover.'

'Well, let's leave it as a surprise then.'

SEVEN

A Cave of Ice

The house was very easy to miss, although not, perhaps, the four times that Andrew managed to miss it, as he drove up and down the same stretch of B-road, squinting and cursing and swerving around hedgehogs, weasels, gnomes, and sprites, ignoring Alice's good advice about turn-offs.

'I can't see how this house can be famous, except for invisibility. It must be some kind of fucking shed, hidden away like this.'

However, once through a cleverly concealed gateway in a thick hawthorn hedge, a smooth tarmac driveway, elegantly lined with poplar, led on. But to where? No house, grand or otherwise, appeared at the end of the driveway, just another Quantock ridge.

'Follow the road,' said Alice, in a knowing way, which Andrew would have resented, if he'd thought about it more. As it was he was too concerned with the coming trials. Would it be the rare first edition of the Audubon, engraved on copperplates in Edinburgh and London, or just the very nice American lithographs of the octavo? Worse still, perhaps it was one of the subsequent editions of the octavo, tinkered about with by Audubon's sons after his death. Not worthless, but certainly not career-making.

Career bum. Andrew hated thinking about a career. How he still longed, when he allowed himself the indulgence, for that vanished ivory tower. Long lovely hours daydreaming in the Bodeleian. Discussing Edmund Burke over tea and crumpets with a pretty student. Delivering his paper on the influence of Burke on Winckelmann (or was it the other way round?), at a conference in Milan; oh yes, the Milan conference, with all the free drinks they pour down you, and the tasty nibbles (Andrew made a fetish of nibbles), and then the dramatic quasi-perverse sex with Steffi, the Swedish professor of what? yes, *Pneumatics*. Ha! But that wasn't to be, and now he'd made his bed, and now he'd rather like Alice to lay in it. Or Ophelia. Or both together. Stop it.

Fuck.

House.

The Merdemobile had seemed to be heading over the ridge, where they would fall, for all Andrew knew, for a thousand feet to the canyon floor below. He stopped himself from making the explosion noise he'd perfected twenty-five years ago when blowing up bridges behind enemy lines. But the road dipped and curved, and suddenly they found themselves facing a wall of glass.

'Jesus,' said Andrew, 'it's a fucking cave of ice.'

'Wonderful, isn't it?'

'I suppose. If you're a modernist goldfish. Or the Snow Queen,' he said, peering through the windscreen. 'No, I can't be too curmudgeonly about it; it's amazing. God I hate the rich.'

The house had been built partly into the side of the hill, facing a broad wooded valley with a suggestion, if not quite the actual presence, of the sea somewhere beyond. The initial impression of pure and solid glass dissolved after a moment into a more complicated pattern of facets and angles, with panes of varying opacity intercut by steel panels and weathered concrete pillars. There was an area of polished granite slabs, like a pool of impossible calm, in front of the house, dimly reflecting the glittering walls and the sky above.

'Who is it, Frank Lloyd Wright?' Andrew was pleased that he remembered the name of *any* architect, and was silently ecstatic when Alice said:

'A pupil of his, actually. Funny how you could tell when it's so different from anything Wright ever built.'

'Ah, yes, em, it's all to do with the, you know, the use of space, and, er material,' said Andrew, anxious to move on before he became more exposed. 'Anyway, how the hell do you know about this sort of stuff? Your land snails I can see, but I never had you down as a *Country Life* subscriber.'

'Mummy gets the magazines. They're always around. And I am, after all, a *girl*.'

That got Andrew's biggest laugh of the day. He was still smiling as he asked, 'Well, Miss Girlie-Girl Alice Duclos, just how the hell do you get into this place?'

Finding the entrance proved a little easier, for Alice, than extracting herself from the car, which took a series of increasingly violent rocking movements, and a final inelegant lunge. They walked gingerly across the polished granite to a tall thin door of beaten metal. Andrew rang the bell. They waited. Andrew rang the bell again. They waited some more.

'You *did* phone and tell him we were coming?' asked Alice, trying not to sound too sceptical.

'Someone did. I didn't. I might have asked Ophelia to do it. But yes, of course he knows we're coming.' Andrew sounded nervous. 'Shall I try the door? Perhaps they can't hear us in the West . . .' waving vaguely, 'whatever.'

Before Alice had time to say 'no', the door opened, apparently by itself, as no head appeared level with their own.

'What do you want?' came a voice from groin level.

Alice and Andrew looked down into a child's face. Six? Seven? Andrew was always rubbish at guessing ages. But a girl, even he could tell that. She had black, very straight hair, and black eyes with grown-up dark smudges beneath them.

'We've come to see Mr Lynden,' said Alice, once more taking control as Andrew wavered.

'He's my daddy.'

'Is he at home?'

'Yes.'

'Can we see him?'

'He's playing music.'

'I think he wanted to see us.'

'I don't *think* so.'

'I promise. He wrote me a letter. He wants me to have a look at some books.'

'What books?' She looked at Alice as though she had come to extradite her Barbie annual.

'A bird book.'

'Oh.'

'Look, little girl,' said Andrew with an unconvincing severity, 'why don't you go and tell your daddy that we're here.'

'I told you, he's playing music. If I go in he'll shout at me.' The girl's serious face lightened for a moment, before she went on, 'You can go in and see him, if you want.'

'It's a trap,' whispered Andrew in Alice's ear.

'Well, it's that or stand out here for the rest of our lives. And it's started to rain. Will you show us the way?' she said to the girl. 'What's your name?'

'Semele. What's yours?'

'I'm called Alice and this is Andrew.'

The girl nodded. 'Do you see that door? Go through it, and then carry on in a straight line, going through each door directly in front of you. If you do that you'll get to Daddy. Don't dare go off on either side, or go through any other door.' Semele then walked calmly away in the opposite direction.

'Creepy or what,' said Andrew.

'She's just a little girl. He sounds like a monster.'

'Let's go and find out.'

They went through the door that Semele had indicated. It led into a large square room with one wall of ribbed, opaque glass, two of white painted concrete, and an enormous single glass plane showing the valley beyond. It was difficult not to gasp. Black massy clouds had begun to form. I bet Alice knows what they're called, thought Andrew. Cumulo-Nympho. The room was sparsely furnished with a single chrome and white leather sofa.

'What do you do in a room like this?' said Andrew.

'Watch the clouds, I suppose,' replied Alice, with her first hint of dreaminess in ages.

They moved on. Each room opened directly onto the next with no linking corridors. All were furnished in the same way, with a bleak, unwelcoming good taste. Chairs to look at, not to sit on. Coffee tables that would never taste coffee. There was no indication that a child had ever played in any of the rooms; no warming human presence whatsoever. The only decoration on any of the white walls was a single picture of a white wall without any decoration.

Three rooms later they found him. Andrew's eyes were immediately drawn to the hi-fi. It was something to behold. Each piece was formed of organically shaped glistening metal, as though of flowing mercury. But there was no music. A figure was slumped in a low cream leather and cherrywood chair in the middle of the room, with his back to them, facing the valley. The glass wall had disappeared, sliding invisibly into some recess, and the wind carried some of the fine rain mixed with larger drops into the room where it misted and splashed on the polished wood floor. The wind caught some strands of the man's long hair, blowing it behind him. He was wearing headphones, connected to the hi-fi by a long snaking lead. Andrew and Alice looked at each other. Andrew wanted to laugh.

'His flashing eyes, his floating hair,' he said quietly to himself.

Alice looked puzzled. Andrew cleared his throat. Instantly Lynden sprang to his feet, with a look like rage on his face. Several things then happened very quickly. The cord from the headphones was pulled from the jack in the hi-fi. Music blasted out from the speakers, placed high in the corners of the room. And Alice fell down. Andrew recognised Wagner, the sweeping, aching chords, wracked with love and death, but didn't know that it was the 'Vorspiel und Liebestod' from *Tristan und Isolde*. Before he could move, Lynden had leapt towards them. For a moment Andrew thought he was going to attack them, but he bent down and picked up Alice, seemingly without effort, and put her down in his chair, all the time with the music swelling louder. It was then that Andrew realised that Lynden's face was not contorted with rage. His face was streaked with tears. He'd been weeping.

'Crying you mean,' said Leo, doing haughty contempt mingled with cunning. 'Whenever people say weeping I want to reach for my loofah. No, okay that's not funny and not clever; I won't use it again. And *fainted*? Nobody really faints. It's always an act. Maybe in the days when a girl's corset was rupturing her spleen, you might have got the odd genuine swoon, but when that happens for real, the first thing

81

you do when you pass out is piss and shit your knickers, and the first thing you do when you wake up is vomit. Jesus, I just can't believe you mix with the kind of people who weep and faint.'

'I'm not saying she completely passed out. She just went all floppy.'

Andrew and Leo were inappropriately drunk in the middle of the day. Andrew was going to have to go back to the office in half an hour, and Leo had already missed the tutorial he was supposed to be giving on the influence of Hegel's master-slave dialectic on later Romantic literature (there wasn't any). Andrew had explained all about the journey and arrival.

'I thought it must be nerves, or some kind of woman-trouble thing,' he continued. 'Lynden shouted to his daughter to fetch some water, and Alice seemed to recover a bit. But I noticed that she didn't look at him.'

'Must have fancied the bloke. What did he look like?'

'Oh, you know. Sort of swarthy type. Old acne scars. Long greasy hair. That cheekbone thing. I don't know. Looked like a miserable fucker to me.'

'Jealousy, thy name is Andrew Heathley.'

Andrew ignored the comment. 'So Alice picked herself up and we got to work. The library wasn't bad. It was the only room with proper walls. He had some good things that he wasn't selling. Mainly early twentieth-century small press stuff. A Nonesuch Dickens set with one of the original printing blocks. Always fancied one of those myself.'

'What about the birdy book? Good or bad?'

'Oh, good. Very good. It *was* the Lizars-Havell edition. Unbound loose sheets, rather than the usual four bound volumes.'

'What a shame.'

'Not at all. Makes it, if anything, more valuable. Able to

flog off the prints individually, sacrilege though that be.'

'And how did you hit it off with the Gyppo?'

Andrew thought seriously about challenging his friend over the lazy racism of that, but he knew he would just fall back on the irony defence. He hated the irony defence.

'Surprise surprise, he seemed mainly interested in Alice. He was selling the Audubon so he could do up that greenhouse of his. Or at least stop it falling down. Not much of a business head. Had no idea what it was worth. Didn't get the impression he'd ever had much of a real job, apart from the looking tragic and moping about the place. We checked the provenance, of course, not that there was any doubting it. I don't know how the hell you'd go about faking a monster like that: you'd need a team of fucking great artists and several years to play with, and if you ever managed it, then good luck to you, you've earned your seven million. But all the papers were there – Lynden's granddad bought it in 1920 for five hundred quid. But anyway, the first bit all went well. The little brat even brought us tea on a tray.'

'Where's the mother?'

'No idea. Couldn't exactly wade in with a "so, wife left you? Or is she dead?" could I? But the way he was sniffing round Alice made it clear whoever the mother was, she wasn't currently co-domiciled with the . . . with Lynden. So yeah, all went well. We had our preliminary look, and then went off to Nether Stowey for the night.'

'And this is where the Heathley Love Machine swings into action?'

'Well, that was plan A.'

'And I'm surmising that plan A didn't quite come off. Gallipoli?'

'Fucking Bay of Pigs.'

'Arse.'

'Arse squared. Alice had obviously been holding herself together by the skin of her teeth.'

'Conjures an image. Not sure it would work, anatomically.'

'But by the time we got into the car she was trembling. I kept asking her what the matter was, and she just kept shaking. When we reached the hotel I practically had to carry her to her room. God knows what they thought on reception. It probably looked like I'd just given her a back-street abortion. She managed to say that she needed a lie down, and that she'd be okay later. It was about six by then, and I said I'd come up and collect her for dinner. So I hit the bar and had a think. Obviously something about Lynden had set her off.'

'I've already said: she fancied him.'

'No, it's not that simple. You don't faint and shake and cry because you fancy someone.'

'Happens all the time, in books.'

'Well this wasn't in books. And if you'll give me a minute I'll tell you what it was all about, because now I know, sort of. So I had a couple of beers in the bar, feeling sorry for myself. It had all gone so well on the way there. She was funny and normal, almost. It was like when she first joined. And you know, I'd swear she was flirting. Not gagging for it, that's not her way. Just letting me know that she thought I was all right, and that if I made some kind of move . . .'

'A lunge?'

'Anything *short* of a lunge, she might not slap my face. And then after she sees Lynden, it's back to square one, or rather square minus one. Goodbye cool smiley Alice, hello mad shaky Alice, plus all of the not-quite-there Alice we'd had to get used to. So, a couple or three drinks later – and Christ, I'd forgotten how they screw you for drinks in hotels, even out there – I went up to her room. She'd calmed down

84

a bit, and we went to a local pub for dinner – I had a strange yearning for chicken in a basket.'

'Getting back in touch with your proley roots.'

'Mm. And I sensed that she might want to talk, which was a new thing, because the cut-off Alice of old never gave that impression. And so after not very much persuasion, and a couple of large gins, she told me the weirdest story.'

'Is this going to involve her darkest, deepest desires?'

'Well, yes and no. No in the way that you mean.'

'Pity.'

'Apparently after a couple of months at Enderby's she saw an accident.'

'What some old git fall over a Ming vase?'

'Hate to be po-faced, but this isn't actually funny, Leo. She saw a boy, a youth, killed on the road near the office.'

'Fuck.'

'And she said that she couldn't get him out of her head.'

'No. Understandable. Must have made a mess.'

'Partly that, but a bit more. It wasn't just the horror of it. It was that she'd, to use her words, fallen in love with this boy. Some kind of erotic fixation. No, that's not quite right. A romantic obsession. Dreamed about him every night. Sort of took possession of her. And oh yes, this all happened the day before our ill-fated date in the park.'

Leo now was serious, and interested.

'So what did you say to all this? Did you give her any big-brotherly advice?'

'Nothing that wasn't written in the Great Book of Cliché. I was going to suggest that she find out more about this youth, confront her demons. She told me that she'd already done that. A friend of a friend had traced his family. He was some kind of refugee or asylum seeker from Bosnia. She got the address, but couldn't actually face seeing them.'

'Yeah, it might seem a bit freaky, some strange woman

turning up unannounced and saying she was obsessed with their dead son. All helps to explain how she was: all that not quite there stuff.'

'Exactly. And the whole thing was all made worse, maybe even partially triggered, by her dad.'

'*Dad?* Where does he fit in? We're not talking Freud here, are we?'

'Not a million miles away, but sadder than that. He'd died when she was quite young. Alice and her father were incredibly close. A sort of pact against the mother, who's half mad, half bad. But despite all that, she said she was trying to pull herself out of it, the weirdness, although I could see that in some ways she was still completely in it, and at some level actually . . . relishing it. But at least she was *trying*, which was why she'd seemed more normal on the way to the Quantocks. And then she sees Lynden. And guess what?'

Leo did an exaggerated 'I don't know' shrug, but he had, in fact, guessed.

Andrew carried on: 'This Lynden looks exactly like the boy. Or rather like the boy as a man.'

'Hence the faint.'

'It was amazing really that she managed to function at all.'

'So she told you all this in the pub?'

'Yeah. It was pretty intense. And although I was half pissed off about the fact that I clearly didn't figure large in her world view right then . . .'

'Like at the end of *The Dead*, when the guy realises his wife's spent their entire marriage thinking about what's his name, with the snow falling on his grave.'

'Yeah, a bit like that. But I was also kind of pleased that she'd felt able to talk to me about it after all. There was a new intimacy between us, albeit premised on her greater intimacy with . . .'

'The Dead.'

'The Dead.'

'So you didn't shag her then?'

Andrew smiled, sadly. He was lucky to have got even the eight or so minutes of seriousness out of Leo.

'No. But we had a hug.'

'That's when you should have slipped your hand up her blouse.'

'And somehow she made it through the next day. We did our stuff, and drove back without talking much.'

'And since then?'

'All quiet on the Western Front. In some ways she seems normal, but things are happening beneath the surface. She hasn't broached any more confidences, but nor does she seem embarrassed about what she's told me.'

'What are you going to do?'

'I don't know. Wait and see.'

'That's my boy. The decisiveness of Nelson! The ruthless martial vigour of Wellington! The tactical brilliance of Marlborough!'

'Fuck you. One last pint?'

After Andrew had gone back to the office, Leo lingered for another drink. Not this time beer, but a large vodka, with ice and nothing else. Five minutes later he was walking through the streets, his head held low, watching the numberless shoes scrape and patter and clump and tap their way on the end-less, meaningless walk of humanity. He felt annoyed about missing the tutorial. Three hopeless cases, but the girl, Patricia Standish, was pretty and intense and had never skipped a lecture. Perhaps she might have been the one. He'd track them down and offer each an extra session. With any luck only Patricia would accept. But no, why should she? And anyway, Patricia was one of the names he didn't like.

Bond Street station wasn't too bad. It was busy, and so nobody had the time to stare. He took the tube out to the campus at Mile End. He had a flat in one of the new student halls. He was allowed to live there rent-free in exchange for 'supervising' his block. It didn't mean much work. One night a week he held a 'surgery' for students with problems. Nobody ever turned up. .Why would they want to talk to him about their little tiffs and traumas? He was thirty-five years old, single, lonely and ugly.

Andrew's research on male beauty had initially drawn Leo into a friendship. They'd met in the British Library, when they found themselves staring at the same very, very short skirt, Leo with a sadness edged with bile, Andrew with a frank and open gratitude that such things could exist in the world. Leo was already an established academic and Andrew just another student, but that didn't stand in the way of their joint love of beer and talking bullshit. Of course Andrew's work was seriously under-theorised, reading like old-fashioned scholarship until Leo helped him out with some spare concepts he'd been keeping for a rainy day. Although he patronised Andrew for the first year or so of the relationship, he eventually came to depend on him. Not as a confidant. Anything but that. More as a field of dreams. With Andrew he could pretend to be the kind of person he'd always wanted to be: confident and outgoing and sexually all-conquering. He made up the stories about nymphet students and besotted older colleagues. He even invented a dose of gonorrhoea. Andrew believed it because he wanted to believe it, wanted to believe in the exploits of his friend, wanted the vicarious thrill of illicit sexual adventure. In reality, Andrew was far more experienced than Leo.

Leo knew everything about love, the endless yearning for beauty and youth, but he'd only ever had one girlfriend. Jean was pretty, but didn't care. And she was as blind to his ugliness as she was to her own attractiveness. They'd gone to see films and whatever plays reached Cambridge. It was a happy time. They were both virgins and fumbled their way to fulfilment, drunk on red Lambrusco.

He never found out exactly what happened, but when she came back after the long holiday for the second year, she wasn't *his* Jean any more. She wore new clothes; her hair was different; she moved in another circle. They never properly talked about no longer being together: they both just knew. At the time he didn't mind too much. Surely there would be other girls? But at the parties, his passes were always taken humorously, laughed off; not with malice, but with an unassailable finality. It was then that he started to look into the mirror, look deeply, look truly. And what he saw was not the average-looking, ordinary guy he expected, the one accepted for his wit and courage by his schoolfriends, the one adored and doted on by his mother, who'd worked so hard to get him to what she regarded as the right school, but a stunted, misshapen, UGLY little man. Sometimes he'd play with his face in the mirror, pushing and pulling at it to try to make it look less strange. And the tragedy was that just half an inch here or there, an ounce of flesh moved from one part to another, and he would have been normal; perhaps even handsome. And with a handsome face, who would care that he was small, and less than perfectly straight? But no. It would never, could never, be. His future history played itself out before him. Only other uglies would ever want him. He saw the frightening academic woman with buckteeth and old-lady hair. He saw how she moved, as if all of her bones had been taken out and replaced completely randomly. He smelt her carbolicky smell, as she came towards him, mouth open, teeth outstretched, and he knew that he didn't want her. Equally vividly, he saw the ones he did want, the girls of the Cambridge glamorous set. He walked past their picnics in the park; he saw them float by on the river; he heard their laughter from windows in the fashionable colleges.

It was in that furnace that the new Leo was forged: the tungsten-hard, cynical, unyielding Leo. He shed those acquaintances that did not afford his kind of amusement; he devoted himself to his studies, soon intimidating even those dons who dared to engage him in debate.

'Hello, Dr Kurtz.'

Leo's key was in the door. He was fumbling. The last vodka. He thought about ignoring whichever student it was and just going straight in. Reflected in the door's glass panel he saw Patricia.

'Ah, Patricia. I um, I um.'

There she was, twenty years old. Perhaps nineteen. Her face so eager, so bright with hope. And her breasts showing through that cheap green dress. What would she do if he just took her by the hand and led her into the little room?

'Can I give you my essay?'

'Yes. I'm sorry about the tutorial. Something came up.' Yes, five pints of beer and a double vodka. 'If you like we could go through your essay now. I have an hour spare.' He tried to smile, but knew it was a mistake. He never smiled when sober.

'Oh, that'd be great, but I have another lecture. It's Professor Connolly on Shelley.'

Connolly, thought Leo. I wouldn't piss on his notes if they were on fire. What had she seen that had so disgusted her that she'd rather go to that old fraud's lecture than listen to him?

'That's very . . . noble,' he said. 'I'll arrange some other time to catch up. Again, I'm sorry.'

He pushed his way into the flat, clutching Patricia's neatly typed essay. That was one good thing about the proliferation of computers: no spidery scrawl to pick through, no fat, clumsy letters to make him think of old women eating pork pies.

As ever, he went first to the mirror in the small bathroom. He turned on the harsh white strip-light. He gazed for two minutes, re-arming himself, closing any chinks in his chain-mail. He then moved into the other room, divided into a study area, with a desk, a hard chair, and two easy chairs, and the sleeping area with its single bed. Everything was precise and neat, as it had to be. He put on the kettle, which perched at one end of his desk, and sat down at his lap-top. Time to work. His book on Hartley, the poor, stunted, lost, drunken son of Samuel Taylor Coleridge. A writer of exquisite sonnets, but a failure in everything he ever set out to achieve. And hopelessly in love with women who could never look kindly at so tiny and odd a creature.

So Alice had enjoyed the three hours of silly chat with Andrew in the car. She was enjoying walking through the beautiful glass house. She was looking forward to seeing the Audubon: partly, she had to admit to herself, for the excitement of touching something worth millions of pounds, but also for the purer pleasure of being near one of the most beautiful and dramatic objects ever made by humankind. She found herself amused by the melodramatic pose of Lynden, who must surely have known how they would find him. And then she saw his face. For a heartbeat she thought it actually was *him*, her Boy. The eyes, the cheekbones, the mouth. But he was so much older; old enough to be the Boy's father, if not hers. And he was crying. Although her mind had remained perfectly clear, her legs lost their ability to support her, and she found herself falling, but in a ridiculous slow motion that added a surge of embarrassment to her distress. Before she could gather herself, the man was bending over her, drying his own eyes with a sweep on his shoulder. She saw Andrew, his mouth agape, paralysed with indecision, and she felt for him. She didn't want to be picked up, and she was pleased when Lynden put her down in the Eames lounger. It was only then that she heard the music, the magnificent, passionate, aching death of it. And then it stopped. There was some water. Lynden had gone to stand in a corner of the room, where he watched the storm pass outside through the now closed window. She saw that yes, he bore some resemblance to the Boy, but only in that they were both of a type. She felt very silly, and forced herself to stand and shrug off the attentions of Andrew. She was fine. She was fine.

'I'm sorry. I shouldn't have skipped breakfast,' she said to the window.

Lynden turned. His eyes were still red, and he looked very fierce. She thought he must be forty, or forty-five years old, but he was still lithe and sinewy. His complexion was dark, whether through the sun, or some southern or eastern blood, she couldn't tell. His nose was strong and very slightly hooked.

'I can't believe the little brat didn't tell me you were here. The child runs wild. I'll have her bring us some tea – Grace isn't here today. How was your journey?'

And somehow Alice got through the afternoon. The Audubon was exquisite. She looked for all of her favourites – the passenger pigeon, the Carolina parrot, the great auk. The ones that were gone. Something about the auk, standing alone, looking rather dim and melancholy, suggested a premonition. And the pair of passenger pigeons, once the commonest bird in the world, the flocks of which could take a week to pass over head as they moved to the woods where they nested, seemed sadly resigned to extinction, full of the knowledge that their kind would be blasted from the sky with cannons, and netted in their millions, until none were left, but the solitary old lady, called Martha, in Cleveland Zoo. If anything the parrot was more poignant. Six red, green and yellow birds squabbled and squawked in a tree, full of life and energy. How could they all have gone from the world? Alice had to fight the unprofessional urge to press her cheeks against the pages to breathe in the artistry and the labour, and the sadness.

Lynden came every half hour to see how they were proceeding. She thought that there was something strange in the way he looked at her. But who could blame him after the appalling thing she had done?

When it was time to leave for the day she realised that she had used up every particle of energy and willpower in her body. Back in the hotel room (how had she got there? Andrew . . . sweet boy), she bathed and lay on the bed, swathed in towels, trying to gather and organise her thoughts. What could it mean, meeting this man, so like her Boy? He was handsome, in a cruel way. She thought about the strength of his arms around her and shuddered. How had it affected her feelings for the Dead Boy? Was this a symptom of her obsession, or a route out of it? And then to her astonishment, as she lay there warm now and wrapped in the clean white towels, she found herself doing something she hadn't done for nearly a year.

She was still flushed and breathless when Andrew knocked half an hour later.

The evening with Andrew had been less of an ordeal than she expected. And she didn't know if it was the drink, or the shocks of the day, but she told him, told him almost everything about the Dead Boy. The fact that she had already spoken about it to Odette made things easier. It was a relief. It didn't sound quite as mad as she feared it might. Sounded, in some ways, too ordinary. She'd seen a boy killed; it had affected her deeply. Of course it would, Andrew was saying. It's only normal. He looked like Lynden, she told him. He'd choked on that, as he munched his way methodically through some enormous meal he'd ordered at the bar.

On the way back to the hotel she had taken Andrew's arm. The skies had cleared and he said something about the stars being God's daisy chains, which she took to be some kind of jokey allusion, but she didn't recognise the source. She giggled anyway. He was a nice person, and she liked him.

The next day Lynden was out for most of the morning. They were admitted by a suspicious-looking housekeeper, who showed them to the library, and stood sniffing for several minutes before shuffling away. Alice assumed this to be Grace. Lynden finally appeared, dressed in a long black coat, just before they were leaving. His hair was wet and his face was streaked with mud. Something about his manner made Alice nervous, confirmed when he said that he'd been shooting mink, which he called 'filthy foreign vermin'. But he thanked them cordially enough as they left.

EIGHT

The Sublime Machine

Kitty was in the sitting room drinking pink gin from a champagne flute. It was half past seven. Alice had come in from work at seven and had decided to talk to her mother. She'd sat on the side of her bed thinking about how she would put it. She'd decided to speak to Kitty because she thought that was what her father had been trying to tell her. The fish had been barely moving in the bottom of the green pool. She asked her father what she should do, and although he hadn't spoken to her, she was sure that he'd wanted her to talk to Kitty. And it didn't seem right that she had told Odette and Andrew the truth, and yet left her mother in ignorance.

'Mummy?'

Kitty turned slowly away from the television. She was addicted to the soaps, to all of the soaps.

'Not now.'

'Mummy, I have to talk to you.'

Kitty huffed and took a long drink from her glass. A little of the pink liquid spilled from the corner of her mouth.

'Very well. But don't drag it out. I'm being collected at eight. Conrad Dosing-Ball is taking me to dinner.'

No, thought Alice, he isn't. Did he really exist, or was he a complete figment? Was it a name that Kitty had read somewhere in a magazine? Or was he an old beau, a lover from before she was married? Either way, she knew that nobody would be coming, not in a vintage Jag, or a sleek Ferrari, or a carriage and four gaily plumed, high-spirited horses.

'Mother, I haven't been . . . well. Some things have happened to me, and I can't . . . I don't know what to do.'

Alice had never spoken to Kitty about anything important. It was proving just as difficult as she feared. Part of the problem was that she didn't quite know herself how to put it into words.

'*You* haven't been well? Alice, I never cease to be amazed at your selfishness and egotism. When have you ever heard me complain about *my* illnesses? You know my heart is weak, and yet you continue to plague and to bother me. Every day I have to face more pain than you can imagine. And where is the comfort, the solace I should expect from my child? I used my influence – *influence* I could have used to help myself – to get you a good position, and what have you done with it? Are you engaged? Is there even a . . . *boyfriend*? I thought it might help you to meet more people, the *right* people. Was it too much to expect that you might introduce *me* to a new circle, to help to enliven my days? But no. All you do is mope and sulk and get under my feet. And do you know the worst thing?'

Alice was looking at the whorls and gyres in the frightful brown carpet and didn't know that an answer was expected.

'I asked,' repeated Kitty, even more savagely, 'if you knew the worst thing?'

'No, Mummy.'

'You bore me.'

It was a familiar theme to Alice, but it hadn't lost its ability to sting.

'Mummy, I'm sorry about everything. But I want to talk to you. I want to . . . some things have been . . .' But then Alice saw that Kitty was lost again in the soap world beyond her reach, and she quietly left the room, carefully closing both the living-room door and the door to her own bedroom to keep out the chatter from the TV and keep in the sound of her own sadness.

'Alice Duclos?'

'Yes.'

'There's a call for you.'

It was unusual for the switchboard to put calls through to her by name. General enquiries would come up just for 'Books', or those specifically wanting her would normally have her extension and dial direct. She'd been working on the catalogue for a sale of original scientific papers. Nothing groundbreaking or famous, no telltale spark of genius: just the routine work of eighteenth- and nineteenth-century toilers in chemistry and physics. It was dull work, but she was the only one qualified to do it in-house.

'Hello, Books, Alice Duclos speaking.'

'Hello, Books, Alice Duclos speaking.' The voice was distinctive. Harsh. Familiar. But not instantly recognisable.

'Who is this?'

'Edward.'

'Edward?' She didn't know any Edwards.

'Edward *Lynden*.'

Alice was sure he hadn't mentioned his first name before, but she should have remembered it from the background papers. She suspected that it was a stunt to throw her off-guard. That didn't stop her from being flustered.

'Oh. Sir . . . Mr . . .' Alice couldn't remember what she was supposed to call him.

'Please, Edward.'

'Edward. How can I help you? Would you like to speak to Mr Heathley?'

'If I'd wanted to speak to Mr Heathley I'd have asked for him. I wanted you.'

'Is there a problem?'

'Do you always assume there must be a problem when somebody wants you?'

'No but I . . .'

'The truth is I'm having second thoughts about the sale. I can't pretend I'm a book collector, but it seems wrong to split up the prints and sell them off. I know they meant a lot to my grandfather. I'm looking into other ways of raising the capital I need.'

This was very bad news. She and Andrew had been lauded since they secured the sale. Parry Brooksbank had paid an ostentatious back slapping, hand squeezing visit, smiling as though for invisible press photographers, and claiming credit for his expert judgement of character in 'appointing' Alice, which rather annoyed her as she'd never previously met him. How pleased she was, now that the deal looked anything but secure, that she had bitten her tongue.

'Well . . . Edward, you know that our main concerns here are with giving the right service to the client, and if you decide that you don't want to sell, then of course we respect that. But there are other issues.'

Alice thought very hard about what they might be. Something to do with scholarship . . . preserving the works for posterity . . . saving Enderby's from bankruptcy.

'Really? Fine. Why don't you come down here and tell me about them.'

Alice was startled. What did Lynden mean? There didn't seem to be anything she couldn't tell him over the phone. But, innocent though she was, she did have an inkling, and it frightened her.

'I'll have to see if . . . when Andrew and I can make the trip.'

'What do we need him for? I could see that you were the expert.'

'Well, technically he *is* my superior.' She didn't at all mean for the 'technically' to come out as 'officially, but not in reality', but she knew it did. Before she could think of how to put things right Lynden had continued:

'Then we shouldn't waste his valuable time. When can you come?'

Without thinking, Alice said: 'Tomorrow.'

'What does the fucker *want*? What *does* the fucker want?' Andrew had been repeating the phrase for about half an hour, trying out different stresses. 'What does the *fucker* want?'

'Andrew, I don't know. All I know is that he says he's changed his mind about the sale. I think if I go there I can change it back again.'

'Oakley thinks you should go. He seemed pretty impressed that Lynden wanted you. Makes me look like a pillock, though.'

Alice was squirming. This was a very awkward situation. She didn't want to tell Andrew that Lynden had seen her as the expert. Nor did she want to tell him that he might be . . . interested in her in some less than professional capacity. Apart from anything else, she might be wrong, and would look a vain and arrogant fool if it transpired Lynden was only pursuing her for her knowledge. It was the kind of thing Ophelia would think, although in her case the interest could *only* be in her beauty.

At the thought of Ophelia, Alice looked over to her desk. Inevitably she was watching, slyly. At repose her lips would always draw back a few millimetres to reveal the tips of her teeth, which gave a wholly inaccurate impression that she was about to smile, and which had led at least three of the boys around the office – admittedly when new and inexperienced – to believe that they might have a chance if they asked her out. How quickly she had educated them as to the depth of their folly and presumption. One, a harmless, freckle-faced youth from the mail room, whose thin shirts always managed to be both loose at the collar and short in the sleeve, was subjected to a tirade so withering that he simply never came to work again.

Now Alice read into her look not only the usual casual malice, but also something more. Ophelia had never attempted to hide the fact that she saw her 'career' at Enderby's as simply a stepping stone to the right sort of marriage. She was content with her relatively junior role, and had no real ambition to excel or become promoted above the point at which she would come into regular contact with 'the eligibles'. She hadn't seemed to mind, beyond the usual background level of malevolence, that Alice and Andrew had gained so much attention with the Audubon scoop; she'd simply left the office with a toss and a flourish of her exquisite head. But now, with the discussion taking such an unexpected turn, a new light flickered in her eyes, and Alice felt as though tiny crystals of something not at all nice had formed in her blood.

'No, it doesn't a . . . a what did you say?'

'A pillock.'

'No, it doesn't make you look like a pillock.'

Clerihew, who'd materialised from somewhere, silently, like a miniature hot air balloon, snickered, and then blew his nose. Alice thought for a moment that he might take up a schoolyard chant of 'pillock, pillock, Andy is a pillock,' and go dancing round the room. Instead he blew his nose some more and floated off.

'I think,' continued Alice, looking at Clerihew's tiny feet in their shiny shoes patter over the carpet, 'we both know that he wants me because . . . I'm a woman, and he probably feels he can . . . I don't know, intimidate me.'

'Yeah, intimidate you into *bed*.' Andrew would have done something about his tone if he'd realised how much like a sulky teenager he sounded. 'Are you sure you're up to it? You were pretty . . . distressed last time you saw him.'

This was the first time either had alluded to the emotional turmoil of the trip. Andrew hadn't mentioned any of it to Oakley, and had praised Alice's expertise.

'I think I'll be okay. I have to do this . . . sort of thing. It's important to face . . .'

'Your demons?' said Andrew, with one of the least subtle ironic looks Alice had ever seen. It made a noise in her mind like an orchestra tuning up.

'My demons,' she replied, flatly.

It was arranged that Lynden would collect Alice at the local station, which turned out to be fourteen miles away. The train journey was pleasant enough, and Alice even quite enjoyed the unexplained delays and sudden, juddering stops in the midst of empty fields. She deliberately avoided thinking about Lynden, swerving away whenever her thoughts drifted towards the reason for his strange invitation; not, however, because the thoughts were unpleasant.

She thought for some of the time about Andrew. Alice had never taken it for granted that anyone would like her. Too many years of snide comments from Kitty had so entirely undermined her self-confidence that she simply could not imagine why any man might find her attractive. Kitty had put her on her first diet at the age of twelve and still occasionally left packets of Slim-Fast prominently in the kitchen, but Alice would never be diet material. If anything, Kitty's snide propaganda worked too well: Alice felt she was too far gone to be salvaged by mere calorie restriction, or even (and she suspected that Kitty might not have dismissed the option outright) bulimia. So, she reasoned, somewhere around her eighteenth birthday, I will never be loved for my body or my face, or my figure; therefore I will perfect my mind.

Not that Alice's quest for learning was some alternative form of coquetry: she never hoped to win love through mental pyrotechnics. It was just that the seed of vanity landed on a ground scoured and rendered sterile.

Besottedness (or even any of the more modest forms of romantic interest) was therefore generally the very last item on her list of possible explanations for odd male behaviour. But after eight months of close contact with Andrew, passing pencil sharpeners, clashing heads over books, laughing together at Ophelia's antics (somewhat bitterly in Andrew's case), even she had detected (without ever raising it to the level of full consciousness) that something was going on. She could feel his excitement and tension on the first trip to the glass house. She had shared it, up to a point. Who knew what might have happened if . . . if Lynden had not looked like . . . the way he did. Andrew had been so sweet to her in the days that followed. He had given her all the credit for the triumph. It seemed faithless somehow: if she were to re-enter the world, abandon the Dead Boy out in the cold, lost forever, surely it must be for Andrew, and not for this new . . . new phenomenon.

But Andrew was Andrew and this was something, someone, very different.

'I'll be in the car park. See if you can guess what I'm in,' he'd said. It turned out, rather predictably, to be a battered old long-wheelbase Land Rover. He shoved the door open from the inside as she approached. There was no polite inquiry about her journey, just a brief nod, and a longer gaze.

'I've a confession,' he said, looking away at last.

'Already?'

'From the last time. When I met you. I wasn't really shooting mink.'

'Really. What had you been shooting? Children?'

'What? No. Not children. Not anything.'

'Why did you say you had?'

'I suppose I was trying to shock you. Or, I don't know, maybe it was just something to say. I did *see* a mink, and I threw a stone at it, which made me slip in the mud. I don't usually lie. It's why I'm saying this now. I didn't want it to be between us.'

'So now,' said Alice, conscious that she was about to say something ambiguous, 'there isn't anything between us.'

Forty uncomfortable bouncing minutes later, Alice found herself again in the glass house. She'd noticed that Lynden seemed hardly more at ease behind the wheel than had Andrew, although she attributed this to a lack of familiarity with the Land Rover. Alice couldn't see Lynden making a living from the country. To break the awkward silence that had fallen (if you filtered out the savage, grinding catarrh of the engine, the buffeting of the wind, and the merciless whining of the dysfunctional wipers), she'd begun to ask him about the estate, but he interrupted her, saying roughly:

'There's no estate at all to speak of now. Most of it had gone before I came into it. Dad and Granddad only ever played at farming. I didn't even play.'

'What *do* you do, then?'

'I squander what little's left of the inheritance.'

It was hard to discern any irony, let alone good humour,

in the voice. But Alice wanted there to be, and she replied jauntily:

'That hardly seems like a proper job.'

Lynden looked at her sharply. His eyes were black, beneath his self-consciously beetling brow. His scowl looked faintly cartoonish, reminding Alice of the famously silly painting of Beethoven, doing a tortured-romantic-genius face, and she giggled.

'You find me amusing, Miss Duclos?' Was there the minutest suggestion of a smile at the corners of his mouth?

'Perhaps if you took yourself a little less seriously, I'd be able to take you more so.'

'I see you can talk in sentences like a Jane Austen heroine.'

Alice blushed, and was still blushing minutes later as they climbed out of the Land Rover. Semele was standing in the doorway.

'Why is *she* here, Daddy?' she asked matter-of-factly, without apparent malice.

'As you know very well, Miss Duclos has come to have another look at my books. Why don't you try to be nice, as you promised?'

Turning to Alice, she said:

'He didn't kill any minks, or anything else, you know.'

'Yes, she *does* know,' interrupted Lynden.

'Did he tell you he hasn't even got a gun, any more?'

Alice was going to say something light-hearted, but then she saw Lynden's face. The Sturm und Drang caricature had given way to something more real and more terrible: an expressionless of utter blankness.

'Go away, Semele,' he said, exercising what Alice could see from the twitching of his fingers was supernatural control. He turned towards Alice and made an unreadable gesture with his hands, which might have been despair, or anger, or resignation, or apology. 'Please . . . wait for me in the library, Miss Duclos. I have to do something.'

Wandering through to the library, Alice found herself deeply perturbed by Lynden's strange mood swings. Initially there had been the tears and anguish she had seen when she first met him, and now this chilling response to Semele's teasing. But she was still enough of a scientist to realise that she had insufficient evidence on which to base any firm conclusions, and so she deliberately closed her mind to speculation.

When she reached the library she found that the Audubon volumes were still on the huge leather-faced desk where Andrew and Alice had left them. There was nothing much for Alice to do except sit and leaf slowly through the magnificent prints. She knew that Audubon originally employed an engraver in Edinburgh, William Lizars, but only five of the plates were completed before Lizars's colourists went on strike, forcing Audubon to look elsewhere. He was fortunate to find Robert Havell in London, who was now generally regarded as the better craftsman. Alice couldn't remember which five of the plates were the work of the Lizars's team, and spent half an hour trying to pick out the inferior work. But it was too difficult. There were so many barely distinguishable warblers and finches, and Alice simply lacked the connoisseurship, that special gaze, acutely focussed, supernaturally alert to tiny variances in the density of a line, or the elegance of a curve. It was a gaze that poor lost Crumlish had acquired, nurtured by long labour and perseverance; it was a gaze that Andrew was developing, almost against his will, through some combination of quick wit and ardent practice; it was a gaze that so many of the auction house fops and dandies felt they must possess by virtue of birth; it was a gaze that would come, perhaps, for Alice, if she lingered for long enough in the world of fine things. But for now the gaze was elusive, and she was beginning to yearn for it.

She wandered around the library. For the want of anything better to do she climbed to the top of a mahogany library step ladder.

'If it's secrets you're looking for you won't find them up there. I'm an enthusiast for the Holmesian doctrine that the best place to hide a pin is in a pincushion. My secrets are all around you.'

Alice nearly fell from the ladder with surprise. She dismounted with as much poise as she could muster. Lynden put down the bottle and wine glasses he was carrying and held out a hand to help her with the last few steps, but she ignored it.

'You were gone for such a long time. I didn't know what to do with myself.'

'What, a book expert at a loss in a library? How curious.' Pointing to the wine he said, 'I thought you might be thirsty after your journey. If you'd rather have some of the local cider I can send Grace out for a keg. I'm told it is very potent.'

With relief Alice noted that Lynden had recovered his gruff good spirits. She decided on a sally.

'For a man with secrets you seem to find it very difficult to conceal your feelings.'

Without a pause Lynden replied, 'There is no art to find the mind's construction in the face.'

'Isn't that what physiognomy is?' she returned, quickly.

'Considered by James I to be a branch of witchcraft, punishable in the same barbaric manner.'

'Are you suggesting I'm a witch, Mr Lynden?'

'That would be to imply that you might have the power of bewitching. And please, make it Edward. "Mr Lynden" makes me sound like your headmaster.'

Alice couldn't keep it up any longer and broke into a giggling blush.

'My headmaster wasn't at all like you. He was small and bald and smelt of taramasalata . . . Macbeth.'

'What?'

'Macbeth. "There is no art". It's from Macbeth, isn't it? I'm not normally very good on quotations from plays, but we did that for GCSE.' And then, on impulse, she added, 'You're an actor, aren't you?'

What had made her make such an outrageous suggestion? Something, she felt, about the size of his gestures. Yes, that was it: it was as if he was projecting his emotions to the back of the theatre, making sure that even the students and pensioners up in the gods could follow the contours of his torment.

Lynden looked surprised but not, as she had feared, annoyed.

'You've seen, somewhere, the pictures?'

'Pictures?'

'The photographs.'

'No, I . . .'

'Oh. Well now I've mentioned them, I suppose I'll *have* to show you.'

He walked across the library and pulled an album from one of the shelves.

'You see,' he continued, 'I wasn't always an idle landowner.'

He had opened the album on a page of carefully posed head and shoulder shots. The face was obviously Lynden's, still baying to be called brooding, intense, melancholic, but there was a playfulness about the mouth, and something that suggested the possibility of hope in the eyes. Old photographs, however jaunty the theme, always made Alice sad, but there was a particular poignancy about the

107

contrast between Lynden's young and not-so-young selves.

'Good-looking boy, eh?' he said, carelessly. But Alice could feel his scrutiny.

'Not bad. What happened to him?'

'Life.'

They both smiled at the cliché.

Alice turned the pages. There were black and white pictures of theatrical productions. The actors were all young, giving a sense of unreality, occasionally even comedy, to the scenes which involved old characters. There was a fairly obvious King Lear, and two suspiciously young tramps hanging around, it could only be, for Godot. Everything about the productions, from the Roman togas to the Elizabethan ruffs, screamed out 'seventies'. Moustaches drooped, flares flopped, hair hung limp and greasy.

'This is drama school, yes?'

'Yes. I was . . . at RADA.'

'Strange how less convincing it is when young people play old people than the other way round,' she said, thoughtfully.

'Well, of course: every harlot was a virgin once.'

'What do you mean?'

'Oh, only that the old have experience of being young, but the young have no experience of being old.'

She found a picture of Lynden receiving some kind of award.

'What was that for? Best leading scowl? Best supporting eyebrows?' Without quite realising how it had happened, Alice saw that she was holding a glass of red wine. She took a gulp. Lynden was already on his second glass.

'You're very funny,' he said, deadpan. 'Believe it or not great things were expected of me. Except by Dad. He always associated the theatre with an habitual preference for the love of boys. He kept expecting to hear about my arrest in a public lavatory. He used to do a comic turn based on it. He did a special voice for the undercover policeman used in the entrapment: "Well your 'onner, the haccused young gentleman approached me while I was engaged in a urinatory capacity and enquired if I should like it up me. I politely declined 'is offer, and read 'im 'is rights as he was writhing and squirming in the piss, begging your pardon your 'onner, just reading me notes, an' clutching at 'is kidneys." He often used to get carried away like that. Suspect he always wanted to be an actor himself.'

This was another new Lynden, and Alice found herself beaming. She didn't know what to make of this rush of eloquence from someone previously so laconic. Although she was pleased that he was confiding in her, she felt that there was something unhealthy in the sudden flow; it was as if the sutures had given way. But she didn't want it to stop.

'What *really* happened to you? I mean why didn't you become a professional actor? I think you must have been very good.'

'You may be surprised to hear that there was a girl involved. I'd been offered a place in the Old Vic company. Nothing earth-shattering, but a good start. I was to hold the spear carrier's spear for him while he carried some other fellow's spear. But before the season opened I met Gudrun.'

'Gudrun?'

'She was Swiss. Still is, probably. I met her at a party. She had this . . . luminosity. I was insane for her. Our romance was intoxicating, and we decided to marry.' Lynden had again ebbed imperceptibly back towards the sombre.

'You know, Edward, you really have no need . . . I mean I don't need to know . . . everything about you.'

'No, no, of course. I'm sorry, I was just trying to explain why I came to give up acting. The short version is that I went out to visit Gudrun in Geneva. I stayed with her family: stolid Swiss mid-bourgeois. They spoke no English and my German was all learnt from comic books. You know, I could shout *schnell*, and *achtung*, and *schweinhund*, but that was it. After a couple of days she took me to the skiing chalet the family kept in the mountains, in the shadow of the Matterhorn. But this was the summer. It was very beautiful, and isolated. We spent three days walking through the flower meadows – remember, it *was* the seventies!

'And then she left me there, on my own. A week passed. She didn't telephone, or write. Nothing. Silence. I thought that I had done something wrong, offended against some unfathomable Swiss custom. I decided to come home. I was desolate. It took me a month. I hitched, took trains and buses, walked, stopping at every bar I could find. When I got home I found a letter waiting for me. It just said: "There was a test and you failed." You see, she'd just wanted to see if my love could endure setbacks. I think it was her father's idea to leave me there without a word.'

'Edward, this sounds very sad, but weren't you just jilted? Doesn't it happen to everybody? I can't see why you couldn't continue your stage career.'

Alice was finding the story of Lynden's woes a little self-indulgent. However, this had the strange effect of putting her further at her ease. She even entertained fleetingly the thought that that might be the purpose of the account. But no, surely no man could be so altruistic as to make himself look ridiculous simply to make her feel more comfortable?

'I was in no fit state when I returned,' he continued wearily. 'I asked for a short break in my contract. They said they'd see. I went to India. I stayed for a year living in a hovel, smoking opium. Then I spent a year trying to stop smoking opium. And then another year looking for spiritual awareness. By the time I got back I was yesterday's man, without ever having been today's. My father was pleased, though.'

'Well, thanks for that. I really don't know what to say. Are you expecting some similar account of my sentimental education?'

'What? No, no. I'm sorry I've been boring you.'

'Quite the contrary; I enjoyed listening to you. But perhaps we should get down to discussing the reason for my visit.'

'Oh yes, my Audubon.'

Alice had carefully prepared her speech. She had sensed that he was an impatient man, and so she wanted to keep it short, her arguments punchy. Even so, there were several important points to make, and she'd timed the full version at eight and a half minutes.

'Edward, I really think that you should reconsider . . .'

'Fine.'

'I beg your pardon?'

'I said fine. I'll reconsider. Or rather I won't reconsider.'

'Wha . . .'

'*Won't* reconsider my original decision to sell. Through you.'

Alice's mind had slowed down, as if she were thinking through treacle. Not reconsidering . . . through you. So he was . . . click.

'Oh. How pleasing. But the phone call? What's changed your mind?'

'You mean why *haven't* I changed my mind?'

'Yes yes.'

'You really don't know?'

Alice knew.

'I suppose it's because you're just a vain and silly man who doesn't know his own mind, and who likes to keep others waiting on his whims.'

111

Lynden laughed. Alice thought that the laugh might have been a little forced to begin with, but after a second its rolling momentum took over, and the eyes began to collaborate. It was a deep bubbling laugh and Alice found it impossible not to join in.

'I genuinely fear I may have been rumbled.'

'So, you admit that this whole thing was a charade to, to . . .'

'Persuade you to come back here.'

Although Alice now knew that this was the case, she was shocked to hear it put so bluntly. Shocked and exhilarated.

NINE

Drinking it Over

'And you expect me to believe that nothing happened? Little girl, all alone in the middle of nowhere, misses the last train – how convenient – has to spend the night, and you're telling me there wasn't a knock on the door, and an "oh, I just thought you might like a nightcap or a hot water bottle", and then out with his tackle and on with the game?'

There was a certain amount of very *un*certain laughter from the small group gathered around Alice's desk. Oakley was there, and Clerihew, and Pam.

Alice herself was paying attention with, at best, half of her mind. That lunchtime she had decided to go back to the crossing. All these months she had been walking miles on elaborate detours to avoid it, discovering new side-streets, and Dickensian back alleys, full of the sort of shops she thought long since banished from London: a saddler's, an umbrella shop, a tiny printer's, complete with a man in an ink-stained apron, a shop selling nothing but fountain pens.

But now she faced it again, stood where she had stood.

People flowed around her; she thought she saw some of them stare at her in that casually hostile way that Londoners save for those who get in their way. She half expected to see him there, frozen as she had first seen him, with the look of wonder and acceptance on his face. She tried hard to remain objective, to study herself, probe her own feelings, as if she were conducting a scientific experiment. And, of course, like all experimenters, she had some preconceptions about what she would find. Scientists always knew roughly what would or should emerge from their work. There were no blind leaps, just a nudging forward in the direction already chosen for you, dictated by myriad other minds, by structures and institutions. But within those limits, a mind could stay clear and open and innocent, could listen for the subtle music of nature, could find a kind of truth.

What she expected was a wash of raw emotion, an unmediated surge of passion and anguish through her veins. She had braced herself for the onslaught, convinced that, if she could just withstand it, then she would emerge stronger, more able to face the world.

And yes, it was painful. Her eyes filled with tears. She wanted to stretch out and embrace the perfect, tragic form of the Boy, to protect him from the bone-crushing weight of the world. But there was something contained, restricted in her sadness, as if the genie were raging inside its bottle. She neither trembled nor sobbed. She knew that if she waited for long enough and allowed the surge to continue, then perhaps it would overwhelm her: yes, she *could* indulge, abandon herself. But that would be her own choice.

A sense of loss, as well as of relief, came with this knowledge of control. She felt almost empty. He was still inside her, but he had lost some of his power, some of his force.

She tried hard to tune back in to the office discussion.

Andrew was camping it up for the crowd, but Alice could sense that there was something serious and not at all nice burrowing inside his brain. It made her feel uncomfortable and annoyed in about equal proportions.

'No nightcaps, no anythings. He was the perfect gentleman.'

'Of course he'd be the perfect gentleman,' said Pam helpfully. 'After all, he's a gentleman, isn't he?'

'Oh no, not a gentleman,' said Clerihew, 'a *lord*. In some ways the opposite of a gentleman.'

'Yes,' said Andrew rather angrily, 'it means they don't bother about dirty lavatories, and swear, and say "what" instead of "pardon". But we're getting off the point. You've as good as told us, Alice, that he only came back on board because he fancied you.'

'Ooooh!' said Pam at the naughtiness of it all.

'I didn't say that and I don't believe it.'

'Well, he sure as f . . . anything didn't want me to come along and persuade him.'

'For heaven's sake, Andy, give it a rest,' said Clerihew, his eyes working feverishly to detect the mood of the group. 'I think Alice has done a jolly good job. She's saved your bacon and you should be thanking her, not not . . .'

'Not what, you nit?'

'N-not being horrid to her.'

'Here here, Cedric,' said Oakley, who'd come along to congratulate Alice, and wasn't happy about what he took to be Andrew's carping. 'Let's remember we're a team, all pulling at the same er, thing.'

'Yes, one for all and all for one,' said Cedric.

'Shut up, Cedric. No one's suggesting Alice hasn't done a fantastic job. I was just . . . I was just . . .'

'Annoying little shag, that Clerihew, by the sound of him.'

Leo was offering support in the Red Dragon.

'Annoying isn't the half of it. Made it look as if I was

115

pissed off about Alice getting the Audubon back – you know, jealous of her success, me putting my own career before the good of Enderby's and the Nagasaki Fucking Investment Bank. Which is completely unfair. I was pissed off about Alice getting off with that posh wanker Lynden – my jealousy was *purely* personal and sexual.'

'How noble. Does he know that he's got a verse form named after him?'

'Clerihew, you mean? Well, he does now. When I first met him I brought it up – well, you'd have to, wouldn't you? He looked at me completely blankly with those nasty piggy little eyes of his. I said, you know, it's an absurd short poem of two irregular couplets, commenting satirically on some aspect of a well-known personality . . .'

'Commendably well put; what a tragic loss to the academic community.'

'Screw you. And he still clearly didn't have a clue. Sorry, I did a rhyme thing.'

'Excused.'

'Ta. And you'd think someone would have mentioned it to him. After all, he went to a public school, like you, you great pansy, and surely one of the masters or a smart boy would have said something.'

'Almost certainly a *minor* public school by the sound of him. And they don't teach much beyond mutual masturbation and algebra in most of those.'

'Bow to your greater knowledge there. Well, I could tell that he thought this, the Clerihew stuff, was all some kind of sly way of getting at him, you know, it's a short and absurd thing, so are you saying that's what I am, eh, eh? Which I hadn't thought of at all, although now I can see that if the dutch cap fits . . . So anyways, I try to give him an example. All I can come up with is,

Bertrand Russell,
Though bulging with intellectual muscle,
Was something of a failure
When it came to genitalia.'

'Nice one.'

'But then he repeated it back, deliberately not rhyming the failure and genitalia, going "fail-*your*" and "genita-*lee-ahhh*" to make me look like an idiot.'

'The swine!'

'It was worse than it sounds. And it's not just me. I'm pretty sure that he had something to do with Crumlish getting the bum's rush.'

'The amusingly fey *fin de siècle* chap, straight out of the Aubrey Beardsley *Yellow Book*?'

'Yeah. He wasn't quite my cup of absinthe – I always reckon that camp humour is a cheat, a way of drawing stuff out to earn you extra time to think of something funny, or just elaborate bitchiness, but that's not a reason to bin someone, not after however many bloody years. *And* he was about the best expert there. You should never sack the talent. Basic tenet of modern management. But the word is – and I got this from Pam who has a finger in most pies, gossip-wise – that the Americans wanted Crumlish out, and so Oakley and Clerihew cooked up a scheme between the two of them. Clerihew suggested that Crumlish made a grab for him.'

'Ouch!'

'Ouch indeed. Now leaving aside the fact that Crumlish had pretty fucking impeccable taste in most things, and therefore wouldn't touch the fat little shit with his silver-tipped cane, I don't actually think he was *gay*. That was his dark secret.'

'Why didn't that come out?'

'The sexual harassment story never officially saw the light of day. It was all just described as down-, I mean, right-sizing. The terms deadwood and new blood were both used.'

'Can't resist a mixed metaphor, your management consultant.'

'And if they really wanted to hack away some deadwood then they could have started with Clerihew who, for all his fawning and his bow ties and his fob watch and his waistcoats, is a fucking idiot; ask him for a valuation and he'll um and ah and start pulling at his crotch, and sweating, with his hair getting lanker and danker, and his Schubert-style little specs misting up, and the next thing you know he's in the corner on his back with his legs waving in the air like a woodlouse, with a keeeek keeeek sound coming out of him.

'*Or*, for that matter, they could have dumped the enchanting Ophelia. Couldn't much bear the thought of not being able to drink her in, I mean just the general loveliness of her, any more, but the fact is she doesn't *do* anything. And I mean *anything*. She looks stunning at a sale, but in terms of work you might as well have an inflatable doll. At least they have three functioning orifices. And while I'm on the subject, there's Oakley, himself who . . . sorry. We're fighting old battles. Point is that Clerihew made it look to everyone that I'm a mean-spirited, back-biting, cock-sucking careerist.'

'Strongly recommend you don't try cock-sucking and back-biting at the same time: that way lies a slipped disk at the very least. So you want advice about how to get back into Alice's good books?'

'God, I don't know. I'm not sure that the thing is susceptible to rational analysis and considered action. If they don't fancy you they don't fancy you.'

'Defeatist! The one thing you have to remember about women is that they don't just go by how big your pecs are.'

'Yeah, I know that.'

'And because it's never just a physical thing with them, you're always in with a chance of winning them round with the force of your eloquence, or your sparkling wit, or, God help us, your *sensitivity*. The negotiations are always, like the girls themselves, open ended.'

'Yes, yes, all fine in theory,' said Andrew, without acknowledging the smut, 'but it's easy for you to go on like that when you have hordes of wanton, nubile girl-students hurling themselves at your lectern like nymphomaniacal lemmings.'

'Ah the poor sweet innocent things. I almost pity them.'

Andrew and Leo fell quiet for a moment as they contemplated the fate of the lemmings. Andrew had long been jealous of Leo's fabled rutting. Easy access to wave upon wave of pretty eighteen-year-olds had been one of the reasons Andrew had set his mind on an academic career. Not the main reason, nor perhaps even in the top three, but certainly top five. He knew from first-hand experience the false glow of allure that attached to any lecturer not actually old, smelly or brown-toothed. His brief brush with tutoring back during his PhD days had shown him that even he, unsure and diffident as he then was, could acquire a fan club. Although Leo was a little oddly shaped, Andrew didn't doubt that his darkly sinister manner and quicksilver intelligence would have the girls shivering with excitement in their dorms, knocking shyly at his door, lingering at the end of lectures, and moaning in frenzied ecstasy as he . . .

'What you need,' said Leo, 'is another opportunity to shine outside the office. Any socials coming up?'

'Well, funny you should mention it, but there is, sort of. I was about to bring it up myself. You know we have these semi-regular, totally crap, Friday-night drinks?'

'Oh yeah, the ones nobody goes to except you and the rubber-band lady, what's her name?'

'That would be the ever trusty Pam again.'

'Pam. Nothing going on there I hope?'

'Oh no no no.' Andrew shivered, ungallantly. 'And it's not *just* me and Pam – there's only so many cake recipes and accounts of who's had who on *EastEnders* you can listen to. No, there's usually a few more of the sadder, less socially adept, who turn up. Not Alice though, even if you'd have to lump her in with the misfits these days. At least not since the first couple of times, before . . . well, her *incident*. Clerihew has been known to show his shiny face, just long enough to sponge a couple of sweet sherries or a crème de menthe, or whatever it is he drinks. And, yes, I know I'm not covering myself in glory here by admitting that I go, but it just seems to me that if there's a drink on, you really should go, whatever the circumstances. Sort of duty thing. Where was I? Oh yes, there's a new found enthusiasm for the idea of team-building social events. All driven by the Yanks, of course, with their chief eunuch, Oakley, in the van. He was jabbering about a weekend in some country-house-conference-centre place, but the mean sods decided that *that* was too expensive. Now they've hi-jacked the Friday evening two weeks away and made it compulsory. They've suggested we bring partners or friends along. Alice has *got* to be there. She looked less than thrilled but said she'd invite along some friend of hers, called Crepe Suzette or Odin or something stupid, not having a *live* partner.'

'She didn't say that?'

'No, but you could tell it's what she was thinking. At least she isn't bringing Baron Arseface.'

'Ah,' said Leo, doing a wily-oriental face, 'a picture is beginning to form. You want *me* to come with you to some boring office piss-up? What for exactly? I mean, what am I supposed to do? Stand around and laugh at your jokes to make you look funny and popular?'

'Well yes, actually.'

'Circulate and tell everyone I speak to what a fine fellow you are?'

'That'd be nice.'

'Generally sparkle so that people will think you have lots of interesting friends and must therefore be interesting yourself, whilst not sparkling so much that I throw you into the shadows?'

'Check.'

'Okay. But it'll cost you.'

'Pint?'

'And a crème de menthe chaser.'

'Beer nuts?'

'Beer nuts good. I was joking about the crème de menthe.'

'Figured. But that doesn't count as sparkling, you know. Barely even *petillant*.'

'Hang on a minute. What were we talking about before Clerihew raised his cherubic head? Your Alice. Yes, what exactly *did* happen?'

'So,' said Odette, leaning over the table in what had become their usual wine bar, 'what exactly *did* happen?'

Alice had finally managed to get hold of Odette; and it was Odette who was full of apologies for straying out of reach.

'Things have been happening,' she said over the phone. 'All kinds of things. Let's meet and exchange stories.'

Alice was a little drunk, but also quite happy. She'd felt instantly comfortable with Odette, who, beyond a tentative initial enquiry, hadn't pried at all about the Dead Boy, as if she knew that nothing productive could come of it. But she had refused to say what her 'all kinds of things' were until Alice had told the full story of the latest Quantock adventure.

'Nothing, I swear. I can't pretend that I wasn't flattered

by the thought that he . . . you know, liked me. Liked me in that way . . .'

'And you're sure that he did? Oh, I don't mean to suggest that he wouldn't but . . .'

'No, I understand. But I'm pretty sure . . . as sure as I can be. It was obvious that the mind-changing business over the Audubon was just an excuse to get me down there.'

'How roguish.'

'But I honestly don't think that *seduction* was on his mind.'

'Oh Alice!'

'No, really. Well, maybe somewhere on his mind, but not at the front bit. You see, I think he was lonely more than anything. He's a bit of a thesp at heart – did I say he used to be a talented actor?'

'If only I'd taken notes I could have told you *exactly* how many times.'

'Sorry. So I think he desperately craved an audience.'

'Doesn't sound like much fun.'

'Oh, I don't mean to make him sound completely self-absorbed and egotistical. He is, a bit, but not only, and not all the time. I think one of the things he likes about me is that I take the piss. He'll be telling some story about himself – he's always the villain of the piece, and it's usually about how his blindness or selfishness destroyed someone's life or led to some great disaster – and all I have to do is raise an eyebrow, or perhaps start humming that awful song, "Tragedy", by the Bee Gees, and he'll furrow his brow for a second as if he's going to start raging, and then he crumples and goes all soft and starts to laugh.'

'Gosh, Alice, I've never heard you talk like this about a man before. When will you see him again?'

'He's having a sort of party in a couple of weeks. Just a few people staying for the weekend. He called it "a shooting party without any shooting".'

'Exciting.'

'Nerve-wracking, more like. I haven't got a Barbour jacket or anything. I probably won't go. It just isn't me.'

Well, thought Odette, it certainly wasn't the Alice of a few weeks ago. Odette was delighted about the Lynden development. It was exactly what Alice needed. Far better than her own idea of tracking down the Dead Boy's family for some cathartic confrontation. How mad was that? What had she been thinking?

'What about that nice-sounding boy in your office? The one who went to the park with you ages ago – I thought he still had some kind of crush?'

'Andrew? It's sad, but I never really noticed him until we went together to see Edward, that first time. We sit together at work, and he just became sort of invisible to me. Especially after . . . when . . . you know, that time.'

'Yes. It's okay. Go on.'

'Well, on the first trip down – he gave me a lift – we talked, and, well, he stopped being invisible. He's funny and nice and sort of hapless, but in an almost-kind-of-sexy way. I think he's a bit jealous about the Edward thing. Not that there *is* a thing, yet, really.'

'*Alice*!'

'Sorry. Anyway, there was an incident at work the other day. I think he may only have been joking, you know, playing up a bit, but it all misfired. There were people around, some of the high-ups, and Andrew came out looking very bad. I hope there aren't any consequences.'

'You still haven't really told me if Andrew has anything to be properly jealous of. You've got as far as staying up late drinking his whisky and swapping stories with the fire blazing and the Cave of Ice all a-sparkle.'

'That's all to tell, honestly. About two, well, maybe three, in the morning, I started to yawn, and he said, "My God, I forget my manners. You must be very tired." And I said I was quite, yes. And he showed me to my room.'

'What was it like? Amazing?'

'As you'd expect, amazing. It was one of the comfortable ones, rather than the bleak and modern ones. It must have belonged to a woman. There were feminine touches. Cushions and things. A four-poster bed, which was a bit of a shock. But it still looked like something out of an interior decoration magazine: I don't mean *Elle Deco*, I mean one of the really flash ones, *Metropolitan Home*, say.'

'And he just left you at the door?'

'I know it doesn't sound plausible, but he did. Gave me a gentle little kiss on the forehead. I assumed that that was a prelude to some kind of lunge, but it wasn't. He just said "Breakfast at eight", and that was it.'

'Oh, how anticlimactic.'

'No, not at all. I don't know what I'd have done if he'd tried to come in. It's been so long. I've forgotten how! And don't say it's like riding a bicycle. For me it was always more like riding a *uni*cycle.'

Both Odette and Alice succeeded in finding this wildly amusing. They did have the excuse of being well into their second bottle of New Zealand Sauvignon. When they had recovered themselves, Alice said:

'Okay, you've had long enough, and I've been analysed half to death. Tell me all about Venice and Matthew.'

'Fine, but just let me catch the eye of that nice young man: I think this needs another bottle.'

TEN

Odette in Venice

'I've booked a weekend,' she said over the lunchtime sandwiches, which they'd started eating together down by the river.

'Oh!' said Matt, in a tone as difficult to pin down as his accent. 'That should be . . . you know. Where did you say?'

'Venice.'

With characteristic thoroughness she had researched and cross-referenced, using every single guidebook in print. She'd found what sounded like the perfect little hotel: nothing too extravagant, but universally recommended for its charm and comfort, and convenience for the Academia. She had even thought carefully about the duration. They would go on Friday and return by the first flight on Monday. She knew that they could get into the office by ten o'clock, and arriving together would signal to everyone that they were an acknowledged couple.

'Wow, Venice.' That 'wow' should have alerted Odette to the possibility of danger. As the mouth was wowing, the eyes were doing something altogether different which, had it taken aural form, might well have sounded like 'nnnghh'.

'Have you ever been before?' she asked, gushing a little.

'No. But I've . . .' He was also going to say that he'd always wanted to go, but it would have sounded limp to repeat what she had just said, and besides it wasn't true.

'You *can* come, can't you? I know it's short notice, but what the hell, we're only young . . .'

'No, yes, of course I can come.'

Odette was at Stansted an hour before check-in time. Twelve-thirty came and went. And then one. She telephoned his flat. The answerphone cut in, and so Odette tried his mobile.

'Matt, where the hell are you? You're going to miss the flight.'

'Oh God, Odette. Look, I can't make it. I was about to call. I've had to come into the office. It's what I'm here for. Stuff's happening. Look, sorry.'

Odette hung up.

The fucker.

She was in shock. How could he just not turn up? What would she say to her mother, who'd told her to be careful, thrilling with excitement at the thought that she might not? Everyone in the office would know. They'd want to see the pictures. In a moment Odette decided that the only thing was to go. She deliberately stopped thinking, throwing her ever-active mind into the almost unvisited neutral. Somehow she found herself in a cramped seat, staring at an over made-up stewardess semaphoring what to do if you get attacked by a shark after ditching in the sea. Strangely, she was in the middle of a three-seat row, sandwiched between a buttock-faced man, and a woman in a crocheted beret, eating nuts. Something about the man and woman made Odette think that they were together, and a little shudder of paranoia ran through her. How had she come to be between them? What were they planning? The airline was one of the budget ones which don't allocate individual seats, and Odette

126

wanted to say that she had paid for two seats, and so should have a space next to her, but that would have involved explanations and excuses, and she didn't have the will.

With the surge of take-off the horror of it all returned to swamp her. Had she done something wrong? Was it because she was too plain, or too dull? Had he been laughing at her behind her back with the rest of the office? Stupid, meaningless taunts from school days clamoured in her ears:

Odette Bach like a dog
Odette Bach like a dog
Nobody will ever snog
Odette Bach, like a dog

She squeezed her eyes tight shut to close out the sound, but a voice came through.

'Are you okay, my dear?'

Odette opened her eyes and found that the buttock-faced man was leaning across her, his paunch pressing into her thigh.

'Yes, fine. Why?'

'Sorry. It's just that you made a noise. A sort of a squeak. You're far safer than you would be in a car.'

Odette imagined herself jabbing a finger into the buttock-faced man's doughy cheek, where it would, she was sure, leave a long-lasting indentation. She shuddered. The bereted accomplice crunched and tutted over her nuts. Odette suspected that they were not nuts at all, but the skulls of mice and shrews.

Odette ordered two little bottles of gin with tonic from the over made-up attendant. The buttock-faced man passed them to her with his fat fingers, and winked. Odette had a particular dislike of winking, which she always thought of as the sex-offender's version of the Masonic handshake.

Somehow she got through the flight. She was determined to make the most of the trip, extracting some cultural capital from the emotional waste, and so read carefully through the Venice guidebooks she had brought, underlining the 'must dos', and asterisking the 'should dos'. She hunted down the best (sensibly priced) restaurants, and worked out itineraries for each of her three days, weaving complicated but utterly rational paths between the eternal beauties of the city. And she saw with pleasure that her true self, the sensible, rational core was still there, dented, perhaps, by the fiasco, but resolute and immutable. Some minor love problem could not bend her heroically straight lines, nor upset the comforting rigour of her thought.

Odette had originally planned to take one of the famously wonderful water taxis from the airport to the city. That was when the wonder and the romance, as well as the absurd cost, were to be shared by two. But on her own, Odette decided on the more prosaic waterbus. At least, she thought, it would provide an appropriately aquatic entrance into the city. She followed the crowd through the various circles of airport hell, trying, and frequently failing, to avoid the buttock-faced man and the beret. She emerged into a wet dusk. A fine rain was falling, seeping its way under her collar, and ruining her hair. She'd had it cut at Daniel Galvin's, but soon she looked like a scraggy teenager, fresh from ten laps of backstroke.

The waterbus was a misery. She tottered over a narrow plank, leered at by unhelpful helpers, who made no attempt to carry her bag. The seats were set so low that it was impossible to see anything other than the dark grey of the sky through the rain-smeared windows. So much for her dreams of arriving like Cleopatra on her barge. After an hour-and-a-half of blind chugging she was disgorged at St Marco. The buttock-faced man appeared at her shoulder.

'Know where you're going?'

She had only a vague idea.

'Yes of course.'

'Don't need any help then?'

'No, I'm fine.'

She wanted to weep, but instead looked around to get her bearings. On one side water, and then an island with a big church; on the other side people, buildings, scaffolding, pigeons. There was no little joyous explosion inside her head at the beauty of it all, just the registering that Venice had arrived, and the knowledge, like an all-body toothache, that a trudge to the hotel was upon her. She consulted the maps in the guidebooks. They were all either too small or too large in scale, fine if she wanted to count the bricks in the Doge's Palace, or find Venice from outer space, but next to useless for getting to the Academia, and her longed-for hotel room.

How much fun it would all have seemed, what an adventure, she thought, if only there had been Matt. For the first time she started to hate him. She decided to tell people in the office about his weak bladder. That helped to lift her spirits as she headed in what she hoped was the right direction. Soon she was lost in the narrow streets, convinced that she was repeatedly crossing the same bridge over the same murky canal. And that was Prada again; or were there two? Finally she did the thing she hated most: asked an American. He smilingly waved her in the right direction and five minutes later she and her suitcase, heavy now as osmium, crawled over the wooden, curiously oriental, Academia Bridge. From there she quickly found her way around the side of the gallery and along the street to her hotel.

'There are two?' asked a not especially charming woman in reception.

'No, just one,' replied Odette, blushing. She remembered

the shame of her first night in a hotel with the lecturer, convinced that the old lady in the bed and breakfast knew and disapproved of their illicit coupling. She smiled grimly at the neat reversal: how she was now ashamed of the absence of carnality.

Her room was small and neat. She quite liked it until she lay on the bed: it was as hard as a butcher's slab. Even the pillows seemed to be made of solid rolls of felt. She curled into the foetus position and tried to cry, vaguely aware that it was supposed to make you feel better. It was six-thirty.

At eight she decided to get something to eat. The hotel restaurant was mentioned as reasonable in the guidebooks, so she thought she'd try it, although she wasn't hungry and was, in fact, beginning to feel clammy and nauseous. Odette was used to eating alone, and would normally have been content to sit and read as she ate, but the dining room was low and oppressive. She found herself blushing whenever she spoke to the overly-attentive waiters, and said too many thank yous and *grazies*. The wine waiter pressed a whole bottle of red wine on her, which she found herself gulping joylessly, like mineral water. She ordered pasta vongole, but when it came the clams had a foetid, faintly faecal after-taste, and she could not eat more than a couple of mouthfuls.

She tried to amuse herself by observing the other diners. They were all, of course, tourists. Mainly middle-aged. Three grey couples (not, blessedly, the buttock-and-beret team); a smattering of late-onset Teutonic lesbians, a man dressed unseasonably in combat shorts whom she assumed to be Nordic, and in the far corner a family, making too much noise. The mother was attractive, perhaps forty-five years old. Four children: two squirming brats responsible for most of the racket, and an older pair – a girl of fourteen or so, and a boy who might have been sixteen. The girl spoke quietly with

130

her mother in a language Odette did not recognise. For some reason she decided it was Estonian, although it could just have easily been Turkish or Hungarian.

It was not, however, the girl who captured Odette's attention. It was the boy. The boy, who remained in silent profile, was the most perfectly beautiful object Odette had ever seen. Odette had never thought it possible for a man to be beautiful. Not that she was immune to physical attractiveness: it was just that the physical qualities she admired in men – boldness, competence, energy – seemed to occupy a different mental space from the world of beauty. She dimly remembered attending philosophy lectures in her first year at the LSE, where the meltingly feminine beautiful was contrasted with the masculine, overpowering sublime.

But now here was a boy, almost a man, who, without having any particularly female characteristics, could only ever be described as beautiful. His hair was long, and seemed to be trying to form itself into ringlets. His eyes were pale grey, saved from any suggestion of emptiness by the slight furrowing of the brow. His face was long with high cheekbones, and the nose was elegantly flared. Odette reeled. She experienced a raging, torrential flood of desire, suffused with a strangely pure affection: she wanted to hurl herself upon the boy, feel his bones crunch into hers, gnash her teeth against his; and yet she also wanted to take his fingers in hers and talk about those things she had shoved to the margins of her life: art, and the beauty of the world, and literature, and philosophy.

And then without quite realising how, Odette found herself sitting on the floor, looking up at the table. Attentive voices were murmuring in her ear. The headwaiter and a dour, middle-aged woman whose role in the hotel was unclear to Odette were looming over her. 'Is it the wine?' a voice said. 'I think the lady is ill,' said another. Odette felt very hot. She wanted to be sick, but she knew that she must not do that . . . here . . . in front of the boy. My God, the boy. She had fallen off her chair right in front of that beautiful boy. Hands helped her up, guided her from the dining room. She looked towards the table with the family. It was empty.

'I shall call the doctor,' said the middle-aged woman.

'No, no, I'm fine,' replied Odette. She thought she was just tired and stressed from the journey . . . from the journey. She smiled at the thought that she had fainted from exposure to the sheer beauty of the boy. Wasn't there a syndrome? A Radio 4 memory drifted in and out. Stendhal syndrome. Fainting from too much beauty. Wasn't it the corsets? But Stendhal was a man, wasn't he?

And then Odette was alone, lying on the bed. The boy's disembodied face hovered before her, his eyes still surveying some distant horizon, but her head echoed with other sounds: the clinking and crashing from the kitchen, which was below her window; the random shouts and guttural noises from the streets; the voice of Matt, with his empty 'wow' and transparent excuses. The sounds would have haunted her all night, but she managed to silence them by focussing on the face of the boy, and his image stayed with her as she drifted into sleep.

It remained with her when she awoke late the next morning. She still felt very peculiar and wobbled as she made her way to the bathroom. She'd missed breakfast, but still wasn't hungry anyway. And she feared meeting the boy. As well as the embarrassment of falling off her chair, Odette was irrationally convinced that the boy would know that she was . . . that she was, well, what exactly? Besotted, she supposed. God, what a mess.

For her first expedition, Odette decided on the Academia, which her guidebook told her held the world's greatest collection of Venetian art. It had the more immediate virtues of being both indoors, useful given the continuing drizzle, and less than thirty feet from her hotel, which was about her maximum tottering range at the moment.

Odette had never really had time for art. She would occasionally permit herself to be persuaded into an exhibition by one or other of her cultural friends, but she always found herself bored within half an hour, and plagued by stiffness and aches in odd parts of her body. The Academia didn't bode well. There was an initial half-hour wait to get in, amid the jostling tourists. By the time she entered the first room she was already soaked to the skin and feeling more light-headed than ever. And then came the procession of skinny saints and stout Madonnas. The artists all seemed to have the same, or very nearly the same, name. Odette found herself entirely unmoved by the displays of devotion, however exquisitely rendered. The toothy yammering of the Japanese, the barking of the Germans, and the uncomprehending murmuring of the English all added to the misery.

'Why am I here?' she asked herself, not for the first time.

'Yes, well, it's magnificent, isn't it?' came a sort of reply. It was, of course, Buttock Face. 'Fancy meeting you again,' he continued. 'Enjoying yourself? Look rather peaky to me.'

'Yes, sorry, feel a bit . . . funny.' Odette couldn't muster the energy to be rude, and besides, it wasn't her way. But why was it always the dullest people, or the weirdest, that we cannot shake off, and never the . . . beautiful ones?

'You know, if you're not feeling well, you can always come back to our hotel for a lie-down.'

Something hideous between a leer and a pout settled on the man's face as he said this. He clearly had some frightful ménage in mind with Odette and the beret lady. She had a sudden vision of whips and thongs and strange harnesses. She knew that if she ever went back to the frightful chamber with them she would never escape alive, and bits of her body would turn up in bin liners, scattered around the city.

'No, no, thank you,' she said, primly. 'Really, I'm fine.' She hurried away into another of the endless rooms. This one seemed to be principally made up of St Sebastians being prettily shot through with arrows. He never winced, not even when a particularly sore-looking one hit him in the shin, or the elbow. As she stared at one frankly erotic Sebastian, his Calvin Klein loincloth barely saving his modesty, she became aware of a dim reflection of a face in the glossy oil-paint, precisely covering Sebastian's pelvis. Thinking that a connoisseur was interested in the painting she moved away and to the side. But it wasn't a bespectacled professor, or an earnest student.

It was the boy.

Odette didn't know if he had been watching her or looking at the martyrdom of the saint. Her lips parted with an embarrassing little 'pap' noise. She wanted to say something, to make some profound or witty remark about the painting, or Venice, or anything. But instead she staggered back into an unruly party of Italian schoolchildren who had just spilled into the room. They were laughing and joking, ignoring their harried teacher, and Odette felt lost and helpless in the flow. She allowed herself to be carried among them away from the boy, away from the Sebastians.

Outside in the fresh, but damp, air, Odette decided that a drink was called for and Harry's Bar seemed the only place to be. She found it without too much difficulty and, as it was the middle of the day, she even managed to get a seat. Naturally, she ordered a Bellini. Naturally, she was shocked by the price, and the tiny size of the thing, but her qualms were banished by the sharp sweet tang of it, and a couple more followed, brought by the crisply dressed and efficiently polite waiters. Venice soon became a little less wearisome.

But Odette still felt strange, and it wasn't just the Bellinis. What on earth could she do about the beautiful boy? She wanted him so badly but she couldn't just go and seduce him, could she? It just wasn't the sort of thing that she did. No, no. Odette Bach was the kind of sensible girl who coolly went about her business, efficiently accumulating capital. Efficiently dumped. Oh God.

That evening, Odette stayed in her room. The Bellinis wore off, leaving her more depressed than ever. She read again through the guidebooks: so much splendour, so much beauty. She felt further away from it than if she had stayed in London. She ordered a sandwich from room service, but still felt too sick to eat. She lay awake again that night, listening again to the kitchen sounds, and her own shallow breathing.

Sunday: her last full day in Venice. She was determined to make the most of it. The woman on reception suggested the Rialto. Odette took the *vaporetto*. The day was brighter, and Venice looked more itself. There really was nothing like it anywhere: the sheer weirdness of buildings lapped by water. Before she came Odette had vaguely thought that there would be some kind of beachy bit in between the canals and the palazzos. But no: it was just there – water and then palace. She wanted to explain this remarkable insight to someone, but she half realised the urge was part of her illness.

Her guidebook had a useful pull-out section naming the major buildings along the Grand Canal, and she ticked off the Palazzo Grassi, the Ca' Foscari, the Pisani-Moretta, and later the Contarini Dei Cavalli, the Grimani, the Ca' Farsetti and the Ca' Loredan. Although she knew she was supposed to be impressed, and did perceive something of the ancient grandeur, she couldn't help but feel that they screamed out for a lick of paint, or just a good tidy-up.

Stepping from the *vaporetto* at the stop just after the bridge, Odette instantly hated the Rialto, which seemed the essence of all that was wrong with Venice. Tourists swarmed amidst the boil-in-the-bag tourist tat, stalls and shops selling the sort of things it was impossible to imagine anyone ever wanting to buy: hideous glass trinkets like fragments of solidified migraine, nylon lace stamped with unidentifiable Venetian scenes; plastic gondolas, complete with string-pull singing gondoliers.

Odette staggered down a side street to escape the inferno, and found herself in a different type of hell. Everywhere there was blood and heads and flayed skin, and the stench of fish. Odette had finally found a corner of 'real' Venice, complete with leering traders, their stubble dense as Velcro, and toothless, black-clad widows, haggling over the price of eels. The air was thick with the strange Venetian accent, well beyond the reach of her phrasebook Italian. Odette thought hard about being charmed, but it was all too real, all too smelly and loud, and she found herself churning again with nausea and revulsion. Hot, despite the still falling drizzle, she leant against the window of a shop facing the market. The glass felt cool against her cheek. And then her eyes focussed on what was behind the glass. Rolls of earth-dark meat; strange cuts she did not recognise; long, curling sausages in the same dark umber, speckled with white fat. And a picture of a gaily prancing horse.

And more. Once again there was a reflection in the surface; the same slender form, the same impression of serenity, lightness, gravity, beauty.

'*Yurluk lie yoor go ña pyook.*'

The boy had spoken to her in his language, exotic and yet familiar.

'I beg your . . . I'm sorry, I don't understand your language.'

'I said, you look like you're going to puke.'

Ah! Not Estonian. The accent was vaguely Northern; Odette thought of Leeds.

'You're in our hotel, aren't you?' the boy continued. 'I saw you the other night when you fell off your chair. Are you sick?'

Odette started to laugh. One of the rewards of honesty and straightforwardness was her inability to take herself too seriously. She was very aware that she had been silly, and unlike many people who would have been embarrassed at the thought, and repressed it, the knowledge gave her no little pleasure.

'Not really. But I haven't had anything to eat for a couple of days, and I feel a bit woozy.'

'There's a place near here. Mum takes us there sometimes. It's good and cheap. Do you want to go for some lunch?'

The cocky little so-and-so, thought Odette, but her nausea had floated away and she felt famished. And even if the boy had lost his mystery, he was still undeniably very pretty.

'Yeah, why not. But aren't you with your family?'

'Oh, they've all gone off to do some sight seeing, now Dad's here. We came a week ahead of him, and he's catching up. He had a funny tummy on the first evening. Something dodgy on the plane.'

The whole family now appeared less romantic. Estonian aristocrats! They were clearly Yorkshire haute bourgeois. Odette mentally moved them from Leeds to Harrogate.

The lunch was fun. The boy, whose name was Peter Todd, was lively and funny. He was halfway through his A Level course, and told jokes about the teachers and other kids in a charmingly egocentric way. He seemed to be used to being the centre of attention, everyone's darling boy. And, Odette realised, he was flirting with her, reaching over, at one point, to wipe away a little smear of tomato sauce from the corner of her mouth, and, more than once, brushing against her foot under the table.

He finally asked her what she was doing in Venice on her own. She gave him a censored account, trying hard not to sound too sad or desperate. But it still sounded quite sad and desperate. Peter seemed genuinely moved by the story.

'The miserable fucker. And you're so . . .'

'So what?' smiled Odette.

'Gorgeous.' He blushed, prettily.

It was then that Odette realised that she was going to sleep with the beautiful boy. She was aware that she was behaving irresponsibly. This boy was more than ten years younger than she was. But wasn't it true that everyone between fifteen and forty was now more or less the same age? Liked the same music and wore the same kind of clothes? It was one of the common themes among her friends, thirtysomethings determinedly clinging to their youth.

She wasn't sure who proposed it, but she found after lunch that they were walking back to the hotel. Peter knew the route well, and told stories (almost certainly made up) about the sights along the way. Here a man was castrated by the irate husband of his lover; in that Palazzo a brother and sister were suffocated in swan down after being caught in bed together. The city was no longer a chore, but a game, and its beauty emerged fresher from the dappling of light amidst the darkness.

He took her hand. She was surprised to find that his was not delicate and light-boned, but broad, and rough and strong. She felt for the first time a rippling of old-fashioned animal lust, so much more energising and thrilling than the curious, disembodied desire she had felt before.

At the door to the hotel, he whispered, 'You can come

to my room. I have some vodka. It's number forty, right at the top. It's the only single room in the hotel. I said I wasn't going to share this time. But we better not go in together.'

Odette found herself impressed, turned on, and not a little shocked by his coolness and apparent experience in these matters. She rather enjoyed the feeling of being in another's control, of not having to act or think.

She went first to her own room, where she applied some lipstick (the only make-up she ever used). She had brought some silly sexy underwear for Matt, mainly as a jokey contrast to her customary utilitarianism in lingerie. But now she slipped on the little knickers with a growing feeling of excitement. Before leaving she popped a packet of condoms into her pocket.

She knocked on his door. The room was tiny, and the sharp fall of the ceiling meant that you could only stand up in the middle. Peter silently approached her and kissed her very gently on the lips, pushing in his tongue, sweet and sharp. Odette noted for the first time with surprise that he was taller than she was. He guided her to the narrow bed. As they sat upon the edge he slipped his hand under her cashmere sweater, and popped the clasp on her bra.

'Very professional,' she said, laughing.

'I used to practise on my sister's – fastened to a chair, of course.'

'Have you got anything?' she said.

'No, but I can . . . I can do a thing.'

'It's all right, you'd better use one of these.'

She was down by now to her knickers, and he was naked but for his Calvin Kleins. His body was completely unmuscled, in the way of teenage boys, but lithe and sinewy. Only his big hands suggested the man he would become. And the . . . well, here it was. Odette was determined to be totally passive – the last thing she needed was a conscience troubling her about seducing children. This way she knew that it was all of his doing. And he seemed to enjoy the challenge of her passivity, straining to tease and stimulate her into a response.

And then there came a knocking at the door, and a voice shouting: 'Peter? You in there? No point pretending, I know you are. Reception said you got your key. Can't believe it. Most beautiful city in the world and all you can do is lie skulking in bed, playing with yourself. Get out of there right now. I want you in our room in five minutes flat to plan the rest of the day.'

Although the door was locked, both cringed playfully beneath the sheets, trying not to laugh.

'Shit, shit, shit,' said Peter, detumescing. 'I hate him. But look, we've got time . . .'

'No,' said Odette. 'It's a lucky escape, really. I shouldn't be here. Shouldn't be doing . . . this.'

'Go on.'

'No,' smiling.

'Please.'

'No,' laughing.

They were sitting up now. The intensity of the moment had gone, but there was no awkwardness.

'You've done this sort of thing lots of times, haven't you?' she said.

'Yeah well, when you look like me, you get . . . offers all the time.' It was said plainly, without vanity. He was just stating the facts. 'You haven't, have you?'

'No. Was I really so bad at it?'

'You were lovely. I mean really sexy. I could tell you were holding yourself back, that something really amazing was about to happen when the dam broke. I wish I could have been there when it happens.'

'Well, you nearly were. You're some boy.'

'Look,' he said, 'why don't you come out to dinner with us tonight? My mum and dad aren't that bad, and they're always picking up interesting strangers.'

Odette thought about her options. What else could she do, alone, on her last night in Venice? There was something about the mother and the elder sister, and even the two brats that drew Odette. They all had that same loveliness which makes you just a little bit happier when it's near. And could the father really be such an ogre?

'Why not,' she said.

Peter called her room to tell her where they were to meet. It was one of the grandest restaurants in Venice, famously expensive.

'It'll be Dad's treat. He's excited about meeting you. I made you sound all tragic and interesting. I hope you don't mind.'

Odette could live with tragic and interesting.

The restaurant seemed to be modelled on the dining car on the Orient Express. It was excessively opulent, and ever so slightly tacky, but that was the way of money in Venice. The family, minus the father, were already there when Odette arrived.

'You must be Odette,' said the mother, her voice placing her reasonably loftily on the Harrogate social ladder. 'Peter's been telling us all about you. You've made quite a conquest there, my dear.' It was impossible to tell if there was any irony in the words. 'My husband is still feeling a little unwell. He'll be back in a moment.'

There followed some pleasant chit-chat. The two little ones stopped fighting so they could stare at the new arrival, and the teenage girl, whose name was Lotte, was very sweet.

'Ah Quentin,' said the mother to a shadow looming behind Odette, 'you're back. Meet Ms Bach, who's been showing Peter the beauties of Venice.'

141

Odette turned and found herself staring into the familiar buttocky face.

'You,' they said together.

'But I didn't know that you were married to this lady. I thought the woman on the plane, the woman with the beret . . .'

'Oh God, and the nuts? But you were sitting between us. Why would you think . . . Never mind. This is a pleasant surprise. Let's have some *prosecco*!'

And to Odette's astonishment, the evening was fun. Buttock Face . . . or rather Quentin, as Odette now forced herself to think of him, was a professor of Art History, a specialist in Byzantine and early Venetian architecture. He loved having a new person to lecture at, despite the heavy sighs and rolling eyes of his wife and children. And Odette found it all, if not fascinating, then at least diverting, especially as it was accompanied by heavy foot-petting from the exquisite Peter.

On the plane home Odette thought about the strangeness of things. Venice had no logic, no reason, no rationality. It just was, and it had endured for over a thousand years, doing its smelly, watery stuff. Her loves, her life, had been one long struggle to make the world behave in ways that could be understood and controlled. But that control had been an illusion. And why had she sacrificed so much in order to work in a place that had no soul, no life, that existed solely to *make* money, to *move* money, joylessly? The relative failure of her trip had shown her the futility of her life in the City in a way that a conventionally, blissfully romantic trip could never have done. She decided to change it, but as yet she had no idea how. She knew that she ought to walk away from the City. She hadn't had time to spend much of her income over the past few years, and she had more money than she knew what to do with in the bank, but she was too . . . too orthodox, too scared simply to walk away. Somehow she knew that she would stay in the City, her career proceeding according to plan, her life withering.

She got into work at ten. Rather than the usual piss-taking, she found the team subdued and uncertain. Had they already heard about the disaster with Matt? Were they sorry for her? She forced some levity into her voice.

'What's happened to you lot? Look like you've all been investing in dot.com stock.'

'If only,' said Philip, one of the guys who normally led the way in the foul-mouthed banter that passed for office wit. 'We're fucked. We've been restructured. It was that cunt Matt. He was sent in to see who could be fucking rationalised out of the picture. It's us, Odette. But you must have known about this. You *were* shagging him, weren't you? Fat lot of fucking good it's done you.'

'So,' said Odette, placidly, 'me too?'

'Yeah, you too.'

'Well,' said Odette, 'that's about it.' The account she had given was shortened, but not censored.

'And what about the boy . . . what was his name?'

'Peter.'

'Peter. I mean, will you see him again?'

'Oh, I don't think so. That's better left as one of those perfect memories. I haven't got many of them, and I wouldn't want to spoil this one.'

Alice looked carefully at her friend. She seemed younger. There was a lightness about her that she had never seen before: nothing dramatic, just a subtle sense of relaxation about the grey eyes, lips that eased into smiles, a calmness

143

of the hands. Alice was pleased. Not, she was aware, the intense pleasure she would have felt before her own life had changed. She had lost that casual affinity with others. No, this was more the distant, passing pleasure on finding out that the earthquake in Lima, or the bomb in Cairo, or the oil spill in Alaska, had not been as serious as first reports suggested.

Alice didn't know what to make of it all; nor what the appropriate thing to say was. She felt horribly guilty about advising her friend to go to Venice, a trip that by any objective criteria looked like a disaster. And yet Odette exuded her new serenity.

'Somehow you don't seem particularly upset by it,' she tried, in want of anything better to say. The 'it' could have been the Matt fiasco or the job catastrophe.

'You know, the truth is, I'm not. I've always tried to take control in my life, but there's something refreshing in being the hapless plaything of Fate. I didn't realise how much I hated the job – no, not hated, was bored by – until it wasn't there. And Matt was never the one. He was just a shell, and my love or my need crawled into it like a hermit crab.'

'But what will you do?'

'They've given me a great fat redundancy cheque. I'll live on that for a while. But I have a few ideas. Well, one idea, really, but I think it's a good one. Or maybe a mad one. I hope not: in fact I've already put it into operation.'

Odette's scheme, briefly told, involved investing a fair chunk of her redundancy money in financing the long-ago ex-boyfriend's business manufacturing garden ornaments. The ex-boyfriend, called Gerald, was actually a perfectly competent, if excessively hairy, artist, specialising in monumental sculptural works. However, with neither a trust fund nor a Tory patron, and lacking the necessary crudity or showmanship to attract prizes or commissions, he had hit, in desperation, on the idea of putting stone circles in suburban gardens. It was a world he knew: his father had managed a garden centre in Woking, a place where Gerald still worked occasionally, and where Odette had met him on a special trip to buy shrubs for her balcony. He'd made his play while loading her Golf with a tightly bound lemon tree and another stripy-leafed thing she'd bought. It had seemed unnecessarily callous to turn down a drink, and besides, he had a muscly, salt of the earth feel to him. She didn't know then about the art.

'Listen, babe,' he'd said on that first and only date, drawing audibly on four millimetres of roll-up, 'people like spending their money on their gardens. It's fucking mental, but it's a fact. I don't believe they actually want gnomes and what have you. It's just that there's not much else, once you've got the bird bath and the cartwheel and the sundial. And you know, I believe that people have a suppressed yearning for the spiritual. The more materialistic you are, the deeper the yearning.'

'I hate that kind of logic, the finding of evidence for something in the very absence of evidence.'

'Stone circles concentrate energy. You ever screw in Avebury?'

'Um, no.'

'Fucking cosmic. By the way, I don't use condoms. It's a vibe thing.'

She hadn't slept with him, but had found him agreeable enough to keep up the relationship on an occasional phone call basis. So she knew that the stone circle business was hobbling along, keeping him in high-grade Moroccan red, but that was about it.

'Well,' said Odette to Alice, 'I'm not sure that it'll ever make us millionaires, but it's all quite . . . stimulating. We have

145

brainstorming sessions where we decide what to make – I've just had the idea of trying a range of glass-topped coffee tables, you know, over the top of the stone circle, and Gerald wants to move into the European market by using selected bits of Carnac, which is the French Stonehenge, only bigger and more straggly. Okay, more Avebury than Stonehenge. Then he goes off and makes the things: a stone original, chiselled out of granite, which he then mass produces in resin, and I do all the marketing and the officey things he can't cope with, being an artist. God, I know the more I tell it the madder it sounds, but I love it. There's no one to suck up to, no one to bitch about, and there's that faint feeling that even if we aren't doing anything especially virtuous, then at least we aren't doing any harm.'

'And what about you and Gerald? The old spark back?'

'No, not at all. There wasn't ever an old spark to come back. He lives with a woman who weaves shawls. Very nice in a tenty way.'

'The shawls?'

'No, her.'

'And you're still on for this drinks thing at my work? I know it sounds terrible, in fact, probably *will* be terrible, but I'll be so much happier if you can be there.'

'I'm actually rather looking forward to it. Quite interested in meeting this Andrew chap of yours.'

Alice looked at Odette with wide eyes.

'Of course! Why didn't I think of it? You'd be perfect.'

'I didn't mean like that,' said Odette, blushing and laughing gawkily. But she did, really.

ELEVEN

Drink to Me Only with Thine Eyes,
or
The Quest for the Historical Noddy

'You look nice,' said Alice. And she meant it. Andrew was wearing a blue velvet suit, nattily cut. It went very prettily with his mauve shirt and lilac tie. Perhaps the sideburns could have done with a bit of a trim, but then Andrew was always reluctant to do that, citing both the fact that his strength lay, Samson-like, in their luxuriance, and, more plangently, the difficulty in getting a straight bottom line when having to do it for yourself.

'Thanks.' They were having a mid-morning tea break, and Andrew took a long, loud (comically loud, he hoped) slurp at his tea. Tea was one of the few remaining areas where Andrew still pretended to be working class or 'of the people' as he usually put it. Hence the ochre-staining, mouth-puckering strength; hence the noise. 'You too.' Andrew also meant it. Alice looked less bag lady than normal. He detected another hand at work.

'My friend Odette has been helping me with clothes.'

'Ah! I *thought* . . . That's the one coming tonight?'

'Yes. You'll like her. She's very sensible. Oh God no! I didn't just say sensible. What I said was glamorous and exciting.'

'If that was meant to undo the bad work done by sensible, I'm afraid it's failed. All you've done is add "very" before "sensible".'

Alice laughed. She'd been doing more of that recently, which both pained and pleased Andrew.

'It really isn't fair. Odette *used* to be famously sensible in our gang.'

'You have a gang?'

'Not really a gang. Just a couple of friends. But then, in one fell swoop, she stopped being sensible and became eccentric.'

Alice went on to give brief accounts of the Venice expedition (leaving out anything that put Odette in a bad light), the sacking, and the rebirth as hippie entrepreneur.

'Okay, I'll gladly give you back your sensible,' said Andrew, faintly impressed. 'And um er what does she . . .'

'Look like?'

'Oh, well, that puts it rather brutally. Yeah, what does she look like: moose or maid?'

'Andrew, I don't find that way of talking amusing. Certainly not when you're talking about my friend. Is that really how you see us? Black and white, beautiful or ugly?'

Andrew was a little taken aback by Alice's response. 'Sorry,' he said, genuinely embarrassed. 'Just, you know, talking.' He wouldn't normally have taken such a po-faced rebuke so passively. But then he wasn't normally in love with the po-faced rebukers. He thought about explaining that she was entirely wrong about the black and white, that he actually had a tremendously complicated and (to his mind) subtle system of classification based on the Football League, but held back on the almost certainly correct grounds that it would just make things worse.

Happy to have made her point, Alice answered Andrew's question.

148

'Pretty,' she said.

'Oh,' said Andrew, looking generally around, before paying particular attention to a frail wisp of cobweb the cleaners had missed in the corner of the ceiling. Had missed, in fact, and gone on missing, since Andrew had joined Enderby's. 'Good.'

By mid-afternoon something akin to excitement was beginning to stir in Books. Each year the whole of Enderby's would throw itself into a fancy-dress Christmas party, but that, with the exception of the desultory Friday drinks different departments might or might not go in for, was, socially speaking, that. Hence the elements of the carnivalesque: Pam had on a new set of curtains; Ophelia's lips had acquired a gloss that could have deflected the high-powered lasers of anything other than the most advanced of alien civilisations; Clerihew had specially buffed his brogues and burnished his leather elbow patches to the point at which you might well, had you wished and been prepared to hunker down, been able to see your face in them. Periodically, Oakley would stride purposefully from his office to chivvy and encourage with ill-judged compliments and oily banter.

At five, Andrew said to Alice, 'How about you and me slip off quickly for a pre-drinks drink.'

'If you like, but it seems a bit, well, indulgent.'

'Don't be such a square. It always pays to hit the ground running, I find.'

'Okay then,' she added, looking around, her gaze taking in Ophelia and Clerihew, among others. 'Shouldn't we ask . . .'

'No,' said Andrew hurriedly, pulling the sort of face he might pull should a nineteen-stone Turkish masseur produce the house's antique anal dildo.

The Mitre, the usual venue for Friday drinks, was an old-fashioned sort of pub, replete with inglenooks and etched glass and complicated lighting arrangements, vaguely suggestive of, without being remotely connected to, gas. The whole thing dated to 1997. Alice hadn't been through its swinging doors for a long time. She'd forgotten how strangely comforting a place it was, as long as you avoided the toilets.

'What'll you have?' asked Andrew, bending companionably towards her, before adding, 'Holy ger-shite, you really couldn't wait, could you?'

Startled, Alice looked at Andrew, and then followed his line of sight to the bar, where a darkly dressed, slightly hunched man was sitting. The figure turned from his beer and bent his face into what Alice assumed was a smile, although the arrangement of features could almost have easily stood in for a range of other expressions: horror; rank disgust; rage; coital disappointment. The voice, when it came, changed entirely her perception. It was like cello music.

'Now there is only one person in the entire world that you could be, given that this is the world of concrete and plastic and junk food and aerosols and boy bands and Lycra. If we were in the world of poesy, you could, of course, as readily be Eloise or Laura or the divine Francesca.'

As he spoke he slid along the bar slowly towards Alice, his motion curiously, but not creepily, serpentine, his black eyes fixed intently on hers, threaded, she suddenly thought, upon one double string. And then he broke off the gaze. 'Will that do you, Andy old chum?' He turned back to her again. 'He said to lay it on thick.'

'I was thinking more of tempora, rather than stucco. *Poesy*? Christ, Leo, sometimes I wonder.'

Alice found that she was smiling. 'So you're the famous Leo. Nice to meet you. Have you ever thought about getting a cloak?'

'What? Oh. Some kind of humourism. Best leave those

to the experts. As I seem to be nearest the bar, why don't I get them in?'

In the hour before the others began to arrive, Andrew and Leo engaged in the sort of competitive male bantering that Alice had only ever seen before from a distance. Most of their jokes were only just penetrable to an outsider, and they made few allowances for the fact that she might not be intimately acquainted with the triumphs of Leo's love life or the disasters that seemed comically to litter Andrew's. It was expected that she would have read (or at least heard of) the books that they had read, and equally expected that she would find their 'insights' into these works appropriately insightful. At no stage did it appear that she was expected to contribute anything beyond admiring gasps, enthusiastic nodding, or appreciative laughter.

Although it was far from boring, indeed flattering, as she could sense that the performance was for her sake, her mind did begin to wander; not so much away from the boys, as above them. She decided to try to think scientifically about the phenomenon, and thinking scientifically was a habit she had lost during her time at Enderby's, so it took some effort. She considered the enchanting bower birds, where the male, rather than dressing himself in gaudy plumes, would make intricate structures from stones and twigs and woven grasses, which the female, like a cultured critic, would study and assess before tipping the wink to the winner. She thought about lions, killing and devouring the young of their deposed rivals to ensure the lionesses would come on heat and allow them to further their genetic ambitions. She thought about the frantic promiscuity of chimps, and the contrasting melancholy brooding of male gorillas, never quite sure when their nuclear family would be hijacked by a bold nephew or an interloping silverback from the next valley.

But it was all no good. How did it help her to understand these two men, so companionable and yet so competitive, each prepared to ridicule and embarrass the other just to gain her favour? All you could ever find in nature were analogues: bits of behaviour that looked similar, and which might tempt you into seeing a common cause at work. But what you really needed were homologues – evidence of the related genes doing the same job across the two species.

And then, as her mind ran through the alternatives, racing back through her deliberations to fill in the complicating and contradictory arguments, Alice felt the sudden, burning wish to be back in the sphere of scientific research, back in a world where knowledge mattered, where problems could be solved if only you devoted enough time and effort, where there were more important things than empty titles and country houses and exquisite old books. It hadn't happened for a year. Pain and longing and anguish had suffocated her science, but here it was gasping and stuttering back to life.

'Spade-no-tash.' Andrew had said it, suddenly, dramatically.

'What?' said Alice, although it didn't seem to have been aimed at her.

'Arse!' said Leo, with feeling.

'I'm sorry, what's happening?' Alice was entirely perplexed.

'Oh, it's just a game we play.' Andrew looked a little shame-faced. The cry of 'spade-no-tash' appeared to be involuntary, and hadn't been part of the showing off. 'You tell her, Leo.'

'Look, it's quite simple. The aim is to spot people with beards but no moustaches. A full Flemish Ruff, also known as the Belgian Bum Brush, or a BBB, scores one whole point, plus a *lot* of kudos, the more so if the desporter is, in fact, a Flem. The classic, fell-walker's chin-cosy still gets you a point and a decent laugh, but hasn't quite got the flourish, the panache, that extra showmanship, that goes with a BBB. A "fashion" quasi-goatee, still, of course, tashless, scores a third of a point. A spade-no-tash worn for ethnic or religious reasons, and generally here we're talking about the followers of Mohammed, scores two-thirds of a point. A false cry of "spade-no-tash" loses you half a point. The games are first to three points, and there are five games in a set and three sets in a match. Got that?'

'I think so. But your scoring system doesn't seem to work very well. What if you've chalked up two and a third points, then lose half a point for a mistake? You'd find yourself with some very peculiar fractions. No, on second thoughts, please don't answer that, I really don't care enough. *That*, I presume, is the spade-no-tash?' Alice nodded down the bar towards a harmless-looking man who'd just been stabbed in the chin with a wombat. 'It looks like it must be the, what was it? Fell-walker's chin cosy.'

'You catch on fast,' said Andrew. 'But then you learn from the masters.'

Shortly afterwards, the office began to arrive. The secretaries and support staff were moderately glammed-up, but most of the experts were still tweeded and frowsty, except, of course, for Ophelia. Most had not, in fact, brought partners. Oakley's wife appeared, walking like an ostrich, almost to the point of her knees going the wrong way. Her face wore the expression of someone about to be given an award she hadn't expected and didn't want, and her hair looked like yellow candyfloss, moulded by a Stasi operative.

'Phwoar!' said Leo, frothing his beer. Andrew had begun to do a little initial circulating, leaving Alice and Leo temporarily alone. Alice wasn't sure if the phwoar had been a comic one aimed at Oakley's extraordinary spouse, or a real one intended for Ophelia, but given a comic camouflage.

'Andrew told me you carry a knife.'

'Really? I must be more discreet with that boy. Did he also tell you about my flame-thrower and collection of Victorian pornography?'

'It seems rather a rash thing to do. The knife, I mean. Isn't it illegal? Can I see it?'

'Look,' he said, seriously. 'It's not a flick knife or a hunting knife, or any kind of stabbing-people-in-a-pub-brawl kind of knife. It's a rather beautiful Renaissance stiletto, and I carry it around because I want . . .' Leo stopped, and then went on. 'Because it's just a nice thing to have.'

'Okay,' said Alice, aware that she might have trampled on some unsuspected area of sensitivity. She'd assumed that so odd a thing as going around the place armed might be something that Leo would want to talk about. She supposed he'd have a funny story about it.

'Who's that vain-looking woman over there, ignoring poor old Andy?'

'Oh her. She's Ophelia. Nominally our art books expert. I expect you're in love with her already. It's usually the way.'

'So that's the fatal Ophelia. Yes, I think I probably am. Why not introduce us?'

Leo had been sitting on a bar stool, and Alice was amazed to find that he was no taller than she when he stood up. Sitting over the bar had also gone some way to disguising the fact that he was strangely ill-knit, not twisted or handicapped in any way, just somehow not quite optimally put together. Had he been less fierce, less caustic, moved with less swagger, Alice might have pitied him.

Andrew had been talking animatedly to Ophelia, an animation she passively absorbed, reserving movement for one

154

arched eyebrow. As they approached, Andrew said excitedly, 'Ah, Leo, I was just talking about you. Why don't you meet Ophelia. You'd never guess it, but she's actually one of our experts.'

Ophelia looked sharply at Andrew, before deciding that he had probably meant it as a compliment.

'So, an expert,' said Leo, looking up into Ophelia's wonderful eyes. 'Isn't that someone who's made all the mistakes there are to be made in a *very* narrow field?'

'I know that, I know that!' said Andrew, making little jumps. 'Niels Bohr, the physicist, isn't it?'

'Or is it someone who knows more and more about less and less. I forget.'

There was a strange little silence after that, as Andrew searched in vain for the origins of the quote, and Ophelia looked at Leo, her face as blank and fearfully beautiful as a pharaoh.

Even Alice, who had only just met Leo, could sense that there was something false about Leo's display of borrowed wit. It didn't fit at all well with his otherwise menacing originality of thought. Ophelia surprised her by speaking:

'And what do you do, little-friend-of-Andrew?' As she said it a lovely smile shimmered across her face, taking, Alice thought, much of the sting away from the 'little'. Perhaps Ophelia was going to be nice.

'Oh, I'm er a . . .' Leo stumbled slightly over his words.

'Let me see,' cut in Ophelia, . . .'yes, I have a . . . hunch.'

Leo's lips had been about to frame something, Alice assumed, witty and appropriate, triumphantly regaining lost ground. She didn't think he had any chance with Ophelia, but she wanted him to keep his dignity and even, she hoped, in an unaccustomed spurt of playful malice, knock Ophelia down a peg or two. But at the word 'hunch' Leo's mouth froze.

'Nothing *ring a bell*,' continued Ophelia, the smile still lingering, but its true meaning now apparent.

'What the fuck are you talking about, Ophelia?' said Andrew, clearly a little too drunk, even this early in the evening, to fully realise what was happening.

Again Ophelia spoke. 'You've come a long way for a drink, haven't you, er, what was it, *Leo*. Is Notre Dame *on* the tube these days?'

Two or three other people who'd been standing around chatting began to pay attention, aware that something interesting might be happening.

Still Leo did not reply.

'I'm sorry, perhaps I was being a little vague,' said Ophelia, sweetening once more her smile. 'If only I had one of my ponies here, perhaps you'd allow me to swap it for your kingdom?'

At last Leo spoke, slowly and quietly, but with total clarity: 'No beast so fierce but knows some touch of pity.'

'If you're calling me a beast, O little-friend-of-Andrew, perhaps you should look in the mirror.'

It was the immense girlishness of this last comment, its very lack of sophistication or polish, that made Alice see clearly what Ophelia was doing. She had assumed that her spite, what might be called her humour, had been for the benefit of those around – a public display of offensiveness intended to in some way enhance her reputation, or at least diminish another's. This was, of course, no defence, but it gave the wickedness a human face – it was part of the long bitter wrangle of mankind. But no. This was something different. This was not intended to amuse, or to affect, in some way subtle or crude, the public perceptions of the onlookers. This was a totally private spite, the simple and efficient delivery of pain with a sublime purity of malice; hurt for hurt's sake. It was then that Alice decided to hit Ophelia.

She took a step forward, with every intention of slapping Ophelia as hard as she could, and then her eye caught a small movement of Leo's hand. He twitched aside the hem of his jacket and Alice saw there in his belt a tiny scabbard, and the black and silver hilt of what she knew must be his famous stiletto.

My God, Alice thought, he was going to stab her!

She looked to his face. Its coldness now matched Ophelia's, although she had already dismissed him from her mind and was turning to talk to one of her handmaidens, a secretary called Anita.

Acting on impulse, Alice placed her fingers quickly on Leo's wrist and, putting her lips close to his ear, whispered, 'I don't know about you, but I could use a drink.' He spun away as if she'd yelled an obscenity in his ear and then paused, blinking. Alice saw the courage and strength with which he regained a measure of control.

He smiled a smile like a fissure in a rock and said, 'What, my round again? What is it about you book people?'

Andrew, who'd remained motionless throughout the exchange with Ophelia, suddenly flew into action, sweeping both Leo and Alice back to the bar.

'Well, that was fun, eh?' he said, looking carefully at Leo.

There was a silence, perhaps only three seconds, but long enough to make its presence felt, before Leo replied:

'Quite a girl. Just the sort of challenge I appreciate.'

Despite the bravado, Alice could tell that Leo had been cut deeply by Ophelia's words. She guessed that his stature and his slight crookedness must have made him an easy target at school, but as an adult it must have been rare for him to encounter that kind of attack. His black eyes had acquired a deep-blue iridescence, like the wingcases of a beetle, although the clinical side of Alice knew that must be a reflection from the blue neon behind the bar. She could taste the dull metallic tang in his mouth, feel the tightening of his scalp, the tingling at his fingertips. Drinks came and Leo drank back a pint of beer and a vodka chaser before she or Andrew had swallowed more than a mouthful.

The pub was now packed. Apart from the odd City type, everyone seemed to be from Enderby's. Many of those who hadn't brought partners had invited friends from other departments, so there was a smattering of half familiar faces: the nasty old lady who dealt with ancient teddy bears and battered toy cars; a large woman in long earrings from Fabrics; a Porcelain man.

People kept waving and gesturing to Andrew, and he obviously felt it was time to circulate. He said to Leo, 'Come on, old chum, let me introduce you to someone that isn't a bitch. There's a mate of mine from Paintings who'd actually *enjoy* hearing your theories about art, unlike the rest of us poor shags.'

'Just give me a minute or two to get properly shit-faced, will you, Andrew? I'm being summoned by Bells at the moment.'

Andrew looked uncertainly at his friend. 'Okay. Why don't I leave my esteemed colleague with you to catch the overspill?' He glanced quickly at Alice, but managed to convey to her a reasonably complex message, along the lines of 'if you keep an eye on him and try to be nice, and don't let him get falling down drunk, I'll owe you a favour the size of Alaska.'

After he'd gone, Leo said to Alice, in a low flat voice, without looking directly at her, 'I wasn't going to do anything, you know.'

Alice didn't know what to say back. She started burbling about Ophelia, telling him some of the stories about her bitchiness and superficiality. Leo interrupted her, talking more to himself, it seemed, than to Alice.

'I like to know that there's a way out.' And then suddenly his mood changed. The electric glitter in his eyes intensified and he said, rubbing his hands together, 'Okay, time to work the room. Let's see: who's pretty, who's clever? Who needs taking down? Who needs dragging up?'

Alice was about to introduce him to some people she knew when she suddenly caught sight of Odette, who she'd completely forgotten about, coming tentatively through the door. She caught her eye and waved, summoning her over, but also went to meet her halfway. They kissed warmly.

'Thank God you're here,' said Alice. 'This is already the most complicated social event I've ever been to, and it's only seven o'clock. I think I need some of your clarity of thought and unflappability. There's a fellow I need some help with. I've never met him before tonight myself – he's a friend of Andrew, who you already know all about, and I've been sort of taking care of him, which is a bit like the rabbit taking care of the fox. He's . . . oh, God, come and see for yourself!'

'Well,' said Odette, with enthusiasm, 'this all seems very interesting. I was expecting a quiet glass of sherry with the tweedies, where the most avant-garde happening would be someone buying a packet of cheese and onion, rather than plain, crisps. But by the sound of it I've walked into a battlefield.'

By the time Alice led Odette back to the bar, Leo had gone, and the pub was too crowded for Alice to immediately lay an eye on him.

'Oh,' said Alice. 'I'm not sure if I'm relieved or disappointed. I'm sure you'll get to meet him sooner or later. In the meantime, let's have a nice girlie chat.'

'I'd love a quick rundown on this lot,' said Odette, nodding towards the crowd. 'I can't quite figure them, at first glance. One of the things about working in the City was that everyone looked exactly the same, but here – well, without going overboard on the individuality, there at least seems to be more than one tribe.'

'That,' said Alice, with something of the refined Edinburgh lilt of Mr Crumlish, 'is because we have displayed before us, the Toffs, the Tarts and the Swots, not to mention our solitary Oik.' She cured Odette's puzzled look by explaining about her initiation, all those long months ago.

Meanwhile, Andrew was trying hard to charm Mrs Oakley, who, disappointingly was not called Annie, but Dorothea. She was very good at giving the impression that she thought he was an escaped serial killer, or at the very least someone likely to give her low-hanging breasts a quick tweak should she drop her guard. In his battle for hearts and minds, Andrew had tried flattering her person, but got no further than 'Oh, I think your dress really is awfully . . .' before radio silence descended on his creative faculties. He then switched to being nice about Oakley, which was yet more of a challenge to his ingenuity. 'Yes, no one has ever disputed his . . . erm . . . er . . . *watchfulness*. Um . . . his tremendous sense of . . .' of what? Of what? How to combine being a stickler for the irrelevant minutiae of office life with a complete inability to grasp what was significant? His way of inciting both fear and pity? How to mix a metaphor like a martini – who could forget his injunction that they should all be singing from the same level playing field? Thankfully Clerihew arrived just then to relieve him of the need to complete his sentence.

'On the stump eh, Andy?' he said, beaming. 'And trust you to pick on the pretty ones.'

Andrew made an audible scoffing noise, but slightly misjudged his airway management procedures and expelled a small amount of mucus from one nostril. Luckily he had a hanky, and was fairly sure that no one had noticed the accident, until he saw Dorothea Oakley's face, half of which was given over to evident disgust at his display, and half to a tittering, hideously girlish appreciation of Clerihew's fawning compliment.

'Oh, Cedric,' she said, fanning herself with a heavily ringed hand, 'you really mustn't be so gallant. What would Colin say?'

'Well, Dorothea,' Clerihew replied, standing to a sort of attention, which involved an attempted redistribution of body mass from abdomen to thorax, 'so long as he doesn't say I can never again eat your simply wonderful food he can punish me as he pleases. Your Sunday roast is the finest I've ever tasted, and I stand by that even though it would break Mother's heart to hear it.'

So, thought Andrew, the little shit's wormed his way into the Oakley family home. Christ, *that's* what I call ambition.

Well, if the gloves are off, let's see what we can do.

'I thought, *Clarence*, that you were a vegetarian? Didn't you make some big fuss about the canteen not having any tofu?'

Clerihew was caught off balance, but only for a moment.

'I, as much as anyone enjoy a joke, but I don't quite understand the humour of getting a fellow's name wrong on purpose, *Andy*. No doubt,' he said, looking meaningfully at Dorothea and also, as Andrew suddenly realised, at Oakley himself, who'd just appeared, 'you've got your reasons. And I'm equally sure that you know that my objection is not to meat, *per se*, but to the hideous industrial effluent that is all too often passed off as the real thing. And Mrs Oakley's table, I can confidently assert, never carries anything other than the finest, wholesome, organic produce. There is simply no other way it could taste as good as it does.'

Andrew detected from a slight tremble from one of Dorothea's wattles that the main organic produce on offer here was bullshit, but he could hardly start insulting her now via an exposure of Clerihew. He mentally doffed his cap to his opponent for the slick move. He then mentally took out a Kalashnikov and splattered his guts over the back wall.

'I've just been talking to a young man whom, I understand, is your friend,' said Oakley in a way that strongly suggested to Andrew that no good was about to come out of this conversation.

'Oh, Leo? Yes, he's a live wire. Brilliant academic, you know. One of the leading minds of his generation.'

The leading *what* of his *what*? Not for the first time Andrew had the feeling that his words were being written by a truly bad playwright. No, it was worse than that: a hack librettist translating a Bulgarian folk opera from the period just before the . . .

'He was talking about Noddy.'

'Noddy?'

As soon as he said 'Noddy' Andrew realised that he should never have said 'Noddy'. It was impossible to say 'Noddy' without sounding like an idiot. Especially if *all* you said was 'Noddy' in a single word sentence, given a rising intonation to turn it into a question.

'Noddy. The *historical* Noddy,' continued Oakley, with an expression midway between curiosity and revulsion, like someone who's found a complicated-looking foreign body up their nose. 'Apparently he's doing some research on the subject. Says the standard view was that the Noddy character was based on a Scandinavian wood-sprite, the Nodal, known for playing humorous, and often explicitly . . . well, sexual, tricks on woodcutters and so forth. Went into considerable detail on the sort of tricks . . . But then there was also a Viking named in some or other *Icelandic* saga, Nodrum Ninefinger, who, oh well, can't quite remember. But this friend of yours, Leo, *his* view was that Blyton was in love

162

with some chap called Lord Nodderington, who was killed in the trenches in the Great War.'

So, Leo was on *that* one. But of course it wouldn't just be Noddy. He looked around, and finally caught sight of Leo, surrounded by an assorted group of experts and others. They wore the mixed expressions of amusement and shock that Leo always attracted when he was on fire, and Andrew cursed himself again for the folly of inviting him. Once spotted, Andrew managed to focus in on where he'd reached in his rant:

'. . . classic Oedipal conflict,' he could just hear, 'father figure wants to drive the "son" out of the family unit; the "son" wants to kill the father to gain access to the females.' Leo was talking with complete authority, and didn't seem too pissed, which meant that something might be salvaged from the evening.

'But that's insane,' replied one of the cleverer young experts, a Map man called Cartwright. Andrew had been meaning to pal up with him for a while. 'Isn't it a chicken-hawk? It doesn't want to fuck the hens, it wants to eat them.'

'You're confusing your Foghorn Leghorn episodes . . .'

'All very perplexing,' resumed Oakley, and Andrew had to rapidly switch back. 'I hardly had the chance to tell him that I'm a collector of the early Blyton stories, and of course they do very well at auction, before he launched into an extraordinary tirade about commerce being such a monstrous thing. Altogether a very peculiar performance and a very strange sort of person to bring along to a, to a . . . to bring along.'

'Mmmmm,' said Clerihew, who'd been waiting for an opportunity to contribute something. '*I* was rather wondering why you brought someone like that along. Unless, Andrew, oh, I'm sorry, is he your *partner*? I really wouldn't have . . . if I'd known.'

'Oh fuck off, Cuthbert. I brought him because Colin

163

suggested we all bring someone, and Leo's about the most amusing and intelligent person I know, and I thought it might be an interesting social experiment.'

There was a pause, just long enough for Andrew to realise what a serious mistake it had been to tell Clerihew to fuck off. Bound to add to the general view that he wasn't a team player, but rather some kind of insane reckless maverick, the sort of person who would, in fact, bring a Noddy-obsessed anarcho-syndicalist LUNATIC to a sedate gathering of book experts and their decent, God-fearing, property-respecting, hatchet-faced, sensibly-knickered spouses.

'Well, *it*, your *experiment*, doesn't seem to be going very well at the moment, young man,' said Dorothea Oakley, whose presence Andrew had managed, with some effort, to forget about. For no good reason that Andrew could see, this was treated by the assembled sycophants as a put-down of Wildean brilliance.

Looking for an escape route, Andrew saw Alice chatting in a corner with a slender, short-haired woman. 'Excuse me, I must um just . . .' he said, and pushed his way through the throng to them, wishing all the time he'd thought of something wittier than 'I must um just' to leave them with. He was only marginally cheered up by recalling his joke about never remembering the phrase *esprit d'escalier* until it was too late.

Alice saw him coming. He looked like one of the miraculously unhurt survivors of a train crash.

'How's it going?' she said. 'This is my friend Odette.'

'I see you made the wise decision to bring someone normal and not a . . . well, a *Leo*.'

'How do you know I'm not a Leo?' said Odette, looking a little puzzled. 'I mean, I'm not, I'm a Sagittarius, not that I believe any of that, but still. What are they supposed to be like, that you're so sure I'm not one?'

Andrew and Alice exchanged smiles, which annoyed Odette. Andrew saw the annoyance and started babbling. 'Oh God, no, it's not the star thing. It's my friend. He's called Leo. The name, Leo. That's what he's called. I'm sure that whatever good things there are about Leos, the star sign Leos, then you'd have them. I mean you've got them. All of them. Fuck. Where's that rent in the space-time continuum, when you need it?'

The babble, as he knew it would, made everything all right.

'Leo's the one I was telling you about,' said Alice to Odette. 'And this is Andrew, who we've already done to death.' She smiled at him to show that this was intended as a compliment.

'Leo sounds like a very interesting character,' said Odette to Andrew, also smiling, her lips neatly together.

'Yes. And sometimes interesting is exactly what you want.'

'And sometimes not?'

'Well no. I suppose sometimes what you want is interesting and safe, but Leo's interesting and lethal. Looks like he might well be on his way to ruining my beautiful career. I blame myself.'

'That's big of you,' laughed Alice, 'given that it is entirely your fault for inviting him. Why don't we extract him from the morass over there and let him loose on Odette. My bet is that she takes some of the wind out of his sails – she's world class when it comes to deflating egos and seeing through people and all that sort of thing.'

'I think that's a bit harsh on Leo. Whatever else he is, he certainly isn't a fraud. He . . . just, well, several things really. He says things for effect, but usually just so he can test them out. And he says things that other people only think. And although he spends all of his time upsetting people, he isn't malicious. He reserves his real hatred for himself. I'll go and get him.'

On his way back towards Leo, Andrew wondered if he'd reached his Marxist analysis of Trumpton yet. The Noddy/Foghorn-Leghorn/Trumpton/jelly baby material began life as a series of lectures Leo used to give to undergraduates to help explain the various interpretative approaches open to literary critics, but he'd found them to be useful ways of annoying the kind of people who ought to be annoyed, and amusing those who deserved amusing. Andrew was secretly relieved that he hadn't come up with something worse so far this evening. Just as he reached the group, he noticed that Clerihew was among the onlookers. There seemed to have been some exchange between him and Leo. Clerihew had said something that had shut Leo up in mid-sentence. In his own way the roly-poly turd could be quite effective. It would be like him to make some veiled allusion to Ophelia's earlier comments. Leo caught Andrew's eye and threw him a wink. Oh dear, thought Andrew. Oh dear. Leo then moved a foot closer to Clerihew and said something quietly to him. The onlookers stopped laughing. Leo then swayed back, a movement exaggerated, Andrew could see, by a drunkenness which was approaching saturation point.

'Clerihew, Clerihew,' said Leo very loudly, and very clearly. 'You really are as . . .'

At that instant Andrew knew what was coming, and it wasn't funny and it wasn't clever. About a month before, he and Leo had been discussing the difficulty in saying anything truly offensive. The various reproductive and excretory terms had been neutered by over-use. Even the dreaded C-word had been rendered relatively benign, although it still topped the tables.

'What we need is a modifier. Something that uses what's

left of the shockability in cunt, but magnifies it.'

That, regrettably, had been Andrew.

'Yes,' replied Leo. 'That's it. We need a metaphor. As something as a something something cunt.'

Between the two of them they hit on a phrase that they were confident would a) offend ninety-five per cent of those who heard it; and b) was flexible enough to be used in a variety of different contexts. And what would it be now, wondered Andrew? As rank as? As fat as? As loose as? As flabby as?

'You really are,' said Leo, '*as slack as an old whore's cunt.*'

Oh Lord. Andrew began to have an out of body experience, floating about three feet above himself before psychic gravity hauled him back in.

Yes, it was the 'whore's' that did it, giving it a Jacobean, no, *Restoration* feel. At least their scientific approach to the subject was demonstrated to be the right one. Scanning the faces from Clerihew round to Pam, encompassing the full range of Enderby's employees, and including, Andrew now saw, The Slayer herself, Andrew perceived everywhere that the phrase had done its work well. Shock was there, and now surely, the outrage would follow, led, the clever money predicted, by Clerihew, camping it up for all he was worth.

But what was this? Clerihew *smiling*. Sadly shaking his head. Walking away. And the others. Also walking away. And then Leo was alone in the middle of the crowded pub, surrounded by a penumbra of contempt.

Andrew sensed that The Slayer's eyes were on him. He'd never met her but she'd certainly seen him on her occasional commando raids into Books territory. If Andrew walked away he could probably, no, not probably, only possibly, get away with the debacle. If it had been *probably*, then perhaps his decision would have been different; but at *possibly* there was no contest. He went up to Leo, put an arm around his shoulders, put his fist against his cheek and rubbed it hard.

'If I didn't love you I'd kill you. Might kill you anyway. As it is there's a top chick to meet.'

Leo looked at him blearily. 'Have I misbehaved?'

'Oh yes.'

'How badly?'

'You know that time when you spent the weekend with me up in Nottingham at my parents, and you got up drunk in the night and went for a piss, and then my dad put the light on because you were in their bedroom, splashing on the Axminster?'

'That bad?'

'Worse.'

'Andrew, I'm sorry. It was that girl. Ophelia. She was so close, I mean sooooooo close to being my absolute personal ideal . . . I mean the Platonic perfect form. And then. I know I should be used to it by now, but Jeeeesus. Andy, I'm in no tit fate. What did I say? Fit state to meet people stuff. Jus' gonna go home. There's always some totty I can . . .'

Alice came to meet them. 'Oh dear, Leo, you don't look very well. I'm sorry I missed the fireworks over there. I'm sure you were being very funny. They'll all be talking about Andrew's brilliant friend tomorrow in the office.' Alice completely missed the for God's sake cut it hand signals Andrew was giving her.

Leo twisted, without violence, away from Andrew and came close beside Alice.

'There something important to tell you. This man here is reality. The real. The world. Your robber-baron down in the country, he's just a trashy fantasy, a bit of Walter Scott whimsy. And,' he said, coming closer still, 'your boy, your boy, he's art. Nothing but *art*.' He spat the word out as if it were poison. 'And you know what Plato said about Art? Art is a lie.'

He staggered away towards the door. Andrew was about to follow him when he saw Alice's face.

'What's wrong? What did he say?'

'You told him. You told him about . . . you told him about it. Who else did you tell? Ophelia? Clerihew?'

'Oh Christ. No, nobody. Look I had to tell Leo. He's my best friend. I needed to . . .'

Alice was crying. Odette appeared. They murmured together for a while, with Andrew looking on, helplessly.

'I'm putting her in a taxi,' said Odette to Andrew.

Andrew's ears were ringing. Was this the worst night of his life? How could it all have gone so wrong? He looked around. At least no one was paying any attention to this latest fiasco, unless you counted Clerihew, who never missed anything, and Andrew had no intention of counting Clerihew. He went back to the bar. To his surprise he found that Ophelia was there. She smiled at him pleasantly.

'I wasn't expecting much from this evening, but I've rather enjoyed myself,' she said.

'Yeah, me too.'

It was all Ophelia's fault, the whole nightmarish, fucked-up, catalogue of dis . . . no, not a catalogue, this was more impressive; this was like one of those great eighteenth-century compendiums, with teams of scholars working for years, or just one solitary madman devoting his life to the project. An *Encyclopédie* of disasters; *Johnson's Dictionary* of . . . But still, her fault or not, she had a minute smudge of lipstick on her teeth, something he'd never seen on her before, a blemish. It made his balls hum with electric desire.

Outside, Odette found a taxi. Alice forbade her to share it.

'No, no,' she sobbed, 'it's the wrong way. Please, I need to do this alone.'

Odette understood. It was still quite early and there were

plenty of cabs around. As she waited she saw something hunched over the gutter across the street. She crossed.

'Are you okay,' she said to Leo. He looked up at her through his fingers.

'Do I look okay?' he said with effort.

'Why don't I put you in a taxi,' Odette replied, matter-of-factly. 'It's what I'm doing today. Which way do you go?'

'Notre Dame. It's not on the tube.'

TWELVE

Country Pleasures, Suck'd on Childishley

The journey was now almost familiar to Alice: the train slowly rattling through grey skies, the ragged lines of hedgerows swelling onto scrubby copses; the occasional flash of strutting pheasant; the cows staring like voyeurs; the scarecrows scaring no crows; the horse in a field of thistles, breaking into a frantic gallop; the Asian family across the aisle, sharing out samosas and poppadoms and Mars bars.

She was still angry and upset at Andrew's betrayal. For all his protestations, she was sure that he and Leo must have been laughing about her; after all, it's what they did about everything. On the Monday following the Friday drink, she'd played it cool, determined that he should not know how much she had been hurt by the affair, but equally determined to withdraw from the relative intimacy of their relations. She'd been scrupulously polite when they met, but said 'no thanks' to the offer of tea.

Whatever punishment she had in store for him, however, soon paled in comparison with the general office reaction to the Friday happenings. One or two of the younger people came up and slapped him on the back, congratulating him on livening up what had promised to be a very dull evening.

Andrew looked embarrassed, stammering something about not expecting his friend to go quite so far over the top. And then at ten-thirty Oakley appeared and asked him to step into his office. Alice, and everyone else, could hear the barking through the opaque plate glass. Andrew emerged entirely drained of colour. The tail of his shirt was, not untypically, flapping slightly from his trousers, which gave the unfortunate impression that he'd been to see the headmaster for a thrashing, lending a certain amount of comedy to the affair.

Alice didn't feel inclined to offer any sympathy, despite the injustice of it: could Andrew really be blamed because Leo had skied so far off-piste? To her surprise Ophelia came over to commiserate, although after a couple of minutes it became clear that it was in such a way as to bring home the enormity of the offence ('yes, I know, they'll probably remember this for ever, you know what they're like').

The whole thing was capped by Clerihew. He marched up to Andrew, thrust out his hand, and said, 'No hard feelings, old man, let's shake and forget it.'

Andrew, startled, didn't quite know what to do. After four seconds of dithering, he took Clerihew's hand, but somehow the impression was given that he had yet again acted in a mean-spirited way. Alice looked towards Oakley's office and saw him standing at the door, watching.

By Wednesday Alice had forgiven him enough to ask about Leo.

'Oh, I haven't seen or heard from him. Don't blame him. Think I might punch him if he did show up. Not really. What did you make of him?'

'I actually rather liked him. Can't say he was particularly *comfortable* company, but he was . . . interesting.'

'I, er, thought your friend, Odette, was very, um, nice. Did she enjoy herself?'

Alice knew that what he meant was, did she mention

172

me? She hadn't forgiven him enough to massage his ego.

'She was having quite a good time until it all blew up. I think the fun went out of it for her when Leo left.'

'Oh.'

'But I haven't spoken to her either, since.'

She arrived in the station at five minutes past five. It wasn't Edward who met her, but Grace, her features as impenetrable as ever.

'Mr Lynden's busy with his guests,' she said, as she put Alice's bag (which she'd almost wrestled from her hand, pulling and twisting aggressively) in the back of her little Fiat. Somehow the term 'guests' was intended, Alice thought, to exclude her.

Alice knew, of course, that there would be other people there, but not how many or who they were. She questioned Grace, but received only cryptic answers. 'Enough to make work,' she said. 'Others like him, of his kind. Had to get the chef from the Wheatsheaf, and two girls from the village. More trouble than they're worth.' With the last comment she looked away from the road and straight at Alice for a good two seconds. Alice looked back at her, studying her face. It was difficult to estimate her age: forty, perhaps? There was some grey in her tightly pulled-back hair, but no more than a few strands. It was a severe face, but not unattractive. She felt it was a face that had swallowed humiliations and slights, and had hardened itself against the world.

The driveway was crowded with cars – a brace of pristine, unrustic Range Rovers; a sleek BMW estate, two different, but equally menacing sports cars, and a people-carrier, looking pleased with itself, and with life in general.

Grace led her in and pointed towards laughter, rooms away. Alice, her heart in her mouth, picked her way carefully towards the sound. When she finally found the right door, it

173

opened into a room dazzlingly bright with sunshine and glamour – even the drinks, carried on a heavy silver tray by one of Grace's unfortunate girls, were brilliantly and strangely coloured. There were at least ten people there, scattered about on the low chairs, or standing in small groups. She managed to take in a confident-looking teenage girl, three smartly dressed women in their thirties, two floppy-haired young men, and two more who could have been in their forties, before Lynden caught sight of her. He was standing talking to an older woman, who seemed strangely out of place here. Instead of the expensive casual rightness of the clothes and hair all around, she was dressed with an uncomfortable formality, in an awkward tweed suit and clumping shoes. Alice could hear her braying voice quite clearly.

'Damned good fortune to turn up just when there was a show on. Offie didn't want to come, of course, but I insisted. Not seen her dear old second cuz for donkey's. Nice for you to have a bit of young blood about the place. Cheer you up. You always were a misery guts. Mother's side, of course.'

Alice wasn't sure how Lynden would greet her. They had exchanged a couple of telephone calls over the week to finalise the arrangements. He'd been weirdly rapt during the conversations; not so much flirting as paying a particularly concentrated attention to her, like an addict contemplating his fix. She'd felt his presence, heavy like fate, at the end of the line.

But now, when he saw her standing by the door, alone, still coated, he just raised his left eyebrow, before returning his focus to the woman. Alice looked at her again. Her first impression was that she was like Kitty, a slightly batty, selfish, hopeless, late middle-aged widow. But there was something intimidatingly single-minded about this woman. Her face, though relatively unlined, looked cruel, or at least as if it were indifferent to suffering. There was something in her manner that made it clear that she was used to being obeyed, that hers was the only opinion that mattered, per-haps even the only opinion that existed. Kitty, despite her folly and selfishness, was ultimately pitiable, but not this woman. She was to be feared.

'Hello,' said a bright voice, interrupting her scrutiny. 'You look a bit at sea. Why not come and meet some of the gang.' The voice, she saw, belonged to one of the floppy-haired men. It continued in a pleasantly mellifluous way, 'I'm Johnny. Johnny Twogood.'

'Is that a nickname?'

'Nickname? Oh, ha ha, I see, very amusing. No, it's a name name, you know, like Smith only spelled *completely* differently. How about getting you one of these things,' he said, holding up a luminous pink concoction. 'Really very effective, you know, at getting you drunk.'

Alice went with Johnny Twogood back to his group. The other floppy-haired youth (who wasn't, when you got close, *that* floppy-haired – he just looked like he ought, or at least wanted, to be), was called Jeremy, and didn't say as much as Johnny, evidently fancying himself as deep. Johnny and Jeremy were paying court to one of the elegant thirty-some-thing-year-old women. They were joined by an older woman, who was almost certainly somebody's mother, and the self-possessed teenager, who was Johnny's kid sister. Alice knew her sort instantly. She'd been told all her life how wonderful she was and now took it for granted that the world owed her its attention. How lucky, thought Alice. She'd never feel inhibited about her oily skin, or bulbous nose, or flagrant dis-regard for the correct pronunciation of the letter r. The way she looked at Jeremy suggested an emotional attachment somewhere between crush and fatal obsession.

None of them seemed particularly interested in who or what Alice was, which was, at least partially, a relief. Alice just stood among them and listened, trying to work out who was who, and how they fitted in to the Lynden picture. She soon gathered that most of the guests were neighbours, rather than close friends, of Edward, of whom they spoke in near-reverential terms. The thirty-something woman in their group wrote the Country Pleasures column in the *Telegraph*, and whenever anyone said something they thought might be amusing or clever (admittedly not very often) they looked over to see if she had caught it. Evidently a mention in the column represented the pinnacle of social achievement in this part of the Quantocks. Whenever she spoke, it was usually to demonstrate how she could have a viewpoint further to the right than any of the others, so don't even think about trying, got that, okay? Her statement about publicly birching hunt saboteurs, was not, it seemed intended as a joke, and she looked sharply at Jeremy when he roused himself sufficiently to suggest that the foxes themselves should be flogged for delinquency before the hounds were sent in to finish the job. Johnny had recently completed some kind of degree or diploma in land management, and his enthusiasm ensured that the conversation continued to lean heavily on matters equestrian, with forays towards more generally agricultural issues, although Alice could see that the ladies, in particular, had little interest in the day to day world of pig rearing, or barley growing. The teenager, who was introduced as 'Miranda', was asked about college, and gushed about the sporting facilities at Lady Margaret Hall.

Jeremy made sure that Alice could see that he was bored.

'You don't look like a country girl,' he said during a round of guffaws in which neither of them were inclined to join.

'No, I suppose I'm not really, any more. But I'm not cosmopolitan either. What do you do?'

'The Law,' he said, and nothing more.

'Do you practise around here?'

'What, suing the vet who's left his speculum, if that's a

176

word, up a heifer's fundament? And those entrancing disputes over water rights and field boundaries. No. My chambers are in Lincoln's Inn. I'm doing some work for Edward at the moment,' he added, as if to explain his presence. He didn't elucidate, and Alice didn't care.

She was becoming very nervous about the whole thing. What on earth was she doing here? She'd only come because she thought that Edward . . . what – wanted her? Needed her in some way? All seemed so improbable now that she was here, with all these people. She began to invent reasons for leaving. She could pretend that she'd been summoned back to London to look after her mother, who'd, yes, fallen off the Stannah stair-lift. But how had she been summoned? Of course, the vibrating alarm on her mobile phone could go off, and she could fake the conversation with the doctor. No, not doctor – it would be a social worker of some kind; that was it, leave it vague, just a bod from social services. Pity about her not having a mobile phone. There was half a Mars bar in her pocket, forced on her by the generous Asian family on the train – could she use that?

And then Edward was there.

'I'm sorry about that. One has . . . family obligations.' Was Edward's adoption of the 'one' form ironic? Alice didn't know. 'But I trust you've been kept entertained.'

There was no mistaking the irony now, as Lynden looked archly at the company.

'It would be nice to know what's happening,' said Alice, trying, and succeeding, just, to look unconcerned.

'But I told you, Alice. Merely a little get-together for my nearest and dearest. Can't live as a recluse forever, can I?'

'Which am I, nearest or dearest?' The voice was familiar, and familiarly low down. Semele was holding a glass of blue liquid, presumably a cocktail of some kind.

'Who gave you that drink, Semele?' asked Lynden, sternly.

177

'Cousin Offie. I asked her for a blue one, and she got it from a tray.'

'She's not your cousin,' Lynden said, firmly taking the drink from Semele's hand.

'Well, I wish she was. She's my favourite.' And then, turning to stare baldly at Alice, she added, 'Why is *she* here now?' It was obviously intended as retaliation for the humiliating loss of the blue drink. 'Are there some more books to look at? Are you going to send her to the library soon? I won't show her the way this time. You can get that Mary from the village to take her and I'll carry the tray.'

'I've told you, Semele, if you misbehave you must go to your room.'

'Let her stay, Edward. We can have a little talk together.' Despite the child's hostility, Alice would have welcomed the chance to escape from the stifling atmosphere of the party.

'I don't want to talk to you. I want to talk to Offie. She's prettier than you.'

'That's it, Semele,' said Edward, now distinctly annoyed and embarrassed. 'Your behaviour is intolerable.'

'Edward, what a stick in the mud you are. Hello, Alice. How nice to see you again out of the office, and still wearing that cardigan. I'm sure Edward would approve of your sort of thrift.'

Cousin Offie. Ophelia. Alice remembered Ophelia's face when the Lynden name had first come up in the office. She remembered the mention of some distant relationship. It didn't stop it from being the sort of shock to the system that could leave you gulping for air like a stranded guppy.

Somehow Ophelia had managed to improve upon perfection, and was looking even more astounding than usual. She was wearing a full-blown cocktail dress that seemed to be woven from mother of pearl and golden fish scales. It was cut low and showed the irresistible rise and flawless skin of her breasts. Even through her surprise, Alice could feel an urge, something only a little short of a desire, to brush them with her cheek, to feel their yielding firmness.

Lynden saw Alice's astonishment. 'You two know each other?' he said, with a note combining suspicion and concern.

'Really, Edward,' said Ophelia, talking in a voice that seemed an octave lower than the penetrating, crystalline tone she used at work, 'if you ever asked any questions about other people you'd know that Alice worked for my auction house.'

'I had no idea that you worked for . . . your mother never mentioned anything. And anyway, I haven't seen you in . . .'

'I rest my case. Of course I didn't want to come and value your birdy books – just wouldn't be professional. Conflict of interest. So I sent Alice and her lapdog. But let's not talk about horrid work.'

Alice was too astounded to point out the flagrant dishonesty in Ophelia's words. Edward, she hoped, would not be so easily deceived. But then Ophelia's beauty had a way of blinding men to what seemed obvious to those not under the spell. And what of the others? Would she be taken for Ophelia's underling? The thought made Alice distinctly uncomfortable, a discomfort given added piquancy by the fact that Alice thought herself above such worldly concerns.

Any plans that Alice had to correct the false impression that Ophelia was giving were rendered futile by Ophelia's decisiveness, and before Alice quite knew what was happening Lynden had been swept away into a far corner of the room. Alice felt a pressing need to disappear. Find a bathroom, she thought. Splash some water on her face. Then . . . go. Yes, go! Just escape from it all. The chance of freedom exhilarated her, and she almost ran through the door. And in the hall she bumped heavily into Grace Harbour carrying a huge tray full of vaguely oriental snacks, complete with a bowl of fluorescent red dip. The tray flew into the air, and fell clattering to the floor. Grace shot her a look of anger, perhaps even contempt, and silently stooped to clear the mess.

'I'm so sorry,' said Alice, and knelt beside her, trying to help. Grace gruffly shunted her out of the way.

'There's no room here,' she said. 'No room for this. No room for you.'

Alice saw now that the look wasn't contempt, or anger. It was something much worse. It was pain. And she wasn't referring to the corridor, narrow though it was, when she spoke of the lack of room. She was completely baffled. Her mind was still back in the room with the party, and its embarrassments, and she couldn't understand why Grace was being so strange.

'Grace,' she said, standing up and trying to get out of the woman's way, 'have I done something, something to offend you?'

Grace laughed, a choking, bitter sound, and continued picking up the little rolls and folds of pastry.

'Some people,' she said, 'some people never have a chance. A chance to show . . . what they are.'

Alice's heart went out to the woman, bent over the scattered food, wiping with her apron at the red pool of sauce. She must hate me, she thought, for being from the town, for coming here and complicating her life. She thinks I'm one of the bright young things. If only she knew. For a moment, Alice was possessed with the urge to tell Grace Harbour that she also suffered, that her life was full of sadness. But she didn't. It would be selfish. Grace had enough to think about, and she would not care. But nor would she move. To get out of there, Alice would have to squeeze past her, through the mess, or leap over it all. Neither appealed. With grim determination, she turned around and went back in to the party.

'You might want to try one of these green ones next.' The voice belonged unmistakably to Johnny. 'I used to have a shirt in exactly the same shade. Always rather regretted it. Do you remember when they said lime-green was going to be the next grey? Or was it some other colour?'

'Do you mean,' cut in Jeremy, 'that it might have been another colour that was going to be the next grey, or that lime-green was going to be the next some colour other than grey?'

'Yes, that's it,' said Johnny, vaguely. 'Well?' he said, looking straight at Alice.

'I'm sorry, I've no idea what you're talking about,' she replied.

'Oh, sorry. I think I was either asking you something about my shirt or if you wanted another drink. Yes, that must be it. I blame the blue one I had. Really very good. At making you drunk, I mean.'

Alice could see Ophelia in the corner. She'd trapped Edward, who was facing the room, but he didn't seem excessively intent on escape. He laughed, and glanced over to Alice, without making eye contact. Alice knew Ophelia must have made some joke at her expense.

'Rather than the green, I think I'll have a blue,' she said. 'Perhaps you could fetch one for me, Johnny. You are Johnny, aren't you?' Alice was a little worried that she might have got her Js mixed up at some point.

'Oh yes, absolutely definitely to that.'

At around the same time Andrew and Leo were settling down to their first pint of beer. Leo had astounded Andrew by suggesting, and then, on encountering resistance, insisting upon a new pub, by which he meant not the Red Dragon of Glendower, in Finsbury Park.

'It'll give us something fresh to complain about,' he'd said, unanswerably.

Continuing that theme, Andrew announced once they'd shuffled their way to a quiet corner, and moved the ashtray overflowing with billowing crisp packets and tabs smoked down to the filter, 'I've got some new things that I hate.'

The things they hated was one of their stock conversations. Over the years it had ranged through Chaucer's verse other than *The Canterbury Tales*, *The Canterbury Tales*, banana-flavoured things that weren't actually bananas, the idle rich, the rich, the idle, *Desert Island Discs*, dancing at weddings, weddings, lady novelists, hardcore Dutch techno, interior design (practice and theory), Scandinavia, Kafka ('people say he's funny but he's just not funny – find me a joke, go on, go on'), the New World Order, gastro pubs, fake vegetarians who eat fish and chicken and, in fact, all animals except those animals which eat other animals ('Tiger? Won't touch it, unless it's at a dinner party and not eating it might cause offence'), the way the news talks about 'rubber bullets' fired by Israeli security forces, which conjures up the big silly red jobs, like something out of a sex shop, when what they mean is rubber *tipped* bullets, which are ordinary, evil little bullets, with a rubber end, and which are very nearly as good at killing people, and especially children, as ordinary bullets; the weirdly uncomfortable sisal or sea grass matting that people put down instead of proper carpet in posh flats; MTV, MPVs, RVP, RSVPs, the IMF and all acronyms, except those which succeeded in spelling something rude, such as the Metropolitan police's Fast Action Response Teams, and the honorary title of Bibliographic Unit Manager, that Andrew had assigned to Oakley in a number of widely-read internal documents.

It was therefore always something of a challenge to bring something new to the table.

'Swimming,' said Andrew, decisively.

'Swimming,' replied Leo, nodding in agreement. 'Of course, how could we have left it out?'

'The thing is that I thought I'd better do some. You know, for exercise. So, blind fool that I am, I went to the Swiss Cottage baths. The trouble was that I'm faster than all the slow swimmers, but slower than the fast ones. I felt too embarrassed to stay in the lanes with the bloody Olympic types overtaking me, but in the dodderers part I got stuck behind some nonagenarian in baggy trunks, so I had half an hour of his fucking old man's scrotum waving in front of my face. But it wasn't just that. It was the whole spectacle. The people who go swimming who patently can't swim, but just sort of paddle along in a more or less vertical position, or the ones where all of their limbs are doing a different stroke, you know, one leg's doing breaststroke, the other the crawl, left arm's sidestroke and the right's the reverse humber. And who invented the butterfly stroke and why? Let's think about it: it's more difficult than any other stroke, uses up more energy, and yet it's slower. And why are there never any attractive girls in the pool, just the ones the East Germans rejected as too beefy to be plausible, or the ones like odd bits of Kentucky fried chicken mould-injected into a Victorian bathing suit? And the water. You expect, and can avoid, the larger items of solid matter: the corn plasters and panty-liners, and the more or less discrete globules of phlegm, but when you look carefully you see that the water's simply swarming with micro-particles, and you don't know what they are until you realise that people take in a gulp of water with each stroke and spit it out again, along with whatever bits they've managed to loosen from their mouths: skin-cells, plaque, pasta, so you're basically swimming in other people's expectorated mouthwash. And the slimy changing rooms full of men with much bigger tackle than yours, and the lockers that take your ten pee, but still won't let you open them. And then there's the athlete's foot, and the fact that they make you, and I mean *make* you, pay three quid for all this.'

Leo had taken it all straightfaced, making sympathetic, sagacious and encouraging noises where required.

'I've one or two new ones myself,' he said when the tirade had run its course.

'Good good good,' said Andrew. 'Pray proceed.'

'I hate the soap that girls use, which instead of getting you clean, makes you soft.'

'Good shooting. What is it with that soap? Why don't they just use proper soap to get clean and then use some other unguent to make them soft?'

'And then there's the thing they do with their feet.'

'Which of the things they do with their feet? Kicking you?'

'No, no. The thing with that rasp they have, when they file off the hard skin on their heels, like grating parmesan.'

'Yeah, what is it with girls and hard skin? I can't help thinking it's locked in with the soap that's supposed to make them soft. I don't think *I've* ever had to file away *any* part of me.'

'And,' continued Leo, after pausing to think for a moment, 'there's something about girls and pop music too.' He chewed it over again for a few seconds. 'I haven't quite worked it out yet, but, well, the thing about girls is that they never really understand about pop music. You put on a CD and the first song rocks out a bit, and they say oooh, this is horrible, or it's too loud, or whatever, and then the next track comes on and if it's a slow one they say, oooh this is nice, I like this one, and then the next loud one comes on and they say oooh this is horrible again, can you please turn it off or down or something. They just can't listen to a whole album, they can't grasp anything beyond the immediate song and whether or not it's too loud.'

'Well,' said Andrew, drinking the middle fifth of his pint in one swallow, and simultaneously deciding to take a moderate, centrist position on girls and pop, 'it's certainly true that they don't understand about how sometimes you have to play things too loud, and *that's* the point of the thing. But you can't say *all* girls are pop-ignorant. I've had girlfriends who could hold up their end, more or less, in a debate on, say, what it is that makes the second Oasis album great and the third a total fucking disgrace.'

'Yeah *sure*,' countered Leo, 'there *are* specialist rock chicks, you know, specialist like the tanks they adapted for D-Day to double as bridges or for clearing minefields with big flails . . . what was I saying?'

'Specialist rock chicks.'

'Yeah, yeah, but the thing is they've all slept with Lemmy from Motorhead.'

'What *still*?' said Andrew, as though Leo had told him that girls still wore whalebone corsets, or used belladonna to make their eyes sparkle.

'Yes, *still*: it's a kind of initiation. And they're always, if not actual goths, then *gothish*, and their whole *raison* is that they're one of the girls who know about pop. There's nothing else to them, apart from enough mascara to blacken an elephant's bum, and frankly I'd rather fuck an elephant's bum.'

'As long as it was a girl elephant.'

'One of the pretty ones.'

'With those nice brown eyes and long lashes.'

'But, no, none of the normal ones – girls, I mean, not elephants – know about pop.'

And then it came to Andrew, quietly, easily, like carbon monoxide poisoning. 'You're in love aren't you, Leo?'

'Yes.'

'With a girl who uses make-you-soft-soap, and grates her feet, and doesn't know about pop music?'

'Yes.'

'And this isn't just some ruse to stop me from whupping

your ass for ruining my life and probably getting me kicked out of my job?'

'Not only that, no. And Andrew,' said Leo, signalling his sincerity with subtle manoeuvrings of eye and mouth, 'I know I behaved like a complete cunt the other night. I swear to God I'm sorrier about it than I've ever been about anything, ever. I lost it. It was Ophelia.'

'Listen, mate, better men than you . . . oh, okay, other men than you, have been fucked over by her. She's the *femme fatale's femme fatale.*'

'But it was no excuse for what I did. I can't believe I wheeled out the tactical nuclear weapons to deal with your chum Clerihew.'

'Let's forget about it. We'll just say you owe me one.'

Leo looked at Andrew. A beer mat had attached itself to the bottom of his pint glass. He wanted to say things to him. He wanted to tell him that he was the best friend he'd ever had; that he made him laugh more than anyone else; that he made him forget the things he most wanted to forget. He wanted to tell him that he loved him. But he also knew that he shouldn't: not only because it would be supremely awkward and embarrassing, but, more importantly, because he didn't have to. Instead he did what men do when they want to show affection.

'My round, I think.'

'Kills me to say it, but it's actually mine.'

'Nah, not this time.'

Andrew looked at him and smiled.

'Tell you what, I'll let you get them in if you tell me the whole sordid tale, beginning to end . . .'

'A blow-by-blow account?'

'A ball-by-ball commentary.'

'I'll endeavour to comply.'

THIRTEEN

Thanks, Rosencrantz and Gentle Guildenstern

Somehow Alice made it through the cocktails. Both Johnny and Jeremy, as soon as it became apparent that Ophelia was not to be lured into their ambit, paid her some attention in their contrasting ways, Johnny with excessive laughter, and Jeremy with unpleasant digs at the others, delivered *sotto voce*. Whatever benefits might have accrued from this were outweighed by the dislike it attracted from the other women. The Country Matters woman probed her for a while in case she might yield a story, but clearly saw Ophelia as more likely material, at least if romance were to be her theme.

'Lovely-looking young woman,' she said, looking towards Ophelia and Edward, who were both firmly in the grip of Ophelia's mother. 'And you work for her at Enderby's?'

'We both work at Enderby's, yes.'

'And she's a relation of Edward's, a cousin?'

'No, not that close. But yes, some kind of relation.'

'Oh, I'm so glad they're not *too* close. There's quite enough of that in the country as it is. You can see it when you pop into the Post Office.' She pulled a surprisingly amusing face indicating advanced rural idiocy. 'And,' she continued, after drawing her features back into line, 'Edward is using Enderby's to sell his library?'

Alice guessed that Country Matters might be working herself up for a piece on poor farmers having to sell off family heirlooms just to buy silage (whatever that was) to keep the cattle going through the winter.

'Not the whole library, no. But I'm afraid I can't tell you any more about it.'

'Oh,' said Country Matters. 'Yes, I'd forgotten you're here on a *professional* basis,' which made Alice feel like a not-very high-class hooker.

Alice added several other colours to her spectrum of drinks; she made a joke about being disappointed on missing out the ultraviolet and infrared. Nobody seemed to get it, but Johnny laughed good-naturedly, as if he'd just got a bargain on a second-hand combine harvester. Although she kept things together externally, Alice was in turmoil within. Lynden appeared to be deliberately avoiding her company, and Ophelia was never more than one body away from him, often less. Alice still couldn't quite work out what *she* was doing. Was this another example of the pure, ethereal malice she had displayed at the office party? Was it simply an attempt to ruin any hopes Alice might have? (And Alice was still herself unclear about the precise nature of her hopes, of her desires, directed towards Lynden.) Or did Ophelia really love Edward? For all Alice knew, Ophelia may have secretly yearned for her 'second cousin' (if that was really their relationship) since childhood. Another possibility was that the spite and love were combined in one package: perhaps the thought that Alice might have him had made Lynden irresistible, and the love had followed the spite, like a hangover follows the binge.

The more she thought about Lynden, the less she understood. How could she explain all of the strange things about him: the weeping, the extreme swings of mood, the things

Semele had said about the gun? And what about Semele herself? Where was her mother? Why was she never mentioned? And Grace: she embodied much of the mystery. So intense, so secretive, so possessive. Too many questions. Too many drinks.

They were going through to dine. Someone had taken her arm. She looked, expecting to find Johnny or Jeremy, perhaps even Lynden, but it was one of the older men. Alice had barely spoken to him; he seemed quiet and reserved. Also very attractive, in a silver-haired, old-fashioned kind of way. His gravity reminded her a little of her father.

'Miss Duclos,' he said, 'we seem to have avoided a formal introduction. My name is Conradian, Alex Conradian. I'm an old friend of Edward's. I've already heard a lot about the beautiful book expert. If I didn't know Enderby's better, I'd have said that you were sent deliberately to entrap dear old Edward.' He smiled very handsomely, but Alice thought his teeth looked slightly younger than the rest of him.

'Oh,' said Alice, 'if they intended a honey trap, they'd have set it with my esteemed colleague, Ophelia.'

'Ah yes. I was forgetting that this is something of a works outing for you. Let me get that chair.'

They had arrived in the dining room. It had the same architectural purity as the rest of the Cave of Ice, but the effect was transformed by the presence of a huge gothic table, in stained oak. Its legs were thicker than Alice's, and it was laden with old silver, and tableware marked with heraldic crests. The light came from fat yellow candles, set in heavy candlesticks. Alice wasn't sure if the clash between the room and the table was creative or destructive, and she was pleased to find that she was enough of a scientist to think of it in terms of wave patterns reinforcing or interfering with each other.

189

'How do you know Edward?' she asked.

'We go back a very long way, all the way, in fact, to drama school.'

'You're an actor?'

Conradian looked disappointed: he'd evidently taken it as read that she would have heard of him.

'Yes. You may have seen one or two of my things.'

He named some reasonably well-known TV series and a couple of classic dramas he'd been in, all dating from the seventies and early eighties. Alice, of course, recognised the names, but she hadn't seen any of them. It resulted in a moment or two of awkwardness, before his natural charm reasserted itself.

'But naturally, you're far too cultured to watch the television; and anyway, that is all ancient history. I sometimes think that Edward's decision to abandon the stage before it abandoned him was a very sound one: stopped him from boring young ladies at dinner parties about old triumphs.'

'I'm perfectly capable of boring young ladies in my own way,' boomed Lynden from the other end of the long table. This was followed by laughter and demurring, led by Ophelia. The conversation then became more general. The crisis in the rural economy loomed large, and there was much carping about metropolitan elites, and their failure to understand how things worked in the country. Thinking of the cars in the driveway, Alice could not resist the urge to contribute.

'But hasn't the crisis in the rural economy really been a crisis for the little farmers, the ones who always only just scraped by? I thought the . . . well-off ones were still doing okay. What with the subsidies, and the hedges you've ripped up.'

Meaningful glances were exchanged in the following silence, ably conveying the sense of 'see what we mean?'.

'I told you she was a tigress,' said Lynden, smiling wickedly, not quite at Alice, but broadly towards her quadrant of the table. Ophelia unfurled her lovely rolling laugh, like a Klimt painting made into music. How, thought Alice, could Lynden not fall in love with her?

He, at least, appeared to be enjoying himself. And then one of the chic women expressed a 'custodians of the countryside' view that had everyone back on track, although Alice couldn't see her as the custodian of anything other than her own nails. Although she was now irritated as much as she had been perplexed, Alice decided not to continue with her views on fox hunting, pesticides, agricultural pollution and so on: there were some gulfs that no amount of educated debate could span.

Given the way the table was laid, Alice half expected nineteen courses, with quails and carp and roast swan and something in aspic and a whole ox and some kind of towering jelly for pudding. Only the ox came close, with the main course, beef Wellington. Alice had no appetite. She turned again to Alex Conradian.

'I don't want you to betray a trust or anything, but are you able to tell me about Semele's mother?'

'Aha, the first Mrs Lynden. Well, I'm afraid I can't, really. Not that it would be betraying a trust, but because I don't know much about her. I never met her – Edward and I went through a period of not seeing each other, and in fact he's always been a bit reclusive, as you've probably gathered. So all I know is that he was married, and then she . . . disappeared, leaving the little girl behind. I understand that there was some kind of an incident . . . a gun.'

Alice very nearly gasped. The drink and the gothic dining room put all kinds of ridiculous ideas into her head. Disappeared? What could that mean? That Lynden had killed her? Not a murderer, no, but perhaps he shot her by mistake, and that was why he no longer had a gun. Other facts fell into place: weeping over *Tristan und Isolde* – the ultimate tale of love and death; the isolation – would he not be shunned, for a time at least, by society, as well as wanting himself to avoid contact with others? But no. This was absurd, truly absurd. She banished the ideas from her mind, and nodded gratefully as Johnny Twogood reached across the table to offer her more of the wine which, she could see from the label, had known the world for longer than she had.

At five minutes to nine, Leo said to Andrew, 'So, that's it. You now know, with all the detail you're ever going to get from me, everything there is to know about us.'

Andrew had chivalrously failed to hide his anguish when Leo told him that he was having an affair with Odette Bach, the once sensible, and now eccentric friend of Alice. Anything other than a show of ill-will on Andrew's part would have been taken (and intended) as an insult: it was standard practice between the two of them to bewail the snaffling of any female above the level of mid-table respectability, using the football-league analogy, on the self-evident grounds that it diminished the pool of available talent. 'A little something inside me dies whenever I see a young girl in love,' was how Andrew had put it.

Still, Andrew's ill-grace had been mainly for show, as he'd only fancied Odette in a purely formal sense, without any real glandular commitment. Nor could he display too much of the real pleasure, amounting almost to joy, that he felt. He had long suspected that Leo's accounts of his depredations on the hapless maidens of Queen Mary and Westfield College were exaggerated. And as, over the years, Leo failed to produce a single specimen of the genus, he began, occasionally, to entertain the thought that they might be entirely fictitious. But he didn't like to dwell on the matter: at times he felt he needed to believe in the myth of Leo's concupiscence and ardour more than Leo did.

Leo's account of the week he had spent with Odette was completely different to anything he had said before. There was no leering; no descriptions of sexual acts proscribed by law or custom; no dismissal of the woman in question as trivial, or silly, or bestially wanton, or dull. Andrew waited but it did not come. It was as unnerving as a bus arriving on time, or a British sitcom with funny jokes in it.

The story began with the taxi ride home after the drinks debacle.

'I sat there stinking like a pub urinal. Before she came up I'd done a certain amount of rolling in the gutter. You know how it is.'

'Been there. With *you* more than once.'

'I don't quite know how, but she got me in the taxi. She looked so perfect. Prim's not the word, but it captures something of it. So untainted by . . . whatever it is that taints the rest of us. And I was huddled in the corner feeling and looking like a Nibelung. And she started to talk. Just about things. Suddenly I stopped being quite so drunk. I can't really remember what she was saying, chatter really, inconsequential, but not trivial, which is a hard one to pull off. Partly about the pub, partly about everything else. And the horror of it all became less real. All too soon we were at Queen Mary's: she'd gone miles out of her way. I asked if she wanted a coffee – no, don't look like that. I only wanted to continue talking to her for a while longer. Then she said it: "I'm free tomorrow afternoon if you want to go for a walk."'

'Incendiary stuff,' said Andrew, accompanying it with a-hot-under-the-collar, boy-it's-baking-in-here act.

'We met up on the Heath. It was only in the daytime

193

that I realised how . . . beautiful she was. Your Alice, I can
see that she's a stunner. And she was incredibly nice to me
at the piss-up, when she didn't have to be, and I'm sure
there were things she'd rather be doing. But with her, it's
like lilies floating on top of a pond, with things happening
down in the murk that you can only imagine. With Odette,
though, there's just pure, crystal water, and you can see forever. If Alice is Keats then Odette is Pope.'

'Ah, the good old Neo-Classic versus Romanticism. Nice
to know you can still be a pretentious shag when you want
to be,' Andrew commented, helpfully.

'A palpable hit,' conceded Leo.

'But,' continued Andrew, warming to his theme, 'it
doesn't quite fit in with Alice the science bunny.'

'Unless we put her in with the Romantic scientists, Goethe
playing with light, Joseph Wright of Derby's Experiment
with an Air Pump . . . we'll come back to it, when I'm not
in mid rhapsody. And so we walked on the Heath, and talked
like I've never talked before. With people like you and me,
life's this huge equation chalked on the blackboard we try
to solve, and we get bogged down in some minor compo-
nent, and end up tying ourselves in knots, and relying on
metaphor to magic us to a solution. Yes, I know, before you
say it, that's just what I've done now, with the equation
metaphor. But Odette just goes straight to the solution, she
reads the equation as easily as a-b-c.

'We stayed together all that afternoon. We had a huge
argument about the City and money, but she was fantastic
about not taking anything personally: it was just ideas that
were clashing, not egos. It was odd, and strangely hon-
ourable, that she felt inclined to defend the system that she's
dropped so spectacularly out of. And then we talked about
culture – yes, I *know*, but this was a first date, although I
didn't know it at the time – and she said that my view of

culture was elitist, and I countered by pointing out who it is that, in the end, benefits from the dumbed-down culture and the race of morons it produces – the *real* elite, the mon-eyed class, who want nothing more than an ignorant, com-pliant workforce to man their call-centres, living on a diet of Pop-Tarts and chicken nuggets, before sitting stupefied in front of *Blind Date* every evening, the extent of their ambi-tion being to get the video of Dad being head-butted in the goolies by a goat with an erection on *You've Been Framed*.'

'Very nice flank-turning manoeuvre.'

'Thanks, except that she just enjoyed it as a *performance*, and then went on to point out the logical flaws and false assumptions in my argument. I think it's then that I fell in love with her.'

'Steady!'

Leo looked Andrew in the eye and said: 'I mean it.'

Andrew had never heard Leo use the four-letter L word before, at least not in relation to a person.

Leo went on.

'And then we had dinner together in Hampstead village. For the first time ever I didn't want to get drunk when I was with a girl. I wanted to hear properly everything she said. She told me all about this mad scheme of hers, making Stonehenges for gardens, with some hairy artist, and I got a bit jealous, and she sensed it, and put me right without making it seem as though she was doing it for my sake or even doing it at all.'

'Okay, I've got the message – she's Miss Perfect, all tact and discretion and brains and good humour and pretty to boot. Let's cut to the chase. Did you?'

'No.'

'You're not holding out on me now, are you? Protecting the lady's honour, and so on and so forth?'

'Her honour did not need protecting. As soon as she let

it be known that she was prepared to see me again I was satisfied. She was busy on the Sunday, visiting parents. She said they were about the only people who didn't think she was mad to change direction so dramatically.'

Leo continued his account with the nights of talk on Monday, Wednesday and Thursday. Friday, to Andrew's relief, was declared a night of rest.

'So,' said Andrew, in awe at so much contact so early in the relationship, which itself explained the week without a word, 'it's been a whole two days since you've seen her. You must be pining. In fact I can't believe you've wasted a night in the pub with me when you could have been discussing Third World development with the Perfect Woman.'

Andrew had now become a little jealous and threatened by Odette, and tried to hide it by sounding a little jealous and threatened.

'Come on, Andrew, it isn't like that. Surely you can't begrudge me a few scraps of contentment in my dotage?'

Andrew smiled. 'Okay, as long as it is only a few scraps. And at least you turned up tonight. I propose that we hunker down here till closing time to celebrate your new found bliss. Hang on, just to confirm, the deed of darkness, the beast with two backs . . .'

'No, none of that. The beef dagger remains sheathed.'

'Christ, you're losing your touch.'

'You know, Andrew, I never had that much of a touch.' There was a pause, and the two men looked at each other. And then Leo continued, picking up the tone as if there had been no gap, 'But as for tonight, I'm afraid that I actually, erm, *have* arranged to meet Odette. We've a table at . . .' Leo couldn't bring himself to speak the name of the restaurant, made famous as the site of the tryst between Gordon Brown and Tony Blair at which New Labour had been con-

196

ceived, '. . . booked for nine. In fact I must be shuffling along.'

He didn't mention that Odette had said that he could, if he wanted, spend the night again at her flat, with something in her voice that let him know that this time he didn't have to sleep on the sofa bed.

'Oh,' said Andrew, unable now to hide his sadness. Leo and he often began and ended a Saturday night drink relatively early, leaving time to get back for the football, or a late film, so he could see that there was no necessary slight involved in peeling off to meet what was, after all, a new and wondrous love. Still . . . still.

'I know it's playing the snake, I'm sorry. But I really wanted to see you tonight, to tell you everything. Odette suggested that, if things go well, I mean if we're still . . .'

'Yeah, I get it.'

'Then perhaps you and me and Alice and Odette could get together.'

Andrew perked up considerably at that.

'Sounds pleasant enough. Certainly don't want to meet you on your own again until some of the ardour has cooled. I had serious issues to discuss tonight, you know, my theory about . . . well, I can't remember now, but I'm sure it was a good one . . . and instead I had to listen to you droning on about how lovely the world is, tra la la. It's enough to make a grown man puke up his spleen.'

Five minutes later they were outside.

'I'm this way,' said Andrew, aiming his thumb westward, down Upper Street, towards the Angel.

'I'm . . .' said Leo, angling head and neck the other way, in the direction of Highbury and Islington station. 'I'll call you in a couple of days to maybe arrange times and places for the weekend.'

'Alice willing.'

'Odette'll sort that. She's good at sorting.'

'I gathered that.'

And then they shook hands, which they never did.

It was only a five-minute walk to Granita. Odette had cheekily suggested the restaurant following a lengthy rant by Leo about the death of politics.

'At least in the eighties,' he'd said, aware that it was not an original line, but impelled to continue, 'you had a real socialist party you could love and despair of and some proper fuck-off Tories to loathe, as well as a melt-in-the-mouth centre. Now what do we have?'

'Prosperity and growth?' tried Odette.

'*All we have now* is the melt-in-the-mouth centre, and policies dictated by what the spin doctors find easiest to sell to the news editors when they meet for gazpacho at . . .'

Yes, Granita.

There was a noise ahead. No not just ahead – ahead and off to the left. Upper Street was busy as always and he couldn't see what was happening. He got to a turn-off, a narrow street leading to a leafy square. In the street he saw two people. One was an old Asian man, bearded and wearing some kind of hat, vaguely ethnic in feel. For no good reason Leo thought he might be Bangladeshi. And about six inches from his face, another face, the face of a white youth, a face contorted with rage. The skull attached to the face was shaven close, nicked and scabbed here and there. Despite the season, he was wearing nothing but a white tee-shirt on his torso, which was knotted and lean. His fists were clenched by his sides. The youth was shouting into the face of the old man, who seemed unable to move. His words were as indecipherable as a drill sergeant's screams on the parade ground.

Walk on, said Leo to himself. It'll blow over. It's not a

mugging: muggers don't scream. Just a thug shouting at a man. He'll stop, the man'll go home shaken, and with another good reason to hate white English youths, but otherwise unharmed. It was the line other people were adopting. Men and women glanced down the road as they walked along Upper Street, and then hurried by, choosing not to see. A couple began to approach from the other end of the road, and would have had to walk right past the screamer and old man, but they turned back and took another route. They were old themselves, and Leo didn't blame them.

Walk on, he said, but he knew from the moment that he saw what was happening that he would not be walking on. Beyond that he didn't know anything. And then his legs decided for him, and took him slowly down towards the conflict. The youth was too focussed on his victim to notice Leo. The first he knew of it was when Leo stepped in between the two of them, forcing the old man out of the way. The youth had had to crane down at the old man, who was at least six inches shorter than he. Leo was shorter still.

The youth's eyes opened wide in astonishment.

'What the *fuck* are you?' he said, his voice cracked and breaking. 'What the *fuck* are you?'

Leo couldn't think of anything to say. He was terrified. He had no plan. He didn't want to fight the youth. He just hoped vaguely that he might go away. It nearly worked. He could see the rage in the youth's eyes fade, replaced by amusement. There was a sublime incongruity in Leo's mute, miniature challenge to the skinhead that even the skinhead was aware of. If Leo could have thought of one of the jokes he'd used at school to make the bullies laugh, then maybe they could all have walked away unharmed. But he couldn't. He just stared back up at the skinhead, meeting his eyes, not thinking that this was to issue a challenge.

The youth's eyes hardened again.

'Go away, you little cunt,' he said, quietly.

Leo did not move. He heard the old Bangladeshi man mumbling something behind him. What was it, a prayer?

Then the head-butt came. It landed not, as the skinhead intended, on Leo's nose, but on his forehead. Worse still, for the skinhead, it was so ill-executed that his own nose took much of the force. It began to bleed. Some of the drops, mixed with mucus, fell on Leo. Disgusted, he took a step back and, emitting a gagging shriek, he slapped the skinhead full in the face.

It took two seconds for the skinhead to respond. His first move was to raise his hand almost gently to his cheek. His second was to punch Leo, this time landing the blow squarely on his nose. He then brought his knee up into Leo's stomach. With Leo bent double, he smashed the same knee back up into his face. Leo staggered back, and the skinhead stepped forward, grabbed a fistful of his hair and threw him face down on to the ground. Without hurrying, the youth put a knee into Leo's back, took again a fistful of hair and ground his face into the grit of the pavement.

What happened next remained in dispute. The youth claimed, and it was later to form the mainstay of his partially successful plea of self-defence, that Leo had reached behind him and pulled the long knife from his belt. It may have been that Leo, calling on some primeval instinct, had made a fumbling attempt to draw the knife; it may merely have been an involuntary twitch; or perhaps the youth had found the knife and made up the story about Leo's movement. Moments before, the old man had hurried away, terrified not only of the brutal violence, but also of becoming involved with police and courts and questions. Leo himself would never be able to answer the riddle.

But what followed had a witness.

Andrew felt that the drink had ended on the wrong note. He wanted to go and tell his friend that everything was fine between them, that Odette did sound like a cracker, that it might well give him his best chance with Alice. He'd run back down the street, and reached the turn-off in time to see the two figures caught in the atmospheric glow thrown by an old corporation street lamp. Something about the shape of the one on the ground, perhaps the neat cut of his jacket, perhaps just its very smallness, told Andrew that it was Leo. For a second he couldn't make out what was happening. The other person, the big man, was crouched above Leo, holding his head tenderly in his arms. Christ, thought Andrew, again only for a second, he's having a shag in an alleyway with a sailorboy. And then he saw the long knife in the man's hand. And he saw the man lift back Leo's chin. And he saw the knife drawn quickly, smoothly across his throat. And then again.

Finally he managed to shout out, feebly:

'Hey, you, stop.'

Even at the time he realised how pathetic an intervention it was. But at the shout the stooped figure looked up towards Andrew. Andrew saw that the front of his tee-shirt was covered in blood, in Leo's blood. Then he threw away the knife and bolted away towards the square, keeping low like a sprinter from the blocks. Andrew ran the twenty feet to where his best friend lay silent, face down on the ground. He began to whimper.

'Oh God, Leo. Oh God.'

As gently as he could he turned him over.

Blood, blood everywhere. His hands were covered in it, rich and thick and hot. He tried to wipe it off on his trousers.

'Oh God, Leo. Oh God.'

FOURTEEN

The Return of the Gothic

At last dinner was over. It had been the longest meal of her life, what with Alex Conradian dropping hints about Lynden that he never followed up, and Johnny Twogood beaming at her from across the table and Jeremy Thingy looking at her strangely, and all the time Ophelia plying her trade with Edward so many miles away, over mountain ranges of silver and porcelain.

At least, as Alice had secretly dreaded, there was to be no separation, the women 'going through' to talk of dancing masters over needlepoint, while the gentlemen discussed politics and porn. Instead it was all on to another room, a new one, where they were served coffee by one of the village girls, who, from her worn face and bent posture, now looked as though she were suffering from a prolapsed womb.

'Dear old Alice,' said Ophelia, surprising her with an approach from the blind side. 'You must come and meet Mummy.'

Mummy was, in fact, right there.

'Hello, Mrs . . .' Oh God, what *was* Ophelia's surname? Remember, remember . . . Andrew had some joke . . .

Ophelia Beautifully Mounted . . . Beaumont! Beaumont!
'Beaumont. It's very nice to meet you.'

'Dear child, Offie tells me you've been working here with
Edward.'

'Yes, we're . . .'

'I've known him,' she said imperiously, and impossibly,
'since *before* he was born. He used to give Offie horsy rides
on his back around the paddling pool.'

'*Mummy*,' said Ophelia, sounding human for the first time
since Alice had met her.

'We've discussed the issue, and it seems clear enough.
There's really no need to drag anyone else into it. After all
it's not as if we're talking about the *Ladybird Book of Garden
Birds*, is it? Not that we aren't very grateful, you mustn't
think that we aren't, and I'm sure that the preparatory work
was competently carried out. And of course Edward insisted,
and it would have been . . .'

Alice was very drunk; her teeth seemed to have subtly
shifted position, making speech difficult; and people's heads
had increased alarmingly in size; objects were nearer or further away than she expected; but some of Mrs Beaumont's
meaning came through. She must be talking about the
Audubon. So, what?

Wait, wait. Surely Edward couldn't be thinking of handing
the project over to Ophelia? Insisting on *her* to the management? It would be insane. Even forgetting any . . . obligations he might have to Alice, Ophelia was totally incapable
of performing adequately the tasks that remained to be done:
writing the catalogue and organising the sale.

In particular her written work was notorious. Verbless
sentences. Sentences that rambled and straggled and ranged
on needlessly, detouring to visit irrelevant byways, often
comically misusing technical jargon in an attempt to show
the intertextuality of her praxis, giving, perhaps, along the

way, the life history of a minor player in the provenance of the book, who'd been lost, say on a doomed polar mission, before inexplicably swinging back in what might have been the right direction, if anyone had still been paying attention, but still without ever making or sometimes stopping just before it seemed they were going to reach the. Everything she wrote had to be rewritten by somebody else – usually Clerihew, who substituted his own crabbed and fussy style for her rank illiteracy.

Of course the catalogue and the sale itself were the showiest bits of the whole process, the ways in which one might gain the attention of the senior management at Enderby's. If Ophelia did take over, then the success of the whole project would be ascribed to her brilliance. Alice didn't care so much for herself; it was Andrew for whom she felt. She had forgiven him his indiscretion with Leo. She knew it wasn't out of malice that he had told his friend about her secret love, and with his helplessness, his charm, his yearning to be liked, she found that she simply could not carry a grudge. And after his recent setbacks he needed some good PR. They had agreed that he would do the catalogue – he was acknowledged as the best stylist in Books – and she would organise the sale. They were a team and would share the glory. But with Ophelia in the driving seat, she and Andrew would be frozen out.

But this didn't seem to connect with Alice's view of Ophelia. Wasn't she always studiedly indifferent to her career prospects? Perhaps the whole thing was simply a ruse to get closer to Lynden. Her mind spun with the effort, not to mention the cocktails, the wine and now, served after the coffee (which had helped only to speed the whirring inside her head), the brandy.

The faces all around her had begun to change as the drink had worked its alchemy. Features were both more animated and yet slacker, eyes flickering but dull. Conversation sub-sided and then leapt into spluttering life, as people laughed loudly at jokes that weren't funny. Alice was relieved that she wasn't quite the drunkest person there: Miranda, the student, had passed out on a sofa. In repose she looked about twelve years old, which gave a faintly disturbing quality to the fact that her head was resting on the knee of Alex Conradian.

Within the space of five minutes both Johnny and Jeremy came up to her. Johnny told her to beware of Jeremy: 'absolutely fantastic chap that he is, he *is* a *complete* and *utter* snake, although I must say what a fantastic chap he is.'

Jeremy helpfully pointed out that Johnny was an 'ass', who, 'couldn't get hold of the right end of a one-ended stick with a big sign saying "hold this end".' At least that's how Alice translated his drawl, drawn out to the point now very nearly of abstraction, and which had sounded like: 'Ghoooud ghold ryetend one nedded stick wibeg sigh seng hhhhhh old thissen.'

The snake and the ass, thought Alice. Sounds like a parable. And the snake saith unto the ass partake of the carrot and not of the worm, and the ass replieth eeyore, eeyore.

'What?'

It was Lynden, standing close beside her. Alice smiled, not as embarrassed as she should have been, which was one effect of her anger.

'I think I may have said "eeyore". Nevermind.'

'I suspect the Pomeroy – it affects people in very different ways. Look, Alice, I wanted to say how sorry I am about today.'

'Which part – the ignoring me all day to flirt with Ophelia? Or the fact that you've told her she can take over all my hard work on the Audubon, making me look completely incompetent to the .... oh I don't really care.'

It was just then, as Lynden's eyes widened in amazement, and his mouth began to work at framing a reply, that Alice realised that she was going to be sick. Her mouth had filled with a thin, sweet saliva and she was peculiarly aware of the disposition of her internal organs. She thought she might have thirty seconds before it happened, but it could be as few as fifteen. She knew where the loo was, but she had no intention of rejoining the party after vomiting. She just wasn't that kind of girl.

'Edward,' she said, 'I need to lie down *now*. Where can I go?'

'Your . . . usual room is made up for you on the first floor,' he said, with a carefully wrought civility. 'You remember, the corridor directly above this one, third door on the left, the room's facing . . .' But Alice had already turned to go.

She felt better with the cool porcelain of the lavatory bowl against her head. She'd had to make loud, piggy, snorting and coughing noises to clear the last nuggets of sick from the awkward space between her nose and her throat, and she hoped, without really caring, that no one had heard. She took some comfort from the fact that only the most muffled and intermittent sounds reached her from the party.

When had she last been sick like that? It must have been at the Sixth Form leaving disco. They'd gone to the pub first and she'd drunk five sweet Martinis with lemonade, and then a gin and tonic to show how sophisticated she was to the boy who'd bought it for her. What was his name? Benedict. He'd always had a thing for her from the moment she joined the school in the Third Form. When the other kids teased her about having come from a private school she could sense that he didn't like it, and was embarrassed for her. She could see him very clearly now, as he was then, with his sandy hair that didn't seem to have a natural grain, but grew in all directions at once; his blazer always too small, showing four inches of dirty cuff or bare, skinny arm. He was the only boy to wear a suit to the disco. Pale grey, cheap. Funny how she should remember him and not the cool boys, the ones all the girls fancied: Gavin Paulie, James Whiteoak, Dave Land. Benedict had asked her to dance at the end to Louis Armstrong's *What a Wonderful World*, and she was too nice to say no. He'd clung to her, his knuckles white with fear and desire, as she looked over his shoulder at the other dancers. She didn't feel at all embarrassed at dancing with the second biggest nerd in the Sixth Form (she might even have danced with Richard Crawshaw himself, who looked like he was pulling a face even when he wasn't). In fact she felt a little thrill at being so ostentatiously and publicly 'nice'. Was that bad? She hadn't thought about it then and she didn't know now. Andrew would know. Or that little friend of his, whom Odette might have liked. Must call Odette. Back then there was so much to look forward to: there'd be nice boys, cool boys, boys who'd love her more than she loved them, and boys who'd break her heart. How easy things were. Kitty was Alice's only problem; her father the only sacred dead.

The dead. How could she have forgotten so soon her own beautiful Dead Boy? She had betrayed him by following this pointless dream here in the Cave of Ice, with her ridiculous Baron. What was it Andrew's friend . . . Leo, Leo, had said? Andrew was real, Lynden was trashy fantasy and the Dead Boy was art. Surely, art was better than reality, better than fantasy. In art the fantastic was made real, the real fantastic. Had Leo understood that as he said it, and was that why he felt the need to drag in Plato to 'prove' that art was deception?

Alice hauled herself up from the bathroom floor, suddenly so tired she thought she might fall asleep where she was on the thick white carpet. She splashed some water on her face and brushed her teeth with her finger – she knew her overnight bag would be waiting in the bedroom, but she couldn't face going all the way there and all the way back for her toothbrush.

The room was as comfortable as she remembered. It occurred to her that the incongruity of the furnishings in some of the rooms must be to do with old furniture kept from the earlier house on the site. How old would that have been? Victorian? Elizabethan? Medieval? She must have read it somewhere, but it wouldn't come back.

She slipped in between the sheets wearing nothing but her bra and knickers. There was a weirdly-shaped pot in the room, which Alice knew had some particular purpose, not a tulip pot, but something like that in specificity. Specificity . . . what a strange word. Must ask someone tomorrow about the pot. Grace might know. Grace. Who was Grace? Who was Grace?

In the night the old house came back. Its walls of crumbling brick and sandstone soft as velvet, held together with moss and lichen and ivy, reasserted their rights to this space. Timbers and whitewashed plaster grew like crystals around the panels of glass and steel, around the concrete pillars. Flying buttresses and high vaults were cast across space like spider webs. Subterranean workings carved themselves again through the rubble of their own collapse. Priests' holes and back stairs and secret places opened like cavities in a rotten tooth. Gargoyles pulled themselves from the earth and scaled the walls to take up again their old places, to summon up, or warn away, or guard against the evil spirits, the ancient ones.

She felt her father come to her through the old house. He held a lantern high, and wherever its light fell the old decayed again briefly into the new. Some niches illumined by the lamp were filled with stuffed birds, the ones she knew and loved, although their names were all wrong. The gyre and the gimble, the petulant, the cave swoft, and the gaily-coloured parasol. When he came into her room, the light was so bright that she could not see his face. He was wearing the white coat she knew he must have worn on his rounds, although she had no memory of ever seeing him in it. Of course, he would never bring something which might be contaminated back into the house, back to her. It was Kitty who had brought contagion. No, this wasn't about that. Her father was telling her . . . telling her the thing he always told her. It was his message. She knew what his message was. It was what he had taught her. The things he had shown her. The message was . . . the message was . . .

'What is it?' Alice had come awake speaking the words. 'Who's there?'

The door closed, cutting out the arc of light that had shown her, for a moment, the figure coming towards her. She heard the man breathing; he was panting, not gasps from exertion, but the laboured sound of someone who has been holding their breath involuntarily, from fear, or stealth.

'Who is it?' said Alice, loudly this time. Her own heart was racing and she was about to launch into a horror-film scream. Only the thought that it might be . . . Edward . . . for whatever reason had stopped her from screaming already.

'Oh crikey, is this where you are, Alice?'

'Johnny? Is that you? What the hell are you doing here? Don't answer that, just get out!'

'Oh gosh, look, I really didn't mean to startle you. Had no idea you were in here. Just wandering around looking for a place to kip. Went for a stroll on my own outside, came back, found all the others had gone off to bed, or driven home, or what have you.'

Alice was no longer remotely alarmed. Even an innocent such as she could deal with a chump like Johnny, she reasoned.

'Well, there must be twenty bedrooms in this house, I'm sure you'll stumble into an unoccupied one, if you keep going.'

'Oh yes, well, doubtless. Only thing is,' he said, suddenly rather closer than he had been, 'I thought that, as I'm here, I might just sort of pop up on the bed for a while.'

Alice laughed. 'Sorry, Johnny, it's been a long day. I've been drunk, been sick, and now I'm sober, with the beginnings of the kind of hangover that you don't want to be around. And I'm really not in the mood to debate the merits of spring versus winter barley with you. Please just go.'

'I'm afraid,' said Johnny, climbing clumsily on to the bed, 'that I just need a minute or two's rest. Recharge my batteries. No need to alarm yourself – I'm up here on top of the duvet, *completely* out of harm's way.'

Until he was on the bed with her, Alice hadn't realised how large Johnny Twogood was. She was still half amused by his antics, and the part that wasn't amused wasn't yet concerned: just angry and already hung-over.

'That's enough, Johnny; I'd like you to leave, now.'

'Not very friendly after giving me the come-on all day. Someone might say you're a bit of a prick-tease.' He moved closer, and touched her hair. 'Unless you're just playing a little hard to get. Don't mind that at all. In fact like that.'

Alice now felt horribly trapped. She couldn't spring out of bed in her pants and bra, and besides, his weight on the duvet had trapped her arms. With one great effort she wrenched her right arm free and shoved as hard as she could, at the same time yelling, 'Get off!' Luckily, he was in the process of shifting his position to enable further and fuller access and Alice's push succeeded in shunting him completely off the bed and onto the floor, where he landed with a clump.

A second after he landed, and before he'd had time to renew his assault, the door burst open. The effort to push Johnny off the bed had displaced the duvet exposing Alice from the waist up. She felt the skin around her nipples pucker slightly with the cold air. Before she had time to pull the duvet back into shape, her eyes met Lynden's as he paused by the doorway. He was wearing a long, dark, heavy dressing gown, lined with white silk. She saw him look down towards Twogood, who was struggling to get back on his feet. Instantly his face took on the look of sublime rage she had seen twice before. Three strides took him towering over Johnny. Without speaking, he clasped hold of his shirt collar, taking with it, to judge by the yelps of pain Johnny was emitting (interspersed with muddled explanations about why he was there), a good clutch of the hairs from the nape of his neck, and marched him out of the door. Alice heard the squeals and whining apologies recede down the corridor, reaching a new crescendo as Lynden dragged Johnny down the stairs. Five minutes later he was back.

'I heard a noise,' said Lynden. 'Are you . . . hurt?'

'Hurt? No. Johnny . . . he came in while I was sleeping. He startled me, that's all.'

'Look, if he laid a finger on you, or threatened to, then it's a matter for the police. I can have them here in twenty minutes. They deal . . . sympathetically with these things now.'

Alice thought for a minute. She couldn't be sure in her own mind if the incident had been more than an inept pass.

'No, I don't think there's a need. He would probably have gone away even if you hadn't . . . What did you do with him?'

'I just threw him out of the door. But I'll tell you one thing. He'll never work in this county again.'

Alice found this rather amusing.

'What are you laughing at?' said Lynden, beginning to smile.

'Oh, just you *grand-seignioring* it. "He'll never work in this county again",' she mimicked, not accurately, but to good comic effect.

'Yes, I suppose that *was* a bit pompous.' He paused for a moment before going on. 'The reason I was able to hear that you were . . . distressed, was that I was coming to this room myself.'

Alice *had* thought it odd that Lynden had appeared so quickly. But what did this mean? What had he come for?

'The thing is,' he said, 'I wanted to apologise properly for everything that's happened today. I really didn't mean to leave you alone with these . . . people. But whenever I tried to come to you, I found I was corralled by the Beaumont heavy squad, or Siân Ellis, out for a story for that ridiculous column of hers. She seems to want to see me as an archetypal country squire, holding the land in trust for everyone. And anyway, you appeared to be keeping yourself amused with your courtiers. Alex Conradian was certainly much taken with your charms.'

'Oh, please, he's old enough to be my . . .' Alice stopped, remembering too late that Alex and Edward were exact contemporaries.

Lynden stiffened slightly, and carried on more formally.

'I also wanted to explain about the Audubon. Ophelia kept saying that you were so busy at work that the Audubon was taking over your life in an unhealthy way. She said that she thought it was selfish of me to insist that you carry it all on your own shoulders, that you'd done enough and that someone else ought to help with the tidying up. I was hardly listening. I certainly didn't see it as any kind of plot. And I thought that with less of a workload, you might be able to see . . . to come here . . . more often. In the end I just vaguely agreed with Ophelia that it didn't seem fair that you had to do so much of the work. I'm sorry if I caused any . . . confusion.'

It was too much to think about. Waves of exhaustion were passing over Alice again.

'Please, please, let's talk about it in the morning. I'm so . . .' and then she yawned as widely and innocently as a child, which made them both laugh.

'Of course. My manners. Goodnight, Alice.'

He bent over her and kissed her very gently on the cheek. His lips lingered there for a second longer than was strictly necessary. As a way of drawing it to a close, but also to indicate that she was no longer angry with him, she turned her face to bring their lips together in a brief, chaste contact, before turning fully on to her side, and burying down in the soft pillow. She pulled up the duvet, leaving space enough for one eye to peep out.

'Goodnight, Edward,' she said, and he left the room.

The next day was sunny and, after breakfast, it was decided that they should all go for a nice long walk. Johnny, of course, had gone, along with several others. Ophelia and Mrs Beaumont were still there, Alice was disappointed to note, as was Siân Ellis, Jeremy and Alex Conradian. Semele joined them, looking grumpy, shaking off Grace's attempt to tie on a hat.

At least Edward was by her side as they set off, down into the valley below the house. Together they led the straggling group, and were soon amid trees, with the sound of water not very far away.

'This is lovely,' said Alice, just to get things going. She

213

looked up at him and smiled, which took quite a lot of effort, given the hangover from which she was suffering. She felt as though the fine old country pastime of badger-baiting was being revived in her brain pan.

Lynden, however, looked distracted, and took several heartbeats to reply, heartbeats that felt like the pounding of the timpani at the climax of some monumental, discordant tone poem.

'Mmmm? Yes. I don't come down this way very much any more.'

He didn't meet her smile, but looked up into the branches of the trees, which held on feebly to the last few leaves.

The tenderness and sympathy of the night before had disappeared as completely as the old house, with its vaults and buttresses and ghosts, had vanished. Alice, annoyed and disappointed, allowed Lynden to stride ahead. She found herself next to Ophelia's mother, who, from the effortful grunts and general air of bustle, had been trying to catch up with her, just as she was falling back towards the pack. She was wearing her usual armour-plating of tweed, and had donned a headscarf. The model may have been the Queen at Balmoral, but the reality was more Romanian beggar-woman. Her face, thickly fleshed, its folds and planes never quite where one would expect, was as implacable and unreadable as ever.

'Ah, Alice,' she said, panting with exertion. Alice was tempted to increase her pace to further discommode the unpleasant old woman. But such pleasures were, sadly, not in her nature to grasp. 'I've wanted to talk to you since yesterday. You are a *cleverly elusive* young lady.'

The phrase, with its subtle suggestion of slyness and cowardice, irritated Alice beyond forbearance.

'Mrs Beaumont . . .'

'Please, *please*, Volumnia. There is no need for formality in the *country*.'

'*Volumnia*, I find it surprising that you were unaware of my presence, when I was so conscious of yours. You are fortunate, I suppose, in having *such* a penetrating voice, which must come in handy for training dogs.'

'Yes, well, I do have my spaniels, which are a great distraction. But I wanted to talk about you, child. Don't intend to beat about the bush. My concern is with family. It has come to my attention that you may have interests here beyond those appropriate to your position at Enderby's. I would have to have been deaf, and I promise you, Alice, I am not deaf, not to have heard the various to-ings and fro-ings of last night. Not to mention the bangs and crashes. And I was so sorry not to have seen young Johnny Twogood over the kedgeree this morning. Quite inexplicable, unless you would care to explain?'

'Yes, I can explain,' said Alice, after considering saying nothing at all. 'He barged his way into my room last night and tried to get into bed with me, despite my urgent and loud request that he go away. Edward heard my complaints and threw him out of the house.'

'Well . . .' said Volumnia Beaumont, filling the word with distaste, as though a stray mongrel had tried to get at one of her spaniel bitches. Evidently, whatever exactly had gone on, it must all be Alice's fault. 'I really can't believe that one of the Twogoods would . . . that Edward would become embroiled in a . . . Oh dear, oh dear, I do hope that Miss Ellis won't be using any of this in one of her *columns*.'

Was that a threat? wondered Alice. Bed-hopping antics of metropolitan elite brought to rural idyll? If it was, it had no purchase on *her*. Conversation stopped for a while as the party picked its way through a boggy bit, which required careful foot-eye co-ordination. Alice noticed for the first time how unsuitable her shoes were for this type of expedition: too sensible for town, too flash for the country. Not for the first time she wished that Andrew was around to give it a proper neatly worked-out, paradoxical form. Or perhaps Leo could work it up into some huge, baroque structure. Alice smiled at the thought of Leo and his stiletto. It must, she thought, come somewhere under the big pink tent of campness.

'What a terrible mess the mud has made of your sweet little shoes,' said Volumnia, marching along in her 1930s, first-white-man-to-reach-the-mountain-kingdom-of-Upper-Bhtwalladah boots. 'I was saying about your romantic intentions vis-à-vis Edward.'

'I haven't got any romantic intentions vis-à-vis *anyone*,' spluttered Alice. 'And frankly I don't see it . . .'

'Alice, I am speaking openly and honestly. It may not be the way of the young, but it's *my* way. Please do me the courtesy of listening. I am told that you value being responsible for organising the sale of this book of Edward's. And I know that Edward has agreed to recommend that Ophelia be handed the project, and I can quite see that that might be a disappointment to you. But a promise is a promise, and I'm sure that you wouldn't want Edward to break his word.'

Although Alice kept trying to correct or challenge her statements, Volumnia Beaumont's way of talking made interruption an impossibility. She continued:

'You may not have noticed, but Ophelia's energies have not always been directed towards furthering her career. She is simply not that *driven*. Sweet natured, other-worldly child that she is, I believe her . . . focus has been more on romance. If she has shown an interest in the Audubon, it is because other . . . influences may be at work.

'Now let me put this bluntly. Edward is a vulnerable and in some ways a wounded man. His own romantic history is not a happy one. He needs now the love of an appropriate

216

woman, one with the right kind of pedigree. My fear is that with your charms, and I do not doubt that they are considerable, you are affecting Edward's judgement about where his true interest lies.' And then Volumnia came to the point – a point that Alice assumed would remain unstated: 'Give him up, go back to London, and the Audubon is yours. Stay here, get in the way, and you know you'll lose out in the end, and you can say goodbye to whatever it was you hoped to gain from being in the pilot's seat on your sale. There you have it.'

Whatever Alice was going to say, and she had decided on something crude and Anglo-Saxon, was blocked by the arrival of Semele. Mrs Beaumont, much relieved, stopped to regain her breath, but not before she had sent Alice a 'think carefully about it' look.

Semele, who had lost her hat somewhere on the walk, said to Alice:

'Do you know about real birds, or just birds in books?'

'I know more about real birds than I do about birds in books, or anything in books. I used to study biology. What I know most about are the birds and animals and plants that live on islands, and how they are different from the ones that live nearby.'

'There's a boy at school called Thomas and he has his own binoculars. He says he knows the names of all the birds in England, and can even tell the little brown ones apart. Do you love my daddy?'

Too much had happened for Alice to be particularly surprised at this.

'I don't know,' she replied, 'do you?'

'Love my daddy? Of course I do. Well, not very much when he's like he is today, all grumpy and moody and off on his own.'

'Semele, where's your mother?'

217

It was brutally put. Perhaps even brutally intended, and Alice regretted it as soon as she had spoken. But that did not mean she wasn't interested in the answer. Mentally, she tossed a coin; what would it be: heaven or the attic?

'Spain.'

'Spain?'

'Daddy sometimes likes to pretend that Mummy's dead, but she's not; she's gone to the Costa del Crime with a convicted credit-card fraudster from somewhere called Hartlepool. What's a credit-card fraudster? *They* won't tell me.'

'It's someone who . . . it's a kind of stealing.'

'Oh.'

Well, that was interesting. Perhaps it even explained some things.

'Daddy won't let me go and see her because he says it's not the right environment. But I don't really care. Mummy comes to see me every few months and she brings presents. And I like Grace. Daddy likes Grace too, but he doesn't show it when you're around.'

The group had reached a meadow beyond the trees. Sunlight was leaking from between the huge and heavy clouds, turning some purple, some bluey-black, and some just black. The effect would have been pretty without the sure knowledge that more rain was on the way. Lynden rejoined them and the stragglers caught up. Alice saw that Ophelia was thick with Siân Ellis. She didn't like the combination.

'I suggest home and something to warm us up before lunch,' said Lynden, his good spirits miraculously recovered. On the way back he practically gambolled. He moved through the group playfully teasing the women and joking laddishly with Alex and Jeremy. None of it fooled or mollified Alice. When they reached the house she asked Jeremy if he'd give her a lift to the station.

'Yes,' he said, 'if you must go. I'd rather hoped you might stay till after lunch: I was planning on offering you a lift back to London. Thought it might make the journey go a jot more quickly. And the trains on Sunday are as rare as hen's teeth, as old Johnny might say. Actually, another reason for the lift was that I thought you might be able to fill me in on the mystery of Johnny's disappearance. Our host was most unforthcoming. Sure you won't reconsider?'

Alice strode up to Lynden as Jeremy went inside with the others to get his car keys.

'I'm glad we have the chance to talk at last,' he began, 'I wanted . . .'

'I'm going back now,' Alice cut in. 'Jeremy's fetching my bag from inside. How long has Grace Harbour been your mistress?'

The clues had been there all along, but it was only with Semele's innocent words (if they *were* innocent: Alice suspected that the slip may have been deliberate) that the truth had stepped forward. And what a sordid, common little truth it was. Alice's anger was more to do with her own embarrassment at inflating Lynden into a gothic hero or villain. How silly she'd been. An ex-wife in Spain, an affair with a plain, but available local. Not very heroic, not very villainous. Just squalid, and ordinary. No wonder he had rages and grumped about the place. No wonder he fancied something a touch more glamorous from the city. And hardly flattering.

Lynden's jaw collapsed. The life and energy drained from his face, leaving him, within a second, a decade older. He made an inchoate sound, which could have become a 'no'. Alice thought he might fall to the ground. With an effort he turned away; not towards the house but back down the valley towards the trees. Alice was concerned enough to ask Jeremy, once he appeared, to return again to tell Alex Conradian that Lynden might need some support.

219

When he came out, Jeremy handed her a piece of paper.

'There's a message. Someone called Andrew. Can you phone him on this number. He wants to get hold of Odette, if that makes any sense.'

Andrew and Odette? Did that boy never give up? Despite her mood, she smiled, but not without some small element of regret seeping in. She'd call him when she got back to London. He could wait for Odette.

Jeremy tried all the way to the station to get from Alice what had happened during the night and that morning to make her leave. But she said nothing. She said nothing because she had remembered her dream of the night before, and remembered, more significantly, its message.

FIFTEEN

Of Monkey Nuts and Hard-Boiled Eggs

'A *paper* knife?'

Andrew spoke with the kind of whining shriek that signalled incredulity.

'A paper knife.'

'A *Jacobean* paper knife?'

'Um, no. Not exactly Jacobean. I bought it in John Lewis. Very good stationery department. Much better than Selfridges. Can't go wrong there, "never knowingly undersold" and all that.'

'I know John Lewis is never fucking knowingly undersold. But still . . . And *completely* blunt?'

'Well, it had quite a sharp point. Do a lot of damage if you jabbed someone in the eye with it. But the edge, no, you'd have a job to carve your way out of a wet paper bag with that.'

'And this Neanderthal didn't realise that instead of cutting your throat in the approved hallal slaughter method, he was barely even giving you a tickle under the chin?'

'Fair play to the guy: there was an awful lot of blood and gore around. At least half of it was his. Perhaps he thought he was slashing his way down to my jugular. Perhaps he knew he wasn't and was relieved. Takes a certain amount of nerve to kill someone like that.'

Andrew was frankly astounded at Leo's good mood. Looking at him now lying in the hospital bed was like watching some footage from a documentary on underground bare-knuckle fighting. His eyes were almost completely closed by the swelling purple flesh around them. His lips were bulbous and misshapen, like rotten plums. He had at least five cuts on his face, three of which had required intricate ladders of stitching, and almost all of the space in between the individual cuts was latticed with angry grazes. But even this was more than Andrew could have hoped for as he knelt with Leo's head in his lap in the narrow street. A small crowd had gathered round them in response to his cries for help, and someone had called for an ambulance on a mobile.

Leo never completely passed out. He couldn't remember much about the beating, but he'd felt the push of the cold steel against his throat, and the hot, sour lager-breath of the skinhead on his cheek. After that he remembered lying face down, under a huge, crushing weight, which stopped him from moving. His mouth was full of blood. And then he was looking up into a face he knew. Why was Andrew there? He was going to the Angel. He'd mumbled, inaudibly, 'Angel'. Another man was asking him what his name was, and if he could move his toes. Why? His toes were okay. There was nothing wrong with his toes. Then a clatter and slide as he was put in the ambulance, and then the meaningless flurry of Casualty, and then a bed, and an injection, and then sleep.

He'd woken into a pain beyond any he had ever imagined. The pain was cunning and crude: it combined an astonishingly high level of general agony, with spots of such intensity that they could, for a few seconds at a time, make him forget the background torture. It was a pain that made him want to be sick, to squirm and writhe and cry. After some impossible-to-estimate time consciously adrift on his inland sea of pain, he began to realise what had happened and where he was. And if this was a hospital, they must have ways of taking the hurt away.

'Hurts,' he'd said, before he could see anything through the narrow slits between his bruises.

He heard a gasp. Doctors and nurses didn't gasp.

He peered fiercely. 'Who?'

A cool, dry hand touched his. A woman's hand. He still couldn't see much, just a blur of whiteness. But then something dark against the light; a face. A face he recognised. The face of Odette.

An hour later, the pain pushed back into its lair by strong drugs, good drugs, Leo was able to listen, and to reply with eloquent grunts. He was wheeled away into a pale, terrifying tunnel for a CAT scan. Doctors came and policemen came. Odette stayed, talking to him lightly about nothing at all. She read him stories from the *Guardian*. He fell asleep when it was dark outside, and she was still there.

He woke up in the middle of the night, raging with fear and pain. People were coming for him. People wanted to kill him. His mouth had oozed blood and mucus, and the nurse had to change his pillow.

Odette came at lunchtime. She brought a brown paper bag, and Leo very nearly burst his stitches when he saw the contents.

'It's the one where Ollie breaks his leg and Stan comes to see him in hospital. Within five minutes Ollie's dangling out of the window, suspended by his bad leg.'

Leo was explaining Odette's joke to Andrew, who arrived that evening, the Monday. Every other word was accompanied by a wince or yelp, or guttural expletive.

'Rings a bell, but you know I was never as much of a fan as you.'

'Well, before the mayhem, Stan gives Ollie a bag with his gift. And what he's brought are *monkey nuts and hard-boiled eggs.*' Leo couldn't stop another ripple of mirth travelling across his face. It looked grotesque and hurt like hell. 'You see I'd told Odette how much I liked Laurel and Hardy, you know all my stuff about love and suffering, and friendship, as well as them being just unbearably funny, and she'd remembered this and brought me *monkey nuts and hard-boiled eggs.* I told you she was amazing.'

Andrew raised his eyes to the heavens, or at least to the strip lighting, and sighed heavily.

It had been a momentous week for Odette. She had found the rampaging Leo of the drinks party exciting and interesting. His small, wiry frame, with the left shoulder lower than the right was, in her eyes, more than compensated for by his face, which she thought the most mesmerising she had ever seen. It seemed to contain whole universes of complexity; geological layers of joy and pain and ecstasy and dread shifted and exposed themselves only to submerge again. But he felt too much like a different species to elicit her desire. It was only when she saw him outside, broken, lonely, that she felt some pang of warmth, and with that warmth, an appetite. She knew very well what she was doing when she took Leo home in the taxi. That it would succeed, in any sense at all, had to wait for the first proper meeting. Almost at once, walking on the Heath with Leo showing off, trying hard not to show off, and then showing off some more, she knew that it was right. Not right, necessarily for ever, or cosmically, but right for now.

Her new business partner, Gerald the artist, picked up that something was wrong, or rather *right* with Odette, after three days of whistling and all-purpose happiness, combined with an occasional irrational grouchiness, which wasn't Odette at all. She told him something about Leo, and something of how she felt. From that point on he referred to Leo as the 'Little Dude', but his sole contribution to character analysis was that he sounded 'a bit flaky'. Fine coming from you, was Odette's silent return.

Every fibre in her being screamed out for a call to Alice to get some feedback through Andrew about what Leo might be thinking. But somehow the same reticence and determination not to spoil their luck that kept Leo away from the phone prevented her from telling all to her best friend. And anyway, for all she knew it might be over by the weekend, and then what a fool she would feel for talking about love.

Frankie had phoned very late on Wednesday night. Odette and Leo had been talking and drinking coffee in the ICA bar that evening. He'd invited her to go and see one of the films in the Tarkovsky season. They'd even managed to get as far as taking their seats, which Leo said were the most comfortable in London, and perfect for snoozing. But after fifteen minutes of the opening shot, which followed a bicycle being wheeled across a bleak horizon, they looked at each other and knew that what they really wanted to do was to sit next to each other back in the bar, poking gentle fun at the arty punters (who would have, as Leo conceded, every right to poke fun back, as he had worn one of his black polo-necks to this, the spiritual home of the black polo-neck), and each playing Columbus and cartographer with the other's mind.

'Where have you been all night, you filthy slut,' said Frankie. She didn't remotely suspect that there might be a boy involved: she assumed working late, or just not answering the phone.

Odette couldn't resist it. 'Oh, you know, just out with the boyfriend down the ICA. Like you do.'

Frankie spluttered, cursed, laughed, wheezed, yelped (the cigarette she was smoking had fallen from her mouth and threatened to initiate an inferno in her ironically-worn, but still very comfortable, pink fluffy mules) and jeered all at the same time.

'I knew it, I knew it! That's why I phoned,' she lied, in her wonderful cheese-grater of a voice, given its broad, lung-lacerating shape by years of Benson's and now finished to perfection by the finer-grained Marlboro Lights. In fact her call was triggered by a more general loneliness and a desire to get the girls together, as they hadn't had a group natter for weeks and weeks. She'd also felt the urge to pass on her enlightening experience involving anal sex while wearing a tampon, but now she thought she'd save that for when Odette's love life with the new beau needed spicing up a little, say next week.

Odette refused to give her any of the gory details; didn't even mention that they'd done nothing more than kiss. And what a kiss: so still, so perfect, so sweet. His kiss was strong magic. But his talk was better.

Odette and Frankie pencilled in two Fridays ahead for a get-together. Odette promised she'd make sure Alice came, and that she herself would come equipped with all the information Frankie could ever want, short of precise measurements of girth, length, and turgidity.

She was, of course, exactly on time at Granita. Leo had spent that one night, the Thursday, in her flat chastely, well, not *that* chastely, but chastely enough, on the sofa bed. She'd made it up for him and they kissed passionately, with her calves pressed against the hard, tubular steel of its frame. She knew then that she had only to fall over backwards

226

and new things would happen. But she didn't. Not then. Nor would she tonight: she had no intention of wrestling with the awkward mechanism, pulling, twisting, folding out, clamping down. She sat and thought through what *would* happen. She had no moral objections to sex early in a relationship, merely practical ones, to do with being hurt and maintaining self-respect. And even they had remained more theoretical than practical, given the lack of opportunities she'd had. Matthew had, of course, been a mistake. But Leo was no Matthew. There was nothing slick or manoeuvring about Leo. His way was always to try to make you think the worst of him, to paint the warts alone. It was only under special lighting that you got to see the faint outline of the masterpiece sketched under the gaudy cartoon.

And half an hour late, that was forgivable. This wasn't his patch. And he'd wanted to have a drink with that nice, amusing friend of his, Andrew. Alice's friend, of course, too. And you could tell that he liked her. What a shame she was still so wrapped up in her morbid obsession with the dead refugee. And then the pointless complication of the aristocrat in the country. Why couldn't people see the world the way it was, the way that *she* saw it?

And where *was* Leo? Forty-five minutes late. She could feel the self-doubt begin to rise in her like damp rot. And the aimless questions: Did he really want me? Was he ever going to come? Was there someone else (not that, surely not that)? Have I been misled again? Perhaps he had only ever wanted a friend, and the unspoken knowledge that they shared that this night would be *the* night had scared him off. He was repelled by the idea of sleeping with her. And who wouldn't be?

She ordered another glass of wine. The waiters were ignoring her; not, she thought, through rudeness, but so as not to make her feel awkward about the non-arrival of the 'friend' she had said she was expecting. What unusual discretion. She'd tell Leo about it when he came.

But he wasn't coming, was he? Had she taken too conservative a line in that argument they had had about the City? She was only playing devil's advocate. He *must* have known that. No, never the arguing over ideas: it was the air that he breathed. If he couldn't like her . . . love her, it would be because she was too dull, too conventional in her thought. That must be it. She bored him, bored him, bored him.

At ten o'clock she took a taxi home, holding back her head to try to keep in the tears.

The next morning she woke early, her mind clear and refreshed. No time to be wasted on brooding or sulking. She brushed her hair, put on her comfortable clothes, a sweatshirt and jogging pants, walked briskly to the bagel place, where she bought three bagels (hungry after last night's missed meal), picked up the Sunday papers, came back and settled down with a pot of fresh coffee. At eleven she took the bus – only a ten-minute wait, which was close to a miracle on a Sunday – up to Pond Street. From there she walked up on to the Heath and followed her usual route, enjoying the late autumn sunshine until it turned into early winter rain.

She was home by two, hungry again. There was nothing much to eat in the flat, but she scavenged a meal of stale muesli and old yoghurt and the pear that had still refused to soften after a week alone in the fruit bowl. As she was eating, she saw the red light beating on her answerphone.

'Er, hello. This is Andrew. We met the other night. I got your number from Alice. I hope you don't mind. It's a bit of an emergency. But don't worry too much, it's not that bad. Well, it is *quite* bad. Oh God, it feels all wrong saying this on the machine, but you should know. I was with Leo last night.

228

He left me to go and meet you. There was a bit of a . . . well, he got into a bit of trouble. They took him to the Whittington Hospital. It's the one up the Holloway Road, near, oh, what's it called, the bit at the top . . . Archway. I think he should be okay for visitors by this evening. Um, bye. Sorry.'

Odette played the message three times again. No need to panic. Not dead, not dying. What could 'a bit of trouble mean?' The idiot hadn't left his number. She tried Alice. She got her mother.

'Alice?' came the voice, astonished and, it sounded, offended that anyone might want to speak to her daughter. Odette had heard it before. 'No, not here. In the country. The *country* . . . What? Back when? No, *I've* no idea. Why should *I* know? She may have said something about coming back, but I can't be expected . . .'

Next she phoned the hospital She got a ward number from the switchboard, and was put through to a busy nurse who wasn't able to say anything other than that no, he wasn't critical, and yes, visitors were allowed, between the hours of 17.30 and 19.30.

Odette wasn't surprised or shocked to find, after a moment or two of introspection, that she was pleased. She did pause, for a moment, in awe that she could be so selfish, but no, it didn't make her a monster, just human. She hadn't been rejected or forgotten, and that was always good. Leo wouldn't benefit from an emotional collapse now, brought on either by girlish horror at his plight, or some existential (if that was the right word – she'd check with him later) posturing about her feelings. He needed good, practical help. And that's what Odette Bach was all about.

The monkey nuts and hard-boiled eggs idea came to her in a flash. Yes, he'd like that. Anything else, anything he *needed*, could wait until she saw him and could assess the situation more thoroughly.

And yes, when she found him, and gave him the bag, he did laugh. A sort of a laugh. He couldn't open his mouth or his eyes, but he made a jolly, choking noise. Even Odette's calmness had taken a buffet when she saw his face. He tried to speak, said something about . . . was it ugly? The effort sent a dribble of pink saliva running down the centre of his chin, which she gently wiped off with one of the coarse hospital tissues from the box by his bed.

'Believe it or not, your handsome face was never the main attraction.'

The once so expressive face was unreadable now – it was a landscape transformed by some terrible natural disaster. Had she gone too far? In their week together, Odette had divined something of Leo's great anguish about his looks. It was a pain that she could see without truly understanding: she had never been on the inside of an anxiety like that. She had felt that the best way to approach it would be by simply showing Leo how much she loved him in his entirety, as a complete person, how she desired him as a whole. And part of that total love would be a lightness directed to where he was most serious. But she was operating by guesswork, by intuition, and these were not Odette's strengths.

There was a noise.

Bliss: again, the gurgling, choking laugh.

And then Odette, sitting on the red plastic chair by Leo's bed, with seven other beds arranged at jaunty angles around the ward to make it seem less institutional, carrying their burden of the old and the dying, mouths hopelessly dentureless, hair awry, pyjamas done up wrong, tubes and drips ascending and descending, bringing in sustenance and taking away the products of decay, Odette had her vision. It was a vision that she knew would stay with her for the rest of her life, its clarity making it simple to compare it with reality, ticking off the points of resemblance, smiling over the details that had not proved accurate. It was a vision of a house in the country, not grand, not even picturesque, but perfect in its way; of a garden thick with flowers, but planted also with useful fruits and herbs, redcurrants bright as arterial blood, sweet basil, rosemary, the never-fruiting lemon tree. And children were in the garden, and Leo playing horsey, one, two, three on his narrow back, all scrambling, all crying for their turn, and Leo, with still something of that choked, hospital laugh, begging for mercy. And again, more years flying and new children, two, blond as angels, and the little girl asking why granddad laughs so funny. And then forward again to the end of laughing, with the garden overgrown, and the ghosts of the children and of Leo playing horsey between the trees, and of her, sitting in a deck chair, in a straw hat, but the cold coming on, and sleeping.

And Leo was sleeping now. She bent over the bed and kissed his swollen eyelids as softly as she could, but still his breathing paused for a second, and his face relaxed beneath the pain, and she knew that he knew.

SIXTEEN

Ghostly Limbs

Andrew had a habit of mumbling as he typed.

'Flyleaves mounted on free endpapers . . . occasional handling creases (predominantly marginal) . . . pale offsetting on versos.'

Alice smiled. Andrew sensed it and looked up over the top of his computer monitor.

'Sorry,' he said. 'Am I . . . doing that thing again?'

'It doesn't matter. I like it as long as I'm not trying to concentrate, or work, or anything.'

'Ah. It's just that I've got to get this exactly right. I know you always find it faintly amusing whenever I get serious about work, but this is all I've got. It's okay for people like . . .' Alice thought that he was going to say 'you', but he shied away from it. 'People like them.' Andrew gave a circular wave of his head taking in most of the room, but seeming to concentrate itself in the direction of Ophelia and Clerihew. 'Nothing ever really goes wrong for you if you're posh enough. There's always a safety net, always the next good thing that'll come along. But if I fuck up here, then what can I do?'

Mentally, Alice and Andrew took the well-travelled bookshop path to Hampstead, Golders Green, Stoke-on-Trent, Hull, Inverness, Stockholm and Reykjavik.

'And after the various um debacles – the Leo performance at the drinks and me calling Clerihew a cunt . . .'

'Wasn't it a fuck?'

'Whatever . . . well, you get my point: I need a gold star
for this one. Anyway,' he continued in his best pompous
voice, 'people'll still be reading this catalogue in fifty years'
time. Can't have any split infinitives or misdescriptions. Not
after all the fuss.' He smiled at Alice and she grinned back.

'They won't really, will they?' she asked.

'It's never properly sunk in with you, has it, Alice? I mean
just how important this all is. I don't only mean to me, or
the Book Department, or to Enderby's as a whole, I mean,
well, *historically*. A new Audubon only crops up once in a
blue moon. We could be looking at ten million here.'

'I do know, it's more that I don't really care. Not about
the money, anyway.'

'Don't let Oakley hear you talking like that. But I
shouldn't have mentioned the money. I agree that's not the
important thing. It's the object itself – its rarity, its beauty.
And beyond that, it's a sort of symbol for America, for an
idea that America has about itself. Savage, free, untamed.
That kind of bullshit.'

'Shame they wiped out so many of them. The passenger
pigeon, the prairie hen, the great auk, the Carolina . . .'

'That's another reason it's so precious. It's a record of all
that's gone. And then there's John James Audubon himself.
As long as you don't look too closely he seems like the very
model of a brave frontiersman, travelling through the
wilderness . . .'

'Shooting things.'

'I thought you liked all that? Death transfigures life into
art, I believe you once said.'

They looked at each other again. As so often in their
conversations lately, they seemed to be on the verge of

something . . . Just friendship, he told himself. A better friendship. That was all.

'I think I'm different now.'

Andrew returned his gaze to the computer. The catalogue was almost finished. He had one or two corrections to make on the proofs, and then it would be away to the Reprographic Unit, who would do whatever it was that they did (no one seemed to know) and then, in turn, send it out to be printed. It was a joy to lose himself in the detail, casting the fine mesh of scholarship over these planes of colour, wider than his outstretched arms. He'd relished everything from checking the watermarks (J Whatman, with dates from 1827 to 1838) to finding the precise terms to cover the condition of each print. Plate 366, for example, had 'some light spotting, minor marginal soiling, title lightly rubbed and a few small ink flecks on the blank area of the image'.

And yet, another part of his mind knew that this description completely missed the point of Audubon's design for the Iceland, or Ger Falcon: the drama of the male, its ghostly paleness flecked with black, hurtling down to ravish the prone, yet still feisty female; the flashing white and black of their feathers, electric against the glowering skies behind. And how did 'colours very fresh, palest spotting in lower margin' come close to the glorious vulgarity of plate 431, the American Flamingo, so like one of those prematurely tall schoolgirls in its gawky elegance? The flamingo had taken him back to the visit to the park with Alice and he found, to his astonishment, a tear in the corner of his eye.

And he knew that Alice had made a sacrifice for him.

It was two weeks prior to this, on the Monday following her trip to the country, that she had marched in to Oakley's office. It was the way she swung the door shut behind her that made people take notice: not a slam, no, not quite a slam, but more than a clunk. About, Andrew calculated, what you'd get if you dropped a large dictionary – say one of the two volumes of the *Shorter Oxford*, or the more compact, but massier *Collins* – from three feet on to a wooden desk. Andrew had no idea what was going on: Alice had dumped her bag, smiled a 'good morning', and gone straight to Oakley.

'What was that all about?' he asked when she reappeared ten minutes later.

'I had to tell Mr Oakley about my weekend with Edward Lynden.'

'I see; so he's your big confidante now, is he?' It was only a tease, but Andrew did genuinely feel uncomfortable. They hadn't had the chance to talk over the events of the weekend themselves yet.

'Not confidante, no, I wouldn't say confidante.' Andrew noticed a hardness in Alice's soft brown eyes that he hadn't seen before. Not a cruel hardness, but more a resolve, a determination. He found it ever so slightly arousing. 'It was business,' she continued, unaware of her effect on Andrew. 'But look, we're talking nonsense and you haven't told me about Leo yet.'

And so Andrew told Alice everything he knew, which helped to fill out the sketchy account he had given her the day before when he had called her to get Odette's number. Alice still hadn't spoken to Odette, who was immovably lodged beside Leo. Alice, of course, wanted to know about Leo, and even more so about Leo and Odette, but she was also pleased that her conversation with Oakley had slipped down the agenda.

'Oh, Alice,' Oakley had said when she burst into his office, 'please sit . . .' thump went the door '. . . down.'

'Andrew does the catalogue or I resign right now. And if

I resign, then my guess is that Lynden will pull out of the sale.'

She didn't need to add that without that sale then not only would he lose whatever credibility he might have with the Americans, but the very future of Enderby's itself would be thrown into doubt.

'This is . . . all . . . I'm not used to people . . .' Oakley was trying to crank up his indignation levels, and failing. His bully's confidence always collapsed when confronted with resistance, and he knew that Alice had the beating of him. For now.

'I've no idea what kind of manoeuvring there's been,' Alice said, ignoring Oakley's guppy-like flapping and gulping, 'and I don't care. Nor do I want to organise the auction: you can throw that scrap to Ophelia and Cedric, if you like. But Andrew must do the catalogue. It's fair, and it's for the best.'

Alice had never before acted with such purpose, clarity and courage. The world had become a strange and complicated place. Odette and Leo, the Dead Boy, Edward Lynden – she couldn't begin to arrange her thoughts or compose a plan of action; but as for the ridiculous idea that Clerihew and Ophelia should just walk in and garner the glory for the Audubon, well no, that she could and would stop. She didn't know quite what she was going to say when she first marched into Oakley's office, nor even did she know what tone she would adopt. She had considered simply resigning, but that would have sacrificed her one bargaining chip without gaining anything in return. She was secretly thrilled with what had emerged.

Oakley carried on blathering: 'We . . . I had no intention of . . . I was told that Mr Lynden had requested that you and Andrew be replaced. I was merely . . .'

'Misinformed.'

'Ah.' Oakley calculated. He had promised the catalogue to Clerihew and the organisation side to Ophelia. He could split things up, keep everybody happy. 'You can all work together on this,' he said, trying desperately to sound authoritative. 'You organise the sale with Ophelia, and Cedric can do the catalogue.' Surely that would keep the girl quiet. She looked as if she might be on the verge of . . .

'Are you deaf? I said I don't care about my involvement. In fact, given the choice, I'd rather have nothing to do with it. Andrew's been committed to this project from the beginning, and he should see it through.'

In the end, Oakley agreed; Oakley had to agree: Andrew, whom he hated and feared with a burning, churning passion of the sort that all insecure managers feel for those below them capable of doing their job better than they themselves, would do the catalogue, with Ophelia and Cedric, *his* protégés, doing the sale.

And Alice mollified, until she could be dealt with effectively.

Andrew was, of course, incandescent when he finally managed to eke out of Alice at least part of what had happened. Two factors prevented him from mashing Clerihew's face into the chromium desk fan he'd insisted upon to help drive away the sheen of moisture that habitually coated his visible parts. The first was the relief he felt at still being in on the project, still doing the cataloguing job he loved. The sale itself was of only passing interest to him, and he wouldn't have to have much contact with the evil duo. The other was Alice's evident lack of concern: she clearly didn't mind being thrown off the case. Seemed relieved, if anything. And there was always, as a third and supplementary deterrent, the faint possibility that Clerihew's boast about being a black belt in karate might actually be true. Andrew pictured himself pinned to the floor, one arm hanging loose and broken, as Clerihew, kneeling on his back, screamed: 'Clerihew Emperor of the World – say it! *say it!'*

Alice didn't tell Andrew about Grace. She just said, 'It's over. It never really got going, and now it's over.'

Andrew would have been happier if he hadn't detected an aftertaste of regret in her words.

On the Friday lunchtime they had gone together to see Leo in hospital. On the way out Andrew told Pam they were going to a meeting, and might well be out for a couple of hours, which ought to cover them in case Oakley came a-sniffing.

On the ward, Alice felt a wave of revulsion when she saw his face. If anything it was more grotesque now, almost a week after the attack. The swelling was still there, but new colours had been added to the shades of purple. He looked, as Andrew said, like a maniac had taken a sledge-hammer to a fruit stall.

'At least I don't wear glasses, you specky fuck,' said Leo in return, his voice now fully audible, but still strange, as if he were being accompanied by a distant kazoo.

Odette was sitting by the bed reading a newspaper when they came in. She and Alice embraced warmly, and kissed on the lips, which made Andrew say, 'Steady on, girls, we don't want Leo bursting his stitches.'

Odette pulled away laughing and said, 'He hasn't got any stitches *down there*.' After a second of mildly shocked silence, they all laughed, and any awkwardness about the Odette-Leo situation dissolved before it had the chance to form.

The timing of the visit was fortuitous: Leo was scheduled to be released that afternoon. Alice and Andrew went down to the grim little canteen to wait for them.

'Jesus,' said Andrew, 'the people down here look sicker than the ones up in bed.'

It was true. The bleak, vinyl-coated world of the hospital canteen was home to as ragged and desperate a collection of souls as Alice had ever seen. Mainly pensioners, their faces folded in on themselves, eyes dull as old ivory. Each seemed to carry a halo of pain and misery. One man, in particular, held a grisly fascination for Alice. He was neat and dapper in his dress, wearing a check suit with a clean blue shirt and a golf-club tie. His hair was white and smartly cut. But something terrible had happened to his face. He was ordinary, no, not ordinary, handsome, from the eyes down to the jaw, but then everything changed. In place of a lower jaw, the man had an expanse of pink, buttocky flesh, its shape and texture completely alien to the rest of the face. It was boneless, formless; nightmarish and comic at the same time. Alice speculated on what might have happened. The best she could come up with was cancer affecting the lower jaw. An amputation. A grafting of flesh from some other part of the body.

She thought of her father, and was ashamed of the revulsion she felt for the old man with his destroyed face. She thought she remembered her father saying something about the only thing that stopped science from being barbaric was love. Without love, the cold eye of the scientist could only destroy. Had he said it in a dream, or was it only something she had imagined, the kind of words she wanted him to think?

'This coffee tastes of fish,' said Andrew.

Alice was still pale from seeing Leo. 'It must hurt,' she said.

'Well, it's an affront to the taste buds, but I wouldn't say . . . oh, you mean Leo. Yes. Hurt like fuck almighty. Pain's a funny thing.'

'What do you mean?'

'Well, when you're in the middle of it, it's all that you

239

are. The way you live in your mouth when your teeth are bad. I remember as a kid I had a perforated eardrum, and for a week I had a pain so sickening, if someone had said look, here's a tablet, take it and you'll be dead and the pain will go, I'd have bitten their hand off. And after it had gone, I mean *minutes* after, not just now, years after, there was nothing of it left, just the words I used to describe it. You see, you can't have a memory of a pain, because a memory means calling something back, experiencing it again, and that would mean having the pain all over again. Sorry, I'm raving.'

'It's okay; hardly anyone's staring.'

Encouraged, Andrew went on: 'It's one of the reasons I've always been obsessed with phantom limbs, you know, when a fellow has his leg cut off, say in a saw mill, or blown off by a landmine, or . . .'

'Yes, I get the picture.'

'And afterwards, when it's been sewn up, they still feel the bit below the stump, still often feel the pain. Their toes might still hurt, even though they're in a landfill in Newcastle, and the bloke's in bed in Manchester.'

'I've heard of it. Sounds horrid.'

Andrew looked at her. He rearranged his features from frivolous to profound. Alice knew that something was coming.

'Emotional . . . pain, anguish, is a bit like the phantom limb thing. Because it exists as pure thought, unmediated by the body, you can summon it back, assuming it ever goes. Fully back, so it's not the memory of a pain, but the pain itself. The thing that hurt you is there like the ghost of the leg you lost. Sorry, is this coming out as comic? I don't think it was meant to be.'

'No. I know exactly what you mean.'

The Dead Boy was her phantom limb, the thing there

240

but not there, an imaginary cause of real pain. His meaning couldn't have been more plain.

'Do you think the fish here tastes of coffee? Maybe that's why everyone looks so ill.'

'The people with phantom limbs . . . does it go away after a while? Is there a way of *making* it go away?'

Andrew looked at Alice, who was staring down into a plastic cup of grey hot chocolate, with a scum on the top the colour of old chewing gum. The harsh strip-lighting emphasised the light and the dark in her face, and made her look . . . vulnerable, was it? Yes, like a face peering out of an old photograph, a match girl or a Victorian child prostitute.

Andrew couldn't remember what happened to the ghost limbs, but he knew what he had to say. 'You have to teach the mind that they're not real. The more you look at the place where the leg isn't, the more your mind comes to accept it. It learns that the body is different now, has a new shape. Stare long enough at the phantom, and it disappears.'

Did Andrew really believe that? It went against one of his most dearly held principles; that the best way to deal with a problem was to ignore it until it went away. If that failed, then you could always try running. He'd dubbed this option 'Acapulco', when he and his friend Marc Dibnah decided that they should flee there to escape the Biology mock 'A' level they were dreading. But it now seemed to him that Alice had some dragons to slay, and running away from a dragon was liable to lead to a burnt arse, at the very least.

'Here they come,' said Alice, looking up.

They drove back to the Docklands in high spirits. Leo kept them amused with stories about the other patients, interspersed with withering attacks on the Merdemobile, which, by some miracle, he had never before experienced in the flesh.

241

'Smells like a fucking aardvark farted in here, died from the stench, and then slowly decayed down to a stew in the back. You should trade up to a chemical toilet. And what is this fabric? It's like the fuzz off a camel's cunt . . . You know, even when it was new this was the car they gave to the sales rep that couldn't meet his quota of surgical supports? If I was a pigeon I'd feel demeaned if I shat on this car. And what's this back here? Pickled onion flavour Monster Munch? Jesus, man, even when I was a kid I knew they were bad mojo. I'm telling you, you're a no-snog zone for a week after a bag of those. But then if this car's your passion wagon then that's not really an issue, is it? I mean what kind of girl's gonna let you within sniffing range if you turn up in this to take her to *The Marriage of Figaro*?'

Andrew let his friend get away with it. He sensed that the stream of invective was the product both of the joy Leo felt on being alive and of the pent-up frustration of a week in hospital-issue pyjamas. And then, he mused, if the Audubon sale went well, there was always the prospect of Crumlish's old job, and the ten thousand pounds a year salary hike that went with it, and that would mean a new car, perhaps something snazzy like a 1987 Ford Fiesta . . . yeah, that'd shut them up, shut them up *good*.

'You're quiet, Alice,' said Odette.

'Am I? Well, it seemed that Leo was doing a whole carful of talking.'

But that wasn't why Alice was quiet. She was quiet because she was thinking about her phantom limb.

The two weeks that followed were exciting ones for Andrew and, externally at least, dull ones for Alice, as she kept things ticking over on the non-Audubon side. The top management, from Parry Brooksbank on up, kept popping down to see the 'Audubon team', which usually meant Clerihew and Ophelia, with Andrew kept on the periphery. Although on the outside things were dull, things were happening inside Alice. She'd known since the visit to the hospital canteen what she would do, but she had to wait until some pre-ordained sequence of internal movement, an almost mechanical falling into place had occurred. Lynden's telephone call was only the last of these events, the final piece of the clockwork mechanism.

She hadn't spoken to him since the weekend, but when she picked up the phone she knew as soon as she heard the hesitation that it must be Lynden.

'Alice, I . . . I had to talk to you.'

'Edward. I thought I made it clear . . .' No, she thought, 'made it clear' was too pompous, too unkind. 'I don't think this is a good idea, for either of us.'

'Please. All I want is the chance to explain. If you'll just listen . . . maybe you can understand. Maybe even forgive me. I can't bear the thought of losing you without a struggle.'

'You never had me.'

Lynden abandoned the tone of pleading: 'Don't twist my words,' he said, commandingly. But then, with an effort that Alice could feel, he controlled himself again. There was desperation now in his voice. 'Look, I'm coming up for the sale next week. Let me see you alone for just a few minutes. You must let me: to know all is to forgive all.'

'I've already forgiven you. No, I mean there's nothing really to forgive. I don't really care about you sleeping with Grace. I find it baffling, I admit, but not hurtful. Why should I?'

'I don't believe you. You do find it hurtful, that's why you left, that's why you won't speak to me. And I know it hurts you because it hurts me. And the reason it hurts me is because . . . because I love you.'

Alice froze. The telephone very nearly dropped from her

243

hand. And then came a rush of ideas, images, impressions. She saw his savage face melting into something younger and softer. Her fury evaporated, replaced by sadness, by sympathy, by hope. A whole new life paraded before her: a life of elegance and ease, and even excitement in the great Cave of Ice. But then she saw Grace waiting in the shadows, shadows she made herself in that house without shadows.

'But, Edward . . . this isn't the . . . time. What about Grace? Tell me about Grace?'

'I must tell you face to face. Let me see you before the sale next week. Please. I . . . beg you.'

Alice paused for a moment. The images in her mind still possessed her, and continued to change. Lynden's face softened yet more, became youthful, and altered in other more subtle ways. As she spoke the transformation became complete:

'Yes,' she said, 'I'll see you,' and the face of Lynden became wholly and completely the face of the Dead Boy.

SEVENTEEN

The Hand that Rocked the Cradle

This time Alice hadn't paused for a moment before the block. It may have helped that it was so bitterly cold, and the rain was taking on the dense, heavy quality of sleet. Alice didn't possess a single waterproof garment and already the chill rain had soaked through her cheap overcoat and was working hard at the frayed cardigan within. It was with something close to relief that she plunged into the pissy stench of the stairwell (the lift wasn't working) and wound her way up to the fourth floor. The walls of the stairway were gashed with red paint, and crude murals: phalluses reared at her like serpents; someone had laboriously etched 'we no where you live' into the concrete with a fine blade. Alice came out into the murk and wet of the day and walked carefully along the row of flats. Some had neatly painted doors and clean curtains, others were crudely boarded; some had great steel plates keeping out the unwanted. A dog barked desperately in one of the flats, but more, Alice thought, with a yearning to escape than a desire to kill.

As she pressed the bell of number 427, she still didn't know what she was going to say. But she did know that she wasn't going to lie.

She had telephoned the woman on the Friday evening ('don't dare spend all night on that phone, young lady,' yelled Kitty, 'there's a call coming through to me from very far away; very far away *indeed*'), saying that she wanted to talk about Matija. How strange the name had sounded in her own ears: she had only ever thought of him as the Dead Boy, never as Matija Abdic, the name on a slip of paper passed to her by Odette. Usually the very name of the beloved takes on an enchantment, becomes filled with magical power. But no matter how hard she stared at the letters, or spoke them aloud to herself, Alice couldn't alchemise Matija: it was too harsh, too jagged. It could never truly be the name of the person she had seen. And so he would always be, to her, the Dead Boy. The woman she spoke to sounded reserved, but not unfriendly. Did she think that she was an ex-girlfriend? Or some official? It was agreed, painlessly, that Alice should come to the flat at four o'clock on the Saturday afternoon.

She expected the door to be opened an inch, held by chains, by fear perhaps, then closed again in her face. Instead, after a startlingly short wait, it was thrown back, and a thin, proud, fierce-looking woman of perhaps seventy years stood before her.

'And you are Alice who phoned,' she said, not a question but a statement, made in heavily accented but otherwise clear English. Alice liked her immediately. She had not the refugee's cowering fear, but seemed indomitable. She could see only dimly the Dead Boy's beauty in her severe features, but in this woman she knew his erect posture, his self-possession. 'You are cold and wet. England, England, England: always cold and wet.' Leading Alice through the kitchen she added, 'You will see that my English is quite good, because in former times it was my subject I taught at school.'

Ten minutes later they were sitting in the small living room, drinking tea. The woman sat as rigidly as she stood, with a china teacup perched on her knee. The furniture in the room was cheap, and Alice feared that she might drop through the bottom of the low, wide chair she occupied. But everything was clean and tidy, almost obsessively so. There were pictures everywhere: blurred snapshots of children on the beach; rigidly posed adults in Sunday best. And yes, there in the corner, a photograph of him: a boy of twelve or thirteen, his beauty still embryonic. He stood, as thin as a wraith, in a pair of tiny, stripey swimming trunks. His black hair sat comically on his head, like a drunk's hat. Alice found herself smiling, but then had to look away before the tears came.

'Tell me please, Alice – am I correct to remember Alice is your name?' said the woman. 'Yes, yes, what is your interest in my grandson?'

Grandson. Of course. This woman was far too old to be the Dead Boy's mother. What could have happened to the mother?

'I am so sorry to disturb you, Mrs Abdic, but . . . I appreciate this sounds strange, but I feel that I know your grandson very well.'

'He did not have any friends. He was a lonely boy. He never mentioned any Alice to me. But I am an old lady and he might not have talked to me of these things.'

'I should explain that I did not meet Matija. Or I mean that I met him only once. On the day that he . . . was killed.'

'This is becoming a mystery.'

Yes, a mystery. It had always been a mystery. Alice closed her eyes for a moment, summoning the nerve and resilience, as well as the words, to continue.

'You're going to think I'm mad, but I saw your grandson just a moment before the car hit him.' The moment came to her again, vivid in the tidy living room of the old woman. The whole seven seconds of their affair. The first look; the glance towards the approaching car, the return; the smile; the terrifying, comic explosion of arms and legs, almost as if some huge demon were trying to burst out from within his body; the thud, like a drum beating, which seemed to follow the impact by an age; the softer noise as the body, already a thing and not a human being, just so much fleshy rubbish, fell to earth behind the car. 'And in that moment, he looked at me, and from that moment everything changed for me. I felt that we had exchanged something, that we had communicated in some way. I'm sorry this is very inarticulate . . .'

The woman smiled. 'That is fine. The language of the heart is something different to the language in the mouth.' It sounded to Alice like a proverb translated. 'And I know that my Matija had a special look. He learned it a long time ago, when he was too young to have seen the things that he had seen.'

'Those must have been terrible times.'

'There were bad times for us. His mother, you know, was killed. And his father. It was why he had only me, and I had only him. And doing what he did, at his age, could only make you special. Special in the eyes. But you did not finish what you were saying.'

'Oh, yes.' Alice felt suddenly trivial and small. Compared to the horrors that her Dead Boy and this woman had lived through, her own experiences seemed insubstantial, weightless, banal. 'Well,' she continued, trying to find a way to express herself that acknowledged the relative insignificance of what she had undergone, and yet gave true weight to its impact on her, 'since then, I've been . . . I can only say *possessed* by your grandson. I can't . . . do anything . . . Be anything. And it's very hard. For me.'

'And what is it you want from *me*?' The woman's tone was neutral. There was no trace of wariness, but nor was there a sense that she was prepared to give Alice the magic word, the secret potion or spell that would set her free.

'I thought that by knowing, by understanding, who he was, I might be able . . . to see clearly again.'

'To see clearly again. How oddly you sometimes express yourself.' She paused and looked towards, but not through, the window. 'But,' she said finally, 'I can tell you the story of my Matija.'

The story ran, at least to begin with, backwards. Difficult times in London; trouble at school; a sensitive boy bullied. Neighbours who ignored them, or sneered, or banged on the door in the night and put vile things through the letterbox. And then back to the war and escaping after the killings.

The woman's tone was matter-of-fact, clear, objective. Her slight awkwardness suggested both that she had not told the story before and that she was keen to tell it, and to get it right. But when it came to the description of what had happened in their town, the things that had made Matija special in the eyes, her words took on an intensity and passion that could only come through pure feeling: rage, anguish, horror.

But the woman's words were not the words that she remembered. She did not, in fact, remember any words at all. What she remembered were images, some moving, some still, and to those she supplied her own commentary.

EIGHTEEN

The Dead Boy

The idea had come from Sarajevo. Its logic was pure; its psychology sound. Executed with courage, tenacity and will, it would never fail. It was the simple perfection of the scheme that attracted: the way that each step followed inevitably on from the next, like a scientific proof. If only socialism had been as clear, as true, as sure.

It came from Sarajevo, but still lacked something. The Sarajevo system had begun with the men: the domesticated type out buying bread, sausage, if there was any, or the morning newspaper, or a toy. But the women eventually learnt not to go to their husbands, dying in the sun. There would be children to look after. Recklessness in these circumstances was selfishness. One was just one, and often none at all, as the men kept to the safe places. So they had switched to the women for the first, the maiming shot. What Slav, Orthodox, Catholic, or Muslim would not go to his woman, lying writhing in the street, a bullet in her thigh, or shoulder? 'No, no,' they would cry, craning back across the cobbles, to the dim shapes crouching beyond, 'please don't come, please don't come.' But of course they would come, and one would become two. And, naturally, two – a refinement was to also avoid killing the husband with the first shot – was an even bigger draw than one. Which brother, or son, or uncle, or friend could leave two they loved dying out on the cobbles, blood working its way slowly, methodically between the stones? And so two had a very good chance of becoming three. Perhaps then evening would come, and three would still be three.

When the idea reached Mostar it was becoming a little stale. And the hate of Mostar, the hatred of Croat for Muslim and Muslim for Croat, craved piquancy just as much as the other hatreds to the West and North and East.

The Mostar variation used, of course, a child. Begin with a child; take the mother; take the father. *Always* at least three, easy as shooting pigs in a yard. And the child would still be there, bleating like a lamb to draw more lions. Skill and care were needed with the child. An adult shot in the gut could live for three hours. *Could,* but only a fool would risk it. Thigh or shoulder, much safer. And no one runs away when they are shot in the thigh or the shoulder. You lie down and you cry like a baby and eventually you die from shock and blood loss. But a child shot in the thigh or the shoulder might die very quickly. Ten minutes. Not long enough. True, you might pick someone up making a dash just to see, but the percentages weren't in it. What you wanted was a shot to the ankle. Asking a lot at a thousand yards. Asking too much, many said. Why are we making sparks, referring to the microsecond of brilliance when the bullet hit the cobble, said one wit, when we should be making widows? But it was an investment, said others. One makes two makes three makes four makes five. Capitalism! Remember, we're capitalists now! Speculate to accumulate!

Training was thought to be the key, but that thought was wrong. You could train a farmer, or a man who worked a lathe, to be a good shot. It took a month, and used up a lot

251

of bullets, but at the end of that month, he could hit a cow's head set up on a stake three hundred yards away seven times out of ten. But an ankle? A *child's* ankle? A child's ankle at a thousand yards? Training couldn't do that. Something inside made the man or the boy who could do that. Something that made him calm and still, and able to feel the beauty of the moment, and so gentle with his touch that he could move the hair from the face of his sleeping lover without waking her.

The boys. It was always the boys. They would go to the streets, to the junctions that they knew were dangerous, overlooked by the ugly high tower blocks, or dark, impenetrable tenements. And they would run. The joy of it was to hear the pretty sound of the bullet as it glanced off the road behind them. They knew that it would mean a twisted ear from their mothers. Worse, much worse, from their fathers; those that had them still. A thick leather belt, and how many cracks on the bare arse? Five? Yeah, in your dreams. Ten? If you're lucky. And there was always a busybody to tell. Some old bitch in black, or a kid sister, trying to buy herself a favour, or the fucking old station master, with nothing better to do now there were no trams.

He had new trainers. They'd come from Germany. He had an uncle there and God knows how, but a parcel had got through. Trainers had always been totemic in Mostar. Only the best athletes, on the books of one of the state athletics bodies, when such things still existed, would have decent trainers. Even the crap ones made in East Germany or Czechoslovakia, from plastic, and not even good plastic, but shitty plastic, lumpy and sweaty, were valued here, in poor Mostar. But oh, a pair of Adidas, or Nike, or Puma! Even the simple recitation of the names was enough to get a shudder, like a milting stickleback down in the Neretva, from any boy. And that was before the fighting. Now boys wore their brother's old shoes, or their father's, or sometimes no shoes at all.

If truth were told he hadn't liked the trainers. They were too flashy: they tried too hard. Too many colours, too many stripes. The sole had a pointlessly thick heel of sponge for extra bounce. He liked a simpler shoe, one that just said, yeah, I can run, not look at me, I cost more than you earn in a month. But the other boys didn't care about that. They all wanted to touch them, smell them, even taste them. One said he'd let him feel his sister's tits in exchange for a go. Others offered food, cigarettes, vodka. But he was thirteen and didn't smoke and didn't drink and still thought (but only just) that there was something effeminate about wanting to be near girls and kissing them and all the rest of it.

It was to quieten the other boys down that he agreed to do it. The traffic lights were long dead: the power cut off, the lights shot out for practice. But they provided a focus for sport. Run the lights, sixty metres, one side to the other. Ten seconds, perhaps, for a quick boy, with time to gather speed in the cover of the eastern approach.

The block that overlooked it from across the river was pitted with shell marks and bullet holes. Its windows were almost all gone on this side. But it was where the best of them lay and waited. How many? Three or four marksmen, perhaps, with their scoped, single-shot sniper rifles. Another twenty or thirty in support, casually sitting around and smoking, playing cards, listening to the radio, their Kalashnikovs and heavy machine guns balanced against the walls and concrete pillars. A handful of families still lived in the rooms facing away from the river.

Midday, they thought, was a good time to do it. A proper challenge. The sun was high and fierce, the shadows short.

253

There were four of them. One of the other boys made him take a gulp from a bottle of aquavit. Another stuck a useless cigarette behind his ear, for later. He hadn't worn the trainers on the walk there, just his old boots. Now he pulled them on, drawing the intricately tied laces tight. And he had to admit they felt good. Soft, and yet they held the foot properly, supported the arch. He couldn't hear what the others were saying. He was quite calm, but knew he would never do this again. He had grown out of the game. Whatever his father said, it would soon be time to take a place in the line, defending his family, his people.

A standing start. He had always been fast out of the blocks. It might add a second to the time, but what was a second? He squatted down, to some jeers: look at him, you'd think it was the Olympics. Those trainers have gone to his head. Joining in the joke, he asked for a starting pistol, for one of the boys to shout bang.

Bang.

There were people around, further down the street. At the shout and the laughter they looked. Madness. But boys will be boys. And look at that one run across the junction, through the old lights. Long legged, starting low, now growing. Good-looking boy, too. And see those shoes of his. Cost a pretty penny.

He was flying now. Five metres. Ten. Fifteen. He took his first breath. Almost into the shelter of the buildings there.

It wasn't the shout of 'bang' that made the sniper concentrate. He'd been concentrating all the time. He was dry, though the men around him sweated in the heat. His pattern was five minutes looking through the sight, five minutes gazing above it, for a wider view.

The trainers caught his eye.

The boy was a little old for the technique. He thought

254

about nailing him in the chest. Or a head shot. The deliberation cost him two seconds. No, those trainers were too tempting. He tracked the runner, and smoothly moved the cross hairs down the slender torso, down the moving line of the thigh to the knee; down further to the ankle. A breath. Squeeze. A breath. Look over the sight.

He didn't hear the shot. The shooter was too far away. At first he thought, with a curse, that he'd tripped, that something had caught his foot. He was spread-eagled on the road, looking and feeling ungainly. The boys would laugh, spoiling everything. He tried to get up, but his leg wouldn't move. And then, after a heartbeat, the pain. He looked down. He saw that his trainer had come off. Wildly, he searched around, and was relieved to see it a metre away. Thank God. He looked back to his foot. It was all wrong. The bottom of his trouser leg was bloody and torn. His mother would kill him for that. They were his best jeans. And his foot, his ankle. Just a mess. Flappy bits of skin. Some jagged white bone, so white, so clean. He tried to drag himself towards the buildings, ten metres away. He was so heavy, so tired. And it hurt so much. And then the unmistakable sound of a bullet hitting the road centimetres in front of his face. Lie still, it said. He lay still.

It was very quiet now. He could hear the fast-flowing river, almost pick out the sounds of individual eddies and little cataracts. He'd played there so often. They all had. Croat kids, Serb kids, Muslim kids. Just kids, then. No one knew or cared what you were. What counted was who dared swim across, or who could piss furthest into the stream.

How long did he lie there? His perception of time kept stretching and contracting, so it could have been days or seconds. The road was warm against his face, but his body felt cold. There was a quick pattering of feet. One of his friends was beside him, lying flat. Insane courage, he thought. Can you move? the boy asked. No. Go away. They'll kill you. Come on, try. Go away, please go away. They've gone for your family. Come on, please try. I can't. Go away. The other boy was crying. Run now. Before they shoot you. But he knew it was already too late; the surprising thing was that they hadn't nailed him already. And then the boy was away, scampering, zigzagging furiously. Waste of time. They'd be up there in the flats, laughing about it, three scopes on him. More bait. But no. He was safe. Why?

Perhaps, he thought, the war is over. He remembered his father telling him about when the Herzegovina Croats had tried to get more independence back in the early eighties under Tito. The Marshal, he'd said, came down and knocked heads together. Compromised with those who were prepared to compromise, chucked out the ones who weren't. That was his way. That was how Yugoslavia had stayed together, no fighting, no real trouble. Compromise, allow self-determination and autonomy within the federal structure, but back it up with an iron fist. But the Marshal was dead. And the world he made, putting two fingers up to East and West, was dead with him.

No one could stop his mother. She ran all the way from their flat to the junction. A mile, in ill-fitting sandals and her housework clothes. She was always so careful about how she looked when she went out. He was proud of her. Some of the boys said they thought she wasn't bad for an old lady. He had a fight with one boy who said he'd fuck her if she asked nicely and gave him cake. She ran, and she lost one of the sandals, and so when she reached him she also had one bare foot. She hunched her body over him, protecting him from the sun, from the bullets, from the war.

They all belonged to the marksman who tagged the first one: that was the rule. Sure, if things got hairy, or if circumstances demanded it, then anyone could join in, but the basic law was that they were yours. He'd let the other kid go because he wanted the family there. Could there also have been something in him that admired the courage of the little one, so scrawny, yet prepared to dash out like that, right under his nose? Or did he know him, from before? No. Nothing cluttered his thinking. He was pure, pellucid.

The bullet entered the mother at the collarbone. It travelled down through her body, through heart, lungs, intestine, liver, bladder; slowed and stopped somewhere near the base of her spine. She was dead before her full weight landed on her son.

His father got there minutes later, with two of his friends from the factory. He was a strong man, broad across the chest. He'd refused to fight. He blamed the trouble on the local bigwigs who wanted to grab as much power as they could from the crumbling wreck of Yugoslavia. They were all the same: all crooks and con men. He wouldn't join the jackals in tearing apart the carcass. They'd tried to bully and scare him into joining the militia, even threatened his family. He'd nearly killed one of them with a wrench, and after that they didn't bother him.

He could see that his wife was dead. The boy had rolled her off him and was stroking her hair. He knew that if he went out there he had very little chance of getting back. He was the real prize: a man, not that slender boy, or the woman. It was two o'clock now. Six hours till it was dark. The boy might be dead by then as well. He turned his back on the scene.

Ten minutes later he returned with the Lada. It belonged to a neighbour. He'd explained what the situation was and the neighbour handed him the keys without question. There was no point driving it out into the junction. If the sniper didn't get him, they'd machine gun it, or hit it with one of the 40mm anti-aircraft cannon they had up there. That'd make a mess of the Lada, hunk of crap that it was. Not even Yugoslav crap, but Russian crap.

He got the men to push it from the side street, building up enough momentum to reach the boy and the woman, with him running crouched behind it. There was a slight incline there, and it should be enough to keep the car moving. His plan was to grab the boy, staying behind the car, and carry on until they reached the other side of the street. The other men had told him, once, not to do it. He said he would, and that was that. They all knew that they'd do the same, in his situation, and he knew that he would have tried to talk them out of it.

He slipped the brake and they all pushed, eight of them now. Soon they were running flat out. A metre before the safety of the buildings gave way to the lethal space, they gave one last push. He tried to steer through the open door, but it was tricky with the car going so quickly. The last thing he wanted was to roll into the two figures, lying together, one dead, one alive. The police would call it a road accident and have him for dangerous driving.

It was going well. They were lined up just right. He'd only have a second to swoop and pick up the boy; but he was strong and the child weighed nothing. He didn't think about his wife, the woman he'd loved for twenty years, loved through the years of passion and fury, through the years of hardship and toil, with her nagging him about his dirty boots and getting drunk. He'd had his chances with other women, and yes, he'd wanted them, but the thought of her rage, and worse, her sorrow, had always stopped him, kept him clean. Well now her toil and fury and rage and sorrow were all gone. But the boy lived, and the boy must go on living.

He saw his father running, crouched low behind the boxy Russian car. He'd always known he would come, always knew he, the famous joker, would think of a trick. He's here, Mum, he said, he's here. He's come for us. It's all right now, it's all right. No need to cry.

The car was level, its bald tyres hissing on the tarmac. Almost without pausing, he scooped his great strong arm under the boy, and pulled him close. He didn't look at his wife. He looked straight ahead to where the buildings were casting their protecting shadows.

The boy's eyes changed when he saw that they were leaving his mother behind. Dad, he whispered. There's Mum. You've forgotten Mum. Don't leave Mum. The man looked at his son. No, of course he couldn't leave Mum behind. He turned and sprang back, still holding the boy. He reached out and grabbed his wife by the hand: he would run dragging her behind him. It would be hard but he could do it. As he began to move again, the last few inches of the car's boot slid beyond him. He would catch up with it in two strides. He stood taller to move more quickly, dragging the woman, carrying the boy, and the one waiting, the one calm and nerveless at the window, shot him in the head.

Of course no one would go out there now. No choice but to wait for darkness. But the men who had seen, and the men who had heard about, the incident decided that it would not happen again: not from that block of flats. The assault began two days later. They got some old artillery pieces from somewhere, Second World War stuff, from the look of it, with just a few shells, and half of them didn't explode. But it was enough to give them courage. A hundred men stormed the block. Twelve died on the flat ground before they reached it, falling and spinning like seeds from a great tree. Five more died as they worked their way up the floors, grenading each room. Any man taken alive was castrated and then disembowelled, left to froth and moan on the floor. They found two women and five children. They slit the children's throats in front of the mothers and then raped the women. It was joyless work; there was no frenzy. The hatred burned cold and deep. Every man there felt the justice of this. When they had finished, the women were given a bullet in the head out of charity for what had been done, and what might still be done.

NINETEEN

The Sadness of Everything

The old woman's story ended. It had taken an hour to tell, with several digressions on subjects ranging from how long to soak kidney beans to the way to make a child look happy as it lies grey and bloodless in a coffin, its throat slit, or its jaw shot away.

Alice closed her eyes. 'Thank you,' she said. 'So the boy, the one who was shot in the leg, that was Matija. And his mother and his father. To see them die like that. The horror of it is . . . beyond me.'

The woman froze suddenly.

'Shot? Are you mad?' She stood up. 'My Matija was never *shot*. There was no bullet swift enough to catch *him*.'

The burning passion that Alice had seen no longer looked like rage. It now seemed, perhaps it had always been, a kind of joy.

'I don't understand,' said Alice, cowering now, as the fierce old woman stood over her.

'Don't understand? Don't understand? My boy, my Matija, he was the best of all of them. He was the one they all wanted to be. He was the finest shooter. He was the most calm, the most serene. He killed more Croat dogs

261

than any man, and he was only a boy.'

Alice now was in shock. Her mind struggled clumsily to absorb and process what the woman was saying. She began to shiver. The flat was icy cold.

'But his parents – you said they were dead.'

'Dead, yes. A bomb from a gun, a mortar, if that is the right word, killed them in their bed on the first night of the war. That is why I sent my Matija to shoot the dogs. He had been the champion of his school, and had represented his region in the competitions at shooting.'

'And how did he escape?' Alice spoke, but the voice came from miles away. 'You said the Croats killed everyone in the building.'

'My boy was not working on that day. He was with me, buying bread. He carried my bags, always such a good boy. But I knew that it was all finished for us in this town. They exploded our beautiful bridge, do you know? It was our symbol of everything. And because his mother and father were dead it was possible for us to become legal refugees, not like these people who sneak here, that I see on the television, brown and yellow and all colours.'

Alice stood up. 'Thank you for your time,' she said, struggling to stay calm. 'I have to go now.'

The woman herself was now entirely normal again: the fervour and fierce pride had passed away.

'I hope it was of help to you to hear about my boy. It is my tragedy to be alive and alone now. Such a silly way to die, on a road like that. After all of the danger he lived in our town. Now it is quieter we could go back. But our bridge is still just stones in the water. I might go back myself. Just stones in the water.'

Alice couldn't look at the old woman. She wanted desperately to get out of there, out into the cold air of the street. But there was something she wanted to know.

'The other boy. The one Majita shot in the leg. The one with the bright training shoes. What happened to him.'

'Oh pah,' said the woman, angrily, making a dismissive gesture with her hand. Alice noticed for the first time that it was knotted and twisted with arthritis. 'What do I care for that boy? He lay there in the road behind the car, with the dog and the bitch, until it was dark, and then they took him away.'

'Was he still alive?'

'More alive than my poor Majita is.'

At the door she said 'Well, goodbye. If you would like to come again, please do. I enjoyed our talk.'

Alice couldn't bring herself to reply.

Alice didn't know where to go, but she knew it wasn't home. She walked blindly through the streets of Hackney, crowded now with people setting out on their Saturday night adventures. Pubs were filling up. Raucous laughter seemed to come at her from every angle.

He was a monster.

He was a monster.

He was a monster.

The boy she had loved so completely had killed women and children, just shot them dead. Dogs, the woman kept saying. Shot them like dogs. But where did people shoot dogs like that? She looked for a rise of feeling, for the overcoming of love by hate: she wanted to feel it surging in her, flushing out the contamination. Hadn't she sought this, or at least something like this? She had finally faced her ghost limb, seen it as a lie, as a phantasm, as a ghoul. Shouldn't everything now be all right?

But there was nothing. The stone she dropped into the well of her heart gave no reassuring plop. Street lights and gaudy neon signs leered at her. People flowed around her, speeding up and slowing down in time to some weird flaw in her consciousness. They weren't really there, they were the fictions of her senses, bundles of colours and forms conjured by the operation of neurones and chemical transmitters in her brain. No, there was nothing, nobody, just the swirl and flux of meaningless sensation.

And then a shape more solid than the others appeared to her. He was back. The Dead Boy was back. She didn't want him back: his presence, once so enthralling, was poison to her now. She tried to squeeze him out, to block his aura. But he came on. She saw his face, his eyes, his special eyes, the woman had said.

She saw the smile.

She saw the complete acceptance of death.

At the time, and ever since, she had thought that his acceptance was simply supreme grace, absolute courage, impossible coolness. But now she could see it as something else.

The boy that she had loved could never really have been a monster. He was a boy whose parents had died, and who was then told to kill by people older than he; people who wanted to use him as a weapon.

A lost boy.

And not, when she knew him, a boy anymore. A man. A man who could look back and see what he had done. Understand it as a man. See again the flash of sunlight on the trainers; see the thigh, the knee, the ankle, caught in his cross hairs. See the mother. See the father. See them, perhaps, every night. See them, as she saw him, whenever he closed his eyes. Saw them all, and was forced to live it again and again through the heartless glee of the grandmother. Might it not be the case, then, that he longed for an end of it? Yes, he said to death. My turn now.

All the time she had thought that he had looked into her

and felt the wonder as she felt it. But now, as she replayed it again, it seemed that he wasn't looking at her, wasn't smiling at her. He was already somewhere else. She was just a thing in his line of vision, as insubstantial to him as these shapes passing around and through her were insubstantial.

And at last the feeling came: She held on tight to a lamppost but it wasn't enough and she sank down to her knees, still hugging the wet metal trunk. She had cried a lot this year, but we never run out of tears, just the feelings that make them. People stopped. An old Rasta man touched her on the shoulder and asked if she was okay.

'Be careful of your purse, lady,' he said in heavy Jamaican. 'It's showing in your bag. This isn't a good place to be havin' a sit down.'

But all she could do was to shake her head and sob and sob and sob at the sadness of everything.

TWENTY

Preparations

At 9 a.m. on Friday 22nd of December a giant took hold of the Enderby building and gave it a violent shake, throwing everything and everyone within it into confusion, turmoil, and flurry. If our giant had peered through one of the narrow, leaded windows above the gothic doorway, he would have seen frantic figures scurrying through the public rooms, some carrying chairs, some with huge, ornate mirrors, others with unidentifiable decorations, elaborate clusters of foliage or *objets d'art*. Disorder ruled, and chaos was disorientingly immanent. Nobody seemed entirely sure of what was supposed to be done, except for the redoubtable Pamela, Pammy or Spam, who stood halfway up the grand stairway in the still magnificent reception hall, directing, cajoling, chastising, her soft bulk energised and thrumming with the joy of it all, like a jellyfish zapped by an electric eel. The hallway, really a magnificent atrium, and the public gallery next to it, called, on this one day of the year, the ballroom, were the twin focuses of the energy and one could just tell, if one squinted and used all of one's imagination, that something wonderful would be happening there.

The frenetic activity was not primarily a consequence of

266

the Audubon sale, quite possibly the most important event in the two hundred year history of Enderby's. That had, of course, made its contribution to the bustle and excitement, but most of the preparations had been made, the main auction room readied, the links for the telephone bids established, the invitations sent, the press alerted, well in advance. No, the commotion was mainly to do with the famous Christmas party, and Pam was its presiding genius. The Americans, ignorant of or uncaring for tradition, had tried to change the date, and had even proposed cancelling Christmas, but Parry Brooksbank, for the first time in his career, had put down his foot, invoked what moral, historical, and financial authority he had, and insisted that the Enderby party was to be, as it had ever been, on the last Friday before Christmas week, and that was that. The Slayer, making quick calculations, accepted that the hassle of running the two events on the same day was probably less than the potential trouble, sulking, and bad blood that would result from stopping the party. She closed her heavy-lidded eyes and numbed the pain of defeat with thoughts of revenge in the form of tiny redundancy cheques.

For twelve years Pam had been in charge of the annual party. She acted as Secretary of the Party Committee, the ten members of which were elected from the various departments, and who would in turn elect a Chair. The Committee would decide on the overall theme, source the fine wines and other refreshments, haggle endlessly over trivial details (the proportion of vegetarian to other buffet items had proved particularly troublesome this year – yes, Clerihew was representing Books), break up in rancour, reform, sample the fine wines, and finally dissolve itself and pass its full authority on to Pam, the Executive to its Legislature. The power invested in her by the Committee made Pam, for the week or so of preparation, the most important, loud, annoying, overbearing, ubiquitous and essential person in the whole of Enderby's. Hers was the task of making sure that everyone properly entered into the spirit of the thing, offering costume suggestions to the unimaginative, and playing Cupid (this her own idea) to potential office couplings, given that, as she insisted on telling anyone who'd listen, 'What's Christmas without a little scandal?' But this all came to a head on the morning of the party, when the stage had to be set, scenery moved, pumps primed and mistletoe artfully arranged.

'You there,' she bellowed to a swarthily handsome man in a long black coat, who stood in the midst of the maelstrom. His stillness could have been the result either of confusion, indecision or passivity. 'If you've nothing better to do, could you help Trevor and Tony with that torso, please? Mmm? Yes?'

As the general public, carrying their useless nick-nacks and gewgaws, their chewed teddy bears, their childhood *Bunty* Albums, for valuation by the bored experts were not allowed into the building before ten, it was perhaps understandable that Pam should have mistaken Edward Lynden for an Enderby toiler in need of direction.

'Actually I'm here to see someone,' he replied, with unaccustomed mildness. But Pam had already refocussed her attention elsewhere.

Edward Lynden had known for a long time that his life had been a failure, measured by the only rule that counted: what use have you made of your talents? He knew that he had been endowed with abilities that, if not great, were considerable. He knew that he could have been a good stage actor. He knew that he had the looks and the raw charisma to have made it as a star of at least middling magnitude in the film industry. Everything had been in place: there had been no disadvantaged background to hold him back: the opposite. There had been the trouble with his father, but then doesn't everyone have trouble with their father? Not even in his weakest, blackest moments, could he blame the old fool for his inadequacies.

So yes, for a long time Lynden had perceived that his life had been wasted. But it was only when he told the story to Alice, back in the library, lifetimes ago, that he fully realised the unattractive self-pitying ring to it. When, how, had he become a *whiner*? He wanted that to stop; he wanted to change. And in his mind Alice became the agent for that change. Her simplicity and directness made her seem like the rock on which he could build a new self. He saw a new life, he saw the chance to slough off the tired old skin. And, of course, she was beautiful: not with the glamorous, head-tossing, show-stopping beauty of Ophelia, or some of the other women he had known, but with a hidden, burning beauty, like a secret shared.

He had even managed to forget, for a while, the other thing.

Grace Harbour had first come into his life after his mother died when he was thirteen. She was barely twenty then. His father wanted someone there all the time to help with cooking, and some other jobs that fell through the cracks. She had never been particularly pretty, but she brimmed with joy and life, and her laughter filled the Cave of Ice. His adolescent fantasies soon took and twisted her into sensuous shapes, only dimly related to the real Grace. In the school holidays he would sit alone in the library or one of the other cold rooms, waiting for her appearances. But he was always too shy to speak to her.

And then, at fifteen, home from school, he had found her unexpectedly in the kitchen, washing dishes. The sunlight came through the window and turned her brown hair to gold. And more than that, its touch gave a transparency to her cheesecloth blouse. He saw the fullness of her breast, and with a groan he realised that she wasn't wearing a bra. Trembling, he stood next to her to fill a glass with water. They touched at the shoulder and hip, and he had to spin away to hide his erection. And then he turned to face her, the blood loud in his ears, and lunged, or fell, towards her clutching with his inexperienced hand for that breast. His lips were on her neck, and then her mouth. She pushed him away, laughing, and he ran from the kitchen and on to his bedroom where, with three savage strokes he came, shatteringly, finally.

And what had most astonished him in the encounter was the knowledge that she had wanted it too, had delayed the push and the laugh just long enough so that she could feel and enjoy the force of his erection against her thigh, and taste his eager tongue deep in her sweet mouth, soft as risen dough, yet cool as rainwater.

The incident was not repeated. Years passed. He went to drama school. Gudrun. India. The wife and the child. All the time Grace stayed on in the house, looking after the old man. And then he died. Lynden returned, lost, brooding, shattered. On the first night she came into his bed, plumper now at thirty, but still an attractive woman; and there, on and off, she had stayed. Not even the short-lived marriage had done much to change the course of their lives. The woman had come; she had her baby; she left. Grace learnt to feel some affection for the child. Soon things were as they had ever been.

He had never made any promises to her; had never hidden his other affairs or infatuations. Perhaps it was his very honesty, the refusal to offer her the chance to dream, that had so dulled her over the years, taking her vivacity and replacing it with a stoicism and rigidity. She had sacrificed everything, and asked for nothing in return; all she had was the cold dark presence, and the weight of him, the weight of him.

She had known, even as Lynden knew, that Alice was different, that Alice might take away even the weight.

'I'm going back now,' she had said, just when he thought that happiness might be within reach. Before she had time to say 'How long has Grace Harbour been your mistress?' he had seen the resolution in her face: a resolution mixed with contempt and scorn. Had she somehow found out about the old intimacy between him and Alex Conradian? But that was drama school: who did not experiment a little there, back in those louche days? Surely she couldn't object?

But no. He knew.

And then she asked the question. With the question came the end of everything. For an hour he wandered through the blighted estate, past broken fences and barren fields. He felt nothing at all. Somehow he found himself in the village pub. He drank beer, and then he drank whisky, and then he drank beer again. At last some feelings came. When he arrived back home, soaking and chilled, the house was silent. He went to the woman, and fucked her out of hatred, fucked her till she cried out in pain, and then ecstasy. When they were finished, Grace pushed him off.

'Go to the bitch,' she said. 'I don't want you.' There was blood on her neck.

He put on his clothes and left the room. The Cave of Ice was always at its most beautiful on clear nights, when the stars and the moon would glitter through the glass walls. But tonight there were no stars and the corridors and rooms were dense with darkness. He found his way to the library and sat at the desk that had always lived there. He put on the lamp, opened a drawer and pulled out a chequebook. He wrote the name Grace Harbour, and then the sum of five hundred thousand pounds. He paused over the date. How long would it take for the money to come into his account from the sale? He dated the cheque for a week ahead, and then scored it out and made it a month, carefully initialling the change. He put the cheque in an envelope and sealed it. He then turned out the lamp and moved to the table where, for so many years, the Audubon volumes had been kept. The table at which Alice had sat, so patiently. He put his cheek to the old wood, and tears flowed from his eyes, although he made no noise. And then he slept for a little while. At dawn he went to the Land Rover and drove into London, where he booked into his usual room at the RAC Club (his membership was a curious family heirloom), and there he'd stayed ever since.

Pam looked unconvinced by the excuse.

'Do they know?' she asked, accusingly. Lynden was spared having to answer by the arrival of Alice, who swept past Pam, and then paused on the last step. It was another of the days when she was paying attention to her appearance. Insisting that she needed something nice for the sale, Odette had helped her to choose a skirt and top that didn't hate each other, and for once her hair looked like it had been cut by scissors rather than secateurs. Alice was self-conscious about the top, which made the best of her neat waist and full cleavage, and she pulled nervously at the neckline, inching it higher. She was even more conscious of the attention they were attracting

'Hello, Edward,' she said, evenly. He looked even wilder than she remembered, and more gaunt. The long black coat was obviously expensive, but it was splattered with mud. 'I've booked a meeting room. It's probably easiest to take the lift.'

At that moment the lift door opened and Oakley stepped

out. He bustled over to Lynden, and reached down to grasp his reluctant hand.

'So pleased to meet you at last, sir. What an honour this is; really what an honour. I'm so sorry I wasn't here to greet you at the door. It was only good fortune that allowed me to discover that you were here at all.' He looked back over his shoulder at Alice, his fawning turning to disdain on the way. Clerihew or Ophelia must have told him that Alice had been called down to the lobby, and why.

'Who are you?' said Lynden.

'Oh, so sorry, sir. Of course we've only spoken by telephone. I'm Colin Oakley; I'm in charge of Books, Manuscripts and Other Printed Matter.' He laughed nervously. 'Alice is one of my girls. A rising star. If you'd like to come and take tea in my office. Or coffee if you prefer. We can talk over the sale. And there're some papers you might like to look at. To sign. Ha ha ha.'

Alice wasn't really paying attention, but she suddenly remembered Andrew's complaints about the fact that Lynden hadn't been asked to sign the contract that would indemnify Enderby's if the Audubon were withdrawn. He had brought the matter up several times with Oakley. 'That's for the riffraff, not a man of this . . . stature,' Oakley had responded complacently. 'And he's hardly going to run away when he stands to make six million pounds. No, he's a gentleman and we have a gentlemen's agreement. You really have a lot to learn, young man, about how to deal with the clients.'

'But it's standard procedure.' One or two people in the office laughed at that. Andrew did, actually, sound a little ridiculous. It wasn't like him to bother with such formalities. Alice wondered if he still felt resentful about Lynden.

'Flexibility, thinking on your feet, that's the new way. Surely you went to the seminar Madeleine Illkempt gave?

We're not a Stalinist bureaucracy anymore. Judgement and discrimination are what we need, not forms and fussing.' He went back to his office, shaking his head and laughing, and Andrew blushed like a girl and called him a cunt twice under his breath.

But, thought Alice, had Oakley changed his mind? Perhaps he'd panicked at the last minute. Or had the Slayer had a quiet word?'

'I'm here to talk to Alice,' said Lynden, quietly, but Alice could sense the barely controlled fury. He turned to her. 'You said there was a room?'

'Oh, of course,' cut in Oakley. 'I'm sure you have some preliminary . . . ah . . . some things to . . . And in due . . . um, we'll see about it later, okay? Sir?' But Alice and Lynden were already in the lift.

TWENTY-ONE

Declarations

'You were going to tell me about Grace.'

They'd been sitting silently in the bright bare little room for what felt like hours, but might have been a minute.

Lynden was stretched out on a hard chair. He looked lean and gaunt and dangerous. A table was between them. Alice noticed with annoyance the brown sticky circles of coffee, and the grey dusting of ash. The room had no windows, and smokers would sometimes sneak in here when it rained outside. Despite the fierce suck of the whining air conditioner, the smell of them lingered. Alice's head felt both full and empty, like a balloon: she had no space to think, no way of getting a perspective.

'Yes. I was going to tell you about Grace.'

And so, slowly, Lynden told Alice about Grace. He began falteringly, but soon his training and his innate sense of drama took hold. Perhaps even the hesitant beginning was part of the performance. Throughout the account he kept his eyes fixed on hers, and she lacked the willpower to pull away. He did not attempt to gain her sympathy, at least not by explicit pleading or obvious, self-serving distortions. The message was rather: this is what I did, I took a woman to my bed whom I did not love, and she stayed there through inertia and perhaps need, but now I have outgrown her and I want you. The bad things I have done were just the everyday bad things that people do; please don't condemn me to unhappiness because of them.

'You *do* know that I love you,' he concluded, with simplicity and dignity. She did know, and she looked down.

'I'm glad you told me all of this. I wish you had told me earlier.' Alice still couldn't think clearly. The words felt thick in her mouth. She wanted some water.

'When? When I first offered you tea?'

That made Alice smile for the first time, and then he smiled too. Alice noticed again that, despite the gauntness, he really was a very, very handsome man. She kept wanting to feel sympathy, even pity for him. She was by nature compassionate, and she felt powerfully for the suffering of others. But Lynden was a hard man to pity – his egotism and habitual belligerence would get in the way. Had she felt pity, although it would have been more difficult for her to dismiss him, as rejection would mean inflicting pain, it would also have meant anything other than rejection would have been impossible: Lynden could not exist for her both as an object of pity and of erotic interest.

She thought again about Grace Harbour, and was taken back to the moment that she realised that Lynden was sleeping with her. Why had she reacted so violently? Lynden had made no promises to her, told no lies. And they had never slept together. Never even, she realised, properly kissed. How strange. She felt as though they had been lovers, and yet they had never even approached intimacy, apart from the time he had rescued her from the inept clutches of Johnny Twogood. He *had* kissed her then, on the cheek. But hadn't she turned her face for a moment and brushed his lips? Was it that she had felt betrayed? No, somehow that didn't catch it. It was something . . . less than that. Something smaller. She thought hard. And then she spoke to him.

'There are things that I haven't told you, either. Important things about me.'

'Only a fool would think that there weren't important things about you that needed to be told.'

They both looked puzzled for a moment about his syntax, but this wasn't the time to dwell.

'Do you remember,' she continued, 'when we first met?'

'Do I remember?' he said loudly, almost angrily, as if he had been insulted. And then, more quietly, he said again, 'Do I remember?'

She took it all as a yes.

'Didn't you wonder about how I behaved? The fainting. All of that?'

'Yes, of course I wondered. But back then, and even now, you seemed a strange thing; a thing not of our time. You looked like you might be the kind that would faint, or swoon for that matter. For all I knew it was your third of the day.'

'Well I'm not – I mean the kind that would faint, *or* swoon. And it was my first of the day. My first ever. It was because I thought you looked like someone.' She had been, despite herself, nettled by the accusation that she was an habitual swooner, and the explanation had come out more directly than she had intended.

'I used to get that all the time. They said the resemblance to the young Olivier was striking.'

Was he joking? It was hard to tell. She took it at face value.

'Not a famous person. You see, some time ago, I saw a boy killed in a road accident. A . . . beautiful boy. And just before he was hit by the car, he looked at me. Or I thought he did. And I fell in love with him. And I thought he fell

277

in love with me. It was an experience that changed every-thing for me.'

This was now the fourth time she had told the story. The first was to Odette; the second to Andrew; the third to the Dead Boy's grandmother. And now Lynden. Something so secret, so private, and yet now so public. Part of her wished that she had never told anyone, that she had let it burn and glow like radium inside her. And what if it had driven her mad? Weren't there worse things than madness? Suddenly she looked up from her own thoughts. She had forgotten about Lynden. What could he make of this? He looked curious; a little wary perhaps, but not . . . well, of course she hadn't finished.

'And this boy . . . ?'

'He looked like . . . I mean you looked like him. For a moment, lying in your chair. You see, I had become . . . I suppose *obsessed* is the only way to put it. There *is* some resemblance, but not profound. Perhaps just the look of, I don't know, anguish that you both seemed to have. But anyway, seeing you, him, there, it was . . . a shock.'

And now, as the meaning found its way home, Lynden did begin to react. How could he not? She had told him that the impact he had had on her was solely because he happened to look like the boy she was in love with. A dead boy. How could a man of his arrogance respond to that?

He began to laugh. She had seen him smile but never heard him laugh. The sound was rich and fruity: a theatrical laugh, but not thereby necessarily false.

'The Dead,' he said, still half laughing.

Alice thought he was referring to the Dead Boy, and his humour seemed misplaced.

'I don't see what's funny about . . . it. A person died.' Again her tone felt wrong, and she feared she sounded prig-gish. She hadn't meant to be.

'No, no. *The Dead*: it's a story by James Joyce. I acted in a radio dramatisation, back years ago. There's a party, and a bumbling, hearty fellow has a rare old time, and there's a pretty wife who seems happy enough with him. But then back home she gazes out of the window, through the falling snow over the hill and the fields to the grave of the boy she's always loved, and the poor lump of a husband just there . . . Well, you see how it all fits.'

'Not really. Well, perhaps, partly.'

But the story did resonate with her. The way minds come up against each other, seem to touch, seem to connect, to communicate, but then you realise that all along the glass was a mirror and not a window; that you were talking to yourself; that the world had closed in around you and you were alone.

And then Lynden's laughter died in his throat.

'But no,' he said. 'I don't understand any of it. Did you ever love me? Want me? Want me for myself? And if you didn't, why were you so concerned about Grace?'

At last Lynden had hit on the heart of it. Alice's instinct was to be kind. And the pity of it, of him, now had come. She wanted to say something that would make him happy, or at least take away his pain. She wanted to give him hope. But that hope would be a lie.

'I don't know what I felt for you, for you as yourself. The tragedy, the grandeur, and now I know that it was a false tragedy, a fake grandeur, well, you became so mixed up with them, with him, with it all, that I could never have teased them apart. And I cannot say that the idea of your beautiful house, and the wildness, and . . . the wealth, did not attract me. But somehow the illusion, the grandeur were shattered when I thought of you with Grace. You became small in my eyes. I wouldn't even say sordid, more just ordinary. What you did was not what I thought my Dead Boy would do. The link with him had been what had captivated me, and now the link was broken. In a way it was because you became real, became yourself, that I lost interest.'

She thought for a moment of trying to explain further the appalling irony of it all: that aching gap between her Dead Boy and the real Matija Abdic; if only *his* worse crime had been the seduction of a serving girl, and the petty evasions and lies consequent upon it. But explanations were pointless, or worse. How would it help Lynden to know that the person he had failed to emulate was himself a sham and a shadow?

'I'm sorry,' she said, as flatly as she could, 'I know all this hardly puts me in a good light, but it's the way it was. I think.'

'I don't care about any of that. I don't care about your Dead Boy or whatever madness you were under, all I care about is now and what you want to do.'

'But surely you must see . . . after what I've just said . . .'

'You haven't really said anything about me.'

'I said that you became ordinary, that I lost interest.'

'But that was before I explained to you about Grace, explained my feelings.'

'Just because you feel something doesn't mean that the world will bend itself to accommodate you.'

'Tell me that you don't love me.'

Alice smiled. The lapse into cliché, particularly one so manipulative, made things easier.

'Okay. I don't love you. I never loved you. I have things to do now. I'll see you at the sale later on. I'm taking phone bids with Andrew. Goodbye.'

Before she reached the door it was thrown open and Ophelia stood there, as vibrant and glorious as an Audubon watercolour.

'Oh good, I thought I might find you here. Mr Oakley

asked me to look for you both. He asked if I wouldn't mind taking care of Edward until the sale. And he suggested you go and do whatever it is you do with your telephone lines, Alice. Apparently you're dealing with Japan. Or is it Europe? It isn't America, anyway, because Andrew's doing that.'

Throughout, Lynden's face was frozen into blankness. But now he started to laugh again. Once more the laugh was theatrical, but now rather than the richness of a joke shared, the laughter was the laughter of a stage lunatic, of a ghoul, of a vampire, of a lost soul.

TWENTY-TWO

Love for Sale

It had all gone wrong. Not horribly wrong. Just wrong. Alice realised, as she left the room and wandered through the high corridors back to Books and her desk, that she had craved a dramatic last encounter with Lynden. She had wanted him to beseech; she had wanted to be tempted, and wanted to resist heroically that temptation. And she knew that it was wicked of her to want these things. It smacked, in its vanity and folly, of Kitty. Nevertheless, she had felt the need for an elaborate endpaper to signal the conclusion of her involvement with Lynden. What she did not want was whatever it was she had just experienced – a clumsy, awkward, embarrassing mess: no grandeur, no tragedy, not even an approach at closure, no satisfying clunk. She had imagined something like the moment of pure silence at the end of a symphony, after the last cymbal crash had died and before the eager chokers had time to insert their braying coughs. The part of her that could lose itself in fiction still thought that life ought to have a pattern, that people could, at least sometimes, say the right thing – right both in bearing some adequate relationship to their thoughts, and right in the more formal sense of sounding *good*. But the rational core in her knew that it was as well to try to paint white lines on the sea as to try to force life into the straitjacket of meaning.

The problem was that Lynden had not played his part. He just wouldn't stay in the role to which he had been allotted. As this thought materialised and presented itself to her in all of its absurdity, she stopped and let out a snorting laugh. It was the crudest noise she had made since she was a schoolgirl. That made her laugh even more. When she finally reached her desk she was wiping the tears away from her flushed cheeks.

'I shit you not, I will have that fucker,' said Andrew, looking at her and trembling with rage. 'What has he done? What has he done?'

Alice hadn't even noticed that he was there, so bleary with laughter were her eyes. His chivalrous bluster was now more than she could take and she sank to her knees, unable even to reach the chair two feet away.

'People think because I work here that I must be some kind of nancy boy, but they don't know where I come from. And I don't care how craggy he is, I'll have him. Oh.' Andrew realised that the sobs were laughter, not weeping. 'Okay. What's the joke?'

Alice finally dragged herself up and sat on her chair. All her hard work in front of the mirror had been undone, and she looked, with her hair and face all a-scramble, like a Lapith ravished by a Centaur.

'I'm sorry,' she said. 'I think I've just had what I think you'd probably call an epiphany.'

'What? Would I?'

'The thing is, I had my talk with Edward, and I was all set up for a tragic, dramatic denouement, and then it never happened. Well, it may have happened for him, a bit. But it just all stopped looking sad to me. And then I sort of saw myself from the outside, and I realised that I looked funny. You know, silly. I don't understand how. I mean all of the facts are the same, but now everything's different.'

'Mmm. Like the duck-rabbit. Gestalt shift. All that. Come on, it's your field. When you have a picture of a duck looking to the left, and then suddenly you see it as a rabbit looking right, with the beak becoming its ears. Stop laughing.'

'Can't help it. Yes, just like the duck rabbit.'

At the repetition of duck rabbit, Andrew started laughing as well.

'You won't, um, mention about the, um, you know, threats to, um . . .'

'Have him?'

'Yeah. But, well, I was . . . I thought that he'd been horrid to you, or something.'

'No, I won't tell anyone. And I thought it was sweet of you.'

'Well, well,' said Oakley, who'd snuck up unawares, 'I do like a good laugh and a joke at work, but there's lots to be doing. Eleven now, sale kicks off in half an hour. Are the lines checked?' He wore a forced smile and looked tense.

'Yes, lines all checked,' said Andrew, soberly. 'I just popped back up here to do a last scan of the email.'

'And yours, Alice?'

'I'm . . .' she began, before Andrew cut in.

'Yes, all checked.'

Oakley looked uncertainly from face to face. 'Good. Well, better get down there. And Alice, perhaps you could have a quick freshen up – you look like you've been dragged through a . . . and there're news cameras and crews and so forth. Lots of attention. First Audubon sale in the UK for . . . since . . . let's all get down there, eh?'

The main auction room was filling up nicely. Andrew was

always interested and amused by the startling variations in type and quality of punter attracted to the different kinds of sale – although of course it would have been strange had they remained constant. Fine art pulled in the trendies to watch and the institutions to buy; pretty girls were not at all uncommon, although horribly outnumbered by grey men bidding for banks. Even within fine art there was a steady change in population, and he could usually tell the period of the sale by spectacles alone: large steel-rimmed for the Renaissance, tortoiseshell for Victorian, rimless for modern. Furniture was older: blue-rinsed and tweedy. The men had port-reddened faces and small, black, shiny, expensive shoes; the women talked in voices like Roedean-educated klaxons. And naturally there'd be a few of the South Coast gays, up from Brighton for a day or two to snaffle a bureau for the shop at Enderby's, and then perhaps to squeeze in a quick shag with a pliant boy in Soho, before retreating back to the grumpy long-term partner, whose looks and sphincters really weren't what they were.

Books tended to be very different and, generally, rather smellier. The joy of books was that even an eminently covetable and collectable rare first edition might be had for a couple of hundred pounds, with plenty of less expensive, but still desirable, stuff from twenty or thirty quid. That meant that ordinary people could get in on the game. Ordinary, that is, in relation to wealth: eccentric in most other respects. Weirdos of every hue proliferated: scholars with dirty collars, academics *sans* academia, twitchers, jerkers, mumblers, fumblers, frotters and feltchers, experts on the Raj, collectors on the rampage. There was a curious anger about the book lot, a conviction that they were being diddled or fiddled or conned; a wariness about the other collectors; a suspicion of the sellers, of the auctioneers, of the world. Andrew had once helped preside over a sale of books about the so-called 'Great Game' played by the world powers in nineteenth-century Afghanistan, when one man had produced a huge, antique blunderbuss from beneath a monumental overcoat, and screamed 'I'll show you a great game. I'll show you a great game, BANG! BANG! BANG!', the bangs emitting not from the burnished barrel of the beautiful brass weapon, but from the pursed mouth of the wielder. It transpired later that the maniac had been driven over the edge by the discovery that his prized copy of Kipling's *Departmental Ditties*, being neither that printed by the Civil and Military Gazette in Lahore in 1886 (£1000), nor the edition produced in the same year in Calcutta by Thacker, Spink & Co (£250), but rather the 1890, Thacker & Co of London edition, was relatively worthless. Yes, passions could rage high in the world of old books. As could the smell. What was it, Andrew often wondered, about book people that made them so neglect personal hygiene? Other types of obsessive managed to change their underwear, brush their teeth, and utilise modern, efficient deodorants, so why not book collectors? Books themselves, of course, could often smell so perhaps there was some semi-conscious attempt at empathy? A brotherhood of mustiness and sticky crevices?

But this was not the usual book crowd, and no pall of odour hung over the room like mustard gas at Ypres. Yes, a reserve of six million quid would tend to keep out the great unwashed. And the Audubon was, anyway, more of an art thing than a book thing. So here were the art crowd, with the more fashionable section excised. Bird paintings were not, after all, at the cutting edge of anything, and so polo-necks and shaven heads were as rare here as auk eggs. This left rather a bland and smug feel to the punters. These were the dull wealthy, and the dull people who worked for the wealthily dull. But a crowd always had something for the connoisseur of amusing visages, and Andrew duly picked out women with heads like cricket bats, and men with features crammed into the middle of their faces like rectums amid fleshy buttocks. He plucked at wattles and toyed with warts; he disarrayed meticulous comb-overs, and came over those in meticulous disarray.

The room held a hundred in reasonable comfort. The best chairs had been brought out, padded red velvet, with carved gilt legs, but Andrew suspected that they weren't as old as they were supposed to look. The walls were hung with paintings of surpassing Victorian tedium: portraits of elderly, empire-building homosexuals and stout women in hats; invented landscapes that suggested a poverty of imagination of a near cosmic proportion: oh look, a carthorse, a haywain, a tree, a sad-eyed doggy.

Thank Christ for Alice, he thought. She was sitting next to him at the desk along the side of the room where they were preparing to take the telephone bids. She had done something to put right her hair and face and once again her rapturous beauty shone forth upon the world – or so he found himself thinking. He was happy that she had sloughed off the aristo, and even more pleased that she seemed so together about it. The new togetherness stemmed from her cathartic expedition to confront the Dead Boy's grandmother. She had told him the story. He hadn't the faintest idea what to say about it, and so said nothing, which turned out to be exactly the right thing.

Well, now everything had been flushed through. No, that wouldn't do. He didn't like the thought of Alice as a WC, albeit it a pretty, Pre-Raphaelite sort of WC of the kind patronised by Dante Gabriel Rossetti, or Burne Jones, or Millais, or the other one whose name he tended to forget. Ah, that was it, yes, she had been restored, like the Sistine Chapel ceiling, and now her true colours could shine

287

through again. Much better, even though you could tell that all of Michelangelo's women were really men in disguise, with their powerful torsos, thick waists, and wide apart, deeply uninteresting breasts.

Not at all like Alice. No one could ever say that her breasts were uninteresting. Not in front of Andrew. Not if they wanted to live. And tonight he had every intention of telling Alice exactly what he thought of her breasts, and all of the rest of her as well, for that matter. Tonight was the great office bacchanalia. Tonight love would stalk the corridors. He had planned what he was going to say. He had to plan it because tonight he was going to use the truth stratagem, and that was always the trickiest to pull off. Yes, he was going to tell her just what he thought; play it honest and up front. Bullshit thrived on spontaneity, but the truth needed devious devices, Byzantine cunning, and subtle words.

Who was he kidding? He was going to get shit-faced on Chablis and tell her he loved her and always had, and pray that he didn't vomit, belch, dribble or piss his pants in the process.

The auctioneer arrived. Dear old Crumlish used to do the job, when he was around, but now Books had to get in that old fart Phillip Quiller from Furniture to do it for them, as no one else was qualified, and never again would be as the training budget had been slashed by the Slayer. Pity, as Andrew always rather fancied the job himself, whilst simultaneously seeing clearly quite how ridiculous it would make him in the eyes of the world. Quiller had quavering, moist lips and a shuffling, uncertain gait, but once he reached the podium he assumed a certain pinstriped authority. Which was only natural, as he must have called the numbers a thousand times and it was all as natural and easy for him as breathing.

The magnificent engravings themselves were placed on a table by the side of Quiller's podium. A video camera was angled down upon them, and the top plate was displayed on a large, obscenely expensive flat-panel screen on the wall behind. Another camera was aimed at the podium, and yet another at the potential bidders, all for the sake of those who wished to follow the proceedings live over the internet. These sorts of technical innovations had come in with the Americans and had, so far, managed to drain what little capital remained in the company whilst having at best a minimal effect on business throughput. Oakley was, needless to say, a great enthusiast. The Slayer herself, along with two other troubleshooting Americans, known generally (or to Andrew, at any rate) as Butch and Sundance, Parry Brooksbank and one other distinguished-looking fellow, who Andrew vaguely knew to be important, were also arrayed at the front of the room. The Slayer, with her bulldog scowl jutting aggressively forward, and her stoutly spread legs, looked particularly uninviting. Something about her posture made Andrew think of an old joke about a peasant woman sitting knickerless in the market. Keeps the flies off the melons.

In addition to the in-house multimedia effort, there was, as Oakley had predicted, a crew from the BBC and another from Sky News, as well as a weedy phalanx of print journalists taking up much of the back row, like naughty schoolboys. It was all really quite exciting.

'I don't know about you, Alice,' said Andrew, 'but I'm really quite excited.'

'Me too,' she replied, and then after a pause, 'After all, I've decided that . . .' but that was as far as she got. There was a noise at the doorway. An urgent murmuring, rising to an insistent whisper. And then a sharp barking noise.

'What the hell's going on?' said Andrew to the air.

Alice looked towards the door. Oakley and two porters in their London Zookeeper uniforms were attempting to bar the way. The person whose way they were barring was Edward Lynden.

The focus of the entire room had swivelled through one hundred and eighty degrees. Some had even, not content with craning their necks, actually scraped their chairs around to get a better look. Oakley's pleading voice came through, interspersed with Lynden's harsh and commanding tones.

'Please, Mister, er sir, Baron, Lynden, you really can't, not at this stage.'

'I can do exactly what I want with my property.'

'But there is an agreement.'

'I didn't sign anything.'

'A *gentlemen's* agreement.'

Laughter.

'Perhaps we could discuss this outside, sir,' said one of the porters, an elderly man called Johns, who'd been there since the war. He gently took Lynden's arm.

'Take your hands off me,' said Lynden, with an unspoken additional clause that said 'or I'll knock you down, old man or not.'

And then he burst through the weak barrier of limbs and protestations. He strode down the central aisle between the two blocks of chairs. Alice thought that he may have glanced quickly out of the corner of his eye towards her, but his head did not move. He looked terrifying and magnificent, and she realised again how close she had come to wanting him, to wanting to be with him. She felt a strong desire to go to him, a pull from within herself, which she recognised as purely sexual.

He reached the table with the Audubon plates. The room had swung back with him to face the front.

'He's going to take them,' said Andrew, again aiming at

290

no one in particular. A smile of incredulity stretched across his face. 'And he hasn't signed the waiver. We're fucked. Totally fucked.'

The smile became an involuntary grin as he worked out the ramifications. He and Alice had been taken off the organisational side of things. All of the paperwork had been 'done', or left undone, by Oakley, Clerihew and Ophelia. His own work had been performed to a high standard, he knew that. And it was far from wasted. The Lynden copy had now been documented and described. It existed for scholarship in a way that it hadn't existed before. His catalogue was still a useful and elegant contribution to the world of books. Alice, was, of course, in the clear. She couldn't be blamed for this mess: she'd secured the sale in the first place, delivered Lynden and the Audubon into the supposedly safekeeping of Oakley.

All the while Lynden was calmly arranging the massive plates between two heavy boards. Quiller was making strange little movements with his red lips, as if kissing the toes of his mistress. Every minute or so he would take a step towards Lynden and then step back again, in rhythm to some ancient, courtly dance. Well, it wasn't his job to go rugby-tackling madmen.

The plates and the boards must have weighed as much as a six-year-old child, thought Andrew, but Lynden picked them up without effort, handling their sheer unwieldy mass with ease. He strode back the way he had come, kicked open the double doors, framed on one side by a rigidly immobile Oakley and on the other by the cowed porters. And then he was gone.

The uproar began the second the actor had left the stage. Andrew swore later that there had been screams; there was certainly a cacophony of jabbering and excited conversation. Oakley was seen to sink to his knees. Clerihew appeared from nowhere and attended to him, Hardy to his Nelson. Andrew saw that he must have come from one of the seats at the back, and now he caught sight of Ophelia, a vacant chair next to her. She was sitting with her legs crossed, her face showing a lack of concern positively heroic in the circumstances. She looked as if she were waiting for the girl to bring her a coffee at the hairdresser's.

'I can't decide,' said Alice, confidentially, 'whether or not this counts as an anticlimax.'

Andrew didn't answer. He was watching the Slayer. She was grinding her jaws in a circular motion, like a Bosch devil chewing the soul of a sinner.

TWENTY-THREE

Complicity

Pam had wanted something traditional: tarts and vicars, sixties, seventies, eighties, Martian invasion, toga. The party committee was in the second hour of its first meeting, back in October, and was becoming restless.

'We did it all poncy last year and look what happened.' Pam had had her hair done specially for the meeting. Its dense and lacquered mass looked solid enough to hold rigidly an arrow or crossbow bolt, should one have been fired by a fellow committee member.

It was true that *The Murders in the Rue Morgue* theme, suggested in an idle moment by Andrew, who was on last year's committee, had been a mistake. Only one person had turned up in an orang-utan suit, and the rest had settled, mystified, for a vaguely 'olden days' look, with bustles and hats for the girls and frockcoats, or street urchin garbs for the boys; but no one had quite known what was going on, and the award for best costume to the orang gained a meagre, scattered applause from the crowd. Andrew was afterwards convinced that his suggestion was only approved by the committee because none of them were prepared to admit that they did not know either who had been murdered on the Rue Morgue, nor by whom.

It was, of course, Andrew who came and triumphed, as the villainous primate.

'But this isn't the Milton Keynes regional office of United Widgets,' said the Chair, Humphrey Palfry, a high-up in Antiquities, famed for his bow ties and dandruff. 'We are a *cultural institution*; a cultural institution of *national importance*. And our party must represent that appropriately.'

'Here here, Humph,' said Ackerly from Paintings. He wasn't high up at all, and generally agreed with whoever was senior in any situation. 'Nor are we the Truss and Prosthetics Manufacturers Association, or a subcontractor making the clip fastenings for Marks and Spencer's support bras or . . .'

'Thanks, Roger, I think we get the picture.' Humph had had enough fawning for one lunchtime, what with Ackerly, and what's-his-name, Cedric or Clarence, from Books.

'Yes. Sorry. But I do actually have an idea.' He didn't: his boss in Paintings, a young Turk called Terence Richardson, who'd recently become a minor TV celebrity after an appearance on daytime television talking about the sexiness of Monet, had suggested it. With his long, dark locks, his velvet suits, and his air of corrupted innocence, Richardson looked like one of Oscar Wilde's less debauched accomplices. Which was exactly what the TV executives and, it transpired, the single mums, pensioners and dolemongers wanted from their art experts. His subsequent appearances were marked by a flickering and dimming of the nation's lights, caused by the power surge as millions of housewives turned up their intimate massage appliances from 'cruise' to 'ramming speed'.

'Oh yes, and what's that then, exactly?' asked Pam, suspiciously. She didn't look at Ackerly, but picked and ate the crumbs from the individual pork pie that had fallen and adhered, by virtue of some kind of electrostatic force, to the phlegm-green nylon of her blouse. Humphrey – who'd once, at a Christmas party years ago, when she was still slender-necked, and before her bust had undergone the Weimar Republic levels of inflation, taken her rather brutally in the mail room – looked on with distaste, and hoped she wouldn't actually root down into her cleavage for a stray, spawnlike globule of glaucous jelly.

'Well, my idea is that everyone has to come as a painting. A famous painting.'

There was a general interested shuffling from the twelve members of the committee. Not at all a bad idea. Perhaps Ackerly wasn't such an arsehole. People threw in suggestions, and then wished they hadn't been so open handed. In the past careers had been made by interesting and original performances at the party. Good ideas were worth their weight in paste and gilt. Clerihew, after a few moments of panic, hit on what he thought would be a sure-fire show-stopper and had to control his urge to shout it out loud. No, this really was a beauty. Too good to share. How they would love him; how they would cheer. One in the eye for Andrew. Ha! Monkey suit!

'But not just paintings, surely?' Tessa, from IT hadn't said anything so far, and so everyone jumped a little at her high-pitched interjection.

'I beg your pardon?' said Richardson, in a good-to-hear-from-you-at-long-last kind of way. For much of the meeting he'd been surreptitiously eyeing her chest to try to work out if the displacement of the white cotton of her neatly-fitted shirt was caused by some seamlike or other protu-berance of her undergarment – a mere bra feature, or, more fascinatingly, an eruption of nipple, raw and chaffing against the shirt fabric, aching for the mouth, longing for . . .

'I mean, we could extend it to statues and stuff. Installations or whatever.'

'Yes, of course. I always meant those too,' said Ackerly, anxious, not to help out Tessa, but rather to avoid having to share the glory for coming up with the concept.

'I still don't see what's wrong with tarts and vicars,' tried Pam, for one last time. But history was against her, and it was not her role to stand in its way.

So, pictures, statues and, improbably, installations it was, or, to give it the resonant title announced in the Christmas Party newsletter (meticulously produced by Clerihew in Pdf format for electronic distribution, with paper copies available on request for the Luddites), ART MOVES AMONG US.

After the aborted sale, Andrew and Alice went back to their desks. The Books people not directly involved in the sale clustered round to find out why they had returned so soon. Heads shook in disbelief. Bemused, embarrassed laughter rippled through them.

'And you know,' said Andrew, 'he hadn't signed the fucking contract. No indemnity. Nothing. The bloke's just taken his toys and gone home, leaving us to pick up the bill, and there's not a damn thing we can do about it.'

'Looks bad for the boss,' said someone.

'Wouldn't be in his shoes,' said another.

'He'll find a way of wriggling out of it. Some other poor bugger's gonna take the rap.'

At that moment Ophelia and Clerihew came in. Ophelia wore her look of studied neutrality, her veneer unscratchable. Clerihew looked like a dog on his way to the vets, given the gift of awareness that it can only mean either the big sleep or the unkindest cut of all.

'So, Cornelius,' said Andrew, brightly, 'another triumph of organisation for Books, eh? And I thought the whole point of you and *Mister* Oakley was that you made the trains run on time?'

'Perhaps you shouldn't be quite so smug,' Clerihew replied, with venom. 'After all, if any names have been associated with the whole Audubon project, then they are yours and Alice's. *I* was just brought in at a late stage, when, it seems to me, most of the damage had already been done.'

If Andrew looked for support from his colleagues, he looked in vain. They began to melt back to their own desks. Oakley remained the man in charge, and Clerihew was still his bulldog. The Audubon disaster might well mean heads had to roll and, if only for the time being, Oakley still held the axe.

Andrew looked, and was, betrayed.

'You know what, Andrew,' said Alice. 'I don't feel like the canteen today. I know it's a bit early, but why don't we go for a sandwich at Cranks.'

'Christ, I'm still digesting one of their wholemeal scones I swallowed last week. Did I ever tell you that they use osmium, the heaviest element so far discovered, in their recipes?'

'Yes, I think you might have mentioned it. But it's not, by the way.' They were in the lift by now.

'Not what?'

'The heaviest element.'

'Really?'

'Really.'

'What is then?'

'Gravitron.'

'*Gravitron*! You made that up.'

'Didn't.'

'Did.'

'Airhead.'

'Bimbo.'

They were out in the street, walking closely together, the sleeves of their winter coats touching.

'I thought you never went to Cranks,' said Andrew. 'Because it was too near to where . . . near to . . .'

'Where Matija Abdic was killed.'

'Yes, there. I don't think I've ever heard you use his name. His real name.'

'It's how I think of him now. And yes, it's near where he was killed. But now I don't mind so much.'

After a few moments Andrew said, 'I still think osmium's funnier. Gravitron just hasn't got that smack of authenticity. Sounds like something Superman's enemies use against him. You know, renders him sterile, or disarrays his coiffure.'

'Don't care. S'true.'

'True shmoo. I'm not risking another scone. Don't like the idea of them hunting in packs inside me. They communicate, you know.'

'What, using electric *currants*?'

'Is that supposed to be a . . .'

'You could always *jam* the frequency.'

'All right, all right, ha ha ha. Scones, currants, jam, I *get* it. Don't you know that punning is for boys? Anyway, I think I'll have some of their cheesecake instead. It's what they use to isolate the core in nuclear submarines.'

They got back to the office at two thirty, but it was quite clear that no work was going to be done in Enderby's that day. From the moment they entered the lobby, now richly decorated with tasteful baubles (some dating back to the very invention of Christmas in darkest Victorian times), ivy, and, of especial interest to Andrew, mistletoe, it was clear that, notwithstanding the shock of the Audubon mishap, from here on in it was going to be party party party.

Books was humming. The women were clustered together talking about what they'd be wearing; the men were joking and generally mucking about. Term was ending, and joy abounded. But not quite everywhere: Andrew could see Oakley pacing in his office, while Clerihew sat and watched. Clerihew looked more worried than ever, but Oakley had his cunning fox face on, which was perturbing.

'I haven't asked you yet what you're going as tonight,' said Alice. 'You didn't seem to bring anything in with you.'

It was true that while most people (including Alice herself) had arrived with large bags and boxes, Andrew had only his usual small rucksack.

'Don't want to give the game away just yet. But this year it's nothing special. You wouldn't believe the animosity you attract for winning the first prize. Everyone hates you. I've been there, done that. I thought just a token effort, this year. But what about you? You could do Joseph Wright of Derby's *Experiment with an air pump*, I suppose. That's science, after all.'

'Is that the one with a long-haired man gassing a parrot, while his family all gather round, and the children crying and all that?'

'Yes. It's actually one of my favourite paintings.'

'Bit hard to recreate on my own though.'

'You could have teamed up: it's what a lot of others are doing. But no, so not the *Experiment with an air pump*. What then?'

'You're being coy, and so will I.'

With the party due to begin at five, the girls started to get ready from three thirty, giggling their way in excited groups to the ladies, from whence they did not return. Alice was in the midst of them, laughing and pushing with the others, which charmed and delighted Andrew. It really did seem as though her burden had been shed. At four, Oakley emerged from his office, with Clerihew in attendance, carrying a bottle of cheap Spanish red wine.

'Quite enough slaving for one day,' he said, unnecessarily. 'Time we all got in the party mood. Open up please, Cedric, and let's er *party*.'

Clerihew then made a meal of opening the bottle, and handing out paper cups to the ten or so men standing around, a group made up of three Toffs, three Swots, an Oik and two porters.

'Can't wait to see what the girls come back in,' Oakley continued, trying to make conversation. 'Lovely peacocks that they er are.'

'I think you'll find that the peacocks – the colourful ones – are the boys. The lady peacocks, I mean peahens, are brown.'

'Thanks for that piece of *pedantry*, Cedric,' replied Oakley, clearly annoyed. Another two bottles of what one of the toffs described, audibly, as 'rank Diego juice', appeared and were consumed primarily by the porters and Andrew. The others were discriminating enough to know that they were about to have something very much better at the party proper.

Andrew spent the time chatting with the porters and Cartwright the Map man, who he still hadn't really got to know, and who proved to be a little dull when you got him off his home ground of maps, and very dull when he stuck to it. Still, nice enough fellow and he laughed at your jokes, which was all you could hope for, ultimately. Andrew had always got on well with the porters or at least the younger ones. The older porters tended to look on any expert not wearing pinstripes as having somehow let them all down. They were the upholders of the ancient traditions: stay at your station, keep your eye on the Fuzzy-Wuzzies, worship the Queen, officers know best, anything other than cheese and pickle on your sandwich means you're a Bolshevik, child-molesting bum-bandit. But the younger ones were okay as long as you kept to sport and girls, and what a cunt Oakley was, which Andrew was always happy to do.

Eventually, after most of the drinkers had gone themselves to dress for the party, Oakley found his way round to Andrew.

'I wonder if we perhaps might ah have a little, you know.'

'Sure. Want to glory in this morning's triumph.' Andrew was already a little drunk.

'Well, that is actually. What I want to talk about, I mean.'

Oakley was sounding, as he often did when under pressure or stressed, as if his language chip had been damaged. Andrew noticed that one of the wings of his moustache was slightly shorter than the other. A practical joke, perhaps, from a barber, annoyed by years of tipless snipping? Or maybe Mrs Oakley did him in the bath, along with his ear-and-nose bristles. And overcome, perhaps, by passion she'd climbed in with him and worked the cheap bubble bath into an ecstasy of foaming froth with her powerful abdominal flexing before she'd properly finished the job. Andrew shuddered.

'Could have happened to anyone. Fucking up completely like that. My sympathy is entirely with you. Bleed for you, in fact.'

'I'm not entirely blind to irony, you know.'

'Shouldn't that be deaf? And anyway, that wasn't irony. That was sarcasm.'

Oakley did an elaborate 'I'll ignore that' shrug. 'I'm sure you'll appreciate that what happened could hardly be lain at my, in any way attributed to . . . However, the events and circumstances could, I think, and if I were you then I would be forced to agree with my analysis on this, be said to stem from, if not originate in, er with, Alice.'

301

'What are you talking about?' Despite the gobbledegook, Andrew had a fair idea.

'Look, I'll be quite clear on this. There are two reports which I could write about the unfortunate events of this morning. Could write and have, in actuality, done so. The first sets out how it was the romantic entanglement of Alice with Lynden that ultimately undermined and led to the abortive failure of the sale. The unprofessional conduct, the leading-on and fickle rejection of, spurning and so forth, that all of us saw undergoing. I have, of course, sought and found corroboration of these facts from the testimony of witnesses closely involved.'

No need, thought Andrew, to wonder who they might be.

'And,' he continued, 'I am quite prepared to see that this was compounded by the administrative oversight in not pursuing more actively the administrative norms and procedures, albeit that the administrators involved could hardly be expected to anticipate that a lovers' tiff would jeopardise the fulfilment of the arrangements.'

So, Alice was to be stitched up for the mess. Andrew supposed that she presented an easier target than he did.

'You said you'd written two reports,' he said, hollowly.

'Two, yes. The second sets out a slightly different emphasis, and one which, frankly, disguises any errors committed by your colleague or colleagues unnamed, by which I mean Alice. It stresses the strenuous efforts undertaken by the Books management team to gain the usual guarantees and contractual arrangements from the vendor, and his continual prevarication. The delicacy of the issue is also greatly stressed, his highly strung temperament and so forth. But great potential gains also to be taken into account. No one directly responsible for the mental breakdown or erratic behaviour of the vendor. And I would be prepared to bear upon my shoulders the responsibility for any errors of minor judgement committed by my staff. That's simply the kind of manager that I am. It, the enterprise, was a brave gamble that, in the final analysis, did not come off. We are risk-takers here, and occasionally those who live by the . . . will also perish by it. After all, who would not rather be, if you'll allow me a classical allusion, Ganymede flying too near the sun than er someone else altogether who didn't try in the first place. Getting near the sun, or, for that matter, airborne in the sky at all.'

'It was Icarus who flew too near the sun. Ganymede was a shepherd boy taken up by an eagle to be royally fucked by Zeus. I believe I know the feeling.'

Oakley ignored the comment. 'The advantages to this route are not only that Alice will be exonerated, at least in the main part, when the issue is considered, but, others might also benefit.'

'Yeah, you.'

'Not only, or even particularly, me. Of course this, second, interpretation of the events requires a degree of unanimity from those involved, directly or indirectly. And you know that the panel will shortly adjourn to decide, at long last, I may say, on the replacement for Mr Crumlish. There are already front runners for that position. Team players. Safe pairs of hands. I have to say that at the moment, you are not necessarily seen as such. Talented, naturally. But not a team player. However, I will be writing reports for those who wish to put themselves forward for the post from within Books, and should you see fit to come into agreement with the line I propose, then any qualms I might have enter-tained about your team-playing capabilities would be shelved, if not refuted. And with a good report from me, or at least in the absence of a report highlighting your weak-nesses, then you'll be on a level playing field with the other candidates and your . . . flair might well show itself to good effect before the panel.'

So, there it was. Back up Oakley and save Alice and do himself a favour all at the same time. Everyone's a winner. So why did it make him feel sick to his stomach? For a moment he considered a flamboyant gesture, but it wasn't fair to be flamboyant with someone else's life. And anyway, he'd always had a streak of pragmatism. There was simply nothing to be gained from rejecting Oakley's suggestion. Oakley had the ear of the Americans. And wasn't there just enough truth in the allegation that Alice's shenanigans with Lynden had had something to do with his withdrawal to convince the neutrals? Something in him almost admired the way that Oakley had pulled this one out of the fire and he made a mental note to remember that being an arse didn't necessarily make you an idiot. He didn't say anything, but the slump in his shoulders was all Oakley needed to see to tell him that he had won his victory.

'Good, good. Now we can all really enjoy ourselves tonight.'

'What are you going as?' said Andrew. He tried to convince himself that he was just making conversation to tear himself away from the unpleasantness of the necessary choice he had made, but deep down he knew that he had simply become another lick-spittle.

Clerihew, the only other person still in the room, looked over and smiled at him, a smile of complicity and fellowship.

TWENTY-FOUR

The Last Party

The tears that Alice had shed the night before were unlike any others that had fallen from her eyes with such unnerving regularity over the past year. These weren't tears of sorrow or sadness, nor tears of desperation or hopelessness. She wasn't crying over the love that she had lost, or the loss of her love.

No.

She was crying, her face screwed up into a bitter conch of anguish, because she couldn't think of anything to wear to the party, and the knowledge that she was upset by something so trivial did not help at all. The problem was that this just *so* wasn't her thing. There were two reasonable illustrated histories of art in the flat and she spent an hour going through them, convinced that she would find *something*. But no: everything seemed either too outlandish or too dull and, more to the point, unachievable, given her limited resources of time and money.

'Stupid, stupid girl,' said Odette, into Alice's ear. 'If you'd asked me a week ago I might have been able to think of something. But for *tomorrow*? Are you mad? Have you tried calling Jodie? She knows more about this sort of thing than we do.'

So Alice called Jodie. They hadn't spoken for weeks and so Alice had to put up with all kinds of gush before they got to the point.

'Based on *art*? What a silly idea. Shame you've got arms.'

'What?'

'Venus de Milo, darling.'

'Please, be serious.'

'Mona Lisa?'

'No. There'll be hundreds of those.'

'Have you got anything eighteenth-century looking? You could go as something by Reynolds or one of those French artists who painted little girls on swings. Fragonard, was it, or Boucher?'

'I haven't got anything eighteenth century. How would I have anything eighteenth century? Have you? Could I borrow?'

'No, sorry.'

Alice had to put up with two more minutes of pleasantries before she could go and get stuck in to her cry. But she did manage to tell Jodie about her plans.

There was a knock at the bedroom door. Kitty came in without waiting for an answer. She wore the look of someone scraping old vegetables from the back of the fridge.

'What's wrong with you?' she asked, accusingly.

Alice told her.

Kitty's face changed. 'What a simply wonderful idea,' she said. Alice looked up from her forearms, stained with smudgy black. She saw that Kitty was smiling. Smiling in a way that Alice had never, she honestly thought, seen before. Not the pinched, forced smile that she remembered Kitty firing at her father whenever he said or thought the wrong thing. Not the half-mad smile she would use when recounting some mythical adventure, or crazed plan. This was a full, broad grin that dragged in the thin white skin around her eyes. Despite the unaccustomed crinkling, she looked younger and softer and, for as long as it lasted, sane.

'I have *exactly* the thing.'

'What do you mean?' Alice couldn't bring herself to hope. The idea surely couldn't be practical, *real*, could it?

'Wait just where you are. No, don't do that. Go and splash some water on your face first. You look like you've been ravished.'

Alice went half sulkily, half hopefully, to the bathroom and stared at herself in the mirror, as she waited for the water to run hot. Something about the face that gazed back at her caught her attention and rather than the usual quick look to make sure there wasn't a bird's nest on the back of her head, or the brief scientific check as she raced around her mouth with the good-value lipstick she always bought from Boots (stocking up whenever they had a three-for-two offer), this became a long, appraising, attentive gaze. How many times had she done that in her life? Not more than three. And never before had she liked what she had found. Now she took in her eyes and her hair and her nose and her lips and her cheeks and her neck and she saw that they were good, as eyes and hair and nose and lips and cheeks and necks went. Perhaps better than good. And that was despite the redness and the smudges from the recent tears. And she could also see that there was a unity about them all, a pulling-in-the-same-direction that further added to the effect. But she could never see, because it required a fonder gaze than she would ever manage, that there was something special, over and above these routine facts of facial geometry and harmony, that transfigured her, the thing that Andrew had once, happily, thought of as the ghost in her machine.

Notwithstanding such intangible spectral presences, the discovery that she was pretty delighted her. She had known that she must not be unattractive because of the attention that she had received from Lynden and Andrew, but that knowledge was both negative, in that it simply ruled out actual ugliness, and remote from her, in that it was an intuition about how others perceived her. Now she saw and felt it for herself. All of the factors that had made vanity impossible for her all through her life were still in place: she couldn't and wouldn't shrug off her history. But now she could see the truth of herself. And who could resist the thrill of pleasure upon such a realisation?

But still, she had nothing to wear.

Water was splashed; teeth and hair were brushed.

Kitty called out as she walked back to her room: 'I'm in here. Come and see. Are your hands clean?'

Alice never usually went into her mother's room. Even as a child it had been a forbidden zone, full of things which must never be touched. Of course she had sneaked in more than once to finger the complex facets of the scent bottles, to caress the powder puffs and stroke the necklaces. But her favourite place had always been her father's study. She remembered holding his leg as he typed reports with one finger, caressing her hair with his free hand.

It was laid out on the bed. Alice thought she'd never seen anything so beautiful.

'How . . .' she said, 'what . . . ?'

'Oh, my mother had it made for her in the twenties when he was all the rage, even here. I wanted to wear it for my coming out but she . . . she thought it wasn't right for me. But I tried it on once and it made me feel like a work of art come to life. But that was back in the . . . well, a little while ago now.'

'But surely it can't fit me if you wore it.'

'Nonsense. I was going through one of my plump phases. And anyway, it's not exactly close-fitting, is it? But before we do anything else, I want to have a go at those eyebrows of yours. I've been meaning to for years now. Can't have you going to the ball looking like a werewolf, can we now?'

After half an hour of agonising plucking (Alice was an eyebrow virgin), Kitty seemed satisfied. It was the most intimate experience Alice had ever shared with her mother. Odd how pain, one inflicting, one suffering, had, if not brought them together, then brought them a little closer. But before she tried on the dress, there were some things that Alice wanted to say.

'Mummy, do you remember I told you what I was going to do?'

'Of course I remember. Do you think I'm senile? Now Mrs Solomon in number 45, *she's* got the first signs. I spoke to her son, who I don't believe *is* a doctor, and he said she couldn't remember the name of her hairdresser.'

'But do you think you'll be all right? Because if you won't be, then I can change my plans.'

'Why wouldn't I be all right? I think I've earned my freedom, don't you?'

'Yes,' said Alice. She thought she'd earned her freedom.

It was all ruined for Andrew. He'd been looking forward to the party all year, and now it was going to be crap. He went to the bogs. There were two other people there: a Laughing (or was it Gay?) Cavalier, trying to stick on his fine, curling moustaches, and an angel, who Andrew presumed to be Gabriel hotfooting it to an Annunciation, but he couldn't even guess at the painting or artist. Both Cavalier and Angel were exuberantly plumed.

He stood in front of the mirror and took, from his jacket pocket, a rubber shark. To be precise it was two severed halves of a rubber shark, conjoined by eight inches of curved, springy metal. He weighed it in his hands for a few moments, considering whether it should go side to side, Napoleon style, or front-to-back like Wellington. He tried it on, both ways. Napoleon, definitely Napoleon.

'Oh, very good. I say, yes. It's that shark chappie, isn't it? Daniel Hurst? Mmm, eh?'

'Yes,' said Andrew, back to the Cavalier. 'And you're Courbet's *Origin of the World*, are you?'

The night before Andrew had been talking over his ideas on the phone to Leo. He liked the Shark but suggested Courbet's *Origin*.

'What is it?'

'A big, hairy, to put no finer point on it, cunt. It's in the d'Orsay, you heathen.'

'Courbet's what?' said the Cavalier, looking worried. 'No, the Laughing Cavalier, actually. Do you think people won't realise? Did this Courbet fellow paint cavaliers?'

'Big, hairy c . . . never mind.'

But Andrew's spirits had already started to lift again. By the time he hit the top of the sweeping stairway, he was raring to go. This may have been helped along somewhat by the fat line of coke he ineptly snorted after the Angel Gabriel and Laughing Cavalier (not looking very cheerful) had left. The coke was a birthday gift from an acquaintance, and was strictly against Andrew's principles: he didn't like what drugs did to the local economies of the producer countries; he didn't like the fact that buying drugs meant, at some stage in the process, giving money to bad, or very bad, people; he didn't like the general smugness and complacency of those who took them, perfectly encapsulated by the insistence on crisp new money as a siphon. He had only ever indulged twice, faintly boring himself on both occasions. But, when all was said and done, these were *free drugs*, and he was loath to throw them away: free stuff was not to be sniffed at. And so the tiny wrap stayed in his pocket for four months (did cocaine go off? Did it lose its potency? No, it transpired) until now finding its way, via the blood vessels in his nose, to the pleasure zones of his temporal lobes, or whichever crinkly part of the brain it was that dealt with that sort of thing.

For a second he thought about launching himself into the throng, like a rock star body surfing over the mosh pit. But no. This wasn't that sort of crowd, whatever the coke was telling him. It was, in fact, quite a spectacle. From up here the initial impression was one of vibrant colour and restless activity, unified yet complex. Like a section through a psychedelic beehive. The spirit of the beehive, the spirit of the beehive. Running swiftly down the stairs he soon found the pattern breaking up into individual units. A young Bacchus, smacking, Andrew surmised, of Caravaggio, his head wreathed in vine leaves, a fake leopard (not, surely, a pyjama case? Yes, surely a pyjama case) over his shoulder, was talking to a plain woman with short hair, in a straight, brown dress, her face made-up to look ghastly and sunken. As he passed her she put her hands to her cheeks and opened her mouth in a silent, haunting scream. Andrew laughed so much he fell down the last three steps, tumbling into a St George. George good-naturedly caught Andrew, and complimented him on the shark.

'Where's the dragon?' asked Andrew.

'He's lighting up outside.'

'Who are you by?'

'Ucello.'

'Bless you,' said Andrew, and wheeled away, laughing at his own crappy joke.

He spied Tessa, looking . . . well, he wasn't sure, but probably quite nice, as a Degas ballet dancer. He decided to go and talk to her, but before he reached her a large man in a strange, misshapen bull mask beat him to it, took her by the

311

hand and led her through to the ballroom, where a DJ dressed as a DJ was playing Abba records. Guernica, thought Andrew.

He found that he was holding two glasses of champagne. How had that happened? Not for long. One. Two. Where's the man with the tray? Before he found him Andrew became aware that the attention of the party had switched, with the weird togetherness of a flock of starlings wheeling through the evening sky, to the top of the stairs. A collective sigh, a lovely sound, came from them. And from Andrew, also. He hadn't needed this to show him that Alice was sublime but now he felt he knew how the mortal heroes of ancient Greece must have felt when visited by the divine Aphrodite, or wise Athena, or rosy-fingered Dawn. *Rosy-fingered what!* he had time to think to himself, scornfully, before he felt himself drawn back up the stairs to meet Alice.

And yes, the dress was magnificent. It was difficult to say exactly which Klimt painting it was taken from. It had something of the iridescent intimacy of *The Kiss*, and more of the languor and sensuality of the *The Virgin*. It suggested to some the flagrant sexuality of *Danaë*, ravished by gold. But whatever the particular work, all those there who witnessed it knew that it was Klimt. Leaping headlong up the stairs to meet her, Andrew was with those who favoured *The Kiss*, and he knew what he must do. He reached her. He gazed for a moment into her eyes. There were flowers in her hair, daisies, he thought, and small blue things. Why didn't he know the names of flowers? Alice would teach him. He felt the eyes of the world upon him, but they acted not to restrain, but to carry him higher. Her dress, dazzling in cobalt and crimson and gold, seemed to cover everything and yet reveal everything. He wanted to be inside it with her. He took the last step up to her and put his hand on her waist. His eyes were half closed. Yes, he was going to kiss her, to taste those lips, to breathe her essence like cool incense.

And then her laughter, her uncontrollable laughter.

'That is just brilliant.'

'What?' He opened his eyes.

'That shark.'

'Oh, yeah.'

'And it's really clever the way it sends up modern British art.'

'Yeah. Sends up modern British art. What?'

'How it's all about having a fairly amusing idea, that you don't need any skill or intellect to realise. Shoddy, shallow, empty. I love it!'

'Alice, you look completely amazing.'

'You know, I think I do. It was my mother's dress. I mean my grandmother's. She had it made to look like she was painted by Klimt. Do you think people will get it? I don't want to have to go around explaining myself.'

This was another new Alice for Andrew. Young and gushing and silly and girly. It set up a charming tension with the ancient eroticism of the dress. He wanted so much to squeeze her.

'Everyone will get it. Except the people who wouldn't get it if you came as the Mona Lisa and carried round a big placard saying "I've come as the Mona Lisa – that's a painting by Leonardo da Vinci".' Somehow the thrill of seeing Alice like this had burnt off the false effervescence of the cocaine. He felt like some more authentic bubbles. 'Let's get some champagne. It's fantastic stuff, yeasty and biscuity. Bet this is the last of the good stuff from the old days. Be Cava next year I expect.'

'Snob.'

'Peasant.'

'Ha!'

'Not that you look much like a peasant. More like some queen in a fairy tale. Maybe even one of the evil-but-beautiful-queens.'

'You should see what's coming.'

'What do you mean?'

'I was in the loos with Ophelia. She's really pulled out all the stops. No one's going to remember me when they see her.'

Alice pouted, and Andrew couldn't make up his mind if it was a joke, or if she really was annoyed. Either way, he liked it.

'What's she come as?'

'You'll have to wait and see.'

By now they were back in the crowd. Several people had already come up to them to admire and touch Alice's dress. A Toulouse-Lautrec prostitute from Fine Arts made a half-joking suggestion about swapping over later on, thereby conjuring all kinds of wickedly enchanting images in Andrew's mind, which he blinked away only with much effort. Whistler's mother was a bit sniffy, but Magritte's pipe broke off briefly from telling people that he wasn't a pipe to blow ecstatic smoke rings around her.

'I think I like parties,' said Alice. She'd decided it was time to tell Andrew. 'Pity really; I don't suppose they'll have them . . .'

'Holy Mother of God!' said Andrew, and for the second time the entire party turned to gaze in wonder towards the sweep of the stairway.

Who else but Venus? And which Venus other than Botticelli's, rising serenely from a scallop like a pearl coracle? No hint from Botticelli of her engendering: no place here for the scythed testicles of Chronos, or Uranus, or whoever it was, tossed to foam in the waves, which then gave forth this Venus. No hint of that barbarity, perhaps, but wasn't there just the suggestion somewhere in all that serenity that this was going to be the world's greatest fuck?

Too obvious now, thought Andrew. Why didn't I guess?

Alice was absolutely right about no one remembering what she wore after seeing this. The illusion of complete nakedness lasted only for a couple of seconds, but it imprinted itself on Andrew's brain, and was sufficient to induce a sudden, dismaying surge of blood to his pelvis, resulting in what he swiftly calculated was three sevenths of an erection. But of course it was a miraculous, tight-fitting bodysuit in some diaphanous, but opaque, substance. Was she naked beneath it? Andrew had encountered invisible, seamless bras and knickers before, but he believed that beneath the gauze, true nakedness prevailed. He ticked off another seventh of turgidity. The wig provided at least some pretence at modesty: Ophelia's black hair lay concealed beneath flowing red locks, with thick strands pinned across and covering her breasts and what Courbet called *The Origin of the World*.

Ophelia paused for a few moments at the top of stairs, basking in the wonder, bathing in the arousal, glorying in the jealousy. How could she not have done so? It was simply in her nature. As well suggest to a rose that this year it might be tactful not to bloom.

And yet that pause proved to be her downfall. She had emerged from the entrance to the right as the crowd looked. But the stairway divided, and another curve went to the left. From that door, quite as grand as the one to the right, there now came a bustle, a flurry, quite palpable before anything could be seen. And then the door opened and Venus was born for the second time that evening.

Pamela, or Pammy, or Spam, as she was known with varying degrees of affection.

Again there was some kind of bodysuit in a flesh, or near-flesh coloured material. But this was denser stuff, suggesting in its wrinkles and folds, the tights of a nineteenth-century circus strongman. There was also a wig, although this one did not fall in endless waves and ringlets but sprang stoutly

315

out, as wiry and fibrous as pubic hair. Each mammoth breast was covered by a comically huge scallop shell, made, Andrew thought, from papier-mâché. Another, even larger, covered the Origins of the World. Beneath her bodysuit Andrew could clearly make out the lines of a pair of giant knickers and, lower down, the ridges of surgical support bandages over her right knee and left ankle.

Andrew rapidly lost his five sevenths of an erection.

Pam did not see Ophelia standing opposite her. What she did see was the faces, gazing, rapt, up towards her. With her great, bubbling laugh she cavorted down the stairs, waving, and miming hellos.

Ophelia. Andrew looked at Ophelia. Surely she must realise what had happened. Even before Pam's appearance Andrew had begun to think that Ophelia's get-up, for all its glory, was a huge, tasteless mistake. She was thrusting her beauty needlessly, humourlessly into your face. But would she now see that Pam had made her look ridiculous? Not only was her vanity cruelly exposed by Pam's colossal, good-natured joke, but somehow she had been dragged in as one half of a comedy double act. She was now Pam's straight man, feeding her the lines, and contaminated with the silliness of it all. She was absurd, absurd, absurd.

But her face betrayed none of this. She stared blankly down at Pam. She saw that no one now was looking at her. She pouted. She tutted. She came down the stairs. So yes, she had missed entirely the brilliance of Pam's unintended deconstruction of her. And yet there was also a magnificence there, the glory of an ego raised to the stature of a goddess.

Alice and Andrew looked at each other. Their eyes shone with the glory of it all. She took his hand and squeezed it. They both said: 'I hate Abba,' at exactly the same time. And so went to dance.

The ballroom was crowded, but Andrew didn't mind as it forced them together. They were jostled by sunflowers and a clumsy Campbell's soup can. Andrew threw some shapes, which made Alice laugh. He was relieved to find that she was a perfectly competent dancer, without excelling. He thought again how rare it was to find a girl who simply couldn't dance in the way that so many men simply couldn't dance; indeed in the way that he couldn't dance. He'd spent long hours agonising whether the correct thing to do, if you can't dance, is to dance or not to dance. He'd finally come down on the side of dancing after concluding that it was better to garner the laughs and instant popularity than to preserve one's cool.

Alice leant over and shouted in his ear: 'I need to talk to you. Can we go and sit down for a minute.'

'After this one. It's the only really great song they ever did.'

SOS was playing.

'What's so good about it?'

'It's the combination of the tragic lyric with the rousing exuberance of the music. What a fucking fantastic chorus.' He joined in, throwing more comically dramatic shapes, and getting the words hopelessly muddled. 'If you hear me baby don't you fear my S-O-S.'

It stopped. *Dancing Queen* came on. 'I hate this,' said Andrew, vehemently. 'Apart from *SOS* it's all camp kitsch cack. Or is that cack camp kitsch. Either way it's shit. "When you've left",' he said, conversationally, '"how could I possibly attempt to carry on?"'

'What?' How could he . . .

'Fantastic lyric. Suicidal. But all the time with the best upbeat pop tune they ever wrote. It's as if *Hamlet* were rewritten as a limerick. What did you want to say? But hang on, let me grab some more champagne before these posh fuckers swig it all.'

317

While he was away, Alice found herself next to Ophelia, in her simulacrum of nakedness. Her features, beneath the wig, were still expressionless and perfect. Alice smiled at her, and a muscle or two twitched in Ophelia's face. A smile returned? Or a sneer called back? Or simply boredom sending out a random ripple?

'Fun party,' said Alice.

'Really? You think so? Brave of you to hide your *pain* so well.'

'What pain?'

'No need to pretend with me, Alice. All girls together here. Did I say how sweet I thought your . . . *thing* looked?' She gestured dismissively at Alice's dress.

Alice still looked perplexed.

'You're hardly,' Ophelia continued, 'the first girl to fail to hold on to Edward, you know.'

Oh *that*. Alice laughed. And she really couldn't be bothered correcting Ophelia. In fact she was sure that Ophelia knew the truth of the matter.

'I suppose,' said Alice, 'that you'll be . . . renewing your interest in Edward now yourself. I'm sure it's what your mother would want.' It was said without bitterness, for Alice found that she felt none.

'Who cares what she wants? No. What on earth would I be interested in Edward now for?'

'Well, I presume for the same reasons you were interested in him before.'

'Just how stupid are you? Why would I want Edward without the Audubon money? Do you think I want to spend my life working out ways to pay for things?'

Alice couldn't help but laugh again. 'Is that really the only thing you were interested in?' There was something delightful in Ophelia's wickedness now that it could not touch Alice herself.

'Look, Edward is a sweet enough guy, when he isn't moping, but frankly there's no money left in his estate. Not a penny. Six million pounds' worth of birdy book would have changed all that. I'm sorry, but I have a market value, and now he can't meet it.'

'You really are some bitch, aren't you,' said Alice with a smile

Now it was Ophelia who was laughing, with her hand to her mouth.

'So, goody-two-shoes knows a dirty word. Look, I'm just honest. We all want the same things: a decent fuck in a decent bed in a decent house. Can't see you getting any of those from your boyfriend.'

Before Alice had the chance to ask what she meant by that, Ophelia's face contorted in rage. Pamela was back. She had been following Ophelia around the party, throwing a heavy arm round her shoulders at every opportunity, and shrieking: 'Could be sisters, couldn't we!' and no amount of unsisterly disdain could shake her off. Ophelia made to run for it, but Alice delayed her with a touch to her arm.

'What will happen to Edward?'

'Oh, he'll be all right. After all, he's got that village idiot woman of his.'

'You know about Grace?'

'Is that her name? Yes, I suppose it is. Of course I know about Grace. Doesn't everybody?' And with that she pulled roughly away.

Andrew returned with refreshments.

'Having a nice chat with Ophelia?' he asked, and then, 'Christ, look who's coming. And what is *that*?'

Alice looked to where Andrew was pointing. Oakley was pushing his way towards them. As far as she could see he was dressed as usual. It was only when he reached them that she could see that he was wearing a tie with a picture of Constable's *Haywain* on it. But behind him she saw the second funniest thing she'd seen all day. Clerihew was following his leader. He had on a sort of loincloth and nothing else. Nothing else, except for several arrows stuck on with Sellotape, and now drooping forlornly. On his plump frame, moist and pink, and with his round tortoiseshell spectacles, he looked, well, like a fat little man with arrows Sellotaped to him.

'Nice tie,' said Andrew before Oakley opened his mouth.

'Ah, yes, well, one likes to make an effort. Important to. Dorothea made the purchase in the National Gallery shop. Where it is. The painting. Turner's ah, constable. His wagon.'

'And you, Cedric,' continued Andrew, shocking everyone by getting Clerihew's name right, 'really excellent. All that work. Did you apply the arrows yourself? Such craftsmanship. And I think what best illustrates the quality of the thinking that went into it, is that the very same idea occurred to our TV star art pundit: Doctor Terry, Richardson.'

'What?' said Clerihew, looking alarmed. 'Where?'

'Just over there discussing Classical mythology with Ophelia. Strange how this has turned into an evening of doppelgängers.'

Alice looked with Clerihew. And there, across the room, stood Ophelia, talking intimately with the gorgeous Terence Richardson. They would have made a striking couple, even if they had not been dressed as they were. His sculptured torso cried out to be pierced by arrows, and *his* darts had been made, by some clever engineering, to stand proud and erect. He looked much more relaxed than Ophelia, who was once again being plagued by Pam, who loomed over her, messily eating a scotch egg. Ophelia tried to ignore Pam, as she fingered one of Richardson's arrows. Alice thought, for a moment, that she was going to suck it.

'Good God!' said Clerihew. 'I wonder if . . . I should never have told her about my costume. She's obviously . . . I must have words.' And with that he started to forge his way to the Venuses and the other St Sebastian, wincing two or three times as a jostle jagged one of his arrows into a soft part.

'Bye bye,' said Andrew, cheerfully. 'What were you saying, Colin?'

'I was telling you about the developments. After we had *our* meeting, that is, the meeting between you and I, at which we reached an *understanding*, I was called into another er meeting. With Mrs Illkempt, and certain others of the Board, as was. The end of the meeting. To be informed on behalf of Books.'

'How very interesting. But as you can see we were just about to go and talk to someone else before you arrived so if you don't . . .'

'I'm afraid this *is* of interest. You see the loss of the Audubon sale was in the way of a final, er, curtain, um straw, breaking the camel's, as it were, back. For the Americans. They've withdrawn, in some sense. Money, it seems, has been haemorrhaging, in their expression.'

'Hang on. You're saying the Americans are pulling out? You mean the Japanese?'

'Withdrawing. Entirely. Yes.'

'But does that mean we're going under?'

'Not necessarily. A new Board has been formed, and there's a new stand-in Chairman.'

'Who?'

'Mr Brooksbank. Which those of us with a sense of history and family can only applaud.'

'Brooksbank, eh? Always seemed harmless enough to me. Bit dim though. What do you make of all this, Alice?' It had occurred to Andrew that Alice had been uncommonly quiet throughout the exchange.

'It doesn't really concern me.'

'That's the spirit! Fuck 'em. Doesn't matter which bunch of tossers decides what colour bog roll we're going to have. We do the real work.'

'That isn't what I meant. I've been trying . . .'

'Oh look,' said Andrew. 'Here they come now. Late to their own funeral.'

Madeleine Illkempt, flanked by Butch and Sundance, was making her heavy-haunched way down the stairs. Behind them, looking altogether more satisfied with life, came Brooksbank and a handful of other Enderby stalwarts. Unlike the Americans, these had made an attempt to get into the party spirit. Brooksbank himself was wearing a squiggly, Jackson Pollock-print tee-shirt. One man had donned a large cardboard cut-out of a drooping Dali watch. A middle-aged woman, whom Andrew knew as being vaguely ennobled, had on a pleasing, sixties-looking dress in Mondrian squares of primary colours.

News of the startling changes at Enderby's had quickly worked its way around the room, intensifying the levels of chatter. The new group's movements were watched with rapt attention. They split up, the Slayer's team going grumpily towards a long table by the wall, stacked with high-grade nibbles. It so happened that Andrew, Alice and Oakley were the first to be visited by Brooksbank.

'Ah, Doctor Heathley,' he said to Andrew, ignoring Oakley who was straining forwards. 'Fine work on the Audubon catalogue. D-damn shame about the cock-up.'

Andrew was surprised and a little embarrassed to be picked out by the man who held, albeit temporarily, the reigns of power.

'Yeah, well. I suppose these things happen.'

'No, dear b-boy, I don't think things do just happen,' said Brooksbank, sagely. 'Things happen because people make

322

them happen. Or sometimes because p-people stop them from happening.' At that point he looked at Oakley.

'Yes, sir, well, that's as may be, but in this case as Andrew, um Doctor Heathley, can confirm . . .'

'I'm sure he could, sure he could. B-But I may as well tell you now that we've b-begun work on a reorganisation, which makes all this seem a little, p-posthumous.'

'A reorganisation? Ah, I quite see that some structure streamlining . . . flatter management . . . ah . . . structures was, is, called for.'

'Yes. It was rapidly agreed that your talents were largely wasted up in Books. We really feel that you were more in your element down in the documents basement.' The eager, thrusting look that Oakley habitually aimed at his superiors changed. His face now wore the blank puzzlement of a severed head, the moment after the axe falls. 'N-naturally,' continued Brooksbank, with remorseless cheerfulness, 'we can't guarantee you your old post back as Head of Document Storage. But I'm sure we'll find something appropriate.'

'Might I ask,' said Oakley in the dismal tones of defeat, 'who will be taking over my position in Books?'

'Yes you may. You see I recalled that several months ago we had effectively dismissed one of the leading experts in the Books department, a man with an exemplary record of both connoisseurship and good business sense, on the grounds, reading between the lines of the report I received, that he had formed what is often referred to these days as a same-sex attachment. Of course that was never explicitly stated: no one was quite foolish enough to make that mistake. But the implication was clear. Well, I'm afraid that I find that entirely unacceptable, and now I am in a position to do something about it. I have made an offer and it has been accepted.'

'You're talking about Crumlish? Garnet Crumlish?' said

Andrew, who was already in a state of such intense physical and mental bliss that he felt he might have some kind
of emission. He looked at Alice who also wore a huge smile.
Alice Sui Generis, she was thinking. *We've recently acquired our
first Oik. And look, he's to be your intimate desk chum. How
affecting*. The same delicious thought occurred to Alice and
Andrew at the same time: Crumlish had been elbowed out
on the trumped up grounds that he had sexually harassed
Clerihew. Now he was being brought back to life because
Brooksbank thought he was a gay martyr.

'Quite,' said Brooksbank.

'But those rumours . . .' began Oakley, only to trail off.
Brooksbank looked at Oakley, waiting for him to finish. But
what, thought Andrew, could he say? 'Those rumours were
baseless, and made up by myself and my cocksucking lick-
spittle, Clerihew?' Oh, the joy, the joy. Oakley seemed to
physically shrink before them, melting like a salted slug.

Brooksbank chatted a little more with Alice and
Andrew, telling them a few juicy details about the fall of
the Americans, and their Japanese puppet masters. He
made little effort to keep the snobbish contempt from his
voice. It seemed that all of the innovations introduced,
and in particular the online auction and other internet-
based projects, were more responsible for the collapse than
the Audubon failure. A little nipping and tucking, he
thought, would return them to modest profitability in no
time. But that wasn't what 'they' wanted, no glory in
modest profits and a stable share of the market, and so
off they had gone.

'Well,' he said, after a few minutes, 'must be doing my
rounds. N-noblesse oblige and all that. Frightfully nice con-
versing.'

Then he was gone. Gone too was Oakley. How had that
happened? He had simply disappeared. Dragged down,

Faust-like, by devils, thought Andrew, to his subterranean document hell. Alice squeezed his hand.

'I've arranged to meet Odette and Leo in the Mitre,' she said.

'What, *now*? But things have hardly got going here. All that free champagne. And I've got to go and gloat. Tonight will be a night of gloating. Don't you see? Nearly all the baddies have been beaten. How often does that happen in real life?'

'We . . . you can always come back. It's . . . I've got to talk about . . . about something important. With all of you. I've been trying to tell you all day.'

At long last Andrew was listening to her.

'What is it?'

'I'll tell you in the Mitre.'

'You *can't* do that. Tell me now.'

'Let's go. We'll be there in a minute.'

On the way out they passed the Slayer and her acolytes. Andrew, now worried and annoyed by Alice, but still exultant over the humiliation and downfall of Oakley, could not resist swaying over towards them.

'I've got it!' he said in a loud and friendly voice. 'I was wondering all evening, and now I see it. Very clever.'

'What are you talking about,' Illkempt replied, glowering at him with her black eyes from beneath her heavy lids. She was only slightly incommoded by the presence of most of a vol-au-vent in her large mouth.

'Your . . . costume. You've come as *Les Demoiselles d'Avignon*. Genius, sheer genius. Can't have too many Picassos.'

He had no time to wait for a reply, or even to see if understanding dawned, before Alice pulled him away, anxious not to keep Odette waiting.

TWENTY-FIVE

Two Interesting Occurrences

Leaving the party when they did meant that Alice and Andrew were to miss two interesting occurrences. The first was the return of Garnet Crumlish, elegantly dressed in a top hat and tails, his patent shoes glittering with the lights of the chandeliers.

'The Degas people will think I'm from a Manet, and the Manet from a Degas,' he'd said as his wife, Jessie, fussed over him, sprucing and defluffing. 'Anyway, what do they expect with such short notice?'

The months had not been easy for Crumlish, or for his wife. He'd made a little money from casual book dealing, but somehow the faintly sordid trailing through house clearances and charity shops on the look out for first editions, felt like one step up from vagrancy. The looks of recognition he got from former trade contacts, the quasi-tramps in frayed shirts and stained ties who'd come in to Enderby's with thirty or forty quid's worth of books, was more than he could take. Would he soon look like them, *smell* like them? Yes, of course he would.

So why not embrace it? He took to whiling away afternoons in the park with a bottle of British sherry, the carnation in his lapel slowly browning.

Jessie could do nothing for him. They weren't soul mates; she looked after him, and there was no way to iron or clean or cook a way out of this disaster. Another year and he might well have been dead.

He entered quietly, acknowledging with polite nods those of his acquaintance who stared at him in astonishment. With each step he took, he gained in confidence, and by the time he plucked his first glass of champagne from a passing tray, performing as he did, an elegant half turn, he felt almost as if he had never been away. His careful eye took in the splendour around him, the glory and chaos of costume, the intricate infrastructure of friendships, alliances, feuds, manifest in the pattern of bodies around him. He saw immediately, the isolated group of Americans, and touched his hat brim with the silver boss on his cane. Illkempt champed, and looked away.

The same careful eye could hardly fail to spot the extraordinary group made up of . . . What? Two Sebastians, obviously: couldn't miss those arrows, and, yes, two Venuses, judging by the beauty of one, and the scallops of the other.

'Pam,' he murmured, smiling to himself. 'You really are a genius.' But he looked sadly at the plumper of the two Sebastians.

He carried in his pocket a bundle of love letters, rather earnest and imploring, craving only that he should think to look the way of his devoted slave, and promising a range of delights almost certainly beyond the young man's abilities to deliver. Crumlish brought them with him not for the purposes of blackmail, or even to support his reinstatement. That all seemed quite adequately taken care of. Of course Brooksbank was an idiot, but at least he was one of our idiots. No, he brought them to return them to the sender, in case he should suffer unnecessarily. Garnet had more than earned his reputation as a wit; perhaps even that of a bitch; but his swordplay, like that of Zorro (a childhood hero), was designed only to leave his monogram cut into the clothing of the victim, and never to eviscerate. He had no intention of harming poor Clerihew.

Nor did he ever get the chance to return the letters, for Clerihew was shortly to be at the centre of the second interesting occurrence. On leaving Andrew, Alice and Oakley, he had gone to stand close beside Richardson, Ophelia, and Spam, where Crumlish now found him.

Richardson was even more annoyed than Ophelia at having a comedy double, and was rather better equipped for dealing with it. When Pam had stopped her good-natured pointing, ooing, and cackling at the new arrival, and when it had become clear that he wasn't about to go of his own accord, he turned smilingly towards Clerihew, whose jaw was clamped tightly shut.

'Exactly which St Sebastian are you?'

'What?'

'Well, you are a little . . . limp for either of the Mantegna's: I thought myself about coming as the Louvre *Sebastian* – the one in the Kunsthistorisches in Vienna gets a horrid shaft in the face . . .'

'I'm just a *Sebastian*. I don't know which one. But it was my idea before yours. You stole it.'

'Please, young man, I haven't finished yet. You really can't be the Perugino, or the wonderful Puget bronze in Vienna. The Hans Holbein altarpiece? No, really, no. What about the Hendrick Terbrugghen? Could be, could be. He has a certain . . . earthiness. But, again, no. You haven't quite the . . . *delineation*.'

Richardson's performance had, by this time, attracted a small but appreciative audience. Garnet Crumlish was among them, drawn into the circle, although he declined to join in with the tittering. The victim had blushed a deep scarlet, and Crumlish was perhaps the only one there who saw it as the mark not of embarrassment, but rage: a consuming, destructive fury. Did Clerihew notice Garnet there, among the crowd? Could that have added to the tempest of emotions bringing him to the brink of action? One would need access to his medical notes, or to the psychiatric report prepared for his trial, to give a firm answer to that question.

'I have it,' said Richardson, finally, 'you're the Antonio del Pollaiuolo *Martyrdom of St Sebastian*, painted in tempera on wood in 1475, and hanging in our own dear National Gallery. Am I right?'

'I told you I'm not . . .'

'Yes,' said Richardson, playing now to the crowd by walking around Clerihew like a tour guide, 'I see now the fluidity of the forms, the graceful integration of the loin-cloth with the supple sensuality, and might I say suggestive *fecundity* of the loins. And, remember, the Pollaiuolo *Sebastian* is set on a high post, and so the archers and crossbowmen must shoot upwards, which helps to explain the curious lack of . . . *turgidity*, in the *shafts* themselves. But most of all we have the magnificent head: serene, beatific, safe in the knowledge that, as the first Christian martyr, he is also the first soul to be saved, the first mortal being to be guaranteed everlasting glory in the presence of God.'

Richardson lowered his eyes in mock reverence, and a ripple of applause passed through the audience, before it began to break up. They may, to be fair, have thought that the whole thing was prepared in advance by the participants: after all, two such contrasting pairs as these Venuses and Sebastians could not, surely, be the product of chance?

It may have been to Ophelia's credit that well before the conclusion of the performance she was bored. Bored and annoyed: if she wanted lectures on art history she could always go to a lecture on art history. As Richardson turned she looked over his shoulder into Clerihew's eyes. And was that a look of sympathy she sent him? Or simply the fleeting absence of active hostility that had so often beguiled and misled her admirers?

But now her eyes acquired another look entirely. Surprise; shock; horror, all within a second.

Clerihew, his face twisted into rage, wrenched one of the arrows from his pink chest and launched himself at Richardson. The point was sharp, but the shaft was of flimsy balsa wood and as Clerihew thrust it into Richardson's neck it broke in two. But now Clerihew was on Richardson's back, screaming like a maniac:

'My idea! My idea! Shaft you, SHAFT YOU, aaaaaaahh-hhhhhhh, shaft you, you fucking shafter, you shafted me. AAAAAAAAAAAAGGGGGHHHHHHHHHHHHH.'

'Get him off me,' Richardson screamed in turn, twisting and writhing, and flapping ineffectually at the monster on his back.

Initially the crowd thought this was all part of the act, and laughed, albeit nervously. It was only when Clerihew managed to pry one of Richardson's darts free and stab him with it several times in the shoulder, chest and neck area, drawing blood from the long, shallow wounds, that they realised that this was not a planned part of the evening's entertainment. In the scramble, Clerihew's loincloth came free, revealing his dimpled buttocks and hairless cleft. Gagging disgust was added to the gasps of astonishment, and shouts of encouragement.

Crumlish acted first. With surprising strength he pulled the now naked Clerihew bodily away. Richardson collapsed immediately on his face. Clerihew also fell to the ground, his passion spent. There was no need for the two burly porters, one dressed as Henry VIII, and one as some or other pope, to sit on him, but sit on him they did, until the police and the ambulance arrived.

'Well, my pretty,' said Crumlish to Ophelia, 'I see a tray of unattended drinks. Perhaps we should go and attend them.'

She took his arm and they walked away.

TWENTY-SIX

The Mitre

The Mitre was half empty despite the Friday night. The Enderby's lot were, of course, partying, or stabbing each other with arrows, and those other local workers who had been in had mostly moved on to brighter lights, or gone home to dimmer. The short walk from Enderby's had been bitterly cold and Alice was glad to take Andrew's proffered arm. There was the usual performance with Andrew's spectacles misting up as they got into the pub, but that was soon settled and they found Leo and Odette sitting together at a quiet table by the wall. Alice took off her coat.

'Well,' said Leo, 'I believe that may be the most beautiful thing I've ever seen.' He kissed her. The dress drew every set of bleary eyes in the place. 'You look like an Aztec goddess.'

'Quite enough of that!' said Odette, sharply. And then to Alice, 'So, you found something to wear then?'

'Mummy let me borrow it. Thanks for coming.'

Andrew got a round in. 'Okay, princess,' he said, setting down the four drinks, spilling a little of each with a tremor which almost certainly signified nothing, 'what's this all about then? You've whipped us all up into a frenzy of expectation, so it better be good.'

'I'm flying to Mauritius tomorrow morning.'

'What,' said Odette, 'on holiday?'

'Great idea,' said Andrew, enthusiastically, although he rather wished that she had thought about perhaps asking if he might want to . . . 'Get away from this shit-hole for Christmas, come back in January with a suntan and a baby-lemur-skin handbag.'

It was Leo who realised that something more significant was afoot.

'I don't think that's what she means,' he said, looking closely at her.

'What do you mean, not what she means?' Something akin to awareness had dawned, but Andrew didn't want to acknowledge it to himself.

'Leo's right. I've planned this for a while. I tried to tell you, but somehow it never . . . worked out. I'm sorry.'

Andrew looked like a whipped dog, but Odette seemed, *was*, pleased. 'So you're going to do your research on . . .'

'Island biodiversity. Land snails of the Indian Ocean.'

'What made you decide?'

'Well you know I'd held over my scholarship for a year, and time was running out. But more importantly, it was what I thought my dad wanted me to do. There was a dream I kept having, and I could never see his face, never quite capture him. But then it came to me that the way I would find him was not somehow inside myself, but out there, in the world, in the way the world *is*. Choose science, he was saying choose knowledge. It was there all the time, but the Dead . . . but Matija stopped me from seeing it. And now he isn't there . . . here any more. My main concern was Mummy, but social services have been very good, and she's having a home help every day. Anyway,' she laughed, 'I wasn't any good at selling books, and even if I had been, it's a pretty worthless sort of life.'

'Thanks,' said Andrew.

'Oh Andrew, I'm sorry. I didn't mean that . . .'

'You did. And it's true. It *is* a pretty worthless existence. You can forget it for a while, but the truth of it always gets you in the end.'

For a moment Odette and Leo vanished from the pub, leaving the two of them alone.

'You know you're the only thing that's kept me sane,' she said.

'Well. I didn't do a very good job of that, did I, you nutter?'

'I mean it. Meeting you, and getting to know you has been one of the most precious things in my life. I love you; I love you all.'

She took his hand, and Odette's, and Odette took Leo's, and Leo took Andrew's, which made them both pull faces, even though this wasn't the time, so they were all joined in a circle, formed around the glasses of beer and wine, and the rings of beer and wine on the table, and the ashtray, full with the ash and stubs of other smokers.

'I know you're doing the right thing,' said Odette, 'but I'll miss you.'

'How long are you . . . does it last?' Andrew was fighting to keep the emotion out of his voice, but it sounded cracked and strained.

'Three years. Perhaps longer.'

'And *tomorrow* morning?'

'Tomorrow, yes. Early. In fact I have to go soon. I haven't packed yet, and I have to spend some time with Mummy.'

'How is she about you going?' It was, of course, Odette, who cared. It was always Odette who cared.

'I think she understands. I mean understands that I'm going, and understands that I have to go. I've done what I can to make sure she'll be okay. I think she may have more friends than I sometimes imagined. Perhaps some of her unhappiness was my fault, and she'll be better when I'm not there. I don't know.'

Andrew wasn't listening to any of that. All he could hear was *go soon go soon go soon*. They weren't holding hands any more.

'What about us?' he said.

Alice looked at him, a little puzzled. 'What do you mean?'

'I mean, what about us? How will we . . . cope.'

Alice forced out a laugh. 'Oh, they'll find someone better than me at books. Maybe they'll give you Ophelia to beat into shape.'

'I don't want Ophelia, even to beat. I want you.' Suddenly his expression brightened. 'What about your notice? Don't you have to give them a month? It's a law, or something.'

'I'm still in my probation year. It's a week for each side. And with the holiday coming . . . I left a note on Oakley's desk.'

'Crumlish's.'

'Crumlish's.'

Alice tried hard to keep the tone light, telling the extraordinary story of the day's events at Enderby's. Leo was worried about his friend, and didn't say much, although he enjoyed the story. Andrew was largely silent. Finally, looking at Alice, he said:

'Do you remember when we met in that park, the one with the wallabies and the bandstand and the flamingos?'

'The ones who were bored with your conversation about plankton?'

'You *do* remember. Do you ever go there?'

'I haven't been since I met you there.'

'I go sometimes.'

'I thought you hated parks. Hare-eyed clerks with the gitters.'

'That's the only one I like. Anyway, isn't that what I am?'

'Fucking hell, Andrew,' said Leo, 'don't be such a tit. From what Alice has been saying you are the Man, when it comes to the world of smelly old books. Sans Oakley and with Clerihew marginalised, aren't you on the way to a glittering career?'

It was true. Promotion was beckoning. He didn't care.

And soon, after another drink (Leo brought over a bottle of champagne, to celebrate, but most of the glasses remained half full), it was time for Alice to go. Odette and Leo had a table at the River Café, and they asked Andrew to join them. He shook his head and turned to Alice:

'Can I see you home? We could walk.'

'Not in those shoes,' said Odette, her laugh forced.

'I think I should get a taxi.'

'Can I ride with you?'

After a pause: 'Yes.'

Before the two couples split to find taxis there was a tele-tubbies style group hug. Odette cried; Alice cried. Andrew didn't cry, yet. But his knuckles were white, and he gripped Leo's shoulder so hard his friend had to twist away.

Andrew and Alice didn't speak in the taxi. Nor, despite the shiny vinyl of the seats, did they slide comfortably together. Andrew felt sick to his soul. They reached St John's Wood. Andrew was paralysed.

'I'm here,' said Alice. 'I'd say come up, but with Mummy there . . . it would be awkward.'

Andrew still could not move or speak. Alice leaned over and kissed him gently on the lips. She then quickly pulled away, opened the door, and fled into the night. The contact was too brief for either to feel the hot salt tears of the other.

336

TWENTY-SEVEN

A Death at Heathrow

Alice knew that she had caused Andrew pain. And she knew
that leaving him was the most difficult part of her decision.
She knew that he loved her, and she knew that she felt
strongly attracted to him. She didn't suffer the agony of love
she had felt for Matija, nor experience the intense sexual
excitement and passion she had sometimes felt welling inside
her for Lynden. What she felt for Andrew was a kind of joy,
a lightness, a sense of harmony and rightness. Did that
deserve less than the pain and the passion to be called love?
Well, if it did, she couldn't let herself use the word. She
knew that she had to go. She could not stay even for . . .
even for love.

Kitty was waiting for her when she came in.

'How was my dress?' she asked.

'Everybody loved it. I think it was the best costume there.'

'That's nice. Now take it off before you ruin it, and then
come and sit beside me and tell me all about your evening.'

Alice told her. She made it sound as grand and as glorious as she could, and Kitty's eyes shone with pleasure. And
then, close together on the sofa, they watched a late film.

*   *   *

As the door to the taxi closed, Andrew came to life. He wiped the tears away with his sleeve and pounded the seat, until the cabbie said, 'Steady on, son.' His mind knew a turmoil he had never experienced before: the churning, grinding horror of love lost, of love lost forever. 'I can't live without her,' he said to himself, and was shocked at the implication of the words.

Andrew had always prided himself in his superficiality. 'Depth is an illusion,' he would say to anyone who would listen, 'surface is everything.' It was only a way of saying that what counted, what contributed to *meaning*, was what people said, how they behaved, those things which changed the fabric of the world. Invisible movement beneath the surface was, he contended, not movement at all. All talk of depth was myth or metaphor, ultimately traceable from Christian thought back through the Neoplatonists to Plato himself, and the invention of the soul, the inner being.

But now he could only think of this dreadful thing that had happened in terms of depth. He had been fissured, pierced to the soul, as much and as deeply as any St Sebastian. He could not shrug off this pain as a passing shower through which he would emerge to dry in the sun of new experiences. He was soaked to the skin, and through the skin to the soul, and now he would never dry out.

He stopped the taxi in the middle of nowhere. He wanted to walk. He thought he could probably find his way back to the flat in Crouch End. And if he couldn't, so what? As he walked he found that he was doing something he hadn't done for twenty years: he prayed. Please God, he said, make her change her mind. Make her not want to go. Make the plane not work. Make Mauritius have a volcano go off, or a revolution, so nobody can go there. But what if he was praying to the wrong god? There were so many. He briefly nodded towards Allah and Jehovah, before going on a whistle-stop tour of world religions, pacing them out with his quick steps. Did Buddha count as a god? Could you pray to him? He tried. Confucius? Softly softly catchee monkey. Probably more to it than that. And which was the best of the Hindu gods? The one with an elephant's head? He always had a soft spot for the one with an elephant's head. Looked sort of friendly. Unlike Baal, who was one of the hard bastards. And Quetzalcoatl, the Plumed Serpent, who feasted on the hearts of human sacrifices. And then there were the big-toothed war gods of Polynesia. You wanted those on your team. Help me, he prayed, prayed to all of them, get together and make this all right. You can do it, you know you can.

He was in Archway, still miles from home.

She wasn't going to stay. There weren't any volcanoes on Mauritius. Just beautiful beaches, and lots of those fascinating snails. How could Alice not prefer that to stinky old England, and stinky old him? If he were her, then he'd . . . go.

Go.

GO!

Madness.

What about the wonderful career at Enderby's opened up for him by the new regime? Oakley gone; the hard-nosed Americans gone. But what had Alice said about it? 'A pretty worthless sort of life.' Did it make any difference now just because the English toffs had turfed out the foreign Johnnies? And wasn't there something *unpleasant* about the way Brooksbank had described the Americans and the Japanese? Something bordering on the racist? Was it really any better to be governed by idiotic snobs, even if their manners and their suits were perfect, rather than the ruthless slash-and-burn merchants of the dollar-yen axis?

No, not really any better. His dad had been right about the Farquars and the Percys.

339

But what could he do if he followed Alice? Was there a university in Mauritius? Of course, there must be. There were universities everywhere. Fucking Salford had one, for Christ's sake. What language did they teach in? Mauritian? Was that a language? No, surely it was French. His French was *trés bien*. Or was it *trés bon*? And even if there wasn't a position for him at the *Ancien Universitaire de Mauritius*, then surely he could teach English as a foreign language, or get a job picking coconuts.

The plans whirled through his brain and, when he reached his flat at three in the morning, he was more awake than he'd ever been in his life. He hadn't used his passport for two years, and it felt as if it took him that long to find it. Finally, there it was, under the sheet of lemon-coloured wallpaper that lined his sock drawer, along with an old tube pass, twenty quid, and an emergency condom, now sadly passed its use-by date.

What was the weather like in Mauritius? Hot, surely. But was it Mauritian winter now, or summer? Hang on, equator. It was *always* summer. Probably the rainy season, though. So, put on his light summer suit, and bring an umbrella. Why didn't he get it cleaned before putting it away in September? Surely to fuck those couldn't be sweat marks under his arms? How did he manage to sweat right through his suit? But wait, getting ahead. If he was to catch Alice's plane, he had to find out when it left, and if there were any seats. You could get tickets at the airport, couldn't you? They always did in films. Cost more though. Fuck it. Not everyday you sacrifice everything to chase a snail expert to Mauritius.

It took him half an hour to track down the right number and get a sensible reply. Eight forty-five. London Heathrow. Air France. Had to be it.

It was five-thirty by the time he'd finished packing. Travel light, he thought. Boost the local economy by buying what he needed out there. He wrote a letter to work, resigning on the grounds, in draft one, of mental turmoil, in draft two, of repetitive strain injury, in draft three, of neurasthenia, and in draft four, of melancholia. He then started again, and asked for a month's special leave to attend a sick relative. No point burning all of his boats. Just a canoe, and a broken bit of wood to use as an oar. In case it all went wrong.

How the hell did you get to Heathrow? He found a map and traced his way with his finger. Fuck, M25. He hated the M25. He had memories of going all the way round London twice trying to find the right place to get off. He washed his face and brushed his teeth, wearing his summer suit, getting toothpaste stains down the front. He wiped it with a facecloth, knowing that the white smear would appear again later on, when the wet patch dried. Didn't care. Hair. Brush, pull, tear.

He put his case on the front passenger seat of the Merdemobile. The boot wasn't opening anymore. He hoped there wasn't anything useful in there. A Mauritian-English dictionary? Snake anti-venom? A lemur snare? Probably not. Just a badminton racquet and some seashells that had been there when he bought it, the relic, perhaps of some disastrous family holiday in Llandudno, or Cleethorpes. Where in God's name was Cleethorpes? He still wasn't remotely tired, though he could feel the redness prickling in his eyes. Not even the tedium of the motorway dulled his thoughts, as he raced at a clattering fifty miles an hour.

Cleethorpes. Wherever it was, it was a long way from Mauritius, a long way from Alice. They were on the beach now under a palm tree. No, the veranda of one of those grass-roofed beach hut things. They were drinking long drinks, and talking the talk. And then she took his hand

and led him into the darkness of the hut. She was taking off her bikini. But it was so dark, he couldn't see. He reached for the light, but there wasn't one. Fuck, the Heathrow exit. Shit. A horn blasted behind, beside, ahead, as he swerved, his bald, flattening tyres gripping feebly at the tarmac. Safe. On target. Remember, he told himself, stay alive. Being dead would never get him to Mauritius, unless Mauritius was heaven.

Amazingly he was almost there. Quarter past seven. Plenty of time. He drove past the model of Concorde, ugly evil-looking thing that it was. Which terminal? Did he know that? Yes he knew that. Parking – long stay or short stay? He knew that too. It was time to say goodbye to the Merdemobile. It was certainly worth less than the cost of parking it, even for a month, should he decide to return, sick relative nursed back to health. Maybe not very community-spirited just to dump it. Would they think it contained a bomb? He'd write a note, explaining that no explosives were carried.

He found a place in the short term car park, and left without getting a ticket. He was running now, and became a little confused, missing the direct route to the concourse. He found that he came out close to the main entrance, where taxis pulled up and delivered their passengers. His head was fizzing and pulsing, and his eyes were stretched and sore. He had to slip between the lines of taxis, and other cars weaving around them, dropping people.

And there . . . . Could it be possible? Was that Alice by the big glass doors? His Alice, waiting for him.

Alice was even more astonished to see Andrew, dressed in a flimsy cotton suit in the freezing wind. She had just got out of her taxi and was waiting for a porter when she saw him. His hair was sticking out all over the place, and he was squinting into the wind. She found herself smiling like an idiot. He had come to wave her away, even though she had forbidden it to the three of them last night. How lovely, how wonderful. She would miss him so much. She stood up. But he was carrying a tatty old suitcase. What did it mean? Her heart began to beat with excitement at the mad folly of it. If, that is, he was doing what she thought he might be doing. The fool. The lovely fool. Perhaps only an insane gesture such as this could have tipped her feelings in the way she now felt them tipping. With each long stride he took she felt her heart overflow. She wanted him to be near her, wanted to feel his silly, silly arms around her.

She wasn't looking for the car. Strangely it was Andrew who noticed it first: some function, perhaps, of his excruciating heightened senses. He saw Alice smile at him, saw her somehow mysteriously open to him, something she accomplished with the tiniest imaginable movement.

But then he knew that it was coming, and he knew that it was, in a way that he could never understand on this side of the veil separating life and death, just and right. He turned to face it. It was a sleek, low, anonymous thing, metallic grey or green. He couldn't blame the driver; he knew that it was his fault, that he had stepped out from an invisible place, coming like an apparition into the path of this thing. Strange, so strange how time slowed: strange only because it seemed the confirmation of the cliché. He tried to replay his life, but he couldn't remember any of it. He looked back at Alice. She saw the look in his eyes. It was a look she had seen before. And then she looked towards the car coming, slowly so slowly.

He had heard the story of the Dead Boy so many times now, and though he hated his memory, and knew that the courage had been false courage, he felt that he must emulate it. He fought the urge, the pointless urge, to throw his arms and the case before him, as if one could simply ward off the car that killed you. He opened to the car as Alice had opened to him, and his only concession was to close his eyes the moment before the impact.

The impact.

The impact.

He opened his eyes again.

Ah.

That exhaustion-fuelled hallucination of slow motion was no hallucination. The car was still coming, crawling round the gentle curve of the roadway in front of the entrance. It rolled to a stop ten feet before Andrew and a head leaned out of the window.

'Out the fucking way, mate: two in here with a plane to catch.'

Andrew jumped onto the pavement, almost knocking Alice over as she ran to him. He threw down his bag. The kiss, when it came, was the most nervous, inept, nose-bashing, teeth-clashing of his life, but he drank deep, and Alice put her tongue in his mouth, and then astonished him by grabbing his buttocks and pulling him into her.

'I'm coming with you,' he said, gulping for breath.

'You'll . . . never . . . get . . . a . . . ticket . . . you . . . idiot.'

'I will.'

'You won't. It was a miracle I got mine. Kiss me some more.'

'I need to get a ticket.'

'Kiss me some more.'

'I'm kissing you.'

'Kiss me some more.'

'I'm kissing you.'

'Kiss me some more.'